Untrue Tales From Beyond Fiction

• Recollections of an Alternate Past •

Book One, Book Two, and Book Three

Teel McClanahan III

Modern Evil Press

Phoenix

Published by Modern Evil Press, Phoenix, AZ

Printed in the United States of America

ISBN-13: 978-1-934516-40-9
ISBN-10: 1-934516-40-6

Library of Congress Control Number: 2007927997

• for love, lost •

Book One

An Introduction To Dodgeball

OR

Conception and Induction

OR

How To Begin An Apocalypse

Sweat beaded on his brow, his eyes were closed in concentration, and his mind was far away from the rhythmic sound of the rustling of the sheets and the immediacy of the reality of his own fingertips on his skin. In his mind's eye she is hot against him, above him, her sweat dripping between them almost melodically with the tandem thrusting of their bodies. Apart and together, cyclically thrusting the proof of their intimacy into hard reality, their bodies rocked each other.

He loved to look at her, to examine the curves of her face as she pulled the arc of her lower lip behind her front teeth, the corners of her mouth just turning upward. Her eyes stayed closed in concentration but he could imagine they were focused hard behind her eyelids, visualizing that sweet spot within her she was driving him against again and again. Tiny creases at the corners of her eyes and the rapid flaring and relaxing of her nostrils belied an intensity that was growing within her even as the motion of her body was coming slower, deeper, more like the gentle rolling of the ocean than the chop of the sea in a storm.

While she was working her way to a personal heaven above him, using him to reach her own particular ends without even looking at him once since her sweat first surfaced on her skin, he was working in his own way beneath her. His hands and eyes roaming, sliding, slipping wet across all the beautiful parts of her that were not already wrapped tight around him. Discovering the gentle nodes of bone distending the slick skin of her back as they protected her spine was glory, and following that line with both hands until he was cupping the rising and falling globes of her smooth, bare ass against his open palms brought every detail of her ribs and the narrow of her waist as it met the width of her ravenous hips concretely into his mind.

His hands continued down and the tightening and shifting of the near-trembling muscles just under the taut skin of her hard-working thighs was like a tactile diagram of her passion for him being worked out calorie by calorie in her reverie as he himself reveled in the beauty of her form and marveled that she could be so happy here with him. He held his hands there on the sides of her thighs as she continued to spell out her feelings for him with every thrust and examined her also with his eyes.

Tanned brown skin crept up from the tips of her fingers which now clenched the sheets at either side of his shoulders, all the way up her arms until as it approached her shoulders the brown of her tan began to give way to something somewhat paler spreading out across her shoulders and down her chest. The giant teardrops of her young, poised breasts were splashing up and back and up and back seeming almost intentionally to imply a meditation on the crests of a hundred waves breaking in synchronicity and harmony before his eyes, and they further brought the foaming excited tips of waves to mind in their intense paleness beside her relatively stationary arms. The very whiteness of the flesh reaching out towards them, veined blue and imperfect in their own little ways but a blur before him, made more extreme the contrast of the roses that were her nipples, floating as though ready to drown in that sea of heavy cream under heavy storm.

His eyes marched a steady line down the valley between those twin orbs of beauty, across the surface of her abdomen, and paused on every bead of sweat making its way down a similar course across and underneath her, pooling briefly at her navel before continuing inexorably towards the mingling with his own sweat. That mingling of sweat was somehow focused in his mind's eye despite the juxtaposition of a mingling of his flesh literally with hers barely beyond it, but it did remind him of another fluid seeking a mingling between them which brought his attention back to that most intense point of shifting contact between them. It was nearly too much for him. He nearly let go just then.

But he could see she was not quite there yet, and he did everything he could to keep that most intense of sensations from usurping the place at the front of his mind and sending him over the edge. His eyes closed, his hands drew casually up over her back and pulled her into him, still moving and sliding above and around him, and he tried to latch onto every detail. He was safe for a moment in the sensation of her hair falling delicately around her face and brushing softly against his face, his neck, and his chest. A thousand points of contact so brief and gentle each that they might go unnoticed but for their quantity and randomness. Not a tickling anymore, as much of her hair was now dripping wet with her sweat, but so light that it was as though hundreds of soft, tiny brushes were painting him with warm rain or sea water or tears. He moved his focus quickly to the friction of her whole body moving across his, no longer a few mere points of contact, but vast curved surfaces gliding in constant connection one body to another. Swaths of nerves used only casually during most of his life were awakened suddenly by the subtle ripples of her ribcage playing out a tune of harmonic sensorial bliss across the undulating surface of his chest beneath her. Their legs were intertwining like the dozens of limber tentacles wielded by two squid locked in deathmatch or lovemaking under the sea, and were nearly as wet with the combined fluids of their exertions. Not like walking or running or a foot fallen asleep, this passionate wrestling of their legs was a wholly unique sensation to him; less a study or a map as some sensations had seemed, this was more a poem or an action statement declaring something brief but beautiful to his nervous system.

The sheets beneath him, the pillow under his head, the single sock the only stitch of clothing worn by either of them, his mind tried to grasp onto these things but could not find purchase. The darkness of the room's lights long off, the silence from the CD player he had forgotten to put on repeat, the mingled twin scents of their bodies conjoined and heady in the air, sensations too much like nothing, too much like something so known it is overlooked, sensations that could not distract him long from her toes beginning to curl at the ends of her legs and her voice reaching a crescendo.

Long enough, it seemed, and his eyes opened and his mind focused like a magnifying glass ready to spark a fire from a single bright point of light, a single intense point of physical sensation and connection, and his own toes began to curl as well. His silence was the perfect contrast to her scream of total satisfaction pealing out into the night air, or at least it would have been – he was silent as his body was rocked with the most powerful explosion of pleasure he had ever known because his parents were sleeping only two doors down the hall and he did not want to be discovered with his "hand in the cookie jar." Even in this most intensely personal moment of overwhelming sensation and the natural urge to make noise backed up by thousands of years of sexual evolution, his self-control and will power overcame, and he made not even the smallest peep or sigh.

The over-stimulated nerves of his fingers and palm pressed hard against another hardness and could feel his body become a sort of pump with a steady whoosh, whoosh, whoosh, whoosh, whoosh of fluid climbing up the back or underside of the stiff hose held within his grasp. At the same time another part of his body became a pump as well, pushing drop after drop of endorphins and hormones into his blood stream and all over his body. The muscles curling his toes and clenching his calves and thighs and ass as tight as steel cables in support of some massive structure began to relax into a jellied state. The same crushed tightness began to leave his abs and back and neck and shoulders and arms all the way down to his fingers loosening their grip and their fist and all of his body was that much closer to a blissful state of perfect relaxation.

Just one more thing and he could roll over and go to sleep in his empty bed. He grabbed the sock he had pulled off for this very purpose and moved to wipe up the inevitable mess created by his 'extracurricular activities.' There was nothing to clean up.

He was sure he'd reached orgasm, more sure than he'd ever been before. He was even sure he had felt his body ejaculating, fluid moving steadily up his urethra with the pulsing of his heart, longer and harder than usual. He was expecting quite a mess. He hadn't been squeezing too hard; he knew that could be painful. There was just … nothing. He switched on his bedside lamp. He looked around to see if there was something on his sheets or his pillow or headboard somehow, but there was nothing. No sign of any fluid but sweat. He tossed the unneeded sock towards the dirty clothes hamper in the corner, pulled off the other one and tossed it to follow the first, then switched the light back off.

That amazing relaxation was diminished by his search for what turned out to be nothing, but he had no trouble finding a restful and immediate sleep that night.

"Are you sure there's nothing I can get you? A glass of warm milk, maybe?"

"No, mom, really. I'm fine. It was just a bad dream, like I said."

"Alright honey, but if you need anything just let us know. That was quite a shock you know, waking up to hear our only daughter screaming bloody murder in the middle of the night. I thought someone had broken into the house!"

"I'm sorry dad. I'm sure it's just the stress of the new school year and my first big test tomorrow. You know I'm prone to nightmares."

"I sure do. But I've never heard you scream like that before…"

"Don't worry about it. Just go back to bed, you two."

"Alright, alright. Goodnight."

"And no more nightmares. You need your sleep."

Her mother switched off the light as they left the room, closing the bedroom door behind them as they went, and she finally began to relax again. She had been sure they would see right through her, know she'd had another sex dream about that new kid in her math class somehow, and they'd ground her or yell at her or something. She knew she wasn't supposed to be having sex and she wasn't – it was a sin. But she also knew that Jesus said that to think about having sex was as much a sin as having it, so dreaming about that boy must be a sin, too. And tonight's dream was so real, and went so much farther than her earlier dreams had, that she was sure she was in trouble.

She pulled her legs up into her chest and rocked back and forth on her back, balled up as tight as she could get, and she prayed for forgiveness while she tried to get back to sleep. She prayed for forgiveness, and prayed that the Lord would save her from the visions and temptations the devil kept putting into her head. She prayed for his help to make it through another day without throwing that new boy to the ground and living out her naughty dreams. She prayed and she prayed and just before the first rays of dawn were breaking across the horizon, she finally fell asleep, curling relaxed onto her right side in a fetal position.

Trevor woke up refreshed. The morning often represented a sort of battle for him, wherein he fought to stay under the covers, to stay out of the light and not have to face the day. Today the challenger, the part of him that wanted to get out into the world and get something done for a change swung out to try to pre-empt his lethargic, apathetic, and usually dominant mode for taking on the world but met no resistance. Trevor literally fell out of bed, he got out of it so quickly. He suspected that he would have a few sore spots before he got very far today, but he didn't let that slow him down.

Underwear, socks, jeans, t-shirt, he dressed in seconds. Comb through his long hair, bottom to top, carefully working out any knots but otherwise ignoring it as usual. Filling his pockets quickly; wallet, black pen, blue pen, red pen, spiral-bound pocket notepad, flat, round stone he'd been carrying with him for years without knowing why, pocket watch, a piece of string and a second rock – to wind the piece of string around. Then he slipped his trench coat on. Its pockets were already occupied. He set down and put on his shoes, tying them carefully. He looked up at his alarm clock, which had yet to go off that morning, and noted as he switched off the alarm that he had got ready in less than three minutes. He moved towards the door.

At this early hour, Trevor was the only one awake in his household. His sister would be rousing in about an hour to get ready for school, and his parents not long afterward to begin their days, but for now the house was silent and empty.

The first rays of sunlight broke assuredly through the windows in the front room and journeyed with deliberate reflection into neighboring rooms and down the hallways and behind and across the furniture, providing a fleeting purity of light that seemed to reveal the truth of color in every thing it coated and enlivened with its presence. Trevor loved the feeling that walking around the house just before the dawn afforded him, that feeling that everything could be renewed and that there was infinite hope for positive change in the world.

The stains on the upholstery, the dirt embedded too deep in the carpet to be vacuumed up, the layered grime of thousands of hands touching and brushing and pushing and pulling on the doors and the doorways and certain places on the walls that may have given the entire house character and made it feel truly lived in but which also made everything feel a little less than perfect were simply not highlighted in this dim yet penetrating light. The light that is so eager to make things appear that it races ahead of the sun and over the horizon before that burning globe of intensity has a chance to show its blazing face, showing only the best and most gentle side of everything it touched as it lit his way to the kitchen for breakfast.

He liked to keep his breakfasts simple – appropriate nutrition and calories to get his body started in the morning, but nothing too elaborate or convoluted. In part this was out of respect for the sleeping members of his family – anything that required multiple plates and pots and pans, griddles and fryers and grills and the oven and the toaster and the blender and the microwave all going at once to produce a sensational delight of colors, textures, temperatures, aromas and flavours to splash across his senses awakening them to the infinity of experience that each new day had the potential to contain would create a virtual cacophony of clatter in planning, preparation and the post-culinary cleanup that it would simply be too much for so early an hour. Especially this close to the shift from summer sleep schedules to school-year hours – no one else in the house was used to or happy with their adjusted early schedules, and being woken to find a gorgeous gourmet meal made for one would not be a beautiful start to their day. Consequently, Trevor pulled a cereal bowl, a spoon, and a box of store-brand corn flakes from the cupboard and combined them with adequate skim milk to make every upcoming bite a moist one. Simple.

As he slowly and deliberately spooned his breakfast bite by bite into his mouth, Trevor took in the contrast of the crunching that seemed so loud inside his head with the silence around him so empty it seemed to press in on him, comforting him in the same way as an old familiar blanket wrapped all around him. He thought about the day ahead of him, of what he would need with him when he left for school. Normality, mostly, and already packed into his backpack left untouched from the previous day.

Paper, pencils, pens, folders organizing everything by subject and already holding his completed homework for the day ahead. Books for class and books to read for fun and books to write in and books to sketch in. His towel. Breath mints, a toothbrush, toothpaste, floss, hair ties, a comb, two clean handkerchiefs. Trevor went over the inventory of his backpack mentally and couldn't think of anything he might need that wasn't already there. Trevor emptied his mind, thinking of nothing else as his hand automatically continued lifting spoonful after spoonful of cereal into his masticating mouth, and he was able to begin the day in a state of peace and relaxation.

Not thinking another thought, Trevor stood and carried his cereal bowl to the sink, rinsed it, and put it into the dishwasher. He strolled to the bathroom, flossed, brushed his teeth, and washed his mouth out with Listerine. He double-checked his pockets, put on his backpack, and walked out the front door, locking it behind him and beginning the walk to school.

Due to certain geographic peculiarities of his neighborhood and some form of what he assumed was gerrymandering of school districts, Trevor attended a school to which the most direct route was a five mile walk, uphill most of the time, walking directly by another high school much closer to his home. Trevor had to leave for his own school so early and returned home so late that he hadn't actually seen who attended the school, nor found out what

14

set them apart that made it worth his time and energy to go so much further to get an education. After the first week of walking by the empty campus twice a day, Trevor didn't give it much thought – it was just another quiet building to meander past on his way one way or the other, hardly more interesting from the outside than any residence or church he passed on the same route. Walking at a casual pace it took nearly ninety minutes for Trevor to reach his own high school from his home. He liked to leave early enough that if he was interrupted or injured or otherwise running late he would still be able to reach the school in time for his first hour, and so as he moved through the growing rays of early morning light towards his destination he did so with the calm and contentment that comes with knowing he will arrive nearly forty-five minutes before he needs to do anything or be anywhere or even begin really to think if he doesn't want to. It was still warm out in the early morning – Trevor lived in a hot enough climate that the heat from the day could not dissipate fast enough to transform into a chill or brisk morning, and it was something he appreciated because it gave him a few more weeks of environmental warmth before he had to button the insulating liner into his trench coat thereby tripling or quadrupling its weight on his shoulders.

Trevor wore his trench coat year-round, and not merely to get attention or to separate himself socially as one might expect – he was intelligent enough and friendly enough that he would get positive attention without the coat, and in the first couple of weeks as a freshman at a new school on the other end of a sprawling metropolis his family had recently moved across, Trevor already counted his friends in the dozens with representation from every major clique and from all four years among them – he mostly liked the multiple deep and mysterious pockets it provided and the unexpected and practically unbelievable way it seemed to actually keep him cool in the summer heat. Through some combination of luck and good planning with perhaps a dappling of careful influence over the people and events that surrounded him, Trevor seemed never to fail to be able to produce whatever he wanted from the pockets of his coat and his backpack during the course of each day. After a few months of owning the coat, Trevor had simply come to understand and anticipate the sort of items people would want or need during the day, and even the most likely items for people to challenge him to produce on a moment's notice – he even had a simple and often satisfying response to anyone who asked for something he could not pull instantly out when he implied to them that he was able to have anything he wanted from out his pockets: "I don't really want that right now."

As he proceeded methodically and with steady pace, Trevor did not detect the precise moment his mind moved from an empty trancelike state to the freeform wandering and daydreaming it was so prone to do, but it was as welcome as the absence of thought had been, not giving conscious ground to the exhaustion his legs might be trying to communicate or the stress his school life might be trying to beat him down with or any other thing that might want to take hold of his conscious mind. Instead of practicalities and realities, Trevor found himself transported to worlds of imagination that were so far-flung that were he ever to try to think of them being conceived by anyone else's mind he would almost surely have come to the conclusion that there was something uniquely foreign about him, totally incompatible with the residents of the world around him in ways he would doubt could be expressed in any language they could understand. Luckily for his sense of belonging, it never once occurred to Trevor that his thoughts might ever escape his own mind, it never entered his frame of thought the idea that his ideas were anything the average person might not have on their own, and because of something he had always considered coincidence, many of his ideas – his best ideas, the ones that could somehow be understood within the frame of reference of modern scientific or philosophical thought – somehow managed to find their way into the world very quickly at the hands of the most qualified to carry them out or disseminate them. An idea for a video game here, in his hands in months, for a new gardening tool, in his neighbor's shed in no time, for a movie or a book or a comic or a web site, it was in his face before he even made the time to write the idea down. All these little instances of serendipity he simply considered coincidences of "great minds think alike" and he didn't spend much time philosophizing about them; it was all just as normal to him as the visions in his head that morning of a rocky mountainside crawling with buffalo-sized chocolate-covered beetles scuttling in complex patterns to create half-toned images visible only from miles away by people wearing heat-vision goggles.

Except that in his mind's eye, the three stranger-looking figures observing the intricate dance on the mountainside miles away were not wearing anything even remotely resembling heat-vision goggles. Trevor knew somehow that they were seeing heat in that red is hot, yellow is warm, green is cool, purple is cold way that modern heat-vision created, but they seemed to be seeing the effect directly with their eyes – eyes bare except for the single pair of coke-bottle-thick glasses that the lankiest of the trio was wearing on his hawk-like beak of a nose, but which Trevor assumed was simply to clear up vision the same way glasses did outside of the impossible realm of his wandering thoughts. He turned back to face the mountain with them – his real body walking as though on some automatic control scheme – and found that he too could see the giant beetles' complex dance as the men did, in intense contrasting reds and yellows and blues, forming images of surprisingly full-color, video-like quality from what should have been a random noise of large and small dots on a dark background.

As his focus moved from the wonder of the improbability of what he was envisioning, the content of the presentation became suddenly clear and surrealistically shocking – it appeared to be a live video image of a young man with long hair and a trench coat walking in morning light with residential housing moving by in the background – it appeared that the beetles in his mind were dancing in such a manner that it allowed the three unknown men he was imagining along with the beetles to watch him as he walked to school. He had never imagined anything quite as mirror-in-a-mirror as this that he could recall, but gladly played along. He turned his real head in the direction of what would have been the camera had the images created in his imagination been real video really being filmed, and as he expected to, Trevor did not see anything there to capture his visage. He did however see his head turn in the beetles' image to face the men directly, and that was such an unexpected yet wholly predictable thing for him to imagine that his physical body nearly missed a step as it came to a stop and turned to face entirely towards the unseen, imagined watchers. As his real body turned, so turned his mind's eye to see the three observers reacting to his apparent ability to see them through the wall of chocolate-covered beetles.

"Can he see us?"

"He couldn't! The chocolate prevents reverse-viewing – I didn't spend weeks hand-painting every scarantula in the forest with chocolate for nothing."

"But he's looking right at us! Something's gone wrong! We've got to get out of here!"

The lanky one with the glasses who had not yet spoken, without turning away from the ongoing mountainside presentation, reached out with one hand and stopped the shorter, fleeing man by grasping the collars of his rumpled and strangely patterned shirt and sweater-vest and pulling him up short. "If he could see us it would be too late to run, Sqrat. Remember though that last night was the first time his power set off any of our artifacts and fetishes – even if he had taken conscious notice of his potential, he couldn't be so skilled with them yet as to see through chocolate. Relax."

"He's right, Sqrat. There's probably just a bird or something taking his notice right behind our vantage. My chocolate is working fine. I'm sure of it."

"Sure," the short one turned back and seemed to relax, though his voice was still trembling quite a bit, "h-h-he's probably just… j-just s-s-standing s-s-s-stock s-still s-s-s-staring at some s-s-small s-sparrow…"

"Sure." Trevor's real body began walking again towards his school.

"Alright, alright, if it will put your mind at ease I'll disband the scarantulas." The lanky one began muttering of chanting something too quietly to hear as he knelt down to the ground and began collecting small marked stones that Trevor hadn't previously noticed from an intricate pattern on the ground, putting them into a lumpy glowing satchel he had been holding. He lifted them from the soil in what was clearly a specific order and at a careful pace, and when the last stone was in the satchel he closed its latching cover with a –click– that seemed to bring the scarantulas – or beetles or whatever they were – out of the trance they had been in and scurrying down the mountain and disappearing into the surrounding forest below. The colored spots which had been forming his image not long before now destabilized into a white-noise-like melting of jumbled activity down and down and down, but at the same time the heat-vision-like appearance they'd had slowly faded to true colors and for the first time Trevor could see what he had earlier known instantly to be true – the gigantic creatures' hard shells were covered completely in another shell of hard, dark chocolate. The lanky one, pulling the strap of his satchel back over his shoulder as he stood up, spoke again to the other two. "Are you satisfied?"

As they both seemed to settle visibly into themselves with apparent relief and thanked him and babbled over each other so that neither could be clearly heard speculating about what might be going on with the young man they had been observing, the lanky one who was clearly the superior of the other two in many ways reached up and pulled his glasses off, moving his eyes' focus away from them. It might have seemed as though he were looking at some interesting bird or other attraction behind them in the distance or merely relaxing his eyes, but really he looked Trevor directly in his mind's eye with a steely but somehow unconcerned – or at least unrevealing – gaze that seemed to say "I know you know."

And as Trevor was about to think about what that might further imply, as his own imagined eyes were locked in an unblinking stare with those that had been hidden behind the too-thick glasses of that strange, angular man, Trevor looked up with his real eyes to find himself standing at his locker at school, and the interesting, engaging, but wholly unbelievable and surreal daydream he'd been having was instantly gone – wiped away by the combination to the lock that momentarily took over Trevor's conscious mind. He opened his locker as he swung his backpack around in front of him so that he could exchange textbooks from his afternoon classes with textbooks for his morning classes. He rattled his head back and forth to clear it, took a deep breath, and carefully closed and re-locked his locker and continued on to the cafeteria where he would pass the remaining time before his first class by completing as much of the next day's homework and reading as he could.

Trevor liked to be the first person into the cafeteria in the morning, to sit at a corner table and watch his classmates slowly file in and take their places, alone of with friends, to eat, to chat, to study or try to get homework done in the fleeting moments before it came due, the noise level gradually increasing from echoing silence to a true din of intermingling sounds fighting to be differentiated and understood. His own constantly growing group of friends came in with random timing and often in spurts, sitting at first at the same table as Trevor, then filling adjacent tables as their number expanded evermore the closer it got to first hour.

The first sound Hannah could recall hearing was not the slamming of the front door, but the rattling of her bedroom window, a startling sound created by a tangible sort of echo in the physical plane that produced sounds of its own rather than simply reproducing sounds the way a traditional echo would. The deepness of her long-awaited sleep had been broken perhaps by the slam itself, so jarring that it was able to tear her from the warm embrace of unconsciousness, but not so quickly that Hannah heard the slam itself - her waking mind seemed to leap directly from fevered prayer to morning light and disturbed panes of glass, not a moment of respite between them. She looked at the clock, finding that she must have unplugged it in a fit related to its persistent reminders that she should already have been sleeping - there was no information to be found in its blank digital face.

20

Hannah rolled over to the side of her bed, leaning her head and arm over the edge to dig through her purse which had been carelessly thrown to the floor the previous evening. In her state of near-sleep, Hannah nearly forgot what she was searching for before her hand grasped upon it in the cluttered mess that the contents of her purse had become. She had to pull its face to within inches of her own before her sleep-creased eyes granted her the comprehension to see what was blinking out across her mobile phone - school starts in ten minutes. Hannah dropped the phone back into her purse, rolled back onto her bed and began to stretch and yawn, lazily waking and only gradually moving to escape the warm confines of her blankets.

She shot upright suddenly, eyes wide open.

"School starts in ten minutes!" her voice strained and cracked as she shouted out surprised into the empty room.

Suddenly she was on the move, leaping out of bed only to find her legs completely tangled in her bedclothes as she tripped up in them and fell face-first to the floor. Groaning anxiously, Hannah carefully freed her feet and legs from the twisted trap of sheets and duvet that linked her steadfast to her bed, nearly taking her pajamas with it as she finally tossed it back onto her bed. By some miracle she managed to pull her pajamas the rest of the way off without twisting her ankle or pulling a muscle or otherwise injuring herself or slowing down.

With no time to spare, Hannah decided to forego a shower, throwing on the first clothes to fall under her hands as she reached into her drawers. She did not waste time looking into a mirror as she rushed out of her bedroom, purse in one hand, backpack forgotten entirely. If she had paused for just a moment she might have taken more time than she thought she could afford by changing into something a little more presentable than the hot-pink bra under thin white shirt above the torn and stained cutoff jeans that were a little too tight for her but that she kept anyway for laundry day, not to mention the mismatched tennis shoes and even less-matched socks she had pulled on in an apparently blind rush to be something other than naked. Had

21

Hannah so much as glanced in a mirror on her way out the door, she may have realized that her hair was a total wreck, tangled and swept up and stuck with sweat and tears and sleep in a coiffure that definitely had an air of the post-coital to it.

She ran out the door, slamming it behind her, but running so fast away from it that she didn't hear the echo-like emanation that was her own window rattling in response. Halfway to school as she grasped her own chest in pain was the first she noticed her unwise selection of undergarments. As she stepped onto campus just in time to hear the bell that signaled she was already a full minute late to class, she had to stop to pull her too-tight, too-worn pants from the crack of her ass, realizing for the first time the unsound decision she had made in selecting them, and that she had somehow totally failed to put underwear on under them.

"What is wrong with me today?" She muttered inaudibly as she ran across campus to her class already in session, "This is so unlike me."

When she reached her classroom, Hannah did her best to slip in relatively unnoticed, but failed rather dramatically. Between failing to tie her shoes in her rush that morning, trying to sneak into the class discreetly to avoid attention instead of just walking normally, and then the unfortunate coincidence of her bag-strap catching on the door-latch catch, Hannah managed to pull off one of those spectacular pratfalls no one expects to see outside of old comedies and vaudevillian stage shows. She flipped around bodily in the air, first half a turn forward as her feet were tripped up under her, then a full turn backwards as her purse's strap recoiled her back towards the still-open but rapidly closing door while simultaneously ejecting the full contents of her purse like shrapnel from a high explosive, showering the class in the bits and bobs and books from the bottom of her bag.

Anyone who hadn't turned at the noise of the door opening or of the inhaling-choking noise she made as she was yanked backward by her bag-strap was suddenly made very aware of Hannah by being hit about the head and shoulders by her airborne assault so that as her head finally reached the hard floor just beyond the door jam with a resounding crack, all other heads in the classroom were looking her way. She didn't move, and neither did anyone else in the room, mouths agape at the unattractively dressed prone body laying apparently unconscious in the entrance to the class - not even the teacher moved from his frozen stance at the front of the room until a few seconds after the automatically-closing door came down hard against the top of Hannah's head, jarring her whole body in a sickening wave of motion that conjured thoughts of molded gelatins jiggling and dropped caskets' shaken contents.

When the teacher did move, he ran over in a rush to where Hannah lay but then stopped short of actually touching or moving her in any way. He could see that her arms and legs were sprawled at what seemed to be unnatural angles, one arm even dangling from her purse, still stuck by the strap to the door-latch catch. She was surrounded by the explosively strewn array of her personal belongings which quite surrealistically created the false image that the contents of Hannah's life had somehow burst out of her own body in physical form and left her lifeless in the process. Makeup here and there, a small Bible and a smaller New Testament which landed closer to her unmoving form, pencils, pens, and a datebook were not further afield, and among the feminine pads, key chains, ticket stubs, knickknacks and a wallet opened to reveal her own smiling face on her ID card, one could get the feeling they really knew all there was to know about Hannah in that single pass of the eyes that each student was slowly making. Time seemed to stand still in the frozen diorama that was Hannah's life laid bare on the floor around her body for each student then - as they all felt their own place in it clarifying - until a single voice that each one there would later swear was not their own said weakly "she's still breathing."

Suddenly the silence and decorum was broken and small conversations broke out all over the room. The teacher managed to prop the door open off Hannah's head without stepping on or moving her, but ended up out in the hallway as a result, away from the speculating students. He tried to

23

figure out what to do; he didn't want to leave everyone alone with her unconscious like that, but someone needed to be notified, an ambulance needed to be called. He leaned into the classroom being careful of the girl at his feet who was taking quite shallow breaths and perhaps bleeding internally and he spoke loudly to get everyone's attention.

"Does anyone have a cellphone?"

"No."

"No."

"No."

Everyone said "no" or shook their heads in dissent and a general murmur rose to the effect of reminding the teacher that having phones on campus was against school rules.

"Come on. You know you're not all following the rules. Betty, I saw you on the phone at lunch yesterday!"

"Sorry, Mr. Morton." Betty wouldn't look him in the eyes.

"She needs help." He looked from student to student plaintively, but none of them was going to be the one to have their phone confiscated. "Someone."

There was a long pause before a gentle voice came from the back of the classroom. It was the new student, a boy Mr. Morton had not yet learned the name of, and who rarely participated in class but who had so far turned in all his assignments on time and aced the quizzes. He was moving, but had spoken so slightly he couldn't have been understood by anyone there. Still, he had something in his hand as he casually approached the door and the injured girl there, not looking down or stepping gingerly but still managing not to set foot on a single strewn item from her purse's explosion.

"It flew out of her bag," the new boy in the trench coat said as he handed Hannah's mobile phone to Mr. Morton.

The flustered teacher didn't even have the chance to say "Thank you" before the strange, long-haired boy turned and returned to his desk, almost unaware of what was so shocking to everyone else about the girl's accident. As the teacher began dialing 911 Emergency Services with the phone of the one in need of those services he was too disturbed by all of this happening in his own classroom to notice the boy had simply gone back to work on his homework for some future class, apparently unconcerned with the health or welfare of his injured classmate. Of course, despite the growing chatter about her from everyone else there, one would have been hard pressed to locate more than a whiff of genuine concern coming from any single person left inside the room. Mr. Morton was the only one aware of the situation with any apparent genuine concern for Hannah, and as soon as an ambulance was on the way he called the front office to notify administration, who he hoped would take over for him in a more appropriate and organized way.

As he stood there looking at the ragdoll-like body captured in the doorway, watched the class as their conversations quickly turned from Hannah to more casual and comfortable topics as though Hannah were not still laying there, as he waited for someone, anyone, to show up and do something, anything, he just kept holding the classroom door open and muttering to himself "I'm a math teacher. I'm not trained for this. I'm a math teacher. I'm not trained for this," and on and on and on for the seeming eternity that passed before he was finally relieved by the paramedics who somehow arrived in advance of anyone from the school's administrative staff.

"Has she been moved?"

"No. I didn't know..."

"Not moving her was the right thing to do, sir."

After that brief exchange, the paramedics practically ignored Mr. Morton. Betty, perhaps feeling bad about lying about having a phone or perhaps because her conscience finally kicked in, had gotten up and begun collecting the former contents of Hannah's purse. When the paramedics had questions, Betty fielded them, ably describing the accident and handing over Hannah's ID and wallet for identification, and then making sure that the reassembled contents, placed back in the purse, went with the unconscious girl when she was rolled away on a stretcher in a a neck brace and strapped down securely. Had the paramedics worked a little faster or had a classmate shared their phone so that the call could have been made a little sooner, Hannah's embarrassment might only have been word-of-mouth from the people who were there. Instead, due to some sort of unending stream of bad luck, Hannah's ill-dressed, unconscious and bound-up body was rolled through the school's hallways just after first hour ended and the living contents of every classroom burst forth, surrounding the paramedics and stretcher as they fought their way to the exit. By the end of the day, nine out of ten students would claim to have seen her with their own eyes and half of them were probably telling the truth. By the end of the week the school's football team had finally won a game against their longtime rival from across town and school spirit seemed to wipe Hannah completely from their memories.

Even Betty was heard to say "How much thought are we expected to give to someone in a coma? Let us know when she wakes up, but until that day, let us enjoy our own, non-comatose, lives."

After her accident, Trevor didn't fantasize about Hannah anymore. He tried, but instead of visualizing her body pressed hot and soft against his own in passion, he could only see her laying tangled and unconscious on the floor of his first hour class with everyone staring on. There was something decidedly anti-erotic about being stared at by thirty pair of uncaring eyes, and for the first couple of nights it was that simple imagery that did him in entirely, stopping any chance of getting himself off. Then, just as the general interest around him dropped off with the knowledge that she was stable and comatose and may not wake up for months or years if at all, Trevor's interest in putting Hannah at the center of his nightly erotic fantasies also waned, and she was soon replaced with less singular, less immersive visions conglomerate from all the most attractive or erotic sights Trevor saw and remembered during the course of his days. The orgasms were less intense and the experience seemed somehow lacking in realism or a proper timeline, but orgasms still felt good, so he kept it up.

As though compensating for the imaginative loss, his dreams and daydreams became more bizarre and intense. Much of the time Trevor couldn't decipher what was going on, and the rest of the time it was as though he were somehow invisibly watching, or imagining watching, normal people's boring everyday activities. It was sortof like the perspective he'd had during the weird beetle-video-thing, where he was an unseen non-participant in his own imagination, but there wasn't anything nearly as interesting as that going on most of the time. Trevor's mind seemed to be intent on imagining what other people looked like when they thought no one was watching them; imagining how people behaved when they were by themselves and not putting on a facade of behavior for the people around them. Whether there was any reasonable connection between what he imagined people were like in their privacy and what people were actually like it would be impossible to say, due to the very nature of privacy. Still, it interested him.

He imagined watching people he'd never seen before, simply eating breakfast and reading the morning newspaper. He imagined watching a woman showering, and it was titillating for a while, but then it gradually became tedious watching her utilitarian scrubbing of herself and washing of her hair and shaving of her legs and then it didn't end there, his mind didn't wander, and he imagined watching her dry off and get dressed and blow dry and style her hair and apply makeup and eat breakfast and drive most of the way to work before he himself got to school on the morning he found himself imagining it.

He also found himself imagining meetings of dozens of strange people and creatures around a geometrically impossible table in a room he knew somehow was not really a room, all speaking incomprehensibly in sing-song clicks and clucks and gurgles and whistles and some form of complex sign language that invoked images Trevor could never seem to make out from his imagined vantage point.

As his imaginings became alternately more realistically mundane and unbelievably incomprehensible,

27

Trevor began to move himself from his former comfortable role as the observer, the entertained, to a more challenging and complicated role as an active observer and perhaps towards becoming an active participant - hoping to bring his everyday fantasies to the level that his erotic fantasies had so satisfyingly operated on when he'd been imagining Hannah, but which normally was not the case with his daydreams.

This first manifested in more conscious control of his point of view of whatever was going on; he could watch someone commuting slowly to work through near-standstill traffic from the passenger seat, the back seat, the hood of the car looking backward, or even straight above the car looking down directly through the opaque roof of the car as though it weren't there at all. He could imagine someone shopping at the mall by themselves, going from store to store, trying on clothes and jewelry and he could follow along with them, but it was no trouble at all to move from following one person in his mind to another, imagining a woman trying on sweaters and then shifting focus to a man trying to choose a puppy from the pet store for his girlfriend's birthday.

Yet still he could usually do nothing more than observe the strange ones from what seemed to be a predetermined vantage. Daydreams of illicit meetings of increasingly unusual people and more and more non-people. The imagined classrooms full of teenagers dressed as oddly as the adults he'd seen, studying subjects he couldn't identify from ... well, they didn't seem to be textbooks, but he didn't know what else to think of them as. The occasionally more mundane look at some lone figure - sometimes someone he'd imagined before at one of the impossible meetings and once it was Sqrat himself - but not doing something really "mundane"; watching an oddly dressed woman build a child-size coffin out of metal with some sort of pen-sized hand-held welder that doubled as some sort of cutting torch when she needed it to be, for example, which she filled with live roaches and then covered with some thick fluid that would have looked like a caramel if it weren't bubbling continuously and cerulean blue in hue. In none of these visions or daydreams could Trevor seem to be anything but a passive observer. He couldn't shift his point of view, he couldn't switch focus from one strange person to another, he couldn't take control of his own imagination and it was driving him crazy.

Over the next month or so, Trevor became more and more in control of his "normal" imagined scenarios - able to change things like which color blouse a shopper would select or to get a showering woman to drop the soap and bend over, or getting a driver to forget himself and miss his exit and be late for work; things they didn't have an opinion of their own about, or just removing thought about something automatic - and he simultaneously became more and more aware of the limitations he was kept under in his "strange" imaginings. It was paying attention to these differences that led him to notice that some of his "strange" visions seemed to be staged for him, like there was something there he was supposed to see, and in others the "players" looked directly at him in the same way the lanky stranger had during the dream about the video-beetle-mountain. Remembering which reminded him of the way he had somehow known what had been going on there despite its oddness and which led him to try to find out what he could know without learning about the things he was imagining.

It turned out to be quite a lot.

Effectively, if someone he could see with his mind's eye knew something, Trevor could know it. The only real limitation on this was in what Trevor could think of trying to know - if it occurred to him to know the color of the car of the spouse of the clerk helping the man he was imagining buying a new drill driver, he knew it immediately as though he had always known that it was dark blue. It was like the recall part of remembering things - anything the people he was imagining could remember if they'd thought to remember it, he could remember it somehow. This was sortof like being in their heads, and it was not long before Trevor tried to shift his point of view directly into the mind of someone in his mind.

A headache and immediate loss of the will or ability to continue his reveries was the result. Trevor did not pursue that option again soon. Instead he tried something a little more aggressive, a move towards taking his daydreams to the level his erotic fantasies had operated at with Hannah. He tried to imagine someone he knew.

At first it was not quite the same as his other daydreams. It was more like remembering the person's image as in a photograph, still or very brief in time and always from the original point of view he had experienced it from. Not moving forward in time, not like watching a story unfold, just a realistic, nearly three-dimensional but unchanging view of the person he was imagining. It was very much like the erotic fantasies he had relegated himself to having since Hannah's accident; he had more control of the elements there than in his standard daydreams, he could imagine their clothes changed to some extent or removed entirely, their hair color and style, their face, and even the environment they were being remembered in to some extent, but it never became the "real" immersive imaginings he could otherwise so easily drop himself into. It seemed like a dead end. An interesting dead end, but he couldn't seem to draw anyone he knew into an active, immersive fantasy in the same way he had with Hannah. In fact, when it occurred to him that he had once been able to do exactly what he couldn't seem to do now, Trevor couldn't remember how he'd got Hannah into his fantasies in the first place.

He tried drawing other young women he'd seen into his sexual fantasies on their own, and sometimes it was good and it was always quite erotic, but it was never quite as real as it had been.

Before that revelation made him begin to lose interest in the less-satisfying sexual fantasies he now discovered he was having, Trevor stumbled on another good idea. If he could move from one person as his focus in the mundane but immersive daydreams to another, perhaps he could keep moving from person to person, location to location, until he came across someone he recognized from reality. Trevor didn't know how long it would take him, so instead of trying it on his morning walk to school he set aside an entire Saturday to spend alone in his room trying to find someone he knew within his imagination. He knew some of the locations in which his day-dreams seemed to take place, such as the local mall and some neighborhoods and stretches of roads and highways he'd seen a hundred times, so he figured that if his mind was populating some version of the real world with people, some of the real people he knew could be found in the parts of that world they corresponded to. That was the theory, anyway, so on that Saturday, nearly two months after Hannah's accident, Trevor spent the whole day in his own mind.

"What are you going to tell her parents?"

"What would you say? I don't even know how to explain it to another doctor."

"There has to be some explanation. Maybe her parents know something that would make more sense of it."

"I doubt that. Have you not met them? They never stop praying and they've got their 60 year old minister in with them praying over her twice a week. From what I've heard there's no chance they know who the father is - she must have been hiding the relationship entirely."

"Has there been anyone else come to see her at all? Some boy who might have ... well, you know... "

"On her first week here, her bible study group showed up, but I wasn't here at the time, so I couldn't tell you. Since then it's only been her family and her minister."

"Is there any chance it was - "

"No. Don't even say that. Remember the details of the ... the situation? Her hymen is completely intact. Totally unbroken. Your little finger couldn't have penetrated her without making an impact - she has not had sex."

"So how did she get pregnant? You think she was fooling around with someone without protection and the healthiest sperm I've ever heard of swam all the way beyond her intact hymen, up her birth canal and fertilized an egg?"

"It could happen."

"Could it really?"

"That's why we need to find out who her boyfriend was, and why I don't know what to tell her parents."

"Why don't you just tell them the facts, unembellished with theories. She's about eight weeks pregnant."

"She also appears to have never had sex. They'll think it's some sort of immaculate conception!"

"Mary was the immaculate conception. She was born without original sin so she could bear the Son of Man in a sinless womb. Jesus was a virgin birth, not an immaculate conception."

"Fine. Whatever. What, are you one of them?"

"One of whom? I was raised Catholic. I went to a Catholic primary school. They make you learn these things."

"Okay, fine, but how can we tell this girl's parents she's going to have a virgin birth?"

"You don't."

"Someone has to."

"Why?"

"She's pregnant, Earl," he was nearly shouting now, but kept his voice low enough not to draw attention from outside his office, "in a couple of months we won't be able to hide it. This can't be kept secret for long."

"There is another option."

"No."

"An unmarried comatose Christian teenager isn't exactly a prime candidate for single motherhood."

"It's unethical! How can you even be considering that?"

"Most pregnancies in comatose patients do not make it to term. It would be easy to document as a stillbirth."

"You're a monster."

"Fine. What do you propose? You can't even talk to her parents."

"I don't know."

"You could wait until she starts to show and they start asking questions. I'm sure that would go over well. I can imagine it now: 'Why didn't we know about this before?' - 'Actually, we did.' - 'So why didn't you tell us?' - 'We were hoping you wouldn't notice.' And then just blank stares and tears and maybe a lawsuit."

"A lawsuit?"

"They're going to claim someone at the hospital did it. Look at her charts - it looks like she conceived the morning of her accident or right after that. No hymen is going to change that."

"We could make new charts."

"And forge a dozen signatures and pay off the nurses and lab techs who know the truth?"

"I don't know. I just... "

"You don't know. I know that. So what choice do you have? Induce."

"I can't."

"I can."

"I... " Earl waited, silently. "I'll assist."

"Okay then."

And they waited until an hour they knew they would not be interrupted and they modified inventory levels on paper so that the equipment they used would not be missed. And late that night they attempted to abort Hannah's pregnancy. They tried three different standardized methods, each more detectable than the last, but the fetus simply would not budge or otherwise react. After four very stressful hours and some further creative attempts involving non-standard tools, the two doctors had succeeded in doing nothing more than completely destroying Hannah's previously untouched hymen. She remained pregnant and comatose despite their best attempts to change that fact. In the end they managed to clean up and get their ineffective implements properly put away before the morning shift arrived to check on her. They waited impatiently to be sure nothing out of the ordinary was noticed, then spoke again in the privacy of Earl's office before retiring home for a couple hours' sleep.

"I don't understand."

"You've said that a hundred times tonight. It doesn't help. I don't understand either, but you don't hear me going on and on about it."

"I'm not sure which is more sane though. Going on about it or remaining silent."

"Sane? None of this is sane."

"That, I can agree with."

"But at least one thing is a little easier now. Her hymen is gone."

"Don't remind me. Uhg."

"I thought you'd consider it good news. It doesn't look like a virgin birth anymore."

"Instead it looks like she was repeatedly violated by two fumbling doctors months after she was comatose."

"Hey. I wasn't fumbling."

"Her scar tissue will say otherwise."

"It will look like she lost her virginity normally to the casual observer. You're the only one who examined her before this, right?"

"As far as I know."

"Fine. Then we're on much firmer ground. We wait a week or two, then just inform her parents about her pregnancy."

"And just ignore the virginity aspect."

"Absolutely."

"Just like that?"

"Just like that. Look, the kid comes out walking on water and curing leprosy and you can tell anyone you want about the truth, but until you see a miracle with your own eyes, this stays quiet, alright? Both of our licenses are on the line if this gets out. You were right about it being an ethical violation. If there had been a stillbirth, that's one thing, but you saw that thing, it wasn't budging. But in trying to get it to budge..."

"I understand. You don't have to tell me. This much I understand."

"Okay. So. You have a week, maybe two to figure out what you're going to tell her parents. She should be sufficiently healed by then to bear a second opinion."

"Alright. Two weeks. I can do this."

"You'd better hope so. If this doesn't go right..."

"I know. I just have to be convincing that she must have been sexually active before the accident."

"You know it must be true, right? People don't just become pregnant. There must have been sexual contact of

some kind, with some teenager with amazingly active sperm.
Something."

"I know, I know, I just... "

"Just nothing. You know what to say."

"I know. I know what to say. I know."

Trevor woke up Saturday morning, ate breakfast and returned to his room. He drew back the curtains so he could see the beautiful blue of the sky as he lay back on his bed and let his mind wander. He was going to try to move within his imagination to someone he knew, to see if his imagination could believably reproduce someone he was familiar with in a way that was recognizably like how they would behave. This was also partially because he was beginning to grow disinterested in imagining only strangers and stranger strangers and nothing he was really very familiar with. Trevor would have liked to know more about what was going on in the things he was imagining that weren't tied to any believable reality he was aware of, but he couldn't seem to control what he saw there and he simply didn't know what to try to remember from the memories of the subjects he was imagining.

As he stared up out of his window at the sparse clouds moving by overhead, Trevor tried to let his mind wander to something mundane - he didn't want to end up imagining another impossible meeting of giant metal men and tiny glowing balls of light. By trying to remember what they were called, Trevor knew the metal men averaged about 10 metres tall and referred to themselves as the Metasanti, but little else. He knew the glowing lights were not will-o-wisps or faeries, but there was something about the way they thought that Trevor couldn't quite get ahold of with his own mind clearly, so he really didn't know anything else about them other than that they were in heated negotiations with the Metasanti over something the Metasanti thought of as the Willowlands. Being unable to understand what was going on in his own imagination made Trevor particularly unsatisfied, so he was specifically trying to imagine anything but the odd.

And then he did. Four people sitting around a table in a huge library, books and papers in front of them, reading and taking notes. Three young women, about college-age, and a middle-aged man. Trevor didn't think to remember how old they actually were or what their names were, he just wanted to get to familiar ground. He moved his mind's eye up and up and up until he had a wide perspective on the entire cavernous room that they were studying in. Dozens of other people were sitting at tables studying and standing at bookshelves searching for books, and then he spotted someone moving towards the doors and Trevor focused on them, effectively zooming his point of view in close to them just as they passed through the doors. As soon as he could see the building and neighborhood from the outside, Trevor knew this was not going to go very quickly; he didn't recognize anything.

He'd barely noticed the gender of the person he followed out of the building before he switched to someone driving rapidly by and was moving quickly away. Trevor was simultaneously passenger and driver in his fantasy today, choosing who he was focused on, but not really choosing where they were going. The driver he was following through a neighborhood he was unfamiliar with was named Tony, and he was heading to the home of the woman he was having an affair with. With a little creative thought, Trevor was able to recall the route Tony had taken the last time he'd done this, and knew there would be a good opportunity to find another subject at the freeway overpass. He was not disappointed, but then found that trying to find a car going someplace he thought would be a good lead was more difficult than he first anticipated.

As Tony had driven over the freeway, Trevor had looked down and selected a car passing perpendicular below to shift focus to, and found his mind whipped sharply in a new direction with a false sense of inertia and nausea. In reality, his body was laying calmly on his bed in his room, his eyes closed. There was no real motion, no reason to react this way except that he so correctly imagined the motion that he couldn't help but feel it. Someone watching his body apparently taking a nap would have thought he was in the midst of an intense dream, seeing his body reacting to the imagined forces it was being subjected to.

As Trevor's mind acclimated to its new direction of motion, nearly seventy imagined miles per imagined hour, he took just enough time to remember where the person was headed before moving to another driver passing by even faster in the left-hand lane. This driver's mind was nearly unreadable to Trevor, not in any normal way. Instead of having full access to remember anything from his mind, Trevor seemed to be receiving a sort of broadcast of tightly controlled thoughts, almost a monologue of thoughts, the way it was always portrayed in the movies. He tried to recall why the person's thoughts were this way, but all he got was that same constant feed of highly edited thought. He couldn't seem to effect the direction the thoughts were going or divine much information from them at first, and it frustrated him enough to draw his point of view right into the car next to the driver's head.

Which was when he noticed that the driver was a nervous young man and there was an attractive young woman looking at him from the passenger seat. The stream of thoughts didn't stop with proximity. Conscious thoughts about careful driving and not wanting to look too cautious in front of Maria. Thoughts about what to say, how to act, what to do, how to be. Thoughts about whether he'd selected the right clothes, about what his breath smelled like, about whether she'd enjoy the picnic lunch he'd packed for them or the scenic overlook into the canyon in the spot he'd spent weeks selecting. Thoughts about what Maria smelled like sitting next to him in the car, the way the light glanced off the blond strands of her flowing hair, the friendliness of her smile, and his good fortune at somehow having managed to convince her to spend the morning with him. The thoughts were a jumbled mess, but controlled by the young man's conscious mind, and Trevor couldn't get much else. He knew enough to know the car wasn't going anywhere he was familiar with, but Trevor wanted to try something else.

He shifted around to focus on Maria, the young woman in the passenger seat, and the voice of the mental monologue changed from male to female, and from fast-paced and nervous to sparse and calm. Maria was not worried that she wasn't wearing the right clothes or had bad breath or any number of other small concerns, but there was a sense of confidence that came across to Trevor that implied to him that she had spent long, careful time making sure that every aspect of her appearance and the young man's perception of her was just as she wanted it to be. She did have thoughts though, that came to Trevor in a steady but less urgent stream. Thoughts about how cute she thought Daryl looked today, about how glad she was he'd worn his blue ringer tee-shirt, and how she liked the way it showed off his firm muscular shoulders and chest by clinging to him in a way she secretly wouldn't mind doing herself. She thought about their next date, what they'd do on the one-month anniversary of their first date, and a few glimpses of thought about what her name would look like in front of Daryl's last name flitted to Trevor.

Through the constant stream of thoughts coming to him from Maria, Trevor found that for some reason he was still able to recall things from her memory in between her conscious thoughts. He found that as long as what he was trying to remember was not far off from what she was consciously thinking about, they came through with much more clarity and detail. Instead of being like other people's memories, which came to Trevor much like the dry facts of an encyclopedia, Maria's thoughts came through like proper memories. He could remember their first date as though he'd actually been there the whole time, as Maria herself. He could remember the taste of the Chicken Parmesan she'd ordered, the lightness in her head after the third glass of wine and the warm feeling she'd experienced gazing across at Daryl over candlelight, how he'd almost seemed to glow with an inner light. He could remember most of their conversation, though Trevor did find some gaps in her memory where she seems not to have been paying attention entirely. He could remember the end of the date, when Daryl had walked Maria home, and what it had felt like to kiss him before she moved inside, and that was more interesting to Trevor than watching a hundred women showering themselves.

He was suddenly very interested in what Daryl thought of that same kiss, and he shifted his perspective back to the driver's seat. Again, the near-constant stream of conscious thoughts shifted in tone and voice as Maria's calm and confident musings were replaced by Daryl's nervous second-guessing. Trevor tried to slip in between Daryl's thoughts to get a glimpse of his perspective of his first date with Maria, and it came only in flashes at first. Trevor tried massaging Daryl's thoughts a bit, directing them somehow back to that first date, and he wasn't entirely sure whether it was his own direction or Daryl's random second-guessing of his actions, but Daryl started thinking about all the things that he'd done wrong on their first date. And in between these intense thoughts about all the things he might have said wrong or done wrong and whether Maria had noticed a crease he couldn't manage to iron out of his slacks, Trevor managed to nudge Daryl's memory of the kiss at the end of their date out of him.

It was much clearer when not through the self-doubting prism of conscious thoughts surrounding it, an unbiased memory that told Trevor what he'd wanted to know. Walking Maria home, Daryl had been more nervous than Trevor himself had ever been in his own life, literally fighting the shakes as they strolled the short distance from the Italian restaurant he had taken her to to her front door. Daryl's mind had been racing much faster then, thinking already about whether he'd screwed up the date and nearly certain that to try to kiss her would get him little more than a laugh and perhaps as much as a slap in the face. Finally, they reached the door and she turned to face him. She looked like she was trying to think of the right words to fill the silence between them but couldn't find them. Trevor knew that that was very close to what she had actually been thinking at the time, that she had been enamored with him and trying to signal to him that she wanted him to bend down and kiss her, and what she'd finally decided to do. From Daryl's point of view, Trevor remembered seeing her moving up towards him on her toes and then felt Daryl leaning down to meet her lips as his eyes came closed blocking out Trevor's vision of the kiss just as it had been in Maria's mind.

As their lips met, Daryl's mind had suddenly gone calm. He wasn't thinking about whether he'd ordered the right salad dressing or if he had some oregano between his teeth. Daryl was just Daryl, just kissing Maria. Which was exactly what it had seemed like from the other side. They didn't kiss consciously, either of them. Somehow all pretense and thought just melted away and they were communicating through contact in a pure way. Trevor let go of Daryl's memory, shifted his focus to the first driver passing by in the opposite direction, and as he adjusted to the near-nausea of the hundred-and-forty mile per hour sudden shift in velocity he subjected himself to mentally, he thought about that kiss.

Trevor had never really kissed anyone that way, himself.

When he finally got his bearings enough to focus on his new driver, Trevor wasn't sure if he was disappointed or relieved that this driver was alone and unconscious of being observed. Trevor had easy access to his memories in that more-familiar encyclopedic way, and didn't have to put up with that movie-like monologue of conscious thoughts coming through, but at the same time he wondered if this new driver had ever kissed anyone in that way before, and if so who, and what were the circumstances, and what did it feel like, and ... and he couldn't quite get to those memories. But he did find that this driver was headed to the mall Trevor was familiar with, a place he would expect in reality to find at least a few people he knew. So Trevor settled into the back seat where he wouldn't have to look at the face of this man who was headed to the mall to try to sneak a peek at young women in changing rooms with a combination of mirrors and guile. Trevor hadn't felt he'd been doing anything wrong imagining watching women in changing rooms or showering or dressing, and had it occurred to him that his driver was imaginary too, and only looking at the people in Trevor's own imagination he might have felt less revulsion to this creepy voyeur.

He didn't think much of it though, instead still reveling in his new, imagined memories of that kiss. Of superimposing one memory over the other, one perspective of an intimate event over the other side of the same event and recalling the subtle details therein. Trevor had kissed before, mostly family on the cheeks or friends playfully, as a greeting, but he hadn't really dated before and definitely hadn't kissed anyone open mouth to open mouth. Hadn't felt that connection, like pure communication, with a real person before. He'd imagined it, with Hannah, and more. He'd imagined kisses that carried that same level of connection and intensity and more than that in them. He'd imagined kisses before, and while he'd imagined this kiss as well, he'd never imagined kissing from both sides of the equation. Not to mention how real this kiss had seemed, how very present and in-the-moment he'd felt, like he had really been the one kissing instead of just being a disembodied imaginer recalling the imagined memories of an imagined kiss two imaginary people had shared on an imagined date.

This was the level of immersion and detail he loved, this was approaching the interactivity and realism he'd come to miss from his erotic fantasies about Hannah, this was going in the right direction for him. As the car pulled into the mall parking lot and Trevor backed up into the sky to find someone moving into the big doors leading to the local equivalent of consumer heaven, he was looking more and more forward to locating someone today that he knew, someone he could imagine the memories of in the very personal way he'd just discovered. He was looking forward to getting a glimpse of a real person, even if the glimpse was just as fake as the glimpses into the minds of strangers. It would feel real. He knew it would. He followed a mother and her kids into the mall, suddenly having to deal with a stream of thoughts about keeping her children out of trouble and scorning her husband for watching his stupid football game instead of watching them for her while she went shopping, and Trevor found someone shopping alone to focus on as quickly as he could.

The mall was crowded in Trevor's mind today. Most of the people who were walking in and out of and between the various stores were with one or more people, so as Trevor moved quickly forward, scanning the crowds visually for someone he might recognize, he found himself practically bombarded with stream after stream of the conscious thoughts he had only recently found his imagined people to have. It was readily apparent to Trevor that these thoughts represented some form of the facade that people put up when they were around other people. All the thoughts about how they're supposed to behave, appear, talk, and otherwise represent themselves to other people formed a constant barricade between Trevor and their raw minds.

On the other hand, if he could find a memory related to their surface facade, he could experience it in its fullness, as real as the rest of what he was imagining, and in some cases as satisfying as his experiences imagining Hannah had been. Passing from person to person, turning around and around and peeking in store after store as he carefully searched for someone he knew from school or around town, he didn't do much to try to get into people's memories, but every new voice that entered his mind had new worries and fears and was just a tantalizing invitation to dig deeper and find out more. That his imagination had this depth of character should have astounded him, but Trevor was quickly becoming used to it, nearly taking it for granted as time went by and he frustratingly did not come across anyone he knew.

Until he saw her. Betty. She was just going into Express with a group of her friends as he was riding along with someone walking by, and he shifted his focus directly to her. A familiar voice filled his head at the same time that it filled the air; Betty and her friends seemed to be able to all speak at once and understand each other somehow. Trevor was almost at a loss, bombarded by a rapid stream of thoughts that seemed to be processing what was coming in and matching it with Betty's memories and opinions and determining what to say and saying it while thinking of other things simultaneously. In addition to this cavalcade of words and thoughts, there were all of Betty's thoughts about

42

shopping and what was hot and what was not and what would fit her and what she would pretend would fit her or diet to get to fit her, and what shoes she had went with the handbag she was looking at, and whether the blouse that Cindy was trying on would look better on Charlene, and on and on and Trevor wasn't sure that finding someone he knew was a good idea, because the real Betty couldn't possibly think like this.

Trevor figured that he must be imagining his impression of what Betty was like into this representation of her. He'd always seen her at school surrounded by her group of friends and it must have seemed like they all spoke at once and continuously, but he had trouble believing that that was really the case now that he was fully immersed in it instead of just passing it by. He couldn't find even a momentary lapse in the constant stream of chatter-thought that was pouring out of Betty's mind to get at her memories. Somehow his mind must have known it couldn't provide a proper experience from the life of a real person for him and was keeping him out. He just watched on in awe at his imagined representation of Betty and her friends moved from rack to rack and wall to wall examining and reviewing and chatting and chatting and chatting about who was seen with who else and doing what, gossip after gossip about people from school, some people whose names he recognized, but no one he really knew enough to know if what they were saying was based on reality or just imagined.

Then Betty finally got to the dressing room with an armload of clothes and Trevor mentally followed her into the quiet seclusion of the small cubicle where all of a sudden the stream of thoughts shut completely down and her mind's barrier relaxed and came down enough to allow Trevor access to her memories the way he was most used to, like a reference book. The contrast of the silence of Betty's mind as she tried on the outfits, with only the occasional burst of surface thought about how she would describe what she thought to her friends, was a shocking one. When Betty was alone, she was much more relaxed and mentally calm. So Trevor didn't waste time, and started digging.

43

This imagined version of Betty had barely given him a thought at all. She didn't remember his name, so Trevor had had to try to remember through her a description of himself, getting vaguer and vaguer before coming upon a firm memory of his handing Hannah's phone to Mr. Morton a couple of months ago. She remembered that he had done it, but Trevor couldn't get her to remember exactly why. He could remember from her mind that she had, in fact, had a mobile phone with her that morning. He could remember from her mind the color of underpants she had been wearing that day, and what she had had for breakfast. He could remember the names of all the boys she'd kissed, and through her memories the scores of every football game their school team had played. Trevor kept going back to the only memories she seemed to have of him, from the morning of Hannah's accident, to see if he could notice a detail of her memory that would unlock additional queries he could attempt to use to figure out what the imagined Betty thought of him, but before he knew it was happening, Betty reached out and opened the dressing room door.

He was still remembering the facts about the morning of the accident that he could think of wondering what she remembered when she set eyes on Cindy for the first time, just outside the door, and her mind's defenses instantly went up and the stream of thoughts tried to start. Except it didn't exactly start the way he expected it to, in a deluge of information about the outfits she'd tried on and the one she was wearing now to model for her friends or any other surface thoughts about whether she was wearing the blouse properly or had selected the right belt to go with the ensemble, and instead he seemed to have triggered her conscious mind to be thinking about the morning of the accident too. There were occasional surface thoughts about what was going on, just enough to turn and smile and comment briefly on Charlene's outfit, but the bulk of what was coming to Trevor from Betty's mind was a full-sensory experience/memory of that morning, exactly what Betty had experienced.

She had heard the door handle turning that morning, and had turned to see who was coming in late so she could gossip about it later. She hadn't really been paying attention in class, either, which had freed her attention to turn towards the door as it opened cautiously. She could tell immediately that whoever was coming through the door was trying not to be noticed, and Betty was prepared to draw attention to whoever it was by greeting them loudly when they were looking for a seat. Except it never got to that point, because the young woman entering the classroom didn't make it beyond the threshold.

Trevor hadn't personally bothered to look up at all during the entire event until he'd helped with the phone, so he saw what had happened for the first time as through Betty's eyes. He could remember, as Betty remembered now in hindsight, seeing Hannah standing on her own shoelaces, about to trip. He could remember noticing as she began her descent forward that her purse-strap had caught on the catch of the door, and in Betty's memory the pinwheeling spin Hannah took through the air was in slow motion right up until the sickening sound of her head hitting the hard floor outside the door, and then things seemed to go very quickly. Almost the next thing Betty remembered was lying to Mr. Morton about her phone. Trevor could hear Betty's self-questioning thoughts as she ran the memory through both of their minds, how she felt guilty for not admitting she had a phone and maybe getting help there sooner. Trevor knew that, for this imagined version of Betty at least, Betty felt somewhat to blame for the coma that Hannah was currently in. She irrationally thought that she should have done more, could somehow have provided whatever additional help would have been required to prevent so awful a state from taking over the life of a classmate. She went over and over the statement to Mr. Morton, then flashed quickly over gathering up Hannah's things and working with the paramedics; she couldn't seem to let herself linger on that - the conscious thoughts she was having about this indicated to Trevor that Betty knew that what she had done hadn't changed anything substantive about Hannah's condition, and that she now felt that she should have somehow done something else instead.

Then as Betty retreated into the dressing room to change back into what she had been wearing when she had come into the store, her memories kept playing in the same fashion for Trevor. Now she was remembering several conversations in subsequent days where she'd said disparaging things about the way Hannah had been dressed that morning, how she'd implied to her friends in private that Hannah's poor fashion choices and regular church-attendance had somehow made the accident inevitable. Betty felt bad now, in the privacy of the dressing room, about having made light of a negative and possibly life-threatening situation, even though she knew her friends expected nothing less and seemed to accept her as before as though she hadn't done anything wrong. Trevor became aware of levels of depth in Betty that he'd never noticed before as he watched her slowly redress herself and replay her memories related to Hannah back again and again in her own mind, unaware that she had an observer of her very thoughts, and he very nearly had a newfound respect for her as a person before he remembered from his own mind that this was simply his own imagined representation of Betty.

He was simply imagining that Betty had a conscience.

As Betty stepped out of the dressing room again, her thoughts slowly picked up speed and her demeanor returned to the impossible level that Trevor had been witnessing until she had been alone with her thoughts, and Trevor found that he had a growing sickening feeling in the pit of his stomach from what he was doing. Before long, Trevor realized that his desire to try to imagine someone he knew with this level of clarity and depth and going so far as to imagine what their thoughts contained and how their memories felt was ridiculous. It couldn't be accurate unless by some stroke of intuition, and most of the details of his manufactured "memories" would have to have been just that - manufactured - not real at all. Trevor roused himself out of his day-dreaming state slowly until he was staring at the dark insides of his eyelids and thought about how these extended sessions spent in a world of his own creation, examining fictional versions of the real people he saw in his everyday life, might somehow lead to false expectations and confusing behavior when interacting with the real versions of the people whose minds he'd imagined reading. He imagined that he might accidentally refer to things they'd only thought in his mind as though they'd actually thought them and as though he'd then had some way to learn them, and he decided not to try imagining anyone he knew anymore.

It was a decision he forgot he'd made as soon as he opened his eyes and saw Sqrat's face looking down at him. Considering that Trevor was laying on his bed and Sqrat was standing beside the bed, looking down, their faces felt uncomfortably close to each other. Trevor was sure he must still be imagining things, that his day-dream had somehow automatically switched over to the "strange" side when he'd let the "normal" one fade away, and he tried to wake up, as it were. He sat up in bed and turned to face Sqrat, who stepped back away from the bed respectfully. In the past, every time he'd imagined Sqrat or those like him, he had been unable to so much as shift his point of view an inch on his own - if his perspective had changed, it seemed to be controlled by a force other than his conscious mind's. But here he was, moving his perspective from laying down looking up to sitting up, looking sidelong at Sqrat's pouty face and rough stubble.

Except that he was definitely experiencing his body, which he didn't seem to be restricted by in either set of his imaginings of late. The last time he could remember having his body there with him in his imagination with any realism was the last night with Hannah, before her accident. It seemed odd that he'd suddenly be able to imagine his own body realistically, and in so tame a setting. He reached up and rubbed his eyes and found that he could definitely feel and hear and taste and smell as though he were actually sitting up in his bed in his room, rubbing his eyes. And when he took his hands away from his face, Sqrat was still standing there, expectantly.

"Well?" Trevor's vague query was met with silence, but the fact that he could hear his own voice was not lost on him - he was beginning to believe that this was actually happening, that his day-dreaming had ended or somehow

47

become real, or ... something. "Are you waiting for me to say something or do something, or... what?"

Sqrat bowed deeply so that his head moved lower than his own waist, then returned to standing and then just continued waiting silently, expectantly.

Trevor didn't know what he was supposed to say, but felt as though the silence was somehow his own fault, and let out another try. "You're Sqrat, right?"

Something seemed definitely to pass across Sqrat's face, a hint of shock or surprise or a simple nervous tick, Trevor could not detect, but he'd had a sort of reaction, anyway. Still, he simply stood there, facing Trevor, waiting.

"How did you get in here?"

This was apparently the right question to ask, because suddenly Sqrat's arms flew up and then sharply down again, and a fast, bright light flashed up from the floor and filled Trevor's vision, temporarily blinding him as though he'd just been staring at the sun. As his vision slowly crept back into cohesion, Trevor found that he was no longer sitting on his own bed. He was sitting at a too-familiar desk in a too-familiar classroom, with Sqrat standing the same relative distance in front of him, by what seemed to be a sort of chalkboard. Trevor began to try to ask another question, and while one did not fully form in his mind as his mouth opened and nothing came out, Sqrat turned and walked out of the room, leaving Trevor alone.

"This has got to still be a dream," Trevor said into the apparently empty room. He tried remembering that his body was laying in his bed, eyes closed, head turned towards the window. He tried to feel the sheets below him, to open his eyes, to somehow realize that this was a dream, that he was really safe at home. He failed. He waited.

As he waited for what seemed like a long time perhaps only because he was alone in a quiet room, as waiting alone in a quiet room for an unknown thing always seems to be, Trevor didn't even bother looking around the room. He was already familiar with it. It was one of the classrooms he'd seen the strange young people and strange textbook-but-not-textbook learning materials he'd seen them using, and after many non-interactive visits to this room in

48

his mind he had become familiar with as much about it as could be known by looking. The layout of the chairs and the images and maps hung on the walls, and the objects all around that he couldn't recognize any better by seeing them with his own eyes rather than his mind's eye held no further interest for him now. If he had someone to ask about them for more information, he may have been held rapt in their descriptions of all these otherwise unknowable things, but as it was, he was no better off than he'd been when trapped in his own mental image of the place. It had turned out that not knowing what something was prevented him from remembering it through the minds of those he was seeing in his imagination, leaving him totally at a loss.

So Trevor sat in silence, waiting in a room that he was simultaneously familiar with and which he had no real information about or understanding of, until finally the door swung open again. The figure that walked into the room seemed familiar, but Trevor couldn't place where he might have seen them before. It was a relatively normal looking woman, considering the setting. She was of average height and medium build, she had blonde hair arranged in a conservative way reminiscent of Beverly Cleaver, and the lines in her skin showed that she had seen at least five or six decades of life without reducing the welcoming, comforting beauty that seemed to radiate from her entire smiling face. She wore an outfit that seemed to have been put on as though by someone unfamiliar with how clothes are worn, but there was no one thing wrong with it, no real aspect of what she was wearing that was glaringly wrong. A simple pastel blouse, conservative, professional khaki-colored slacks, understated jewelry and makeup - Trevor couldn't quite put his finger on what was wrong with her appearance, but he knew it wasn't exactly right. She walked over to where Trevor was sitting and extended a hand to him, palm facing down parallel to the floor, as she looked him directly in the eyes.

"Welcome to my school, Trev."

Trevor reached out to take her hand as though to shake it, but at the last moment his hand corrected him on its own, turning so that his palm was flat opposite hers, face up

49

parallel to the ground about half an inch beneath her hand, and as his right hand swept under hers from right to left, she swept hers as well in what he instantly understood was a normal greeting. As their hands passed directly over one another there was a brief flash of light from in between them, though Trevor did not flinch back or feel a shock or a warmth as it happened and neither, it seemed, did the woman standing before him. She turned away and began again towards the door as she continued speaking.

"Let me show you around." He stood without question and followed her out the door which he noticed for the first time as he walked through it seemed to open and close on its own. The hallway he stepped into was a conglomeration of familiar and unusual elements that was jarring and just as he would have expected at the same time.

The floor plan was familiar - it was like every school he'd seen, with rows of lockers broken up by doors to classrooms, wide hallways to allow many people to move between classes at once but in such a way that between classes or on weekends they seemed cavernous and excessively large. There was something different about the place, too - a sort of foreign feeling to the construction or design, as though it were a school in a different country and culture that he was unable to place. There were also a familiar sort of hand-made posters on the walls in between more professionally made ones; the professional ones encouraging studiousness and attendance and the hand-made ones apparently in reference to upcoming student elections of some sort, being in support of or speaking out against someone with a name very similar to Trevor's name, he realized as they continued down the hall.

"I apologize for those," the woman said, apparently reading his mind, "they were supposed to be taken down before you arrived, but we weren't expecting you until Monday. Your little stunt this morning was vindication for some and an outrage for others. Personally," she looked backward over her shoulder at him briefly as though to be sure he was paying attention, "I thought it would come to this much sooner." Her head turned forward again as she continued walking down the hallway. "We had a little pool

50

going between the teachers here, and I had you down for three weeks ago. Of course, considering the nature of your first incursion it was either going to be within weeks or not for decades."

Trevor wanted to speak up, to ask the woman what she was talking about, but he didn't even know her name or how he should address her. From her greeting, he guessed she was the Principal or Dean or equivalent of the school they were walking through, but how ought he to begin? And was it prudent to reveal his ignorance? And would it be worse to keep his ignorance a secret and perhaps get himself deeper into difficulty? Again, she seemed to respond to his thoughts as they stopped and turned to face a door near the end of the hallway.

"This is my office, and that is the way out." Indeed, the end of the hallway was that familiar bank of double-doors that seemed perfect for letting hundreds of people escape the building at once at the end of the day, but seemed like overkill for his own singular departure. He looked from the diffused light coming through the frosted glass panes in the exit doors to the office door they were standing by. Painted onto another rectangle of frosted glass in her door were ornate but formal words that read "Sunshine Charming III", and below that "Principal Intendant, RMS" and then "Dean of Special Studies" and then "Head of Invocations" and finally, in tiny print near the bottom of the window, "Chief Operator in charge of Emigration and Normalization within the Southwest Region" - Trevor decided to call her Ms. Charming, figuring that Sunshine or Principal might be awkward.

"Ms. Charming," he asked with as even a voice as he could muster under the circumstances, "What's this all about?"

The answer was apparently inside her office. Without a word, the door opened and she stepped inside, walking around to sit behind her antique-looking hardwood desk as Trevor stood in the hallway. The door seemed to be waiting for him to make up his mind and go one way or another, and Trevor's natural inclination was to not keep it waiting, so he walked nonchalantly into the office and took a seat opposite the Principal.

"I realize this must all come as a sort of shock to you. Still, I think you'll acclimate quickly to our way of life. It should come naturally to you, like the handflash did. If you just relax and take it all in, I'm sure you'll be wondering how you ever lived any other way within a few weeks. There's so much for you to catch up on to really fit in here that some of the elders in the community tried to push you into one of our Elementary Education programs, but you don't think that will be necessary, do you?"

She seemed to be waiting for his response, so he tried to give a reasonable one, "I ... I have no idea. How much material are we talking about here? Is it stuff I can learn from books, or will I have to be tutored? Is it even in a language I'll understand? From what I've seen..."

"I know what you've seen, for the most part. That was ... unfortunate, but unavoidable. Your mind is somewhat more resilient than many expected, and some of the people on the regional board were ... not up to the task of hiding from you, let's say. Frankly, there are a few that would be removed from the board if I were in charge - they have no business being there. But here as well as there, politics end up making decisions that are not in the best interest of the most people, and no one has found a spell yet to change that.

"But I haven't answered your question, have I? Pardon me. Most of the material requires a combination of reading from books, being taught by experienced individuals how the things you read about can be applied in meaningful ways, and practice outside of class to reach your own personal best level of use with each item. Obviously, if we have to go through it that way it will take a very long time and a lot of work for you to catch up to the others your age who have been doing this coursework their entire lives. Which is part of why I have you alone today. I have an idea about how to get around all that and get you started Monday morning as though you'd been here the whole time." She smiled at him conspiratorially.

"What's your idea?"

"Well, that's part of the problem. I'm not allowed to suggest such a thing, and I'm certainly not allowed to teach you how to do it, but ... let me just suggest that based on ... what Sqrat saw, let's say, you know what to do." She winked at him, "so while you think about what I've said, I've got some paperwork to go over to get you enrolled for Monday morning if you don't mind." She looked down to some paperwork on her desk and began shuffling through pages, making notes and filling out information where it was needed, certain that she had told Trevor everything he'd needed to know to move forward.

The only thing he could think of that she might mean was that she wanted him to imagine something again - that was what he'd been doing when Sqrat had first seen him. So, hoping that it would become clear sooner rather than later, Trevor closed his eyes and tried to relax and not think of anything at all. To let his mind wander. And his mind did wander, right back to Sqrat, who was pacing silently back and forth in the hallway outside the door to Sunshine's office, apparently waiting for something. Trevor hadn't noticed Sqrat in the hallway as he and the Principal had walked from the classroom he had appeared in to her office, and had no reason to believe he was really out there now, except that almost as soon as Trevor began imagining him, Sqrat stopped walking and turned to face in the direction of Trevor's bodiless point of view.

Just as quickly he looked away as though not to reveal that he knew what was going on, and he moved towards the office door. Trevor's imagined point of view moved along with Sqrat into the office where - and this took Trevor by surprise even though it should have seemed the obvious thing - he saw himself sitting where he was actually sitting, with a calm expression on his face and his eyes closed, and he saw Ms. Charming behind her desk with that same paperwork in her hands, looking up to see why Sqrat was interrupting her meeting. She spoke "Yes?" and there was a weird sort of non-echoing echo, not exactly like an echo because instead of a sound following a sound, the sound of her voice seemed to come simultaneously from two different places. In his imagination, her voice seemed to

53

come from where he could see her, and at the same time the same word in the same voice came from the position that was relative to his physical body, but superimposed over the imagined scene. The sound continued on that way as they conversed, and as had happened that morning with the "normal" people he'd been following, as soon as Sqrat had entered the presence of others, that conscious voice of his barrier thoughts came streaming forth, mostly about not wanting to be here today.

"I was just wondering what you wanted me to do about the shipment delays of the cold iron."

"How late are they saying it will be, now?"

"Two more weeks," their conversation continued like this as Trevor realized that he was listening to the wrong person's thoughts. He moved his focus to the Principal, and the voice of thoughts he heard shifted from Sqrat's nervousness to Sunshine's matronly timbre, saying "I knew you'd get it, Trev. Now remember with me."

And suddenly Trevor was remembering Sunshine's formative years from her own perspective at what seemed like an amazing rate of speed. They went through everything from early childhood, including her learning of three languages before ever setting foot in a school as was common in her family, through every day, hour, and minute of her experiences growing up, going through elementary school and middle school and even into High School, and as she caught up to the middle of High School and seemed to be trying to stop thinking about it all in such detail, Trevor really wanted to keep it going. More information had entered his mind in that short moment than the sum total of information that he'd learned from all other sources in his life before coming here, and where someone else would have been overwhelmed, Trevor was hungry for more. He tried to remember through her mind the rest of her education, every day in every class of the rest of her High School career, and at first she seemed to be resisting, so he pushed, mentally. He hadn't tried this with Betty or the couple in the car, he had simply nudged their minds gently to get at what he'd wanted, but based on what he'd just absorbed from fifteen years of experiences and living, he expected that this woman could take more than he could possibly have dished out, and he pushed.

Whether he had pushed hard enough to break her will or she willingly relented, he was suddenly awash in what he would eventually realize was actually around eighteen hundred years' worth of experiences. Centuries apprenticing in time-dilated pockets of the universe with ancient masters and wise old creatures the likes of which he had never set his own eyes on in real life. Years working for equal rights for men alongside her husband, trying to buck an engrained matriarchy despite it supporting her own gender, and coming out on the winning side only by sailing to the "New World" and creating a new system of governance for their people, only to then lose her husband in an unexpected battle with the surprisingly powerful and theretofore unknown shamans of the Americas who resisted what they had incorrectly assumed was a legion of powerful evil spirits taking over their lands. She had then worked to normalize relations between those whose land they were sharing, and her efforts led to the integration of tribal magic into common usage before 1820.

If he was imagining all of this, it was enough fantastic and amazing alternate history to fill an entire series of novels, and if Trevor was, in fact, reading the mind of a real person who had really done all these things, it had implications he simply could not yet fathom. Her mind kept on rolling out every aspect of her experiences for Trevor in an unending cavalcade that was as real and complete as every memory he had of his own comparatively short life. He remembered her first kiss as easily as her last day with her husband and the decades it had taken for her to get over his death, and the emotional toll it had taken on those around her as she tried to heal. He remembered every time she had had sex, every meal she had eaten, every outfit she had worn, even up to putting on what she was now wearing. He knew then why it looked a bit off; it was an outfit she had selected with the specific intention of appearing normal to Trevor that morning, and bore no relation to what she normally wore from day to day. He even remembered the controversy leading up to his coming here at all, and suddenly all those meetings he hadn't understood as he'd watched them were clear to him - she had been present at many of them, and knowing the languages they were communicated in made a world of difference. Every scene he had imagined that wasn't mundane had been either about him or to intentionally keep him from realizing that what he was imagining was indeed reality. They had thought that if they showed him things he was unfamiliar with, it might throw him off the right track, and they were right - he hadn't really considered that the things he was imagining were actually happening until it was so obvious, until he'd thought of it all from Sunshine's point of view.

And then Sqrat and Sunshine had run out of things to talk meaninglessly about, and Sqrat left the room. At once as thought and spoken aloud, she told Trevor "Open your eyes," and he did.

"So, as I was saying before we were interrupted, I think you'll acclimate to life here pretty readily. In fact, I don't mind saying that you went too far just now, which is what my colleagues were worried about, as you know - that you would pose a threat or get access to information they wanted kept secret. For reference, the aggressive assault you made would be enough to endanger the life of someone not prepared for it as I was by my study with Maheu'le. This is why your extraction this morning was so urgent, to keep you from unknowingly injuring anyone. You could have put another young woman into a coma."

"Hannah's coma wasn't my fault. She hit her head."

"That's what the doctors are saying, but based on our observations her mind was in a weakened state due to your ... contact, and the concussion's effects were amplified by the ... resonance you left with her."

"I remember, now. You visited her at the hospital just after the accident. You found ... that can't be right."

"You know it to be true. You remember what I saw, what I sensed."

"And it's mine. But how is that possible?"

"You know. Try not to work from your old frame of reference, you can integrate mine with yours safely."

"Alright, I'll try." He tried to work it out, to think not just from what he would normally have known, but from all that she had known. "Well, that night was the first time your community really became active about my existence. The first sign that I might be aware of who I really am. Which you don't really know."

"But we know enough to know that you needed to be monitored."

"Sure, in case I did something catastrophic. From what I gather, it's believed by some that I'm the antichrist, is that right?"

"Only the extremists. Most refuse to state their beliefs in such an obtuse fashion."

"Fine, fine. Why exactly do they put so much faith or fear in the my supposed ability to bring catastrophic harm or good to the world? I mean, what started all this?"

"I'll remind you. Do you remember the map room downstairs?"

"Yes."

"Do you remember the Map of Power, the one that showed concentrations of spiritual and magical energies everywhere in the world?

"Right, yeah. And there was a hole in it."

"Marking the location where you were conceived, the moment your soul first entered this world in a physical way. The burst of power the map was trying to represent was so intense that it burnt straight through the material of the map with its heat and energy."

"And then, if I'm remembering correctly, my path through the world practically erased all trace of former points of power as I went. Jurrin thought I must be absorbing every ounce of energy I came across, didn't he?"

"Jurrin didn't know what he was looking at."

"But I can see how people might interpret that as potentially scary."

"Sure, if you want to leap to conclusions. The more rational among us just kept an eye on you, waiting to see what would happen."

"Until this morning when I went too far."

57

"You didn't hurt anyone. You may have made Betty a little down about Hannah, but she should recover."

"Oh, yeah! Hannah. What ... what do we do about that?"

"We wait. It's a very tricky situation. It was made a little less difficult last night, but her parents reaction when they find out could be anything. Our best experts on Christians don't really know how they will react to this situation. If she were healthy, it's our experience that they would put her in a home for troubled teens until she gave birth, then give the child up for adoption so that Hannah could return to what they considered to be a normal life."

"But," Trevor responded, working from the Principal's frame of reference, "since she's already out of sight for the community, you don't know how they'll deal with the shame of having a daughter who - for all intents and purposes - had premarital sex despite her conservative Christian upbringing. Since she's already out of the public eye, they may not take action at all until or unless Hannah wakes up. But she isn't going to wake up, is she?"

"No. Not any time soon. The Board decided that since the expectation was that her family would take no action as long as she was comatose, they would keep her comatose until they could make a more informed decision about what to do about the child."

"What gives them the right?"

"They give themselves the right. You know that. You know I've been fighting that elitist view since the day I won my seat on the Board."

"Okay, so. The issue of Hannah is really out of my hands right now, even though it's basically my fault. And I'm supposed to start school here on Monday morning, even though I basically know everything the normal coursework has to teach me and more. Is there no better alternative?"

"There's a certain way things must be done. And there are things you can learn here. I don't hire teachers that don't know more than I do about their subject matter, so there should be something for you to learn in every one of your classes. I'm not guaranteeing that you'll be kept interested all the time, but as far as anyone here knows you're a fifteen year old boy who has never seen anything beyond the world of the mundane, so we've got to keep up appearances for a while."

"What are we telling my parents? It was uhh... "

"Some garbage about being a magnet school. Same as we're telling your school district. You're switching schools because you've got a special talent and we're the best school for helping you master it."

"And you're telling them my talent is ... telepathy?"

She smiled, "No. Psychology. It turns out you have an unprecedented ability to understand what's going on in other people's heads."

"I guess that's one way to put it."

Sunshine gathered up the papers she had been working on as they'd talked and handed the top sheet to Trevor. It was the letter to his parents explaining his change of schools, that there would be no extra cost or need for them to do anything differently, and that Trevor was already aware of the changes. Knowing his own parents the way he did, Trevor realized it would be more than enough to get them to go on ignoring his career as a student. He doubted they would care that he was going to one school rather than another, they were so wrapped up in their own lives and careers anymore.

"So I'll see you Monday morning, then?"

"Right. Just be careful not to go meddling in anyone's minds for a few days."

"No, I know better than to do that now, thanks to your own mistakes and hard years of study. There are things I'm much more interested in trying out than that. Nothing that should draw any attention, just ..." Trevor turned his palms face up in front of him and a ball of light jumped from his right hand to his left hand in a perfect parabolic arc, disappearing into his flesh with a burst of color. "Little things."

"Sure, sure. Just don't do anything too obvious where too many people can see."

"Not that they'd notice."

"True, most people ignore anything they don't understand. Remember when I had to walk that scarantula

59

down 8th street in broad daylight? Not a single person who looked at me seemed to see me; their minds simply reject to integrate anything out of the ordinary. It works greatly in our favor most of the time. Just be careful."

"I will. And thank you. I'm glad you were an advocate for me when so many were reactionary and defensive. I might have had to face a pretty dangerous attack if the most extreme had had their way, and years before I was ready for it."

"I think you could have handled yourself. I'm sure there are depths within you no one has imagined, just waiting to be discovered. Don't limit yourself because of the limitations of my life; seek out what you are most interested in, and lead the life you want to lead no matter what they say."

"Well, we'll certainly have to wait and see what they say - Monday morning could be pretty difficult, the way people were going on last week around campus."

"I think you'll be alright."

They exchanged pleasantries and she walked him to the row of double-doors that led out of the school, but Trevor continued from there on his own. As he stepped out into the midday light, he found that, just as his memories of Ms. Charming's memories had led him to believe, this was the school that he had passed by every morning on the way to what he could now only think of as his "old school". It was less than five minutes walk to his front door, and then Trevor retired once more to the privacy of his bedroom. He drew the blinds and began to play with his newfound understanding of the magic and energy that had always been at his fingertips, waiting to be harnessed. Time flew, and before he knew it he was called to supper, forced to act as he had before, as though he were "normal" in front of his family. As he had expected, his parents took the news of his impending change of schools as though it were nothing, and signed the letter with hardly a glance. This was the beginning of what promised to be a very interesting time in Trevor's young life.

★　★　★

"How could you betray me like that, Sqrat?" The lanky stranger's tone was as fierce as the grip he had on the shorter man's lapels, lifting Sqrat up off the ground to be properly shouted at, face to face. "You gave him everything. He would have been hopeless on Monday, but you gave him exactly what she wanted!"

"She made me do it, you know she did! I had no choice." Sqrat whimpered uselessly.

The tall man growled in frustration ascendantly as he shook Sqrat like a ragdoll, then tossed him aside. There was a definite sharp, wet snapping as Sqrat's arm struck the brick wall of the tiny hovel they had met in, and before he reached the ground he was certain that his arm was shattered.

"I forgive your failure; you are, after all, only human."

"Thank you, sir." Sqrat was trying to prop himself up on his remaining good arm, trying to rise from the mud and straw and scum of the floor without taking his fearful eyes off the tall figure now marching bitterly out the door of the hovel, "Thank you."

Sunday went by in a blur and suddenly it was Monday morning. Trevor inevitably woke up at his normal time, despite the fact that it would now take over an hour less time to walk to school than it had taken him to walk to his old school, and also despite the fact that he could move there with even less effort, disappearing from his bedroom in a flash of light and appearing almost anywhere he could think of, with just a thought and a gesture. He had been practicing that little trick off and on, bouncing back and forth from one side of his room to the other, from standing next to the door to sitting at the desk, from laying on his bed to hiding crouched down in the closet, and once, after everyone else was asleep, he even went directly from his bedroom to the bathroom and back again without walking the distance between. He had never tried it at further distances, but based on Sunshine's experiences he should have been able to find himself instantly on the other side of the planet, or even on the moon.

He lay still in his bed, flat out under the covers, and as the light slowly grew to fill the room with that beautiful quality of near-sight that Trevor so appreciated, he began to levitate straight up off the surface of his bed, his blanket and sheet draping down towards his bed to create that look that illusionists seemed so fond of when simulating that very act, extending the contours of the side of his body, leg and arm. The sensation wasn't exactly like weightlessness or floating in water, it was like something in between, with the force of his will holding him up instead of the water, but the tug of gravity still felt all across his body in the weight of the air and the bedclothes above him. It was new and old at the same time, it was a feeling he could recall, and part of an activity he could remember doing a thousand thousand times in Ms. Charming's memories, but it was also something he had never felt with his own nerves, his own skin, flying over his own bed. "This will take some getting used to."

The sound of his own voice leaving his throat took him enough by surprise that he lost his balance and began spinning downward in the air, first spilling his blanket and sheet down in a line onto his bed, then spinning faster and faster as he slowly floated diagonally down to the ground beside his bed, drifting in the direction of his spin. He could have willed himself to a stop, could even have reached out with his arms and grabbed hold of his bed or the floor and put a stop to his near-frictionless spinning and his gradual descent from the air, but he was trying to try new things. Better judgment in the future would lead him to try new things that were less likely to lead to nausea. Just before he reached the floor of his room, his stomach seemed to reach the breaking point, and just before he let loose a spinning spiral of vomit all over his bed and floor and walls and perhaps even the ceiling as well, he disappeared, reappearing kneeling in front of the toilet. It was a lucky thing that Trevor hadn't had anything to vomit and merely experienced a sort of dry heaving as his body tried to get its non-rotational bearings; the toilet seat he was perched in front of had the cover completely down.

He wretched and shook and held onto the toilet bowl as though for the sake of his life, and then when his stomach seemed calmed again, Trevor rested his face cheek-down on the cold white cover of the toilet, breathing deeply with closed eyes. "This day has got to get better from here," his voice echoed gently off the hard tile of the shower stall, reminding him that he should probably use his extra time to be extra-presentable to his new schoolmates. He stripped of his pajamas, locked himself in the bathroom, and stepped into the shower.

There was something about having seen so many different people showering candidly from the perspective that he was just now fully realizing was not an imaginary one that gave his own showers an entirely new sort of atmosphere to them, and which changed the very steps he followed to get himself clean. On one hand, every time he moved or bent or twisted or reached or scrubbed or rinsed off, Trevor remembered having seen someone else, someone real, doing that very thing, and as these memories came rushing back to him they had an altered character. Whereas when he had thought he was simply imagining people showering his thoughts had seemed nearly antiseptic and logical to him - as though he had simply been trying to work out the optimal methods for showering a variety of body types in a variety of showering facilities - his adventures now came across as some extreme form of invasive voyeurism, dirty and depraved at their most innocuous and an extended exercise in violating the assumed rights to privacy that people expected in their own homes and especially in their own bathrooms. Still, all the time spent thinking about it from the first position had, in fact, given him some ideas about what the best and most efficient ways to cleanse one's body were, and he had modified his routines with much success and increased overall effectiveness, even at cleaning hard-to-reach spots and maintaining the health of his hair and skin. In addition to all of these complexities were the remembrances of every shower Sunshine had taken in her entire life, every detail, each routine and shift in routine as technologies and soaps and shampoos and shavers and moisturizers had advanced around her, the net sum of which was that before he realized what he was doing, Trevor had routinely shaved his legs and underarms bare, and was working on shaping his bikini area when his hand stopped mid-stroke.

"Fuck."

Trevor saw no reasonable choice but to finish the job and with a somewhat less effective and inexperienced conscious hand, managed to do so without opening an artery. When he was done, his pubic hair was in a neat triangle and his testicles were completely hairless, hanging between his now smooth legs. The sight of it was strange and erotic at the same time, and as the blood began to lift his penis from a shrivel to a staff, Trevor thought that his new haircut seemed to make it look significantly larger than he had thought it was. Standing still in the steady waterfall of warmth, Trevor took his trembling tool in his hand and quickly discovered that the slick sensation of his smooth legs sliding across each other hairlessly readily took the place of the fantasy that he wasn't sure he wanted to try to conjure; he came hard and fast and was quickly cleaning up and rinsing off and out of the shower altogether. He grabbed his pajamas and disappeared directly to his empty bedroom in a hurry, where Trevor found that his suspicions had been correct and wearing pants, while effective at covering his hairless legs from easy discovery, also generated a plethora of constant and new sensations for him to have to deal with. He was erect again before he'd finished dressing, but his time was running short and he tried to ignore it as he finally exited his bedroom to go eat breakfast.

Walking was something else entirely, and his underpants seemed totally different against his newly exposed skin as he moved. He barely made it through preparing and eating breakfast without returning to his bedroom, but that restraint got him to a point where Trevor was almost entirely sure he could get through the rest of the day without embarrassing himself. Almost. He did go take a few more minutes for himself after finishing his breakfast just to be sure he would be okay, then hurried out the door with his backpack in hand, and his pockets double-checked as normal. He did not allow his distraction to distract him so much that he was not meticulous and methodic as he prepared for school and left his home.

Trevor's mind didn't wander at all as he made his way to his new school that morning. He thought about what it would be like, what people would actually think of him in person, what his teachers would be like during classes, and so many other things that he knew would very likely be subtly or entirely different from the way he remembered them. His only experiences with the students and faculty of the school were the secret memories he shared with Sunshine Charming III, a respected community member and leader to most of the faculty and an imposing authority figure to most students. The way teenagers behave when the principal is around is usually not the way they behave when she is not, and Trevor realized that their behavior may seem almost entirely foreign to him. More importantly, the relationships he remembered having with the faculty could not easily exist between a student and teacher, and it was likely that his expectations would be unable to match the coming reality of classroom life.

None of which took into account the way the community was divided against him, or the way that rumors of who or what he really was would have shaped people's impressions of him before he ever had a chance to make a first impression. He knew to expect the unexpected, to expect difficulty and subversion, but he had no trusted frame of reference with which to build those expectations, so his trepidations and fears about the enormity of what he was about to walk into completely occupied Trevor's mind until he reached the edge of campus.

There were already other students beginning to arrive all around him, and many of them did not bother to mask their reactions to his presence. Mostly they just stared at him as they walked by, some giving him looks he wasn't sure the meaning of. A few were already in groups and were whispering behind their hands to each other as they eyed him warily or pointed at him. Trevor did his best to ignore their attention as he walked as normally as he could - considering the way his pants felt rubbing on his barren legs - up the stairs to the row of double-doors he had walked out of two

65

days earlier, and into the school. He could see Sunshine standing at the door of her office, waiting for him, and he walked directly to her.

"Are your old textbooks in there," she asked, indicating the backpack slung over his shoulder with nary more than a flick of the eyes, "all of them?"

"Yes."

"Good," she reached out and took his backpack as she handed him a large leather satchel that he recognized as her husband's favorite, "here are your new materials. Keep the satchel. I'll have your books returned to the other school and have any belongings you left there in this backpack waiting for you before the end of the day. Are you ready for your first day here?"

Trevor looked around at the familiar faces who were seeing him for the first time and acting the same way the students outside had been. He glanced around and listened to the din of the dozens of conversations and was sure he could hear his name echoing out of every one. He looked back to the Principal, locked her eyes in his and replied as he reached out and confidently handflashed with her, "I am" - the handflash was as lightning in the eyes of every carefully watching student, the likes of which they had never produced themselves, and the hallway was silent for a moment as Trevor turned to walk towards his locker.

The locker was his, he knew it was his because he remembered Ms. Charming setting it aside for him before the school year had even begun. It was a locker long reported to have unusual properties among the student body and thus shunned - no one wanted to put anything in it for fear that it would not come out, or would come out transformed or alive. There was a lock on it much larger and more ancient than the locks on the other lockers to its left and right, covered in runes and with no visible dial or keyhole for opening it. According to rumor, that lock had been affixed to it for the protection of the students after an entire arm had been lost to the darkness of the locker. It was believed to have stood unused for more than a generation before Trevor's hand reached out to it, and no student had dared attempt to unlock it, not even to prove their bravery or prowess. Trevor reached up, took the lock in his hand, and spoke two words to it, the same two words he had last spoken, and it disappeared along with the entire front of the locker, revealing a black emptiness within just beyond where his hand hung empty in the air.

Trevor did not flinch, did not react, he behaved as though this whole morning was going according to a long-standing routine, and the students all around him pretended they were not watching as well as they could without blinking or moving their eyes from the feared locker. Trevor reached his arm fully into the locker, far past the depth of the wall and the normal depth of the lockers adjacent to his, and it sounded like a hundred throats gulped at once as a hundred pair of eyes saw his arm disappear into the darkness up to the shoulder. A moment later that felt like a year and a month and a day to the frozen assembly and like a clever joke to Sunshine, watching on from down the hall, Trevor pulled his arm back out of the locker with one of the textbooks that weren't exactly textbooks that he hadn't known the name for just days before. It was a first-edition copy of the self-updating, self-aware information compilation tool that all the students were using modern editions of, handwritten by Echelar and Spink themselves, and dedicated to Trevor - something that he would not notice right away himself - and everyone there knew what they were seeing when he pulled it out. It had been missing for over thirty years, and Trevor had apparently known just where to find it, and also apparently how to create a collective gasp erupt from the crowd.

He placed it carefully into his satchel as people tried to return to normalcy without getting themselves too far away to see how Trevor closed the locker. They would all agree later that it had been obvious, but as he reached up to where the lock had hung before and spoke "I was" it seemed a revelation that the lock and the front of the locker were reappearing. All over school, as the other students turned combination locks and keys in locks to get at the contents of their finite, standard-sized lockers, they felt jealous or scared or just in awe of what they were now becoming a part of. Trevor just wanted to get to class.

His first hour was still math, which was a coincidence of only passing interest, but math had always been one of Trevor's best subjects, and he looked forward to seeing how he would do in a somewhat familiar subject matter. There was a very real possibility that the overlaps and assumptions that were created by the complex interweaving of the Principal's memories and experiences with his own would create new types of unpredictable problems for him, in the same vein as his automatic shaving in the shower had, and Trevor was trying to determine how reserved he would try to be once class actually began, and how involved he may have to be to just keep up. He walked to the classroom as he remembered doing a thousand times before through Ms. Charming's many walks around campus, through the door, and directly to Mr. Glip's desk.

"Good morning, Mr. Glip. As you may be aware, I'll be joining your class today. I understand you use assigned seating, so I wanted to see where you'd like me to be." Trevor tried to be as straightforward and clear as possible without coming across as entitled or self-deprecating in any way. Mr. Glip's response was to refer to a complex equation scrawled on a chalkboard at the back of the class that Ms. Charming had somehow not been aware of.

"I assigned the class that assignment on Friday after the vote passed. Class starts in seven minutes, and anyone who has solved it knows where to sit, and anyone not in their new assigned seat will receive a zero on the assignment and will not be allowed to attend class until they have solved it and each subsequent assignment sufficiently." Trevor looked at the equation, and at the other students who were filing in and sitting down confidently as Mr. Glip continued. "Your classmates have had all weekend to work it out, but have been instructed not to assist you in any way. Oh, and just so you don't try to wait it out and see which chair remains empty, there will be six empty seats in the finished equation. Good luck."

Mr. Glip turned his attention back down to a stack of assignments on his desk, leafing through page after page of what appeared to be differential equations combined with some form of runic writing that Trevor would have been able to recognize from Sunshine's memories had he not been thoroughly distracted by trying to work out the equation that he now realized took up an entire chalkboard. This was well beyond anything Mr. Morton had been teaching at Trevor's old school - mostly because it was well beyond the lowest common denominator of the students in attendance there. Still, Trevor read over each line, each formation, and tried to comprehend the meaning of several symbols and arrangements he had never been taught on his own. He wanted to figure it out without drawing on the experiences he had borrowed from another's life.

More and more students came into the room and sat down, some of them spending more than a moment counting desks carefully before sitting down at their pre-calculated locations. One student, who Trevor would have recognized as Nirgal if he had tried, sat in the wrong desk - this became obvious almost at once, as his sitting in the wrong seat seemed to cause him to disappear altogether, taking with it his truncated yelp of realization. A murmur went around the class that Nirgal had probably forgot to factor in the mass of Mr. Glip's desk in his calculations, and they speculated about whether he had been disappeared to detention or someplace more horrible. Some began to whisper and speculate about whether Trevor would be able to solve the equation in time, and soon there were wagers being leveled and raised. None of those who were speaking up as time wound down and Trevor stood still at the front of the class simply staring at the chalkboard behind the rest of them seemed to have been able to solve it in less than three hours, and some had struggled with it all night and day to avoid Nirgal's fate of missing out on Trevor's inevitable humiliation or exultation. Finally, a one-minute warning bell rang out through the school, and it seemed to bring Trevor out of his trance.

Trevor walked confidently over to the desk that Nirgal his disappeared from and sat down there, pulling a pencil and paper and his recently acquired copy of Echelar & Spink's book from his satchel and placing them neatly in front of him on the desk. Many nonspecific voices made that whining "Awww..." of disappointment that he had

69

somehow figured it out, and as the second hand ticked down the start of the class, new speculation erupted that Trevor had somehow had some help. Mr. Glip hadn't even lifted his head from his work, though a careful eye might have seen a subtle smile form on his face as the crowd had voiced its frustration, and did not stop shuffling papers until a sudden clatter of noise came from the hallway outside the class, rapidly approaching.

Nirgal's face could been seen frantic outside the door, and the handle was rattling as though he was so nervous he was unable to turn it to get the door open. Finally, just seconds before he would be too late for a second chance, Nirgal burst through the flung-open door and ran around the front of the desks and across the room towards another empty desk. Just a brief moment before Nirgal reached his destination, Trevor spoke.

"Not there." Nirgal stopped dead in his tracks, frozen as a deer in headlights.

"But, but... my calculations... I..."

Trevor indicated an empty seat at the front of the class, directly before Mr. Glip's desk. "Here." Mr. Glip made no motion to agree or disagree or to try to stop Trevor from helping or hindering the other student.

"Are you... are you sure, Trev?"

"Here. You're nearly late."

The final bell rang three times, with Nirgal's narrow bottom landing hard in the seat Trevor had indicated just as the third chime reached everyone's ears, and a half-second after that, every unoccupied desk in the room disappeared. Including the one that Nirgal had been about to sit in when Trevor had stopped him. Mr. Glip stood up as Nirgal tried to catch his breath after running from who-knows-where to get back to class after sitting in Trevor's seat instead of his own.

"I'm glad to see everyone managed to work this one out. It shows you've been paying attention. We'll spend twenty minutes going over the proper solution to that, and I'll answer any questions. Then we'll move on to Chapter Four." Everyone's Echelar & Spink flipped itself open on their desks and paged itself open to Chapter Four at the sound of Mr. Glip's voice. Trevor's, and some of the higher-end models that a few of the students were using, had understood even better and placed their own ribbon bookmarks on the specified page and re-closed themselves for easy use later in the class.

A class that was unremarkable in its remainder, as far as singling Trevor out from the rest of the students went. He worked along with them as they went over the problem, the prior week's homework - which he did as they went over it, even though it wasn't collected - and onto the new lesson. This was a shift for Trevor, who was often so far ahead of the class that he paid only the smallest amount of attention required to be able to answer any question the teacher could ask, usually working on something for another class, reading a book for pleasure, or writing in his journal. In this new class, at least on his first day there, Trevor found himself actually engaged and interested by what was being covered.

The fact that the math they were doing seemed to integrate assumptively the pre-calculus he had been studying at his old school with a form of runic magic that allowed this mathematics to approximate the world more fully than mundane mathematics could have may have had something to do with it. Mr. Glip's teaching also seemed more engaging by an order of magnitude from what had been going on in Mr. Morton's class. The students were more involved, asking informed questions and able to follow along ably with the material instead of being held back by the incompetence of one or two students - a difference that illuminated for Trevor the fact that the system at his old school did not effectively advance students or keep students from advancement, ending up with classrooms that were not generally at the same level of comprehension. This classroom seemed extremely well grouped, with multiple students being enlightened by the same questions and the pace remained a steady one as they moved forward through nearly half of the fourth chapter of the mathematical unit of their Echelar & Spinks.

Better still for Trevor, the process of going over the material in class was not the potentially boring and repetitive task he had expected it to be in consideration of the fact that he had already studied all this and more through Sunshine's life, but more of a sort of dreamlike review of the material - it was really the first time he was consciously going over it, even though it was already in his mind, and that made it very much like a new experience somehow enhanced and made more interesting by the fact that he could remember learning it all a little differently a long, long time ago, too. As the math class drew to a close and the homework for the next night was assigned, Trevor looked forward to the rest of the day with less apprehension than he had had at first. He hoped that every class that day would be as interesting, engaging, and mentally stimulating from as many levels as this one had turned out to be, and looked forward to finding out whether that good luck could possibly be his. It certainly wouldn't hurt, considering how his morning had accidentally gone.

The first bell rang and everyone gathered their things together and worked their way out of the room. After spending the hour with him, seeing him learning right along with them, interacting on the same level they were, perhaps just seeing that he wasn't an abomination or a snob or any of the other things they had imagined, his classmates paid Trevor little mind. A significant change from the way they had acted on the way into class, and for the better, so Trevor left on an entirely upbeat note.

"See you tomorrow, Trev," said Nirgal, still trying to force his Echelar & Spink into his ratty bag at an impossible angle at the front of the room as Trevor reached the door.

"You too, Nirgal. Good work on the seating arrangement, by the way, working out where I was supposed to sit."

Nirgal became flush, but smiled, "Thanks. I just ... I just wondered. Then I mixed up my results. Thanks for pointing out this one."

"Don't thank me, thank Mr. Glip," Nirgal looked in the teacher's direction, but Mr. Glip didn't turn away from enchanting chalk dust down from the chalkboard, leaving it an astonishingly deep black. "It was a very efficient algorithm he designed." Nirgal looked back towards Trevor, but Trevor was already gone from the doorway, on his way to his next class. Literature. With Mrs. McCallum.

As Trevor walked from class to class in the throng of the other students, he realized that he was already half a head taller than most of the crowd, as he could see easily over the sea of hair and hats that swelled and shifted and churned all around and in front of him, just as they had at his old school. He might not have noticed it except that a few heads rose imposingly above the crowd with him, plainly visible, and it seemed to draw out the contrast of the taller with the shorter. Only one of the other heads above the student body seemed to notice him as he made his way to Mrs. McCallum's classroom, that of the man he now knew to be the head of campus security. It was the third man he had seen watching the scarantulas, the one who had clearly been beholden to the lanky one and who had apparently hand-painted thousands of scarantulas with chocolate. It was Mr. Feagan Trask.

Feagan watched Trevor with a careful eye, as though expecting him to erupt from every pore with blood or millipedes at any moment, as though Trevor was up to no good, but really as though Feagan suspected that Trevor knew what he was really involved in and was about to reveal him for what he was. Trevor knew, to a point, what had been going on with him, inasmuch as Ms. Charming also knew, but there were layers of deception there that were hidden even from the lanky stranger that Trevor wouldn't have bothered to guess. In fact, aside from the fact that he recognized the wizened man at all, Trevor did not react to Feagan in any readable way as they passed in the hall. If Feagan didn't already know what had found its way into Trevor's head, Trevor wasn't going to reveal it so easily on his first day. Feagan didn't break his steady stare at Trevor as Trevor passed by and continued away, but Trevor didn't hold his end of it, just looking away casually before they had even passed and never looking back. He just wanted to get to class.

The students in the halls were still mostly hyperaware of Trevor as he moved among them, some giving him a wide gap of personal space at the expense of their own. Those who had just been in class with him, and those who had spoken to them, seemed less interested in whispering back and forth between themselves about him

73

than the rest, but the hallways still echoed his name as he moved through them, perhaps in spite of the new and noticeable lack of posters debating his own right to be there. Had Trevor bothered to think about it, he might have been able to pick those responsible for the bulk of the attacks on his character from the crowd using Sunshine's memories, but he was too busy trying to remember the details of Ulysses for his next class to think about such petty, past battles.

Trevor arrived at his second hour class as the one-minute warning bell was ringing, and most of the class was already seated. "Would you mind closing the door, Trev?" Mrs. McCallum addressed him immediately as he came in.

"Sure thing," and Trevor closed the door behind him. "Do you have a preference for where I sit, Mrs. McCallum?"

"Oh, no, no, no. Sit anywhere you like." She gestured broadly at the room as though every seat were empty and available for him to choose. In actuality there were only a small handful of seats to choose from. Two were in the front row, and while he wanted to try to integrate himself into the student body as quickly as possible, Trevor chose to sit up front. He knew Mrs. McCallum would appreciate the gesture, even if it didn't carry on to the next day. "Good, good. A real go-getter. Welcome to my class."

"Pleased to meet you."

"Now class, I'm sure you're all already aware of who our new student is, so we won't bother with introductions, but Trev, are you aware of what we're studying? Do we need to give you a proper introduction to the text?"

Trevor leant over and pulled a well-worn leather-bound copy of Ulysses from his satchel and opened it to the section they were working on. "Ulysses, right? I'll try to follow along. I'm pretty sure I get it."

"You'd be the first one in this class to really get it, if you do, but we'll see. Okay everyone, open to page 90 and let's take a look at the symbolism of the cat."

A voice from the back of the classroom, "What cat?"

"See, Trev, I told you they didn't get it."

They dove into the material, discussing the
understanding or lack of understanding that each student had
come to in their readings, and despite her hopes and his
access to Ms. Charming's memories, Trevor wasn't
anywhere near grasping the complexities that Mrs.
McCallum was trying to get everyone to see. Luckily, he
was not alone in this. Again Trevor found himself well-
matched with his classmates in his reading level and capacity
to understand the material, even though they all seemed to
fall short of the teacher's highest hopes for them that
morning. Instead of continuing to hammer on the same
missed points over and over again though, Mrs. McCallum
quickly turned the classroom's discussion to investigate what
the students had actually thought about as a result of their
readings, and there was a lively and well-informed
conversation about the things that different students thought
might be behind the ideas they'd read.

At his old school, Trevor's English classes hadn't
done much more than regurgitate the contents of their books
without really getting into any critical thinking about what it
might mean, or how that might relate to the time and place in
which it was written. Here he found that they not only tried
to examine the meaning of the book and the setting in which
it was written, but tried to intuit what the author's intentions
might have been - not just overall, but with individual
passages. It wasn't anything that could be backed up or
verified without somehow asking the author himself, but it
seemed to add depth and it definitely brought the students
more actively into a developing a personal relationship with
the work.

There wasn't really a consensus about what it all
meant before the class ran out of time to discuss it, but
everyone agreed that they were interested enough to try to
finish the book before class met again, so they could discuss
the resolution, and the rest of the book in its context. It
wasn't exactly a homework assignment, it was just what the
entire class had agreed to do - by this point in the discussion,
Mrs. McCallum's role seemed mostly to encourage everyone
to get involved more than to direct the students in a
particular direction of thought. The bell rang to dismiss the

class, and not everyone wanted to leave immediately, they were still trying to argue their views to those who had seen it another way. Trevor was interested, but was sure the conversation would pick up where it had left off the next morning, so he gathered his things together and re-entered the throngs in the hallways with the voices of his classmates still going on and on behind him.

Next up was P.E. and Trevor walked quickly to the gym, and into the boy's locker room where he was expected to change clothes and be ready for whatever was planned within five minutes of the final bell. Mr. Klaw, the P.E. teacher, was well-known even to Mrs. Charming as being tough on students who showed up late or out of uniform. Luckily for Trevor when he got to the locker room, it was clear which locker contained his uniform - someone had scrawled graffiti across it in runes. Whoever had done it was effectively referring to him as lower than the fungus that feeds on the slime between the toes of retarded ogres, though it hadn't been put as eloquently as all that in the short burst of profanities on his locker.

Trevor didn't bother to give it a second look as he opened the combination lock on the locker on the first try, and he didn't try to recall whose handwriting it was by drawing on the Principal's memories, but from the way the students were reacting - in shock rather than the bravado he would have expected at his old school in a case like this, especially in a boy's locker room - he thought it might be one of the faculty. Regardless of who had thought it appropriate to defile school property to harass a new student, Trevor was glad to find that his uniform was intact inside the locker, unharmed by the attackers. He began to disrobe.

Pulling off his pants, Trevor realized what was underneath them and nearly stopped himself. Not wanting to appear timid or self-conscious in any way in front of the other students, he forced himself to strip normally, as though everything were as it normally was down there and he had nothing to be ashamed of. Trevor quickly replaced his pants with the provided pair of short pants, apparently woven from a single piece of fabric and heavy, like canvas or burlap, but soft like a kitten's fur - the short pants stopped just below his

76

knees when he stood, and thus his hairless calves were still visible as he continued to change. He pulled his normal shirt off over his head and pulled on a shirt that was cut like that sort of undershirt that had no sleeves, but which was made from the same material as his short pants. Next Trevor pulled the underskirts of the uniform on over his head. They were the perfect length to ride just above his hips and barely touch the floor below him, and they were multilayered but light and cool and loose, allowing easy movement and reasonable protection. Next was his underrobe, which was made similar to a duster or other large, long coat, covering him from the neck down to about six inches above the hem of his underskirts, and all the way down his arms long enough that his hands were concealed when his arms were at his sides, plus it buttoned up the front with four large round buttons drawn diagonally across his chest from shoulder to hip. The underrobe was a relatively heavy material compared to the underskirts, and appeared to be deceptively warm - it was still very light and breathed well enough and moved easily enough to allow for broad motion unrestrictively. Finally, he pulled his overrobe on over all of it, completely concealing the rest of the uniform and now also concealing his head as the hood flipped up. The overrobe made him look somewhat like the stereotypically imagined monks, it was thick and dark and with the hood up it hid his face along with the rest of his body. The primary purpose of the overrobe, Trevor knew, was as a sort of armor and padding for the most intense activities he might participate in, and he also knew that in the most intense situations that might call for it, it was considered a sign of weakness not to discard one's overrobe as though unneeded.

Trevor doubted it would be needed today for P.E., but he also knew that Mr. Klaw was a stickler for proper uniforms and saw that all the others were either already wearing their overrobes or were still dressing - though he was the only one with the hood up. As a last touch, Trevor put on the heavy leather boots that stood waiting for him at the bottom of his locker, pulling them up all the way to just beyond where the short pants ended under his underskirts. Like all the other clothes, they were a perfect fit for him and

77

already broken in, clinging perfectly to the curves of his smooth legs as he shifted all his layers down around and over them.

"One minute, people!" Mr. Klaw's voice echoed into the locker room from the door, reminding everyone that there was a reason they were dressing so quickly and while those who were already dressed moved out through the door, Trevor among them, a few stragglers, including Nirgal, were still struggling with getting their robes and skirts and boots in place on time. Trevor stepped out of the flow of properly dressed students on their way to see what Mr. Klaw had in store for them to help Nirgal get ready.

"You don't have to do that, T-T-Trev." Instead of the simple flustered way Nirgal had been at the start of Mr. Glip's class, Trevor detected actual nervousness. Whether this was because Trevor was lacing up his boots for him while he pulled on and straightened out his underrobe and overrobe or for some other reason entirely, Trevor didn't know. "You don't want to be late."

"We'll be fine. Is that what you're worried about?"

"I've been l-l-late ten times already. K-K-K-Klaw said I'd be running laps around the BOTTOM of the pit if I was late again."

Trevor didn't have to draw on Sunshine's memories to know that Mr. Klaw wouldn't really send someone to the bottom of the pit for something as simple as being late. "Look, your boots are on, your robes are on, come on. You look fine. Let's go."

Nirgal looked down at his hands which were still trying to get his uniform ready, only to realize that he already was ready, just as Trevor had said. "Oh. Okay." They were the last two out the door, but with Trevor's help, Nirgal was going to be on time for a change.

"Glad to see you've decided to join us on time this morning, Nirgal. I hope I'm not going to be having the same trouble with you though, Trev. There's nothing worse than being late. Actually, now that I think of it, worse than that is to be consistently late like Nirgal." Some of the students laughed at this, and if Trevor hadn't already been aware that Nirgal was not the most popular student around, this

situation might have made it clear. It also helped clarify how
Mr. Klaw treated the students he didn't like. "Now Trev,
since you've never attended my class before, in fact have
never attended a single hour of proper Physical Education in
your life, I'd like to go easy on you for today."

"Oh, there's no need for that. I'm sure I can keep up
ably."

"Good," Mr. Klaw's preplanned statement had less
bite in light of Trevor's polite one, "because I can't go easy
on you, and I wasn't going to. You don't deserve special
treatment, and you're not going to get any from me."

"Good."

The other students, standing all around them in their
layers and layers of robes, looked like a stunned group of
underage monks who were witnessing acts of intense
blasphemy - they simply could not believe how well Trevor
was reacting to Mr. Klaw's attitude. Any one of them would
have cowed to him already, or bowed their heads in shame.
Trevor was acting like this was nothing, and it earned him
quite a bit of credibility and respect in the eyes of his
classmates, all of whom had had to put up with Mr. Klaw's
punishment at one point or another.

"We're going to start with three laps around the pit,
two running and one levving. Then we'll choose teams and
practice dodgeball."

"Awesome!" Whoops and hollers broke out from
the other students at the sound of this, excitement all around,
and for good reason. Dodgeball season was coming up and
they all wanted to have a chance to make the team, but
freshmen were only allowed to play by special selection.
Special selection was only made when the coach saw a
student playing at what he considered to be a level good
enough for competition, and since Mr. Klaw was the coach
and didn't watch games outside of his own P.E. classes and
official matches, this would be one of their only chances to
show off for him. Trevor was aware of all of this somewhere
in the back of his head, but Nirgal interrupted him from
trying to remember the details by sighing heavily.

"Dodgeball..." Nirgal sounded disappointed,
dejected, and destitute all at once in that word, and as the

other students rushed outside to the pit for their laps, he walked sluggishly with Trevor at his side.

"You don't like dodgeball? Don't you get knocked out right away?"

"Have you ever played dodgeball? I mean, real dodgeball? With fire and lightning and scarantulas all flying at your head while you're just trying to conjure a simple mudball before you get concussed or torched? Usually my own team tries to take me out before the other team can throw me for a conversion, and then I'm back to zero for getting out of the game and they just keep it up..." Nirgal was clearly not a fan of the game, as they closed the distance to the pit his ranting became incoherent and frenzied.

"Okay, okay, I get it. Well, not really, you're right, I've never played dodgeball like that, but I hear you. It sounds like they've developed a sort of side-game to play with you instead of really focusing on their core game play strategies. It also sounds like we'll be on a team together before long, whether we get picked by the same side or not, so once we are, why don't we work together and show them what teamwork is supposed to look like?"

They were standing at the edge of the pit, and while Nirgal seemed to be thinking over his suggestion, Trevor looked down into the pit with his own eyes for the first time. He had been thinking about it off and on since Nirgal had first mentioned it, thinking back to the original selection of this site as a way to keep the people who would never allow themselves to understand what was in this pit from getting access to it, and how it had gone through several variations of inauspicious and uninteresting facades before Sunshine had finally decided to build a high school here all around it. Trevor looked down into the darkness long enough to begin to make out the glinting and glistening of the slithering and shifting forms that seemed to form its walls, but there was no easy way for him to observe anything within it in real detail in the daylight - as the arc of the sun penetrated the pit its inhabitants naturally shifted into the shadows or disappeared entirely - what was illuminated just looked to be the carefully carved wall of a large open pit or mohole.

"Yeah, sure, you can try, but we'd better get running."

So they ran their laps around the edge of the pit. As they ran around it without speaking, Trevor kept running the numbers in his head, trying to estimate how far they were traveling based on the size of the students directly across the pit and the average length of his stride and whatever other things he could come up with. Trevor estimated the diameter to be just under two hundred and eleven yards across, as far from edge to edge as a two football fields end to end lengthwise, and it seemed perfectly round even as he and Nirgal finished their second lap around it without slowing down to transition from running along the ground to floating along just above it. They levitated inches above the ground and continued forward at running speed, 'levving' all the way around the pit one more time. If Trevor's calculations were correct, this massive pit was exactly the size he wished it wasn't. If Sunshine had known, she hadn't thought about it much, but that was alright for Trevor, who liked doing math for fun sometimes. The fact that the math distracted him sufficiently that he had missed the transition from running to levving was probably a good thing, because as they reached the end of their final lap and Trevor had to come back down onto the ground, the experience of levving for the first time in his own body was enough to toss him tumbling to the ground.

"Are you okay?" Nirgal bent down to help Trevor up, and looked around to verify that they were far enough behind the other, more eager students that no one had seen his fall. "I don't think anyone saw that."

"No, no, no problem." Trevor was practically laughing as he pulled himself up with Nirgal's arm, "I've just never really levved before that. It was a bit of a shock to find myself ... levitating."

"You've never... how is that possible? When we were running, you took to the air without missing a beat or changing speed - you're a natural for the track team! It took me until I was eight before I could start levving without falling on my face or flipping around in the air."

"I ... I don't want to get into it, but ... well, you saw me coming down. Not exactly the most graceful landing."

"It comes with practice. It's like ... " Nirgal was trying to think of a way to explain it to make it easier on his new friend, and they walked casually back to the gym where they could already hear the other students picking teams. "Okay, I know. One time my family took me to the uhh... the ... is it airport? Yeah, so, anyway, we were just going to go pick up some distant relative who had gotten too old to reliably disappear. Actually, she could disappear just fine, it was the reappearing where she'd meant to go that didn't work out so good. So anyway, she was coming to visit my father or something, and she had to travel across the country by airplane, so we had to go down to the airport to pick her up. And she smelled funny. I know I was only a little kid, but this smell stuck with me, it was like kardiff dung and mildewed leather and ... well, old people, but all rolled up together. You wouldn't believe this smell. But ... wait, what was I talking about?"

"You were going to tell me what coming down from levving is like."

"Oh yeah! So, anyway, we were at that place, the airport, and there was this one long hallway we went down with mechanical floors that moved along on their own, to carry people from one end of the hallway to the other. I'm still not sure why they bothered; those things barely moved faster than I could walk, but I guess when we were all walking along on the moving floor it was a little faster than just walking normally. But then all of a sudden the mechanical floor ended and I had to go from walking at double-speed to normal speed, stepping down off this weird raised mechanical moving floor at the same time. And I saw the people ahead of me doing it, and I was worried I was going to trip up or fall down or snag on the mechanical floor somehow, but I got there and it was just like coming down from levving and I didn't miss a beat, because I had been practicing it all summer. Have you ever been to the airport?"

"Yeah, I know just what you're talking about. I'll try that next time."

"I'll take Pilty." A skinny student that Trevor recognized as Corvin seemed to be the head of one team, and a shorter but very muscular other student that Trevor couldn't seem to place was picking for the other side.

"Fine, then I want Jawnee."

"Okay, but here comes Trev, and he's gonna be on my side, aren't you, Trev?"

"Sure. Why not?"

"That's not fair!" The built one was clearly of the opinion that Trevor playing on the other side would mean certain defeat for his own team. "If you get Trev, I get an extra player!"

Corvin addressed Mr. Klaw, "What do you say, Mr. Klaw? I'll agree to that."

"You're probably going to be disappointed. I doubt Trev has ever even seen a match played, have you boy?"

"No, sir. I've never even had the game described to me. Is there a rule book I could take a look at before we..."

"Not today." Mr. Klaw happily interrupted Trevor to deny his request before he'd even finished making it, "Fine. Corvin's team gets Trev, and Boden's team gets an extra player. Boden, who do you want?"

"Martin and Hortis, obviously. Do you think I'd really want Nirgal on my team?"

"Of course not. But I thought you might like to shore things up, get a bad player on each team. Go ahead and take all three." They nodding in grudging agreement, and Nirgal went over to Boden's side while Trevor stood at the edge of Corvin's group. Then Mr. Klaw went over the basics.

"I want a good, clean game. No sissying out, Nirgal, you've got to put up a fight this time. No wide angle illusions, any of you - keep it focused on a single opponent if you can - and no tackling today. Well, unless you're going for Trev. He deserves a few lumps to make up for lost time. I'm short a grouper and a guard for the new season, but I want to see how you work as a team, so keep it to invocations, summons, and other magics as much as possible, and show me how you can work together. We've got about half an hour left, so I expect to see full point

83

matrices on both sides and I've set the court's timer to automatic." Mr. Klaw looked around at the two teams, eager to get started, "Is everybody ready?" He held a red rubber dodgeball the likes of which Trevor was quite familiar with out in front of him, and as he said "Go!" he tossed it straight up in the air and instantly disappeared to the edge of the court. Just as the ball reached its apex it burst into flames.

Suddenly everyone was moving, getting into positions, watching each other carefully and shouting to each other in a sort of dodgeball shorthand that Trevor wasn't familiar with. He tried to stay out of people's way as the game got started with competing blasts of energy trying to force the ball of flame in the direction of various players in a weird sort of non-contact volleying. As the fireball was volleyed back and forth between the increasingly scattered players - the playing field for dodgeball seemed to be slightly larger than an indoor football arena - Trevor tried to get the gist of the game from Ms. Charming's memories. But he couldn't.

She had apparently never been interested enough in the game to pay attention to it, to play it even once, or to watch any single game from start to finish. She understood that it was popular, that Mr. Klaw's team brought home trophies from regional competitions most years, and all the administrative aspects of having to deal with students more interested in winning the next big game than passing the next big test, but she had never really learned the game. Trevor was really at as much a disadvantage as everyone's lowest expectations had predicted he would be, and instead of the fulfillment and confidence he had felt in math and literature he felt a sense of dread that he would lose a lot of ground with these students if he didn't do well. So instead of trying to remember anything about the game, he tried to learn the rules as it went along, and he turned his full attention to that fireball.

Good thing, too, because just as he became decisively determined to figure the game out and focus on the fireball, it was headed his way as fast as he'd seen it go. He tried mimicking the motion and invocation pair he'd seen and heard the other players using to deflect the ball at

84

another player, but he must not have got it quite right because instead of the ball moving away from him, it seemed to pick up speed towards him. At the very last second before it was supposed to hit him, with his arm stretched out in front of him as though to catch the flaming mass at arm's length, Trevor reflexively seemed to shift his center of balance to where the center of the fireball was, and rotated sideways and around it as it continued towards where he had just been, his body moving in an impossible, almost-floating-spin akin to what he had experienced getting out of bed that morning. Two distinct syllables came out his mouth as the ball reached the point where it would have either left the relative spot just inches from his palm or pulled him with it towards the floor, and his spin continued around with all the force he had picked up in rotating around the fireball, but now his center of mass seemed to have moved back to his actual center and the fireball remained in the same relative position to him as he did so, which meant that when the third syllable of the invocation was uttered at just the right moment of the spin, the fireball was released with significantly more velocity in a direction that was away from Trevor instead of towards him. The fireball flew a very short straight line for the side of the head of Boden, hitting him hard enough to knock him to the ground.

From what anyone else saw, the whole thing was elegant and graceful, a single smooth reaction. Those who were watching the ball rather than preparing for the next phase of the game saw the ball fly directly towards Trevor's hand as though in a slow pitch intended to be caught. Then they saw what looked like Trevor's grabbing the ball without touching it, spinning around in a wide circle like a discus thrower and releasing the fireball with velocity and accuracy rarely seen outside of professional matches directly at the captain of the opposing team. Even Mr. Klaw knew that it had either been a powerful show off of advanced skill at the game intended to win Trevor a place on the dodgeball team or a spectacular bit of beginner's luck for a player who didn't know the first thing about what he had just done. Luckily for Trevor, the first strike signaled the beginning of the second round and all Hell broke loose across the court before anyone could take the time to see the surprised but pleased look on his face.

A look that very quickly turned into apparent awe as lightning balls and fireballs and giant spinning insects and speeding spheres of water and mud and that strange bubbling blue goo he had seen poured over live cockroaches trapped in a child-sized metal coffin and a few balls he couldn't figure out the type of appeared entirely out of nowhere and at quick pace crisscrossed the court. At first, Trevor couldn't make much sense of what was going on or who was on which team and just did his best to bounce anything flying towards him back in the direction it had come with the invocation he very quickly got right. Slowly though, he figured out enough of it to take control of his role in the game.

Trevor had never had much interest in sports generally, so any correlation to sports he may have been exposed to before was lost on him. The layout of the court, the positions that each of the other students seemed to be doing their best to be filling, the techniques and scoring rules, all of it was a mystery to him even by the end of the game. Which did not stop him from playing along as he found patterns in behavior, or from working with Nirgal as soon as he had the chance. From what he could discern, different players' roles were to generate different, specific forms or groups of balls. The players nearest the back of each side seemed to be the only ones generating lighting balls, and these seemed to have propulsion of their own, usually arcing high above the players on their own team and falling almost directly from the sky onto the players of the opposing team - much like lightning really would. There were players who seemed to stay towards the front corners of their team, off to the sides of the court, but close to the center of the court, and they were the ones in control of the fireballs. The fireballs' purpose seemed to be to take the core group of players by surprise before they could finish whatever they were trying to conjure or propel, coming in sidelong and interrupting chants, gestures, invocations and the like either by getting the player to jump out of the way, deflect it magically, or take the hit - and usually taking a tumble from the force of the hit. The third main set of players that Trevor noticed was that core group of people in between the fireball throwers and in front of the lighting casters. They had plenty of room on the huge court, and stayed relatively well-spaced, giving them all plenty of room to avoid incoming projectiles and to avoid their own teammates with their own. These players seemed not to be specialized in what they used to try to take out the other team, and the different balls they used seemed to be not just for show or out of a personal specialty, but had different outcomes when they actually hit players. Trevor could see enough to know that different projectiles had different outcomes, but had not begun to try to catalogue the types of balls and different levels of results - the mudballs Nirgal was invoking, spinning up to speed, and hurling at the other players rarely made contact, but when they did, it was more impressive a result than most of the other ones, splashing wet mud in a sort of creeping field all up and around and across the entire surface of their robes in a thickening layer that seemed to slow them down significantly. When the mudballs hit them in the head, their heads became completely enveloped in mud hood and all, blind and deaf and holding their breath until they could break through the quickly hardening shell or otherwise disenchant the substance entirely. Trevor could see why Nirgal had focused so singly on that one type of ball; if one is going to only rarely hit, one would want it to be the most effective, and from what he could see from the looks on their faces and their rate of fire, lightning balls were proportionally more difficult to invoke as they were successful offensive tools.

The look of the court in the heat of the game, when he paid closer attention to the other players than his own potential danger, seemed to Trevor to be one of careful concentration as each player was effectively continuously performing their most advanced "spells" over and over again. Sure, they were also trying to maintain that concentration with other people's spells speeding towards them, but getting their own spells off seemed like the primary concern of the bulk of the players. Until Trevor noticed that two players on each team seemed actually to be

87

using defensive techniques primarily, he was sure the game was an exercise in bullying on par with a primitive version of the deadly "wizard's duels" Ms. Charming had seen too many times in her life. But those four players seemed to be doing enough to try to protect the other players on their teams to make up for the bulk of each team's actions being entirely offensive. Blocking, disintegrating, and rebounding balls approaching nearby teammates so they didn't have to stop their own conjuring, chanting, gesturing, or invoking, these players seemed to be the result of perhaps fully two thirds of the airborne projectiles at any one time despite the fact that they almost never created one on their own. To Trevor's increasingly positive impression of them, they even seemed to be able to stop some of the lightning balls from coming down - flashes of light intersecting with literally lightning-fast balls of light and heat, both bursting into explosive showers of sparks falling all around the protected players. They didn't always get the timing right, so sometimes they just tossed a flash of light just beside the ball lightning that came down hard on a player's head and threw them smoking and twitching to the ground, one point closer to a conversion.

Which Trevor didn't really grasp, either. He could see that there was some sort of automatic accounting of points being done, and he could hear the different players shouting and taunting and bemoaning their own scores, but he didn't really put much effort into figuring it out. He gathered that a single player being hit by lightning balls three times in a row without hitting another player with a ball of his own seemed to "convert" the player automatically to the other side - the players were literally disappeared from their position on one side of the court to an equivalent location on the other side, facing the opposite direction and their new opponents, their old team. Some running balance accumulation of lightning ball strikes could have the same effect despite successful hits by a player, but Trevor wasn't in the mood to try to discern the mathematics involved while dodging and repelling a variety of projectile attacks. Especially in light of the apparently similarly complex calculations regarding offensive and defensive hit balances

88

that, when a player reached a sufficient marginal deficit of offensive hits resulted in the player being disappeared off the court directly to the benches on the sideline, unable to continue playing. What the margin required to get someone out was, Trevor had difficulty detecting - he would have had to keep track of every shot a player made and every shot made at them while keeping track of his own fate, and Trevor simply didn't care enough to figure it out.

What he did figure out, or decide anyway, was that the defensive players seemed up to the task of defending his teammates from the sidelong fireballs and most of the other attacks, and that the core players on both teams were just about evenly matched with each other skill-wise - though Nirgal did go back and forth a couple of times before Trevor figured the game out enough to do anything about it - so Trevor decided that the lightning ball casters were the most important players for him to try to take out, with the defensive players coming in at a close second. No one on his team was communicating with him, so he couldn't tell what their strategy was, or even if they really had one, though it was clear they had all played together before. So he just went forward with it on his own until Nirgal switched back to his side. He didn't know how to generate exactly the types of balls everyone else was using and didn't want to break any unknown rules, so instead of trying to figure out a new set of offensive spells from the basis that he had in more commonly used and rare spells that Sunshine had known, he decided to take a more team-player tactic.

He took to grabbing, through force of will, deflective force as though the balls were giant flying billiards, and whatever other means he could think of, the balls already going back and forth between the two teams. He did his best to mostly use balls the other team had sent their way so as not to cut down on his own team's offensive hits, but as long as there were balls moving in the air between the teams, Trevor had plenty to work with. He managed to redirect one of Nirgal's mudballs with a burst of wind that threw it from too close for the defensive player on Nirgal's own team to get out of the way of or really even to see clearly before it began enveloping his head entirely in thick, hardening mud.

The fireballers on the edges of Trevor's team cheered and whooped as they made hit after hit against a suddenly half-undefended team, and those hits kept Trevor's own team from being distracted long enough that suddenly a dozen projectiles flew at once from all around him, many making solid hits. Among the hits was a lightning ball strike against Nirgal that disappeared him to right next to Trevor as the defensive player got the mud off his face and play began to get back to normal on both sides.

"Good one," Nirgal panted, out of breath, "Trev." He tried to catch his breath as Trevor blocked any balls headed in their direction, then spoke again, "that was a lot of hits."

"Thanks." Trevor knocked a flying, volleyball-sized scarantula that was hurled at him away with his bare hand, and it scuttled away across the floor towards the sidelines, disappearing as it passed over the line marking the edge of the court. "I have a plan. Can you defend me while I take out the guys at the back over there, the ones with the lightning balls?"

"I guess so, but how are you going to ..."

"Don't worry about that. Just give me a chance to concentrate; these guys," Trevor gestured at the defensive players on his own team, "are not helping me out at all."

"Okay." There was a decidedly unsure sound in Nirgal's voice, "but I've got to warn you, I'm not the best at defense."

"Just do your best, it'll be good enough."

"Okay." This time, Nirgal blew back a rounded stone the size and weight of a bowling ball with a flash of light that seemed to turn it to dust as it reversed direction, which was cue enough for Trevor to get to work.

First, he held his hands out it front of him as though there was a dodgeball-sized ball between them, and stared at the space between his hands while muttering a simple chant. The chant just came naturally to him, but whether that was because of Ms. Charming's memories or not, he was beginning to be unable to discern - her memories and experiences were blending with and fading into his own unconscious mind to such a degree that, like showering or walking to school or writing in his own handwriting, the source wasn't as important as the result. There was no really discernible ball forming between his hands as he continued to concentrate and chant quietly to the space there, but there was a sort of rippling visual distortion increasing in size steadily outward from the center of that space - like ripples distorting the reflection on the surface of a pool of water, a sort of three-dimensional, spherical distortion was rippling out in waves from the center of the space, the sort of effect one sees in movies all the time, but real and right there in front of him. Nirgal saw it and was slack-jawed almost long enough to miss a fireball thrown his way, but froze it out at the last possible moment and increased the intensity of his defense, apparently wanting to see what it was that Trevor was planning.

The distortion between Trevor's hands continued increasing in intensity and reach after he shut his eyes, and his muttering continued even as his mind separated and went into that state that he had mistakenly believed before to be immersive imagination; he was focused on the mind of Nirgal, whose constant thoughts were shotgun-fast and scattered, barely able to keep up with the increasing pace at which the opposing team was trying to hit him or Trevor. Trevor shifted his view back and upward to get a better look at the entire court, and it became clear that the players had all begun noticing Trevor standing still with his eyes closed, muttering at an increasingly intense distortion of reality. The players on his own team were trying to take advantage of their distraction, but at the same time were giving Trevor a wide berth, keeping plenty of distance between themselves and the sphere of rippling distortion approaching four feet in diameter. Trevor tried shifting his focus from the single mind of Nirgal to the entire team at once, something he had never before attempted, but something that apparently worked just as easily as any other thing he could do during these experiences.

The thoughts coming to him seemed to be just those tuned into the "channel" in their minds focused on teamwork. Their other thoughts and fears and memories and such were there, but muted to just below the level of

Trevor's perception, which was interesting but not really what Trevor cared to think about just then. Instead he tried to frame the message he wanted to get into his teammate's minds in a simple and direct enough way that it would come through clearly, but without giving so much information as to cause confusion or doubt. With Ms. Charming's long training at reasonable levels of thought projection under his belt as though it had been his own training, Trevor first sent the simple idea to all the players on his team to "Be ready to fire," and it seemed to come across ably, because anyone not already preparing something to lob at the other side began doing so, all at once, and none of them let loose, waiting for something. From the thoughts coming from their minds, Trevor could tell that they all seemed to think his projected thought had been one of their own, natural thoughts - which was exactly what he wanted. When he saw that everyone was ready, he projected another thought at the same moment that he opened his real eyes to the world, "Take the rest down."

With his eyes open, Trevor could see the lightning ball that was headed right for him, and was glad that Nirgal had no hope of blocking it. Trevor gently motioned as to toss the non-ball between his hands up into the air to meet the ball of lightning, and stepped backward quickly so that he could jump up just before the center of the distortion and the lightning ball intersected. At the precise moment that the distortion reached the lightning ball, Trevor's arm came down and forward against the lightning ball as though he were trying to volley the sphere of electricity like a volleyball back to the other side of the court. Except that as the distortion and the lightning and the palm of his hand all came in contact, the eight foot diameter rippling waves of distortion came suddenly crashing into the ball of lightning, and the force that Trevor applied through his striking hand drove what was suddenly not one lightning ball but over two dozen streaking towards the other team with ferocious velocity. The two defensive players were able to block one lightning ball each, but they were both struck down with the rest of the front line players and several of the sidelong fireball throwers, some of them by multiple lightning balls, and all quite literally knocked to the ground and stunned.

Which was when the second round of balls went flying, one from every one of Trevor's teammates, all prepared by his projected thoughts for taking out the players left standing. The fireball throwers and the core players repeatedly struck the lightning ball casters who were now almost defenseless - they could deflect some of the incoming balls, but not nearly all of them. The lightning ball casters on Trevor's side directed their lightning balls to the already downed players who had not been disappeared to their own side already, and there was an almost wholesale conversion of players from one side to the other before any of them had a chance to get back to their feet, wondering how they had been overcome but somewhat glad to be on what was rapidly apparent to be the winning side. They got their own balls headed towards their former teammates as quickly as they could, and the lightning ball casters were all pretty efficiently moved to the sidelines, leaving the side Trevor was on with no one left to play against.

The students seemed unsure as to what they should do next, and some of them looked to Trevor while others looked to Mr. Klaw for some sort of direction. Trevor just shrugged.

"I don't know. Is that not right?"

There was general muttered agreement that there hadn't been anything against the rules in what had just happened, and it was clear to Trevor that despite that, something wasn't right. He leaned towards Nirgal and spoke softly.

"What's wrong? Why is everyone standing around confused?"

"The game isn't exactly over..."

"Nirgal, you know I've never played before. What's supposed to happen next? How does the game end?"

"It's timed. A normal match would be three twenty minute games, and for P.E. we usually just play one twenty minute game. I guess we just have to wait for the twenty minutes to be up."

"There's no score or anything? No rules about what happens when there's no one left on the other team?"

"I uhh... The score is calculated based on the players' scores and conversion points, total and by the side scored for, and on the number of conversions made and the number of players knocked out during each game, and then at the beginning of each game the players start out again on their own sides and play again, and at the end of three games the three matrices of scores are combined and compared reduced to determine pairwise defeats in various categories of scoring using the Condorcet method with CSSM for ambiguity reduction in the case of no clear Condorcet winner, which gives us the final winner for the match. But ... I don't know of any rules about one side ending up with no players, except to just wait it out."

Boden, now on Trevor's side, spoke up. "In the National Dodgeball League, end of game is called when there are no more players on one side, but in school-level competitions, we're supposed to wait out the time. They're talking about changing it for the games this year, but there's a lot of argument on both sides."

Corvin, still on Trevor's side and apparently quite happy to have selected him, joined in. "There are some people in the Atlantic Division that want to get the National Dodgeball League to start using the same rules as the EU Dodgeball Quorum, on account of the new time-dilation and non-visible attacks that are coming into common use."

"Sure, but who, at a High School level, is going to be using a time-dilated attack or casting a hovering invisible lightning ball? Those aren't exactly easy to do." Boden seemed to be in favor of cutting games short.

"I bet Trev could, couldn't you, Trev?" Corvin patted Trevor congradulatorily on the back.

"I really don't know how to play, guys. I'm sure this was just beginner's luck."

Dissenting voices broke out all around him, and Boden said "I've never seen anyone play like that before, that's for sure. How did you do that?"

"I just ... did it. I don't really know. I just thought of what I wanted to do, and did it."

94

"Dang! It took me months to get a basic lightning ball down, and you can fork it twenty-five ways on your first try. Maybe we shouldn't have let you come to school here after all - you don't need it."

"No, no, I'm sure it's just beginner's luck." Then, the twenty minutes buzzer went off and everyone who had been unable to step onto the court rushed out to join the crowd.

"That was amazing!"

"How did you do that?"

"Mr. Klaw is sure to offer you a position on the team!"

"I just wish I'd still been in the game for that! It was so cool."

They went on and on until Mr. Klaw reached them, and then suddenly everyone in class fell silent, waiting to hear what he had to say.

"Good game, everyone. Get cleaned up and get out of here. Trev, I need to speak with you." Everyone else moved back towards the locker rooms, some of them disenchanting the remnants of the game still clinging to them and their robes as they went, leaving Trevor and Mr. Klaw standing at the middle of the dodgeball court alone. Mr. Klaw waited until the last student was through the door to the locker room and the door was closed before he spoke.

"You used psychic communication to coordinate that last big offensive."

"Is that against the rules? You wouldn't let me learn the rules before --"

"No, it's not against the rules. There is an understanding of sorts among competitive teams at the high school level that Mentalism won't be used. Most high school students can't handle it, either projecting or receiving, and coaches are discouraged from projecting instructions because they want to keep the games based on the players' skill levels. But no, there's no actual rules against it."

Trevor didn't know what to say. He just waited for Mr. Klaw to continue.

"I don't know what position you could play, and it's pretty clear you have no idea how to conjure regulation balls, but I'm thinking of offering you a place on the school dodgeball team. From what I saw, I can't tell what kind of a team player you are, or how you'd do in a real game with broad illusions, good groupers, and tackling, so it's hard for me to say anything. What do you think?"

"Honestly, I've never had much interest in sports. I just wanted to try to hold my own out there. You know how important my impression on everyone is today."

"True, true." Mr. Klaw put his hand on his chin, and for the first time in Trevor's or Ms. Charming's memory, looked thoughtful. "I'll tell you what we'll do. Instead of the normal P.E. program, we'll go through basic dodgeball instruction for the next couple of weeks, and you can decide whether you like playing and winning. When we have our first practice matches next week, will you come, at least to watch?"

"I guess so. I just want to be clear that I don't expect to be interested in playing competitively. I won't rule it out, but..."

"No, no, I understand. That's fine. Go get cleaned up. I'll see you tomorrow."

Trevor walked singly back to the locker room. As soon as he was through the door, his classmates, in various states of undress and redress, accosted him excitedly.

"Did you make the team?"

"What did he say?"

"What position are you playing?"

"Did he say if anyone else would make the team?"

"You're gonna be great!"

"I told him I wasn't interested." Trevor's statement elicited a loud gasp and several shouts of "No!"

"You turned him down?"

"Why would you turn him down?"

"Do you have a contract with a pro team?"

"What's wrong with you?"

As Trevor reached his locker and began peeling off his robes, everyone kept asking him questions he didn't want to try to answer, and Nirgal came over to talk to him more discreetly. "That really was amazing."

"I couldn't have done it without your help. Thank you."

"Hey, I'm just glad I wasn't everyone's focus today. Sometimes it's like standing in a thunderstorm with a lightning rod on my head."

Trevor was nearly undressed, down to his short pants and undershirt and was unlacing his boots when he leaned in towards Nirgal and spoke softly, "I don't see a shower, and I'm sure I need one. Where am I supposed to get cleaned up so I don't smell for the rest of the day?"

"Oh! You've never... Right. I keep forgetting you were, well... you know. Before today."

"Right. So. What do I do? Is it some invocation or chant, or a mathematical proof, or what?"

"No, no, nothing like that. The short pants and undershirt do it for you. When you take them off, they take any sweat and dirt and odors and anything otherwise unwanted with them. Try it."

He did, and as he pulled the undershirt off over his head, Trevor was pleasantly reminded of a sensation he remembered experiencing countless times in Ms. Charming's body after a lightball match. "There's a lot of stuff like that around here. It's why I seem to be so comfortable and natural in such unfamiliar circumstances; most of the time it seems like if I don't try to figure it out, if I just go along with what everyone else is doing, I'm successful. If I'd just got undressed without asking, I'd have seemed like I knew that the clothes would do that all along."

"Well, no one but me knows. They're too busy trying to figure out why you turned down playing on the dodgeball team, and who Mr. Klaw will find to be a new grouper or guard. They don't care if you don't know about clothes with CleanGuard protection. Of course, with the way you took out Kyl with a mudball from his own team just about puts him out of the running for the guard position."

"Speaking of that, what does a grouper do, exactly?" The bell rang, signaling the end of the period, and Nirgal had barely started undressing.

"I'll tell you later." He ran back to his locker and tore franticly at his clothes. Trevor was dressed again and

97

tying his shoes as the other students walked by him to get to their next class, and most of them made some sort of comment of approval to him as they went by, like "good game," "see you tomorrow," or "awesome first strike." Trevor did his best to respond in turn with "thank you" and "see ya" and the like without losing track of his shoelaces. It seemed more difficult to him to keep looking up politely and responding while tying his shoes than deflecting the fireball to score the first strike had.

Finally he got his shoes tied properly, grabbed his satchel out of his locker, and headed towards the door, turning back towards Nirgal on his way out, "I've got history with Mrs. Leeds next, you?"

"Advanced runic poetry with Ledbetter. It's uhhh... like a college level language class. I've always been good with magical languages."

"That's pretty tough stuff. Do you like it?"

"I didn't think I would, but I've found out that a lot of the most powerful and effective ancient spells that you don't hear about anymore are hidden in runic poetry. Those mudballs are something I developed out of a mud gollom invocation ode I found. There isn't anyone else that can do that, as far as I know."

"Can you invoke a gollom, too?"

"I'm not supposed to, but ... Yeah, I probably could if I tried."

The one-minute warning bell rang. "Do you think we'd get in trouble for disappearing from here to our next classes?" Trevor asked Nirgal even though he already knew the answer from the Principal's careful knowledge of school rules.

"They'd rather we didn't do that, but they'd much rather we were on time than late, so ... just appear around the corner from the door and walk the rest of the way. Lots of seniors do it. Wait, can you do it? I wouldn't trust myself to pop up closer than I started, from here."

"Yeah. Here, you want to get to Ledbetter's class? I can take you."

"You can disappear me with you? That's pretty advanced unless... are you using an artifact or enchanted item?"

"Just me. I've never tried two people, but it can't hurt, can it?"

"Yeah."

"You wanna try it anyway?"

"Yeah."

Nirgal grabbed his own bag just in time to find himself standing just around the corner from Ledbetter's classroom with Trevor by his side. "Is this close enough?"

"Yeah."

"Okay. I've got to go, myself. I'll see you at lunch in an hour, right?"

"Yeah."

Trevor laughed, "yeah." and disappeared to around the corner from his own destination. There hadn't been anyone there to see him and Nirgal appear in the other hallway, but this time there were several young women standing in a group chatting about something who gasped and went on talking when Trevor appeared before them, changing only the subject of their continuous conversation to Trevor's possible role as a troublemaker. He did his best to ignore them and walked around the corner to get through the door of his history class just before the final bell rang. There was only one seat available, at the back of the class, so Trevor quickly went to and sat down in it as quietly as he could.

"This week we'll be continuing our examination of the Fall of the Great Matriarchy. Your research papers are due at the beginning of class on Monday. Trev, I know you haven't been here, so here's the assignment," she passed a sheet of paper down the row of students to him as she continued, "basically I need you to show in seven pages the unsavory background of the rebels who undermined the core of our society and describe, in your own words, how much better the world would be today if not for the events of the Fall."

Trevor had suspected it would be this way. He knew the history between Mrs. Leeds and Ms. Charming from only one side, but his views on the subject were strongly held. Having memories of witnessing historical events unfold created a strong bias within Trevor for the history books to reflect the truth and facts that he felt he had experienced firsthand. Mrs. Leeds took a less strict view of history, he knew from Sunshine's experiences with her, and was more than happy to interpret the events of history through the colored lenses of personal prejudices. Trevor knew that if Mrs. Leeds had not been the next in line for the throne, deposed in part by Ms. Charming's actions, she would not be given the freedom and power over young minds that she enjoyed here. The Principal felt bad, in part, for tearing another person's entire future away and thought that doing what she could at the school to offer an alternative future was a reasonable way to begin to repay Mrs. Leeds. Measures had been taken, of course, to ensure that all students received both sides of the histories that Mrs. Leeds was teaching, with more fact-based teachers in the mandatory Sophomore and Junior level classes, but Mrs. Leeds still had a large influence on the way all the students thought about their own backgrounds and histories.

Unfortunately for Trevor, Sunshine's memories created a seething emotional state whenever Mrs. Leeds opened her mouth in class to speak. She presented only the parts of the historical record that supported her points or that could be distorted to appear to support her points. Anything that had happened that she didn't like or didn't like the result of, she either ignored entirely or painted as negatively as to stand equally with the likes of Hitler's death camps and the Byzantine fae massacres. The largest number of words that her voice forced through the minds of her students were baseless claims, opinions, and outright lies.

"Fuck."

"Who said that?"

Trevor tried to look as innocent as possible, tried to put on the appearance of wondering who had said it, and it seemed to work.

"Well, whoever it was, please keep language like that to yourself. This isn't the Navy, you know. Now where was I?"

Trevor thought of what he wanted to shout at her, and barely contained himself. He wished someone else in the class would speak up, say something - anything. He hadn't been able to contain his first outburst, Mrs. Leeds' lying had just forced it out of him. She was looking around for someone to remind her where in her lies she had left off, and called on a student at random, "Sam. Surely you were paying attention, where was I just then?" Trevor imagined Sam saying what Trevor knew he mustn't say on his first day in class, what he mustn't say but was compelled very strongly to say, what he wished Sam would have the guts to say.

"Uhh.. " Sam cleared his throat and looked down at his notes, "You uhh.. well," Trevor's stare was nearly burning a hole in the back of Sam's head, "Well, your head was stuck so far up your ass I couldn't understand a word you were saying." Sam's hands flew up to cover his mouth as soon as he heard what he'd said. Mrs. Leeds' jaw dropped, her face went slack, she was frozen. Trevor was fighting a huge grin from tearing his face open from ear to ear, was watching Mrs. Leeds carefully now to see how she would react. It appeared that she had never been confronted by a student before, from the speechless way she stood there. The thirty silent seconds ticked by for what represented far too long for her not to say anything to such a comment from a student.

"How dare you," she whispered, still shaken, "how dare you... Do you know who I am? How dare you say that to me?" Her voice was quiet, trembling, as though she was on the verge of crying. "I... I..."

"I'm sorry, I'm sorry. I don't know where that came from! I meant to say you were telling us about the vile cannibalistic rituals of the insurgents who overthrew your, err... who overthrew the crown. I don't know what came over me."

"I... I just don't know what to say." Mrs. Leeds' voice was barely audible, her skin drained of all color, and she was slumped backwards against her desk, just broken.

"I do." Trevor couldn't believe that the entire class was so apologetic to her, every face painted in shock and awe at the disgracefulness of Sam's forced comment. He couldn't not say something. The students all turned around to the rear of the classroom to see who had spoken. "I know just what to say, and I should have said it myself. Sorry, Sam. That was my fault." Everyone seemed to be looking even closer at Trevor now, as though he were some sort of freak or powerful enemy to be frightened of, and Trevor thought maybe they were right, but that what Mrs. Leeds was teaching represented a more immediate and lasting threat.

"What?" Mrs. Leeds, still not understanding how Sam could have spoken to her that way, had clearly not grasped what Trevor had said.

"You're filling these students' heads with lies, Mrs. Leeds, and I can't stand it. I know you were there, you saw some of what happened or heard firsthand reports of it, so I know you must know that you're creating a false version of events in these students' minds. This shit isn't close to what actually happened. I know Ms. Charming feels sorry for you, but I don't, and I know better than to let you taint the minds of so many. How dare you abuse your position here to try to put yourself back into power? You're supposed to be helping us to understand the past. You're not supposed to be building an ideological army to make you feel better or stand by you in another bloody revolution. If I have to take this class, I'm going to challenge every single little lie you tell, starting now. Those so-called insurgents you were talking about? They were regular people like all of you. They didn't perform cannibalistic rituals, they didn't mutilate babies, they didn't kidnap anybody. They reformed the Matriarchy from within its own regulations, first by helping to shift public opinion, then by passing laws through the parliament to broaden men's rights, and finally by reframing the entire basis of government to give equal rights to all sapient beings capable of requesting them."

"That's not how it happened." Mrs. Leeds was still on the verge of tears, now looking at Trevor as though he was threatening her very life. "You weren't there, you don't know."

"I know a lot more than you think, Abby. I know you murdered your sister so you would ascend instead of her, and look what good it did you. Turning these young minds into blind-faith believers in your hate-filled rhetoric, perhaps even someday returning to power, none of this will bring her back or redeem your actions, and you know it."

Mrs. Leeds hit the ground hard in a dead faint before Trevor finished what he was saying. More than one female student who had apparently been won over to Mrs. Leeds' side leapt up from their desks to rush to her aid, fanning her and trying to get her to come to. Trevor closed his eyes and imagined telling the Principal what had just happened, then reopened his eyes to face half the students staring back at him. Their faces were a mix of apparent emotions: shock, anger, resentment, fear, pride, joy, and less clear expressions. The rest of the students were focused on the action at the front of the class, the students trying to figure out how to conjure smelling salts or at least invoke their scent, one girl holding Mrs. Leeds' head in her lap, up off the floor. Just as Ms. Charming came in through the door, an intense room-filling odor that was definitely not smelling salts filled the air, and Sunshine had to fight her way in through the rapidly evacuating tumult of students trying to literally get a breath of fresh air.

Sunshine wrinkled her nose at the scent, then just waved her arm back and forth in a gesture that represented the brushing aside of an idea, and the foul odor was rapidly transformed into a light floral bouquet of fragrance that was reminiscent of a walk through a field of wildflowers on a warm summer's day. The Principal pointed at the two girls who had stayed by Mrs. Leeds' side despite the smell, saying "You two, get your things and go to lunch. Class is dismissed." The younger one began to carefully lay Mrs. Leeds' still-unconscious head back down onto the ground, and with a flick of the wrist, Sunshine had a pillow there to soften its landing. Once the two girls were out of the room and Sunshine was left alone with Trevor and the lifeless body on the ground, she spoke again. "I thought this might happen."

103

"I know you did, and I'm sorry, but you know how she gets."

"I know, I know. But she deserves something. I can't just turn her out onto the streets."

"You know she'd never end up on the streets. Replacing the monarchy with an elected executor didn't exactly leave her family penniless; your partners were very generous. More generous than most would have been, considering the way they were treating you."

"She has a place on my staff as long as she wants it."

"Can't you at least require her classes be fact-based? Seventy-five percent of what she said was outright lies, and the rest was bullshit. There has to be a way to get her to stick to the facts. Or better yet, teach another subject. Couldn't she teach girl's P.E. or something?"

"I told her years ago she could teach what she wanted, and I don't go back on my word. You know that."

"How can you let her do it this way? She's doing everything in her power to undermine yours, and she's molding young minds to reject the need for truth and perspective, not to mention freedom or equality, which she treats like bad words."

"I... I don't want to discuss this with you right now. I've come to let her know I'm taking you out of her class. Instead of having you in here causing her more pain every day, you and I will meet privately for Special Studies. If you're still with us next year, you can take Basley's world history - he's more ... fact-based. But from now on I want you to avoid Mrs. Leeds, and try not to talk to anyone in her classes about her, either, or about any of this. She's had a hard enough time already, and I don't want you aggravating the situation any further. Now go to lunch before I wake her."

"Fine. But if the next generation rises up to create an oppressive regime, you'll know why." He stood up, satchel already packed, and disappeared.

It was still several minutes before class was supposed to be let out, so when Trevor appeared in the hallway outside Nirgal's class there was no one there to see him. He tried to calm down, to cool his thoughts and stop fuming over the injustice that Ms. Charming was allowing to occur within her school's walls. He thought about the rest of his day, about the fact that he didn't have to ever share a classroom with that woman again, and that his last two classes, after lunch, should be interesting. He thought about how lunch might go, too.

He knew that the students, like students everywhere, formed into little closed cliques and clusters socially, and that the lunchroom was the sort of place that made this behavior the most obvious, students literally segregating themselves into half a dozen tiny nation-states with well-defined borders - these tables were for the dodgeball team, these were for the nerds, those for the preppies, and so on. Trevor had been able to break that tradition at his old school pretty easily, quickly attracting people from all the different groups and cliques and taking up a non-standard, undefined corner of the world map that was the cafeteria. He hoped he could have similar success here, and was not really worried about not sitting with the right people or at the right table on his first day - he wanted to sit with Nirgal because Nirgal was the student he had connected with first, not out of political or apolitical motives.

Eventually the bell rang, releasing the students quite happily to the high school equivalent of recess, and the hallways instantly went from echoing silence to discordant resonance. After every other student had exited the classroom, Nirgal trailed out, still fumbling with his things. Instead of being glad to see his new friend, Trevor still felt bad from what had happened with Mrs. Leeds and Ms. Charming. He and Nirgal walked along together towards the cafeteria, but Trevor wasn't paying attention to what Nirgal was saying about runic poetry. Trevor was grinding away at his own insides, mentally clawing at the dark, sucking emptiness that seemed to be growing in the center of his gut, going over and over in his heart and mind his frustration at the situation he had found himself in and unable to effect. He could imagine his insides turning black with rotting, festering anger at the Principal for allowing Mrs. Leeds to go on like that, for simply taking him out of her class instead of addressing the issues that made it such a bad situation for every student she didn't pull out, for being so blind to the truth she knew so well. He had hoped to be able to let it all go, to walk into the cafeteria happy and hopeful, to get through at least his first day without a real incident or problem with the teachers or the student body.

"One down, one to go," he grumbled as he and Nirgal reached the back of the line of students waiting to buy school lunches.

"What's that?" asked Nirgal.

"Oh, nothing. Just thinking to myself. I'm sorry, I didn't hear a thing you said just now."

"No problem. What's on your mind?"

"Mrs. Leeds."

"I don't know why they let her teach here. I hear she's awful."

"I do, and it's not a good enough reason."

"What is it?"

"I shouldn't say. But it doesn't matter, it's not going to change, there's nothing that could be done to get rid of her that wouldn't hurt the school overall, I think. At least I don't have to deal with her personally anymore."

"What happened?"

"I called her out during class for propagating lies, she fainted, and the Principal took me permanently out of her class. I'll be doing Special Studies with Ms. Charming every day in fourth hour instead."

"You should ask for Advanced Runic Poetry."

"I think I'll just wait and see where the rest of the day takes me before I start worrying about tomorrow." They were approaching the head of the line, where Trevor would have to make a decision about what to eat. He knew what Ms. Charming had always liked, but doubted their tastes would match. More than that, he felt awful on the inside just then, like he'd drunk a quart of used motor oil and half a pound of rusty nails just before getting in line, just from having to deal with Mrs. Leeds for forty minutes. He doubted he would be able to eat much at all. "Hey, Nirgal, I'm gonna go find a place to sit. Here's ten bucks, just get two of whatever you were going to get so I don't have to think about it today, and your lunch is on me."

"Do you care what I--"

"Just whatever you normally get. I'm sure it will be fine. Is that okay?"

"This is way too much money."

"Bring me change. I'm not feeling well, I just want to get out of this line."

"Sorry, yeah, go ahead. I'll find you."

Trevor realised that he really was getting claustrophobic, crushed in line between too many eager students, the din of voices and plates and forks and the occasional burst of magic coming from every direction, the sense of unsteady motion all around him as people moved this way and that way and around to their various destinations, and it was all giving him an awful feeling about the world around him that was beginning to match the feelings he was having on the inside. He ducked under the strap that delineated the line for food from the main area of the cafeteria, and looked around for someplace he and Nirgal could sit down. Trevor was unsteady on his feet as he walked towards a small cluster of empty tables in the corner, and it seemed to him as though the ground itself was unsteady, tilting back and forth like the deck of a boat in a heavy storm. He had to reach out and clutch at the edge of the tables he was passing, had to lean on the shoulders of students he was passing, felt he was losing strength in his legs to stay upright as he marched onward, just hoping to get to an empty chair before he collapsed on the floor. The world seemed to be eating him from inside and out at once, rotting and churning and turning everything black around the edges and turning him black from the inside out.

His hand found the back of the chair he was heading towards, he was nearly there, just inches from sitting down and regaining his bearings, but it was too late.

His satchel dropped to the floor, slipping off his shoulder as he slipped slowly from consciousness, and his legs gave out underneath him so that he collapsed forward onto his knees. His hand had a sort of death-grip on the back of the chair that seemed to be keeping the rest of him upright, but then the growing infestation of hideousness began boiling and bubbling and welling up within him, he

107

couldn't take it any more, couldn't resist it, and a wide and impossibly steady and voluminous spray of thick, black, horribly rotten-smelling goo erupted uncontrollably from his mouth and nose, covering the surface of the table he had been planning on eating at and splashing down all around. The black substance kept flooding out of his mouth and nose as he became too weak physically and too far gone mentally to keep his grip on the chair and the world, and he collapsed forward, hitting his head hard on the edge of the table and being deflected to land on his side on the ground, the black substance still pouring out of him. Whatever it was he was expelling seemed to be corrosive or a rapid rotting agent, and the table was quickly melting and falling apart, and the chairs it had splashed onto were covered in a growing, creeping blackness that also ate away at their surfaces until they were crumbling into moist chunks on the floor all around. The floor where Trevor's body eventually stopped spewing the black wretchedness also appeared to be becoming soft and rotting away, and as the thick fluid slowly crawled across the cafeteria floor, it also crawled up the legs of tables and chairs, rotting and consuming them as it went.

Everyone in the cafeteria who had not been watching Trevor stumble and fall over to the table had their attention drawn to the growing black mess by the odor it gave off, more pungent than what had filled Mrs. Leeds' classroom, more like rotting, wet, mold, death, and what unease would probably smell like if it could be smelled. Those nearest to where Trevor was twitching and sinking into the rotting floor moved rapidly away, if only to keep themselves and their belongings from being consumed or destroyed by whatever that goo was. The students further away were trying to get a closer look, but also keeping the nearer students from getting away. A ring of bodies quickly formed, and eventually someone who knew what they were looking at said it aloud, word traveling quickly around the circle and to the back of the crowd. "Mrs. Leeds."

Nirgal was getting out of line, trying to balance two lunches on two trays and find Trevor, and he didn't care to see a fight or whatever the other students were looking at. He heard their murmurs, discerned what they seemed to be saying, that Mrs. Leeds had attacked another student, that the floor was rotting out again, that no one was going to risk getting the student out for fear of their own safety from Mrs. Leeds' dark magic. Nirgal had heard that Mrs. Leeds had done that sort of thing to students before, but thought it was just an urban legend, the students saying she was worse than she really was. He found a table where he could set his trays down while he looked for Trevor, and then it finally occurred to him that it might be Trevor who they were all talking about. He fought his way into the crowd.

When Nirgal reached the inner edge of the crowd and could see clearly what they were backing away from, he didn't really know what to do, so he just did it anyway. He levved over the rapidly growing ring of black decay, holding his breath to save himself from the stench and weaving in between the rapidly crumbling remnants of the tables and chairs and lunches being consumed by the dark magic with Trevor's unconscious body at the center. As he reached the spot where Trevor lay he could see better how Trevor himself was being effected.

The black that was consuming everything else in the room that it touched, the goo that had come from Trevor himself, seemed averse to him. It had covered his hair and his clothes, but stopped just short of creeping across his face or other visible skin, growing up to the edge and then shying away from touching Trevor himself. Stranger perhaps than that was the fact that Trevor's trench coat seemed similarly unaffected by the expanding devastation of the dark substance, which seemed actively to be advancing across and dying and falling away from the surfaces of the coat in a way that his other clothes were not lucky enough to experience. Seeing the coat driving away wave after wave of corrosive growth gave Nirgal an idea.

He bent down carefully, not losing his position levitating in the air over Trevor, and at moments when the black goo was driven back from them each in turn, grabbed the ends of the coat's belt. Then, using all his concentration not to lose altitude or run into anything, he levved away, dragging Trevor's limp body along through the slimy offensive mess that the cafeteria was becoming, towards the

109

edge of the crowd. Trevor's body was becoming heavier and heavier as it pulled along more and more of the rotting black matter that represented the incoherent remnants of the cafeteria floor and contents. By the time Nirgal was nearing the edge of the crowd, the floor was collapsing towards the center of the expanding circle of corrosion. He called out to the people at the edge of the crowd, "Can any of you levitate him? I can't lift things his size yet!" Blank stares from the people he was nearing did nothing to calm Nirgal. "Anyone?" He looked around, not wanting to drag Trevor and the mound of rotting cafeteria with him into an unaffected area, not knowing what else to do. "Well has anyone at least told a teacher? Or Feagan? Someone?"

"What's going on in here?" An adult's voice was coming from the rear of the ever-widening ring of onlookers. "What's the commotion? I've got alarms going off all over my office, telling me someone's using dark magic, but no one here would -- sweet heavens!"

"Mr. Trask! Over here! Can you levitate him above this stuff? He's out cold and I can't lift him!" Nirgal was clearly straining, at the edge of his ability, and might have given up if Feagan hadn't shown up in the nick of time.

"Oh, my, my, my. What has Trev gotten himself into now? Ms. Charming can't forgive something of this magnitude." Feagan seemed pleased with Trevor's predicament, and did little more than move closer to where Nirgal had dragged him.

"Would you please just help? I don't know what to do with him, and no one else is doing anything."

"Fine, fine," Mr. Trask begrudgingly reached out his arm and with a simple upward gesture raised Trevor's body limply to a height where the ends of his dangling limbs were still in the deep, dark goo. Then with a flick of the wrist he seemed to shove Nirgal towards the edge of the crowd and down to the ground just beyond the blackness, stumbling forward into a none-too-happy crowd of onlookers. "I suppose I should summon the Principal. Everyone, be sure you keep clear of that stuff. No knowing if it'll be as kind to you as it seems to have been to Trev." The students all around had been giving the sludge a wide berth, but now

110

took a collective step away from it. Feagan pulled a small artifact from his pocket and whispered a brief command to it before replacing it into his pocket. Sunshine Charming, Principal Intendant, appeared almost before he had the artifact out of sight.

"Oh dear." She closed her eyes for a moment, as if in deep thought, and though they didn't feel any apparent compulsion to do so, everyone present blinked at once, and everyone present opened their eyes at once, including Ms. Charming. Everything that had been black was gone, and the odor that it had replaced the air with was itself being rapidly replaced with the same enchanting scent that Sunshine had filled Mrs. Leeds' classroom with not half an hour before, much to the relief of every nose in the room. Still, the cafeteria was a disaster area.

Every surface that had been touched and rotted out by the black substance had disappeared when the blackness had gone. Tables, chairs, books and book bags, lunches and lunch trays and an unknown number of small personal effects that people had been too rapid in their evacuation to rescue, all were removed. The floor that had been blackened and rotted was gone, too, leaving only a semi-round cavity that went straight down through the foundation to the soil beneath. The growth of death had reached the walls in some places, and there was an odd pattern of missing matter that implied the devastating nature of what had come and gone without hinting of any structural instability in the building that was left - everything seemed to be left standing that was left to stand.

Levitating above the hole in the floor, arms and legs and trench coat dangling down below him, facing down unaware of what was going on around him, was Trevor. He was no longer covered hair and body with the blackness that had been trying to consume him, and if not for the coverage of his unaffected coat, his body would have been entirely uncovered - his clothes had been a complete loss. As soon as she saw that this was the case, the Principal disappeared Trevor and herself directly to her office, with his body now laying face up on her couch and tastefully covered by his instantly closed coat. She knew who had done this to him,

111

but not what to do to wake him, so she disappeared back to the cafeteria to work with Feagan on replacing what had been damaged by the dark magic.

✫ ✫ ✫

In a lightless cavern deep beneath the ground stood the lanky stranger by himself. The walls and floor of the cavern would not have reflected back a single whisper of light had the tall man bothered with a lamp, candle, flashlight or other such device – their surfaces, like most of his body by this time and everything else in the room, were coated in a thick layer of an impossibly black substance the consistency of tar or peat. Luckily for the long-limbed stranger, one of his specialties was seeing the unseen and the unseeable. He tuned his mind's eye to detect all that was around him, regardless of whether light was able to return to him from its surface, and thus he could see that he was surrounded with strange-looking things.

Most of what he saw trapped within the dark confines of the sticky tar were tables and chairs and half-eaten lunches, some of these not entirely present in the muck as though largish creatures had taken sizeable bites out of things before discarding them into this inaccessible pit. There were also books and stationary, pencils and pens and papers and folders and all the detritus of learning, encased in unmoving, unyielding darkness. He searched carefully through the objects frozen in this slow-oozing blackness until he found what he had interrupted his morning with such awfulness to get his hands on. Trevor's satchel, suspended above the stranger's head by the sticky black substance that made up the entire space there, was almost in reach.

The tall man's long arms slowly, gradually forced their way upwards, fighting against the black substance's unwillingness to budge or let him budge as he reached for the satchel. When his arms reached their apex there was still a matter of several feet between their grasp and the black-encased satchel. He strained mentally against the taffy-like blackness that anchored him where he stood, trying to levitate up to within reach of his goal, and slowly he did rise, stretching but not breaking the dark bonding agent keeping him tied to the black, covered floor. As he crept upwards, groaning with the pain of his flesh being painfully pulled at by the thick goo he was struggling against and from the exertion he was making to try to reach his prize in this detestable situation, he began to notice in his peripheral extended vision that some of the trapped items were disappearing. Table and chair legs with no tables or chairs to support at first, and he wasn't sure anything had gone at all. Then whole sections of what seemed to be concrete and flooring was no longer in the sticky blackness. He didn't have much time.

He roared in anger and pushed harder against the resistance he was surrounded by, inching slightly faster towards his goal. Within his range of view, the long man made apparently longer as his arms stretched up and his body seemed to turn to an elongated formless putty that reached down to the ground and all around could see that the items were disappearing from the blackness with a steady and deliberate pace. Someone was undoing this dark magic the hard, fast way instead of the slower more complete way – they were recovering items one at a time from the effects of the rotting darkness rather than dispelling the entire effect. Finally the man's outstretched hands reached the blackness at the ceiling that held the satchel within its grip, and he kept straining upward, hands plunging slowly into the goo above, which was apparently a cue to that goo to begin its own way down his arms. He did not seem worried about the enclosing blackness, but about not reaching the satchel before it was too late. His worries did him no good in his quest, for just as his hands felt the edges of the satchel between them and he grasped it, he felt a tugging sensation pulling it away from him. He tried holding on, pulling back, but by then the blackness had completely enclosed his body and he had almost no freedom of movement whatsoever, even just to bend or retract his arms. The satchel was pulled away from him harder and harder, and then was gone entirely, leaving him stuck there, stretched out in a solidifying cylinder of blackness from floor to ceiling, his toes pointed down and his arms and hands pointed up and all of him quite totally stuck.

He tried to disappear, to escape this disappointment the same way he had entered it, but did not disappear. He tried several different incantations and mental exercises that should have had some effect on his predicament, but nothing worked. His face was completely covered, like the rest of him, and he knew he could only hold his breath for a limited amount of time before he absolutely had to get free. He tried to think a way out before his brain ran out of oxygen and he lost the ability to think altogether.

✯　✯　✯

"I think that's everything," Ms. Charming said to no one in particular. She had spent the rest of the lunch hour restoring the cafeteria piece by piece, and then a while after that as well until she was satisfied that everything that had been consumed by the rotting black substance had been recreated or replaced. She held the satchel she had given Trevor earlier in the day in her hands and was looking at it closely – it appeared to have two sets of black fingerprints on it as though the resistance she had felt in recovering it was not just because it was so much more complex and magical than the rest of the items she had more easily brought back, but rather that someone had literally been trying to keep it from her. She looked around one last time to be certain that everything was in order, then disappeared directly to her office, sitting behind her desk with the satchel standing upright on its surface.

She could see that Trevor was still unconscious, though now dressed in his own recovered clothes, and did nothing yet to try to rouse him. Instead she opened the second drawer from the top on the right-hand side of her desk and pulled out a marble cylinder about thirteen inches long and one inch in diameter, closing the drawer after it. She held the unadorned stone shaft upright with both hands, one above and one below. She spoke clearly a simple arcane phrase, then moved the shaft slowly from right to left across the surface of the satchel. As it passed over the finger

114

marks, they disappeared. She spoke a single syllable, then levitated the satchel, rotated it so that the other side of it was facing her, and set it back down gently onto the table. Another set of arcane syllables, similar but distinct from the first phrase, escaped her lips just before she passed the shaft left to right across the surface of the satchel, thumb marks this time disappearing as it went over them. One more arcane phrase smoothly formed by her lips and tongue and she set the stone down on her desk and levitated the satchel over next to where Trevor was laying.

Ms. Charming reached down to the bottom drawer on the left-hand side of her desk and after opening it and before closing it, removed a larger marble cylinder from it. This one was nearly fourteen inches long and looked to be three inches in diameter, but instead of a solid stone, this one had an opening in one end approximately the same size as the stone she had just used on the satchel. She placed it standing up on the desk with the hole facing the ceiling, and lowered the smaller stone into its place in the larger one. It fit perfectly, and she rotated the center stone until the grain of the marble matched up, creating the appearance of a single solid stone before her.

This motion appears to have been all that was needed to activate an automatic process within this strange artifact; as soon as the stone appeared to be a single solid stone instead of a stone within a stone, a slight grinding sound came from its untouched insides, as though the one were still turning within the other – though no visible trace of this motion could be detected from the outside. After only a few long minutes, the sound stopped. Ms. Charming lifted the large, heavy stone in both hands, one above and one below, and turned it end over end so that the inner stone slid out of the larger one as she separated her hands. She set the larger, outer stone cylinder aside and while still holding the smaller stone shaft in her left hand pulled a large sheet of blank paper to the center of her desk. She laid the smaller stone cylinder down on the edge of the paper, parallel with the edge, and began to chant a guttural utterance over and over to compel the stone to slowly roll across the surface of the page she had laid out, stopping only once the stone reached the other edge of the paper.

As it had moved along the page, the stone seemed to be leaving a trace of black instead of taking one as it had done to the satchel, leaving the blank page turned into a detailed illustration of a man's face, head on and in profile as though it were a mug shot rather than a magically rendered drawing. She looked hard at the face depicted before her, but did not recognize it.

"Who are you?" She spoke aloud to the face on the page, musing. "What did you want with Trev's satchel? And why were you willing to risk being trapped in a prison of the residue of dark magic to get it?"

She stared on at the page in silence for a while, wondering, until a knock came at her door. "Mrs. Leeds, please come in. Shut the door behind you." Mrs. Leeds did as she was told, and set down in a chair across from the Principal with no trace of emotion on her face at all, but an aura glowing red hot with pride all around her for anyone attuned to such things to see. "We need to talk again, about the boy." Ms. Charming indicated Trevor's unconscious body at the side of the room.

"I heard he caused some sort of commotion at lunch. Considering the way he was behaving in my class, it's no wonder."

"Indeed." Sunshine shined a look of distaste and disappointment at Mrs. Leeds, who still refused to show her true feelings on her face. The Principal looked down at the face still laying out in plain sight on her desk, made sure that Mrs. Leeds got a good look at it, and then rolled it up and put it into her top drawer with the smaller cylinder that had created it. As she did this, she watched Mrs. Leeds' face and aura for any sign that she had recognized the face on the page, but saw nothing. "This isn't the first time something like this has happened, Abby, and you know we're going to be able to trace this back to you."

"Whatever could you mean?"

"Cut the crap, Abby. I'll source the spell right now."

Suddenly the tone of Mrs. Leeds' voice shifted a little, trying to stay even, "You haven't already dispelled it?"

"Not yet." The Principal's eyes were locked onto Mrs. Leeds', like a predator watching its prey.

"But I went by the cafeteria; everything seemed to be in order…"

"I spent a fair amount of time on that. But seeing as you aren't willing to admit anything," Ms. Charming spoke a few arcane words, a shortcut she had invoked earlier to refer to a much longer spell she had already begun, and suddenly Mrs. Leeds' skin caught fire and she pulsed with an unnatural seizure and fell out of her chair onto the ground where she continued to burn as her body became paralyzed. A disembodied voice, loud and strong and deep like the way they do the voice of God in the movies, briefly filled the room, reporting the completion of the sourcing of the dark magic that had been wrought against Trevor; "Abigail Rottendam Leeds", it boomed.

As Mrs. Leeds' twitching subsided and Ms. Charming stood up to walk around the desk to see her, Trevor began to rouse. He still had a nauseous look on his face as he sat up on the couch where he had been laying for nearly an hour, but seemed calm and composed as he surveyed his surroundings. He tried to speak, and his voice croaked at first, words failing him as Sunshine came around to stand over Mrs. Leeds' body. His second attempt was more successful, "Why is Mrs. Leeds on fire?"

"It's her own fault, really. She retaliated against you with an intensely dark magical attack. I simply sourced it back to its creator, which she happened to be, and the natural effect of a sourcing is that the originator of the effect being sourced is effected in kind to what she did, and what type of effect she was using. Had she not attacked you at all, she would have been fine. Had she used a less severe spell, her pain now would be worse. Had she used a different class of spell, she might not be burning and paralyzed, but covered in insects or jolting with electricity or … do you remember what happened at the Raidsonne Manse to those murderers?"

Trevor grimaced a little more than he had been from the nausea at the memory, "I do." He very nearly threw up at the thought of what Sunshine and her husband had found when they'd finally been able to successfully source the criminals who had been terrorizing the Raidsonne clan. Perhaps luckily for him, the darkness that had erupted from him earlier, combined with his failure to eat lunch, had left him with nothing to expel. "Uhg, but they deserved it."

"And so did Mrs. Leeds. She should know better than to attack a student. If this were the first time, if you were the first one to push her over the edge, that would be one thing, but this isn't even the first time this year. She gave another student hives over a simple mistake in class during the first week of school."

"Oh yeah, Boden misspelled her family name on a pop quiz."

"And this isn't the first year it's happened, as you'll recall. Why do you think I was surprised that you had acted that way in class, knowing all this?"

"I haven't exactly gone through every single memory you've ever had in detail yet. There's no shortage of them, compared to my own memories. Really though, you haven't sat in on a class with her in years. I doubt you could stand being quiet through it for as long as I did."

"That may be the case, but I still … you know how I feel about this. It's complicated. And I was prepared to give her leeway, same as I always do, until I saw what she did to you. You probably don't remember any of it, do you?"

"Not really. I remember feeling awful, and … I think I might have dreamed I was vomiting a vast sea of something awful, but then it all goes black."

"I won't go into the details, but you'll probably hear enough about it in the next few days from other students to satisfy your curiosity."

Trevor didn't press the issue. He rubbed his eyes and face as though waking from a long sleep, then asked "How long do you think she'll be burning?"

"Hard to say. But I don't want you to be here when she comes to. You can get to the last twenty minutes of your Ethics class if you hurry, and then you can finally get to your first real magic class. I apologize for her behaviour today. You shouldn't have had to put up with all this on your first day here."

"I'll survive. It could have been a lot worse."

"Good attitude. Now get out of here, and don't forget your satchel. I'll see you tomorrow."

"Be fair."

"I'll try."

He left her classroom via the door, but as soon as it was closed behind him, he disappeared to stand directly outside the door of his Ethics class so he could walk right in and get seated; he was still feeling a little woozy from his recent unfortunate experiences. Mr. Tauer, the Ethics teacher, didn't miss a beat as Trevor came in.

"…the very nature of magic itself, as evidenced in the power origins required to generate it. A very good example of this occurred today with our new student, Trev. Trev, welcome to class, have a seat right over there," Mr. Tauer indicated an empty seat to his left; the desks were arrayed in a double-horseshoe pattern around the room so that everyone could see most everyone else – it was something that Trevor knew Mr. Tauer did to try to keep his students engaged actively in his classroom discussions – and Trevor moved as normally as he could to the indicated desk. "We were just discussing the inherent nature of magic as being non-ethical, and how individual uses of magic can infuse different spells and effects with an ethical charge. The example you provide is a fairly clear one. Would anyone like to proffer an explanation?"

Several hands shot up, but most of the students either didn't know what had happened exactly or didn't dare attempt to discuss it in front of Trevor. Trevor himself was fairly aware of where Mr. Tauer was going with this, but since he couldn't remember what had happened and didn't really feel like talking anyway, he remained quiet and still. Mr. Tauer handed the attention stick to a young female student Trevor couldn't recall the name of from Sunshine's memory. Trevor did manage to recall that the attention stick had no special or magical properties, only the social powers that Mr. Tauer had assigned to it; in class, no one could speak unless they were holding or pointed at by the attention stick, and everyone was always to give their full attention to the bearer of the attention stick. In Ethics and other

Philosophy classes it was an effective tool at keeping heated arguments from getting out of hand.

"Well, I'd say that the primary effect we saw applied was probably based on a simple expurgative effect of neutral basis. If it had been used with positive intent, it might only have helped to rid the recipient's body of unwanted toxins or other dangerous elements. If it had been used with negative intent, it might have forced nutrition or internal organs or other desired elements out of the effected system. The expurgative effect itself is neutral, carrying no ethical basis of its own. There was a second effect combined with it though, a sort of decompositional element. If I were to guess at a positive use of such an effect, it might perhaps be used to speed the decomposition of compost for fertilizer, or to rid an area whose natural ecosystem had become unbalanced by expanding human contact of uninhibited growth vectors through a natural biological process."

"And the negative?"

"That seems obvious. It could be used as it was in the cafeteria, to destroy desirable goods and materials, to weaken structures, and possibly to destroy life. The corrosive appearance of the decompositional process indicates that in this particular effect the consumptive nature had been tweaked or enhanced to accelerate it, which I believe multiplies the negative or unethical nature of the core effect by the same order of magnitude as the effect itself is multiplied, right?"

Mr. Tauer took the attention stick back from the female student who was apparently quite the bookworm. "That's correct. And don't forget that the expurgative effect was also multiplied far beyond any normal level, not to mention one other thing about it… anyone?"

"The color?"

"We'll get back to that, Byron. Something else… Something obvious…"

"It was expanding."

"A lot."

Mr. Tauer smiled. "That's right. Without modification, any magical effect will only effect the specified recipient. So if you want to create an expurgative

120

effect, it doesn't cause everyone in the room vomit, just the person you intend, and if you generate a decompositional effect, it doesn't keep spreading beyond your initial specifications, consuming and consuming endlessly. Usually the area or subject range effected is based on how much power is available to the caster, and how much of that power they are willing to devote to the effect for its duration. Does anyone know how expansion enhancements work?"

"Don't they usually require material sacrifice? Like, burning incense for simple spells and vaporizing gold for the high-end spells?"

"That's correct, Blayn, and is this ethical, unethical, or non-ethical?"

"Doesn't it depend on the spell you're enhancing, and the material sacrificed?"

"Exactly. The enhancement itself is non-ethical for most materials, and has any ethics it takes on from the nature of the core spell multiplied according to a power function depending upon the amount they enhance that core spell. Is that clear to everyone?"

"So… if you enhance to expand a spell for unethical reasons, the inherent ethical charge of the spell are increased exponentially based on the factor of increase of the core spell's effect?"

"Correct. And can anyone give examples of sacrifice materials that would add automatically to the negative charge of their core spell?"

"Burnt offerings, like … animals?"

"Okay, good… anyone else?"

"Human sacrifice?"

"That's where I was headed. Thank you Gean. In order to create the most expansive enhancements of effects, human life must be sacrificed. This act has an inherently unethical charge so great that no spell or combination of intentions and effects has been found that can offset the negative charge that sacrificing human life for expansive enhancement creates. That's not to say that the overall effects of these vastly expanded spells has not been overall positive and vastly more positive than they would have been

121

without the benefit of human sacrifice, but that the casters were unredeemably burdened with negative ethical charge."

"You're talking about the Spanish Inquisition, aren't you?"

"Not exactly, but you'll learn more about that in your history classes than I have time for here. Let's bring the focus back to what happened with Trev today. So far we've covered that whoever cast the effect," several students whispered under their breath "Mrs. Leeds" as Mr. Tauer continued without naming names, "combined an expurgative effect with a decompositional effect, right?" Everyone nodded. "And we've determined that beyond basic power multipliers that could have made Trev vomit longer or more volume and that could have caused that vomit to consume things faster than normal, there was also a general expansive enhancement on the combined effect applied, correct?" Nodding all around. Trevor just kept listening carefully. "We've also discussed the fact that expansive enhancements can have an inherent ethical charge in addition to their exponential multiplication of an effect's inherent charge. Now, considering the fact that the effect in question was clearly an attack on Trev, and not intended to compost the cafeteria or induce the expulsion of tainted food, what is the basic ethical charge of the core spell?"

"Negative."

"Very negative."

"Probably as negative as a spell gets without multipliers and enhancements."

"Alright," Mr. Tauer continued, "assuming that that's the case, what scale of multipliers would you guess the overall power of the spell created? We'll assume that the normal level of the decomposition was merely twice the rate of natural decomposition, and that the expurgative effect at a standard power level would merely induce enough vomiting to remove a small amount of tainted food or poison from the stomach."

"Three times."

"No way, did you see it? It must have been at least ten times."

The female student who had answered at length earlier was doing calculations on paper to try to work it out while everyone shouted answers back and forth, then she said "I've used a double-speed decomposer at home, and based on the rate things were crumbling I'd say it was…" she double checked her math, "forty-six times a double-decomposer. I don't know much about expurgatives though, so I can't say for sure."

Everyone looked to Mr. Tauer for confirmation. "I spoke to Feagan afterward, and his measurements of the effect indicated between forty-five and fifty times multiplication of energy, plus the enhancement. Anyone care to guess what had to have been sacrificed for the scale of growth we saw? Betty?"

The female student that Trevor had been unable to identify, the one who was clearly a teacher's pet, was apparently named Betty, and responded, "a cat?"

"No. Anyone else?"

"A baby!"

"No, where would Mrs. Leeds get a baby? It was a big dog!"

"Let's not get into accusations, class, we're trying to do an ethics calculation here."

"A toad!"

"Three cats and a rabbit."

"Two coils of incense and a brick of solid gold!"

"Her own left arm!"

"Okay, okay, we're getting off track here. Let me see if I can guide you at all. To determine whether the enhancement's sacrifice was material only or also included organic matter or even life, what do we look at?"

"Color, odor, and pH."

"Don't tell me you measured the pH of that stuff, Betty!"

"Of course she didn't," Mr. Tauer was thinking he'd have to put the attention stick into heavy use instead of just pointing to students in turn, the way this was going, "but she's on the right track. What color was it, and what did it smell like?"

"Black. Like death."

"Totally black. And I thought it smelled like wet, rotting wood and smelly feet."

"It smelled like a rotting corpse. I saw one, once."

"Definitely like death."

Trevor finally spoke. "I didn't get much chance to smell it, but it tasted like anger, unease, and like someone had put a cemetery and a bunch of cremated remains into a blender with swamp water to make a horrible smoothie."

The class was silent for a moment, but Mr. Tauer picked up after only a beat and a half, "Good words, Trev. Anger, unease. Very good. Did anyone else notice that?"

"I didn't want to say it smelled like anxiety, I thought it sounded funny."

"It does sound funny, but it isn't wrong. All the things you smelled were generated by either the spell itself, which is where the rotting and fungus-like smells came from, or by the caster and the enhancements, which is where the smell – and taste – of death came from. The black color, the smell of death, we know the enhancement included the sacrifice of some form of life. We're running out of time, so I'll just tell you that based on the information we have right now, the caster paralyzed thirteen large snakes so that they were stiff like sticks, then arranged them into a campfire-like configuration for a fire sacrifice. This arrangement helps keep expansion even in all directions and reduces the ethical charge somewhat, because while the sacrifice is live, it does not feel the full extent of the pain of its death. The factor of expansion in this case was nearly eightfold, no need to look that up, you'd never find it in time, but can anyone but Betty, who I can see already has the answer, can anyone tell me what the total ethical charge of this attack would be? Assuming, as we said, that the core effect had an ethical charge of fully negative one?"

Most students went hard to work trying to get the answer, and before anyone other than Betty had their hand raised, the end-of-class bell rang. No one moved, they all wanted to know the answer, and they all looked to Betty.

"Alright, alright. For tomorrow's class I want you all to check Betty's math. I expect a one-page proof showing how this is arrived at, plus three examples of how such a negative charge will effect future castings. Betty?"

"Eleven thousand, seven hundred and seventy six units of negative ethical charge, based on the assumptions you gave."

"Wow" and similar exclamations went around the classroom as people tried to conceptualize the sort of person that could withstand such an intense negative ethic and packed their bags to get to the last classes of the day. As everyone began filing out, Mr. Tauer moved over to where Trevor was still sitting.

"I had no idea Ethics required so much math. It's interesting." Trevor was exaggerating; as they had started going into the calculations of ethical charge he had wracked the Principal's memories of studying Ethics in school and found that the bulk of it required math, but that once the basic principals of the math were mastered it went back to being a mostly philosophical endeavor.

"Glad you like it. I just wanted to be sure you're alright. I didn't expect you to be up and around so quickly after … well, after what happened. I'm glad to see you're doing alright. How do you feel?"

"Thanks for your concern. I guess I'm okay. Still a little nauseous, a little woozy walking in, but I'm still alive."

"Which is a miracle, considering. I heard that the substance that was consuming everything else it came in contact with actually seemed to be repelled by your skin and your coat. Now, either your coat has a greater negative ethical charge than Lucifer Morningstar himself, or it's been accumulating energy from you as you've been wearing it. Where did you get it?"

"My coat? No one knows where it came from. A few years ago I decided I needed a coat to wear around and my dad told me to check the trunks in the attic for something of my grandparents'. It turned out my mother had donated everything in the attic to the Salvation Army just weeks before that. The only thing I found in the attic was dust and this coat. Exactly what I was looking for and a perfect fit that I'd swear has grown with me, so maybe it is absorbing my energy."

"Which is a conundrum in itself. Had any other student here stuck so much as a toe in that stuff, they'd probably have lost a limb before it could be dispelled. It was actually a decomposer selected specifically for its ability to rapidly consume human flesh, from what we can tell. Obviously, more time will tell us more about it, but from our basic analysis you should have been destroyed or at the very least transported to an underground cavern and trapped in what amounts to a sort of physical representation of negative ethics until the entire effect was sourced and dispelled, and even then there's a good chance the dispelling itself would kill you. Except… none of that happened. You were basically unharmed."

"I don't know why. And I don't mean to be rude, but I've got to be going. You know how Goldberg treats students who show up late."

"Oh dear, yes. You'd better disappear there post-haste. Are you feeling well enough to disappear properly? Yes? Okay. Here's a disappearance pass, in case he asks. We'll talk more tomorrow." Trevor took the pass, grabbed his satchel, said goodbye, and disappeared directly to his seat in Mr. Goldberg's class, made confident by the pass in his hand. Mr. Goldberg wasn't even looking at the class when Trevor appeared, so the pass was useless just then. Trevor slipped it into his satchel for later, and didn't have long to wait for the one-minute bell and then for class to start.

This class turned out to be the least engaging one Trevor had been in all day, lunch included. Mr. Goldberg's style was really just rote memorization of the rules and principals, vocalizations and chants and proper mouth shapes, plus the arcane vocabulary words needed for this level of invocations, summonings, et cetera. It was everything he'd hated about spelling homework in elementary school and biology homework in middle school; he could never understand why he was forced to write a word ten or twenty or fifty times if he already knew it, he didn't understand why he needed to memorize the binomial nomenclature of every plant and animal that had been named, and he didn't understand why Mr. Goldberg spent an entire hour having the class repeat the same eight arcane words over and over and over. Worse than the repetition and lack of actual learning for anyone more intelligent than a stump was the fact that because Ms. Charming understood this material so well, Trevor knew it all much better than the back of his hand; he knew it as well as the curve of Sunshine's hairless legs. A lesson in the dangers of absorbing repetitive memories wholesale from other people's lives he would not soon forget, if only because he would have to wait weeks or months for his leg hair to return to normal, and that was if he managed to keep from shaving them again. Just thinking about it made his crotch itch.

As he sat there in Mr. Goldberg's class, muttering along with the rest of the students who had got the hang of these arcane syllables quite a long while ago, Trevor thought back through the Principal's memories of all of the teachers and classes on campus that he might be more interested in and more engaged by than this inane repetition of what he had assigned as homework anyway. Advanced Invocations, A.P. Summoning, A.P. Mentalism, Advanced Enhancements, The Devil's Arithmetic, A.P. Binding, or even something like Artifact Creation and Enchantment would be interesting and engaging to him, and would clearly offer him access to insights and magics that he didn't already have through Ms. Charming. The fact that they were all senior-level classes and he was enrolled as a Freshman with no prior magical experience was probably why he was here in what amounted to a remedial invocations class. He tried to keep paying attention to Mr. Goldberg's monotony, but his mind wandered.

As he had recently learned, this wandering was not just into the realm of fantasy, but into real life and into the real parts of life that would pass for fantasy to most people. As his lips continued to mouth along to the same eight arcane words over and over and over again, his mind traveled out into the hallways of the school, peeking into the windows of the classes as it went by. No particular focus was held, Trevor was simply exploring the school; this was something that Sunshine had spent a long time mastering, and where he had had difficulty staying in this state without a mind to latch onto before, Trevor was now free to treat it like the out of body experience it truly was. He passed by the English class that Nirgal was in, and thought about maybe seeing him after school let out. He saw other faces he recognized in other classes, intent on what was being taught or bored or in some cases intent on the developing members of the opposite sex sitting in various poses all around them.

Then, as he was looking with his mind's eye through the glass window of a classroom entirely full of people he didn't personally know, many of those people turned towards him. Trevor realized that there must be something else catching their attention there, someone at the door perhaps, and he turned his point of view around and around to see who they might be looking at.

But there was no body there.

He moved his point of view into the classroom itself so he could turn around and face the direction they were; perhaps there was something on the wall worth seeing. Except that there wasn't anything interesting on the wall near the door. And now almost everyone in the class was looking directly at where his mind's eye's perspective was coming from. He tried to focus on one of the students who was looking impossibly at him, but felt a backlash, like being struck hard in the face. He tried to find a teacher in the room, but all he saw were students, so he tried to do what he'd done during dodgeball earlier in the day and focus on the entire class as a group.

There was a lot of silence there, and not like a lack of thoughts, but he could sense that many of the students seemed to be intentionally preventing him from accessing their thoughts, while the rest – while trying – were not doing as good of a job. The occasional snippet of thought came though quietly to him, not really giving him a good idea of what they were thinking of as a class. He thought about trying to remember Ms. Charming's training, and it came to him what he needed to do; he stopped trying to read their minds altogether. He stopped trying to think what they were thinking, stopped trying to remember his training, stopped trying to wander around the school when he should have been paying attention to Mr. Goldberg's inanity.

And then the voices started coming through loud and clear, with a teacher's voice among them, guiding them, "do you sense what he's just done, there?"

"…let go… of intention, right?"

"…like he stopped trying to read our thoughts and instead just started reading them…"

"How's he do that? I want to do it that easy."

"We'll get there eventually. Did anyone glimpse what he remembered just before he stopped the bulk of his mental processes?"

"It didn't seem to make sense. I got a flash of Ms. Charming."

"Me too. It was weird, like he had stopped being him for a moment and was her, and then nothing at all."

"I think what we're seeing is that he's absorbed her memories wholesale, and is drawing on her experience to supplement his own inexperience. Is that right, Trev?"

Trevor responded automatically in thought so that the rest of them could hear/think his thoughts – he hadn't meant to or tried to, it had just worked. "That's very close. Sorry to interrupt your class."

"Oh, it's no problem, Trev. I've been hoping you would stop into one of my classes this way all day, actually. We've all heard the rumors of your abilities, and now we can see that they're not far off."

"Is this … let me remember … A.P. Mentalism, right?" Several of them thought the affirmative before he continued, "I should have guessed. Is there any way I could get transferred into this class and get out of Mr. Goldberg's Monotony 101?"

"I'll see what I can do, but even if Ms. Charming agrees, the rest of the class has to vote on it. Since we're all sharing access to each other's minds, it has to be unanimous that everyone accepts you into the group. As you can see, a few of the students are keeping up around-the-clock mental blocks to keep you from thinking their thoughts. Personally, I think they're overreacting. Would everyone like to take a vote?"

There was a pause of sorts, still full of thoughts but no consciously projected ones like the conversation had been, as every last member of the class consented to a vote. Then they took the vote in a very particular matter. Every student began to clear their minds, removing all blocks and guards and prejudices and thoughts about their plans for after class and their girlfriends and the next dodgeball game on TV, until every mind was like a stream of white noise, empty of thought. Then, clearly from the teacher, came a sort of mental version of a query, an algorithm of thought that every clear mind responded to instantly and automatically based on the actual preferences therein instead of what the mind thought the mind wanted or what the mind thought was best for it or its compatriots. No votes could be given to one side that were not intended for that side, and no votes could be taken away either. No conscious thought was involved in giving the vote, the algorithm was designed in such a way that the only possible outcome could be that mind's actual, honest response, with zero layers of nuance.

It was a unanimous yes, much to the surprise of many there who thought before the vote that their minds would have voted no. Suddenly the mindscape was awash with thoughts all over the spectrum of what might be next in their class, with Trevor on board. The teacher seemed to take Trevor aside, and the others' thoughts quieted as their own thoughts became less thinkable to the rest of the class. "Now, I've got to confer with Ms. Charming and Mr. Goldberg before you're officially in, but I don't think we'll have any problems. Worst thing that could happen is you have to take a test with Goldberg to prove that you already know everything he could possibly have taught that class before the end of the year, which with all of Ms. Charming's memories in your head should be a piece of cake."

"Sounds good. So… I'll hear from you tomorrow?"

"In a manner of thinking. Now go back to your class and at least pretend you're paying attention. You should know how important proper enunciation is for effective spell casting."

"Okay, okay, if you say so. Thanks for this opportunity. I'll see you tomorrow."

"In a manner of thinking."

And Trevor did as he said he'd do, and went back to his body and to the useless repetition of sounds he already knew better than would have been possible in his own relatively brief life. Knowing that he would probably not ever have to sit through it again made the remainder of Mr. Goldberg's class somewhat more bearable. Before he knew it, the final bell rang and the first day of classes at his new school was finally over. He gathered his belongings in a daze and found that as he stood he was feeling almost entirely better than he had only an hour before, that walking was not a constant challenge and his stomach was beginning to feel hungry instead of the opposite. He walked through the emptying corridors to the front of the school and out again into a world that didn't even want to know what went on all around it.

The next day was rather more uneventful than the first one had been. When Trevor had gone to Ms. Charming's office after learning some basic dodgeball tactics in P.E., she accompanied him to Mrs. Leeds' classroom, where she filled in for the absent teacher. He didn't ask, in fact no student had to ask, and the Principal didn't say where Mrs. Leeds had gone, or why, or when she would return. Suddenly their history classes were based in fact instead of propaganda and bias though, and that took some students quite a bit of getting used to. Lunch was only interesting in that by his second day, Trevor was already quite well known and popular among the student body. Trevor made sure that everyone treated Nirgal with the respect he deserved, and as teenagers are wont to do, it was rapidly forgotten that they had ever treated him any less than well. Math and Literature and Ethics were still engaging and interesting, and after a brief meeting between classes with Mr. Goldberg and Ms. Charming, Trevor was moved into A.P. Mentalism where he seemed to belong.

Classes went along normally like that for a couple of weeks, and Trevor was really much happier at his new school than he had been at his old one. The bias and fear of him that so many had held before ever laying eyes on him seemed to evaporate as soon as people got to know him, got to see that his intentions were only good. No more dark magical attacks disrupted his school days, he made more and more good friends, and he continuously better-integrated Sunshine's memories and experiences into his own and into a more natural and accessible mesh of what came easily to him. Everything was going smoothly until his second Friday there, just two weeks into this new experience, during his Ethics class he received an urgent mental message to meet Ms. Charming in her office after school.

One day earlier at the hospital, the doctors had informed Hannah's parents of her condition.

"Mr. And Mrs. Walker. Good morning. Is there anything I can get you? Coffee?"

"No, thank you. We just want to know what this is all about. Has there been a change in Hannah's condition since last night? We've been praying for her day and night."

"No change, I'm afraid. But I do have some new information for you." The doctor paused. Every moment since Earl had come to him on Tuesday with this information had taken its toll on him. He wondered for the first time how Earl had talked him into telling her parents about her condition, and now that they were sitting across from him he knew he had no chance to deflect the responsibility back onto its source. "After carefully monitoring her these past months, we've discovered that your daughter is pregnant. Our best guess is that she conceived around the time of her accident, so if the fetus makes it to term, she'll deliver in June. I should warn you though that in most cases the unborn children of comatose mothers do not make it to term."

"What are you saying? How is this possible?"

"Our Hannah isn't that sort of girl!"

The doctor had suspected they would react poorly. He could see that Hannah's mother was on the verge of tears, and wondered if that was a normal state for her to be in as he tried to calm them both down. "I can't begin to tell you exactly what happened, and I'm certainly not trying to make any claims about what sort of person your daughter is. All I can tell you is what we know from a medical standpoint, and right now, that's that Hannah is pregnant."

"Why didn't you find out sooner? Shouldn't you have known when you ran her blood tests, months ago?"

"I've gone over the records myself, and it looks like the evidence was there when she arrived at the hospital, elevated hormone levels and other chemical changes, but it was all overlooked somehow. The attending physician at the time made note of it and suggested that it be followed up on after her initial work was done, but … well, no one followed up on it, it seems. I apologize for that, but we know now, and that's why you're here."

"Better late than never, is that it?"

"Oh, honey, let the poor man be. He's just doing his job, after all."

"Fine, fine. But what happens next? Do we need to do anything? Does she need to be cared for differently?"

"That's all being taken care of. In addition to her normal nutritional intake we've already added a pre-natal cocktail. Folic acid, vitamin A, anti-oxidants, nothing you wouldn't find in an over-the-counter pre-natal supplement. She's already been looked at by our two best OB-GYNs, and they tell me that everything looks good. If the fetus makes it to term, she should have no problems birthing it, comatose or not. There's nothing for you to worry about, we'll ensure that she receives only the best pre-natal care we can offer."

"That sounds … good, I guess. I still don't understand how this happened."

The doctor was beginning to wonder if he was going to have to explain the basics of human reproduction to them before the father spoke up again.

"I suppose you'd tell us she was sexually active before the accident, to avoid a lawsuit. Of course, how could we prove anything without a DNA test? How soon is that possible, by the way?"

The father was savvier than he let on. "Not until the end of the second trimester. But I don't believe that will be necessary." He lied, but after hours of practice, did so without a trace of it being revealed on his face, "The admitting doctor's examination noted that she had been

133

sexually active prior to her admittance here. It's all in his initial reports." He waited to see if they bought it.

"I just don't understand. My baby. How could she do this to herself?" Now Mrs. Walker really did start crying.

"It doesn't matter now, dear. What's done is done, and she's already being punished for her sins. We have to start praying twice as hard for her, and again as much for our new grandchild. Doctor, is there anything else you need to tell us? We'd like to go see our daughter right away."

"No, nothing, go ahead. If you have any questions, here's my card. You can reach me at this number day or night."

"Thank you. Honey, let's go." Mr. Walker stood, taking his wife's hand and helping her stand, still weeping. They walked out of the doctor's office and, once the door was shut behind the two of them, he let out a deep sigh of relief at his having made it through that situation. Still, he thought they had seemed fairly guarded the entire time, and he was not entirely sure they believed that there was no reason to file a lawsuit. He would have to wait and see. He would also have to get back at Earl for sticking him with this situation. He hoped the worst had passed.

✧ ✧ ✧

"Trev, come in, come in." Ms. Charming welcomed Trevor into her office, where several figures he recognized as members of The Board, including Jurrin. He took the proffered seat uncomfortably, surrounded by adults and ancients who were left standing after the seating room had run out. Something was definitely up, and it wasn't just the further delay of the shipment of cold iron.

"What's going on?"

The Principal sat at her own seat behind her desk and addressed him directly. "It's Hannah. She's gone missing."

"Missing? How? Did she wake up?"

"We don't know. She's just missing. Has anyone contacted you?"

"Only you, about this meeting. Do you think she's been kidnapped?"

"It's a possibility." Jurrin's voice was clearly upset, but that was not far off from his normal tone in meetings of The Board. "There are forces in this world worse than you, and they'd be more than happy to get their hands on a power similar to what you represent."

"But right now," Sunshine interrupted, "we have no evidence of wrongdoing. Yesterday Hannah was in her bed as normal, her family came to visit her off schedule, but when they left, Hannah was still in her bed. The paperwork to have her signed out of the hospital was never completed, there's no record of an ambulance moving her to a different facility, and while they admit they don't know where she is, the hospital itself is admitting to no wrongdoing. Our people have checked every room on every floor, all storage areas, everything with standard senses and enhanced senses, and they came up with nothing. There's no trace of her left in the hospital."

"There is still a trace of you there, though. The room she was staying in is practically coated with an energy signature roughly equivalent to the one you give off – we detected it coming from her before, and assumed it was actually coming from the fetus. It's the only trace of magic left anywhere in the hospital." Trevor didn't have to turn around to know who had said that; it was the security expert adjunct to The Board, Mr. Skaphe. His word on this matter could be trusted.

"What about her parents? Have you checked in on them, maybe asked them if they know anything?" Trevor was just trying to be helpful without really knowing everything that they'd already done, and they appreciated that he seemed concerned.

"That was a good idea, but ..."

Sunshine filled in the blanks. "Their house is as empty as her hospital bed. No people, no sign that they'd left. Their belongings are still there, intact and even their luggage is standing unused in their closets. Their cars are still in the garage. The Walkers themselves are the only things missing."

135

"And we're working on a final sweep, but initial intelligence indicates that no magic was used to remove them. If they left, they left of their own free will, carrying only what they had on their backs and in their pockets, they didn't lock their doors behind them, and they left either on foot or in someone else's vehicle. Whatever happened, it happened during the night – they were seen entering their home by neighbors last night, but not leaving for work this morning. Their bosses each said they hadn't heard from them."

"Okay, what else? Have you tried mapping her? If the fetus shares my energy signature, shouldn't it come up on a Power Map somewhere?"

"It should, and it used to, but we can't find it on any of our maps now."

"What kind of surveillance were you using?"

"We had people looking in on her three times a day, but … she's in a magical coma that we'd know was dispelled, we didn't exactly think she needed constant surveillance."

"Reasonable. Who saw her last?"

"I did." It was someone Trevor did not recognize.

"And you are?"

"I'm uhh… uhhh… I'm …"

"That's my son, Tack," Mr. Skaphe said, "I've been training him, and I had him assigned to do the evening check. He saw her last night at 10PM, still in her bed."

"You saw her with your own eyes, physically, right Tack?"

"Y-y-yes, sir."

"Alright. And when the 6AM check looked in, she was gone?"

"Right. It was as though her bed had never been slept in. Clean sheets, no charts, all personal affects removed from the room. And no one on the night staff saw anything."

"So what you're telling me is that we have nothing. We have no idea where Hannah and my unborn daughter are, and we have no leads. The strongest opponents to my right to life are here in the room, just as worried about this as I

136

am." Trevor looked Jurrin in the eye as he said this, but knew what he was saying was true from the color of Jurrin's aura. Jurrin really wasn't involved, and didn't know who was. "What's next? We wait for a ransom note?"

"Just about," Ms. Charming said honestly, "there's not much else we can do. The top three sensitives on the planet are carefully going over every living being on Earth and seeking out any sign or knowledge or trace of Hannah or your child or anything that may lead to them. They started locally, and are working quickly, but you know how complex a matter this is. There are over a trillion living beings on Earth right now. This could take several weeks, and considering our current results… it isn't hopeful."

"Is it possible she isn't still on Earth?"

"We're investigating that avenue through known portals, but it's very difficult to trace something like this. Especially if you consider that they may have passed through an infinite loop portal."

"Is there anything I can do?"

"That's actually why we're all here. We want to let you know we're all in agreement on this. We want you to try to reach her directly."

"The same way I did before?"

"Whatever works. Whatever it takes, if you can contact her, that's far enough, and … Ms. Charming tells us you'll be able to find out where she is once you've made contact, is that correct?"

"If I can make contact."

"So you'll try?"

"I'll do my best. I haven't really … made contact since … since that night. I can't promise anything."

Sunshine smiled warmly, confidence glowing upon him, "we have faith that you will do your best, but we realize that if our best efforts are fruitless, you may experience the same thing. We do not mean to put any pressure on you. That would be counterintuitive, yes? We just wanted to suggest that you try." Her voice washed over him in calming waves, and even knowing what she was doing and how it worked, Trevor simply let her do it, wanting to be calmed.

They wrapped things up quickly after that, most of those in the room simply disappearing in turn to wherever they needed to be, until all that remained in the room were Sunshine and Trevor. She wished him well in that calming way and sent him home for the weekend, both of them wondering how things would go for all of them from then on. Trevor did not look back to her as he walked in the direction of home.

✛ ✛ ✛

In a city far from where The Board had had its informal meeting stood a cathedral. Built far from civilization, the cathedral was now buried deep in city streets and towered over by modern skyscrapers, overlooked by most eyes as a relic of a bygone need. It was a complex construction of solid stone the likes of which modern engineers would have had difficulty expressing the manipulation of to achieve the same effect, and it stood in majesty and antiquity, an icon of religious power.

Underneath the cathedral, into the surface of the earth, was dug out a mirror image of the cathedral, extending towers and gargoyles down into the soil to exactly match the towers and gargoyles stretching into the sky. Every detail of the two cathedrals was equivalent: one cathedral reached down as deep at the other reached up, and somehow the very effect of gravity was reversed in the lower one so that the rows of pews in the church above were mirrored on the relative floor of the one below, the candles burning above with smoke curling away towards the ceiling were matched by candles burning below with smoke curling down deeper into the ground and finding the same arch of stone as their counterparts above, and on and on unto every detail, matched below in a mirror representation of what was above. With the simple exception that every detail praising god and good above was matched by a detail cursing god and praising evil below, and instead of the brilliant colored light that streamed in through the stained glass windows of the church above, the light seemed drawn out of the matching windows below, creating therein an unnatural darkness that even the constantly burning candles could not penetrate more than a few feet.

Whenever a mass was held in the church above, a black mass was held in the church below, to keep the careful balance of powers within the walls of the doubled cathedral. This balance of power, hidden from the eyes of the world, created a way to hide things from the sight of those who saw with more than just their eyes, a fact that had been used to the advantage of generations of evil men who had secrets to keep. Unknown to even most of those who knew of the existence of the church were most of its secrets, and on this day the church had taken on one such secret more important and more needfully hidden than all its other secrets combined.

In the church was a stone crypt that had lain empty since the church's construction, unused and waiting. It was inaccessible through any physical means, though its contents would be kept alive and healthy through ancient magic embedded in its very stones. It was at the focal point of the cross that the cathedral formed, perfectly balanced between the church above and the church below, effectively beneath the main altar of both churches while remaining hidden from both. Its contents were suspended in a weightless state, no forces exerted on them by the pull that would have kept people in either cathedral stuck to the floor, and in complete darkness.

The balance of the mirrored churches made everything within its walls invisible to prying eyes, hearts, and minds, and this kept Mr. and Mrs. Walker from being detected by any of the parties looking for them. The perfection of balance of the crypt in which Hannah was now kept was able to hide even the true nature of the child growing within her a secret from even the most skilled and powerful of forces. The family's twin ministers had joined them on alternate days during the week to pray over Hannah's comatose body, and had simultaneously reported back to their respective bishops what they had detected growing inside her individually. The information had worked its way up the two parallel hierarchies at the same rate and reached the twin popes in the same moment. In the very next moment, their course was set and they took coordinated action without conferring – such was the connection between them. It was less than an hour later that Hannah was entombed within the balanced crypt and her parents were safely hidden in the inner rooms of the church above with a representative couple tracing their movements in the church below, and less than a day later that the dual churches deployed the second phase of their plan, dozens of ministers walking two by two outward through the city, finally putting into motion what they had waited so long to begin. Soon the ignorant public would turn its back on a church it had never known, their hatred for one church carefully balanced against the hatred held by another for the other, generating the energy they needed for the ritual soon to unfold. The time of the twins was nearer that night than it had ever been before, and there was no one with the power to stop it.

Book Two

The Twofold Invasion

OR

Penetration and Destruction

OR

How To Make Love With Twins

"I'd somehow managed to go this long without once thinking about what it would be like to kiss you." A fireball crackled with searing heat as it flew within inches of Trevor's head, his robe's hood down, his hair blowing back with the warming wind of the passing danger.

"What?" Nirgal was so distracted by Trevor's strange comment that he nearly failed to burst a lightning ball that would have converted their best player to the other side.

"Nothing. Sorry." Trevor had an idea forming as he ran over to help Jode get a scarantula off the back of his robes without either of them being hit by incoming projectiles. He shouted back to Nirgal who was redirecting a series of fast-moving visionballs away from their right-side cluster of fireball throwers, their Burners, "I was just thinking about a girl from my old school."

"Is that such a good idea?" One of the visionballs got past him, and a Burner was down. Nirgal had been hit with enough visionballs to know what his teammate was seeing, and that what he was not seeing was more important – until the visionball dispelled, Nirgal was the only person keeping Saeto from being hit by every single thing the other side decided to throw their way. "We are in the middle of a championship dodgeball game. What would Kay and Elle think if you lost the big game because you were thinking about someone else?" Nirgal suddenly jumped away from the cluster of Burners, ducking and rolling along the ground to miss a very close freezeball that would have slowed him down significantly. "Maybe you could daydream later? AFTER we win?"

"No, no, but it gave me an idea. I'm going to need some help." Everyone who heard Trevor say he'd had an idea looked his way, at least for a moment. His own teammates had learned to just trust him and hope for the best. Eight times out of ten his ideas won the game for them, and the other times… well, they hadn't ever gone so wrong as to cause a total match loss. The other team tried to prepare for the worst, word spreading fast among them to get ready to try to distract Trevor or lose big – only one team had ever been able to break his concentration, and they had disqualified themselves in the process. And the crowd, the crowd roared louder and louder in excitement, then hushed to a startling silence in anticipation of something unexpected. "Everyone aim at different players... just ... figure it out, okay? We want every one to hit."

They all got projectiles ready to loose, and then Trevor seemed to disappear. And then their projectiles all seemed to disappear. And then Trevor reappeared, holding nothing in his back-cocked arm, and shouted, "Now!" Everyone threw nothing. Nothing flew across the courts at the other team. Some of them tried to block nothing, a few of them tried to move or leap out of the way of nothing, the guards tried blasting nothing out of the air. "Get ready for another set of shots!" Trevor already had a fireball blazing just off his hand as he said this, and it seemed to be enough to get his teammates to stop just watching to see what was happening on the other side and get them back into play.

What happened was, excepting one player whose leaping had got him just out of the way of the invisible mudball Nirgal had thrown at him and one player who had never been kissed, all the players on the other team got hit by invisible balls and then just stood there with their eyes closed and smiles drawing across their faces.

The other team's coach was at the edge of the court, screaming at the referees, "He's playing with their minds! He can't do that! They ruled against Mentalism in the playoffs and you know it! What kind of a referee are you? That monster is in there flagrantly breaking the rules and you're just going to let him do it? How far up your ass has your head got to be not to see what he's doing out there to my boys?" He went on and on, saliva spraying on the referee's face as he screamed and turned red and tried to get the referee to make a call in his team's favor. The constant barrage of hits raining down on his players did nothing to distract them from whatever was going on in their heads, some of them literally being knocked to the ground by lightning balls or multiple hard hits, and there were fewer and fewer of them smiling happily as they lost the game.

"What did you do, Trev?" Harrison, the team's captain, threw marble ball after marble ball at the remaining players as he implored Trevor for an answer. "You know you're not allowed to use Mentalism in the playoffs. Are we going to be disqualified?"

"I don't think so." Trevor always felt like a weakling when he tried to heave balls of solid marble twelve inches in diameter across the court, so stuck to fast fireballs as he also continued playing. "I read the ruling pretty carefully, and it only says I can't communicate or otherwise directly interact with the minds of the players on either team. So I modified everyone's balls to do it for me."

"What did you put in their heads, exactly? They seem pretty happy to be losing, maybe you could do the rest of us after the match." Harrison grinned, hoping it was something troublingly erotic.

"Oh, nothing special. I just triggered a looping memory of their most emotionally significant kiss. Pretty easy, if you know how to create mental loops."

"Is that because of the emotional content?" Their conversation was fairly relaxed, since no one on the other team was trying to hit them with anything. "I'm studying to get into Mentalism 1 next year, and I think I read something about emotional memories being the easiest to get people to replay."

"That's a pretty good way to put it. I think we're about done here."

"But we've still got to wait for the end of the game. Could you do me?"

"After the game, Harry."

"Okay."

"Do you want to do the cascading balls trick again, while we wait?"

"Yeah." Harrison began grinning a conniving grin.

"Tell the others; I'll get ready."

Harrison gathered all the players who weren't trapped in reverie together at the center of the court in three concentric circles around where Trevor was sitting cross-legged and floating just above the floor. Everyone, even the players that had been converted from the other side, got into the energy of it as the three rings started moving in alternating directions around Trevor; the smallest and largest circles moving clockwise and the other circle moving counter-clockwise, all of them facing in. A sphere of distortion, like a three-dimensional rippling of waves in the fabric of reality radiating outward, was already large enough to encompass Trevor and was growing and growing to take in the other players. As soon as the entire inner circle was inside the distortion, the players within appeared to turn into a blur of motion around and around and around Trevor, who sat perfectly still in the center, windblown. The sphere of rippling distortion expanded and expanded until eventually all the players and a big chunk of the floor below them and air above them were contained within it, and then it maintained its size and rippled slower and slower until its surface was like the perfect clear surface of a crystal ball.

Within this strange sphere, the three rings of players were spinning in a blur around Trevor, who could just be seen through their partially transparent vagueness. Then Trevor opened his eyes and seemed to turn into a blur himself as a constant stream of light began pouring out of the air in front of him and cascaded up into the air above them all until very quickly there was a half-sphere of white light curving out like water from a fountain, flowing from Trevor to the inner circle of players. And then a second burst flowered out of that one, a yellow fountaining of light and energy reaching the second circle of players, but less visible so that the light from the white, inner sphere was still visible to the crowd. Finally a third fountain of multicolored light flowed forth from Trevor to the outer circle of players, a constantly shifting rainbow of continuous color forming a half-sphere of light with the multilayered backlighting of the inner half-spheres within it. This gorgeous display of light continued for a few moments, and then the crystal-like sphere around all of them suddenly exploded outward to encompass the entire stadium and everyone inside it as the last few seconds ticked down on the clock for the third game of the match that would decide the national dodgeball championship. As soon as the clock was inside the sphere it seemed to stop altogether, and as soon as the nearly silent audience was inside the sphere, they gasped and cheered to see what was really going on.

The players were still slowly circling Trevor in alternating directions, but now everyone could see that the solid half-spheres of light they had seen above the blurs of players had actually been various dodgeballs being passed back and forth between the players in a complex pattern that could not have been achieved by anyone without a fairly high level of skill. Different colors of visionballs were moving across the highest arcs between the players of the third circle. Fireballs were burning their way back and forth in careful arcs between the players in the second circle, and lightning balls sped still blindingly fast between the inner circle of players, the best of the lightning-ball casters from both teams showing off their skill and dexterity. The crowd ooh-ed and ah-ed and cheered and clapped as the players' circles slowly expanded. The outer circle took two steps back, carefully maintaining the constant motion of dozens of visionballs, the second circle took one step back without losing a single fireball, and then all three circles began taking simultaneous steps outward until the outermost players were heaving visionballs across the entire width of the court to reach the players on the other side.

Trevor was now standing, and as soon as they reached the edge he shouted out, "Ready?"

The entire team shouted back in unison, "Ready," and the balls began flying faster.

Trevor raised his arms into the air and shouted "Set" as he whipped his arms back to his sides. The nearly forgotten crystal-like sphere of distortion came rushing back in on him in an instant, time speeding back up to normal with three seconds left on the clock. Everyone caught the balls in the air and held them floating in front of themselves as they turned to face the audience. When they had all turned with held balls, they shouted back to him, "Set."

The clock ticked down to one second and Trevor shouted "Go!" – Each player heaved his ball towards the crowd in long, slow arcs through the air, a rain of fire, lightning, and color streaming towards the thousands of onlookers who all leaned back in their seats, even the ones who had seen this same show at earlier games, as the danger approached. The clock hit zero before a single ball reached the audience, and as the buzzer rang out through the air every single projectile still in motion disappeared at once and the audience let out a communal breath of relief and joy. The cheering and clapping and whistling and roaring of the crowd rose to an unbelievable level and players and families and fans rushed onto the court to congratulate the obviously winning team, raising the players onto shoulders and backs above the crowd and carrying them around in celebration. They all knew the final display was a bit of showboating, but since it didn't elevate any one player above the others and emphasized teamwork and skill above grandstanding, even including players converted from opposing teams, the referees had been more than glad to allow Trevor to show off a little when there was time left on the clock. Though he was loath to admit it, Trevor found he liked playing dodgeball after all.

At the same time that Trevor was trying, as politely as he could, to get the three strangers who were carrying him around like a trophy to set him down, two young women were weaving their way through the crowd trying to reach him. The two women and Trevor met their goals at almost exactly the same time, so that he seemed to fall out of the sky to stand directly before them just as they were coming to a stop.

Kay smiled her proudest smile at Trevor, said "Good game, Trev," then leaned up and forward and kissed him gently on the lips.

Elle smiled her identical smile at Trevor, leaned forward and up and kissed him gently on the lips before saying, "What did you do to those guys at the end? It all went so fast, and then they stopped playing!"

"Thank you," he nodded to Elle. "Thank you," he nodded to Kay, took them one to a side, arm in arm, and began working their way out of the still-raucous crowd. "Nothing that would seem too fancy to you two. I slowed down my personal time so I could turn everyone's balls invisible and then give each ball a single mental command to transmit to whoever they hit without running down the clock."

"Invisible so the other team couldn't block them," Elle began.

Kay finished, "but what was the mental command?" Both girls smiled their mischievous smiles at him as they continued their slow way through the crowd, and he knew they wanted the same thing Harrison had.

"Are you sure?" They nodded synchronously. "Okay, I'll give it to you in a minute." Their smiles drooped a bit. "It'll take you two a few minutes to recover, I'm sure. I'll give it to you when we part ways at the locker room." They nodded in grudging acceptance. "Are you two gonna stick around for the co-ed game?"

"Of course we are!"

"We want to be sure you treat those girls right."

"No funny business." She reached out to poke his side, tickling him.

"But don't throw the game, either."

"Of course not, Kay. You know I would never mistreat anyone, whether they happened to be the national champions of all high-school level women's teams or not. Though I can't actually promise 'no funny business.' You remember how the quarter-finals went, Elle."

All three of them laughed at the thought of the way the court had looked at the end of the quarter-finals, with banana cream pies splattered across every player on both sides, the floor, the walls, and most of the audience. It had been a close game, decided without a clear Condorcet winner at first, but in Trevor's team's favor after all, despite no points or conversions being scored for either side after his area-effect spell had begun to work. Before the three of them had really caught their breath from the memory of Trevor's "funny business," they reached the locker room entrance, and Trevor unhooked his arms from those of the young women on either side of him.

"Well, I guess I've got to change my robes before the co-ed game, and Mr. Klaw will probably want to talk strategy with everybody, even though we're already the champions. Your seats up front should still be reserved, but be sure you're in them before the game starts, or they'll give them to someone else. Now, I'm going to give you the

151

mental command, and I don't know how long it'll last, exactly, but I have a feeling you'll want it to last longer, so… Well, here goes, I'll see you later." He held out his hand and generated a red ball of light, imbuing it with the same mental command he had used earlier. He held it up to his face and kissed it and then, as though blowing the kiss to them, blew the energy ball out of his hand in their direction. It split into two glowing balls as it lazily crossed the distance between them, and before the balls landed gently on each girl's smooth cheek, transferring the mental commands to them, he turned around and went into the locker room, leaving them standing there just outside the door reliving their most emotionally significant kisses over and over again.

It is perhaps an unfortunate thing that he did not stay to look at the expressions on their faces or to look into their minds to experience what they were remembering in such vivid detail, for it might have changed the entire course of future events for dozens, perhaps billions of people. For most people, their most emotionally significant kiss would be a pleasant memory, where the emotion had been happiness, joy, love, or some other warm and fuzzy feeling that one would want to experience again and again and again in a loop of true experiential realism. In the case of Kay and Elle, the primary emotion of their most emotionally significant kiss was identically different from what most people would have expected, and as the remaining players filed into the locker room they passed quickly by twin faces of frozen terror.

"What did you do to Kay and Elle, Trev?"

"Nothing they didn't ask for." Trevor smiled, thinking what he'd done had been quite pleasant for them, and didn't see his teammates' puzzled reactions because he was pulling his undershirt off over his head to freshen up between games. "Do you want the same?"

"N-no. No." Everyone who had seen the girls was shaking his head, fervently imploring Trevor not to put him through whatever had put that expression on their faces. Some turned their backs on Trevor, facing their lockers, and others just busied themselves with changing their robes or looking though their playbooks, but no one wanted to make eye contact with him. They knew he didn't need eye contact to get into their heads, but there was something psychological about looking someone in the eyes that seemed like an open door to mental manipulation.

"What about you, Harry?"

"What?" Harrison was caught off guard by Trevor singling him out; he thought they had been on good terms at the end of the game. "No, err… No."

"Whatever." Trevor didn't understand the sudden cold shoulder everyone was giving him. They usually liked to goof around after a game. He began to wonder if he'd done something or said something that had upset them, but Trevor had been pretty sure he'd made winning the game a team effort, and he certainly hadn't intended to or felt he had received any more praise than anyone else on the team after the game. He pulled off his short pants and then pulled them right back on as soon as the CleanGuard enchantment had done its work of returning him to the state of cleanliness he had been in at the start of the game.

Trevor remained silent, trying to work out why everyone else was so quiet, as he changed into his new robes for the final game. Instead of the school colors, these robes were the traditional dark brown of proper magicians' monk-like robes, with the symbol of the national championship winners proudly emblazoned across their backs. It was supposed to be a secret, but these one-time-use overrobes were also supposed to enhance reflexes and act as power multipliers for any magic they used as they played – fireballs would burn hotter, lightning balls would shock more intensely and convert players faster, and all magically propelled balls would fly faster and hit harder. It didn't give them a real advantage, since the young women's team would be wearing equivalent robes, but it made the last game a real blast. Literally. Mr. Klaw finally came into the locker room to give the team some guidance for the final official dodgeball game of the school year.

"None of the prophecies have been fulfilled yet; how can you still be thinking he's the one?" Feagan was clearly beginning to doubt that the tall, lanky man with coke-bottle-like glasses standing before him. "He's powerful, yes, and the stars are coming into alignment, but nothing else seems to fit."

"Forget the prophecies! They were lies when my predecessors wrote them, and they're still lies! That doesn't mean he's not the one they were warning us about." The dark stranger spoke with a burning intensity that literally showed in his eyes, tiny flames licking up across his irises towards his pupils as he roared back at Feagan. "He's a danger to all of us, and if we don't do something to stop him soon … you know what could happen."

"I'm not sure I believe that part either. Why would he do something that would destroy Earth as we know it? He's not exactly suicidal or quote-unquote evil." Feagan made finger quote-marks in the air as he emphasized the word "evil" verbally. The lanky man rolled his eyes in response, but Feagan continued, "So he can read and control minds with an unprecedented level of skill, so what? So he's got a copy of Sunshine's entire life history to draw on, and who knows who else has let him into their minds by now to add to that, there's nothing he could learn from someone that could make him any more of a threat than the person he learned it from already represented to us."

Sqrat, who had been standing so meekly to the side that he seemed hardly to have been noticed by the other two, spoke up. "I've watched every single dodgeball game he's ever played, written down every play and studied what he's done – he uses magic no one has ever used before in almost every game, developing strategies and complex spells spur-of-the-moment to suit his moods. When he does use traditional magic, he rarely uses it the way everyone else has been using it for eons. I heard Echelar & Spink has been planting a man in the audience at our games and have already begun to update their texts with as many of his plays as they can before the new school year."

The tall man's glare focused through his giant glasses and seemed intensified like the sun's light would have been intensified through the lenses to rapidly create a fire, and would have been burning a hole right between Sqrat's eyes if it were more than just a glare. "What does that childish game have to do with anything, Sqrat?" As the lanky leader said "anything," Sqrat's bushy, connected eyebrows actually did catch fire, and he quickly reached up to slap at his own face to try to put out the tiny blaze.

"Aaahh! Aaa-aahh.. ahh… Ow." Sqrat calmed down when his face was no longer on fire and tried to answer, "if he… if he's that powerful just playing a .. a... childish game, imagine what he could do in a … a… a ..b-b-b-b… b-b- b-b b-b …"

"A battle?"

Sqrat let out a huge breath in relaxation. "Yes. A real battle. I'm on your side, sir." Sqrat reached over and put his hand on the scar where his bone had broken through his arm and remembered the day he had first introduced Trevor to their world.

"Good thing, Sqrat." He turned back to Feagan and continued to try to quell his mutiny, "what do you say to that, Trask?"

"I've seen him play, too, and if he's using the full extent of his abilities in the game, they're impressive, but he wouldn't beat you on your worst day in a proper duel." The tall one seemed nonplussed about having his ego rubbed by Mr. Trask, but didn't interrupt again. "Just because he's powerful and can do things no one has ever seen before doesn't make him the one talked about in the prophecy. If he wins the championship tonight, it almost means the opposite, since the one in the prophecy isn't ever supposed to achieve notoriety before the end has already begun."

"You're not listening. I told you the prophecy isn't the point anymore. Stopping the boy is."

"You've been telling us from the beginning that the prophecy was all that mattered. All the work we've done has revolved around the prophecy, and now you say it's all a lie, it doesn't matter, that the prophecy is not the point? If the prophecy isn't real, why am I talking to you at all?"

"Because you know I'm right." The tall man's voice was becoming more even.

"You got me to believe in the prophecy for nothing, then?"

"Do you still believe I'm right about the boy?" His face was becoming more relaxed.

"He's not the one in the prophecy."

"Do you believe me about the boy?" The formerly imposing figure now seemed forgiving, imploring rather than demanding.

"…I…" Feagan Trask was no longer looking at an angry face, a menacing beast defending himself, and if the tall man was so calm and assured about it … Feagan wasn't sure what to think. "We should keep watching him."

"We should stop him." The lanky figure was determined, but not oppressive.

"Stop him from doing what? If the prophecy can't be trusted, what exactly do you think he's going to be doing?"

"Just because we don't know the path he takes to get there doesn't mean he's not going to destroy life on Earth as we know it."

"It doesn't mean he is, either."

"He is. You've seen the look in his eye. You've touched the surface of his mind. You know he's not like us."

"You're such a xenophobe. You're worse than the native shamans were."

"And if he's the advance scout of a colonization effort of thousands or millions more like him, like we were when we arrived on these shores? Do you want to be the one that welcomed him and his people to take over our planet?"

"Is that what you think is going to happen?"

"You know we can't know the future with that much detail. All we can do is speculate and calculate and observe him until we see the moment to stop him."

"But if he's not the risk you claim, what sort of ethical charge do we get for stopping him?"

"You're worried about ethical charge? You. That's a joke, right?" The thin face's composure finally broke into thundering laughter.

"Stop laughing at me." He simply laughed louder. "You don't know what I've gone through to get back to a

156

balanced charge after what we've done already. Sunshine does random charge sweeps of her entire staff, and I'm not about to be singled out or lose my position there because of your … experiments."

The tall man couldn't seem to stop laughing, apparently thinking about the sheer scale of community service and positive social work Feagan must have done to make up for their dark activities of the last decade. He laughed so hard he nearly fell to the floor, shaking and bending over and clutching his skinny belly in pain from convulsions. He laughed and laughed and laughed and the other two men didn't try to speak or leave, they just watched and waited. Sqrat chuckled a little, but more for the tall man's benefit than his believing Feagan's actions had been funny. Sqrat had done quite a bit of work to balance his own ethical charge; he just didn't consider bringing it up to be a wise idea. Finally, the lanky man began to catch his breath, and spoke again.

"How many little old ladies do you have to help across the street to make up for murdering a room full of children, exactly?"

"You know that wasn't my fault! I never meant for them to die! What about your sacrifices? How many hungry mouths do you have to feed, how many lives do you have to lift out of poverty, how much human suffering do you have to erase from the world to make up for just one of your human sacrifices?" He barely paused to see if the tall man would try to defend himself, "Oh yeah, that's right! You can't! Ever! Bring back a human sacrifice! You can't ever balance it. At least I have the opportunity to try."

"You know you're asking for trouble, right?" The lanky man's voice was calm and even, and his face once again had no readable expression. "You're not the only one who can do the Devil's Arithmetic. A tweak here, a tiny change in your instructions there, and next time the balance of the charge will land on your shoulders."

"There won't be a next time. You think I'd work with you again on something like … that?"

"You'll do precisely what I say you will. My runestones have a record of every effect they've ever played a part in, and can be source-routed back to everyone who had a hand in their use. If the right stone were somehow misplaced and ended up in the hands of The Board, you know it wouldn't take them long to detect one massacre or another lingering on it."

"You'd never allow that. You'd be sourced, the same as me. They'd know what you've been doing, and I could tell them I only acted under duress."

"Are you sure they could source it back to me? Do I need to remind you of my true name?"

Feagan's lack of a reaction beyond silence told the bespectacled man that he had reasserted his power sufficiently, and the mutinous thoughts of his colleague were at an end. He returned to his appropriately tall seat at the head of the table, waited for the other two men to take their more humble seats, and began again.

"The real reason we're meeting today should be obvious. You haven't found the girl yet. You haven't found out who took her or who wanted to take her. All you've proven is who didn't take her, who didn't want to take her, and that doesn't actually help us. She's less than a month from natural birth, assuming a standard gestation, and we need to find her before The Board does and before she gives birth. Whoever took her will probably just discard her when they have what they want from her, and her dead body doesn't do us any good at all. So. What news do you have for me?"

★　★　★

The final buzzer for the final game went off, and the crowd sat in stunned silence, staring at the scoreboard, staring at the teams, trying to decide whether to cheer or boo or just go home. Down on the court, the players were tired and sore and the players from both teams, when they had caught their breath after the final buzzer, walked to the center of the court and shook each other's hands almost silently. The sounds of their boots on the floor of the court and the shuffling of the crowd in the stands echoed in the empty air; no one even coughed to fill the silence.

The game had been a perfect tie.

There would be no way of knowing which team would have won if Trevor had not been playing, or had not been allowed to use his Mentalism, but the way it played out gave the appearance that the young men's national champions were exactly matched with the young women's national champions. Every player on both teams had exactly the same number of hits against them as they hadmade against another player. Every player that had been converted from one side to the other was converted back again. Every block was matched with a block on the other side. Every single thing that was tracked about every single player and action in each of the three games was precisely matched between the two teams. There was no way that either team, based on the match they had just completed, could be said to be the winner over the other team.

Trevor remembered what Mr. Klaw had told them before the game; it had been brief. He had said that the young women's team was significantly better than they were, more talented, more skilled, and based on scoring for the entire season, if they played according to the same rules that had been used for the playoffs, Mr. Klaw assured them all they would lose two or three to one in every scoring category. Women are simply more naturally magically inclined, and had better intuition and teamwork, he'd said. And then he'd addressed Trevor directly, saying that the women's team, the judging officials, and the league president had all agreed to allow Trevor to use his mental powers during the match, and that Mr. Klaw wanted him to go "all out."

And that had been it. He'd had what had felt like a really long time by himself to think about what he could do or should do during the game. He could have not used his mental powers at all, and his team would probably have been severely beaten, even if he did pull off a big play at the end of the game, because of wins in a majority of statistics. He could have used his mental powers to lead his team to an overwhelming victory, even just by standing in the background and giving his teammates instructions about when to dodge and block and dip and when to throw or not to throw and who to throw at, giving them an excellent advantage in timing and precision and a relatively easy win. It was something he'd always avoided, so that the team's winning was about their own skills generally, rather than his playing the entire game for the entire team as though it were merely a mental exercise. It was something he still didn't want to do.

In considering it, Trevor also considered the implications of many possible outcomes. If he was allowed to use his Mentalism and didn't, his teammates would hate him and the crowd would just watch them get smashed. If he led the team to a stunning victory, the other team would hate him and all the work he'd done during the season to make the team the focus instead of himself would be lost in a little over an hour; it would be pretty clear to everyone playing and watching that Trevor's Mentalism was the difference between winning and losing for the young men. Trevor wasn't sure where the idea came to him from, but he decided to attempt to create an outcome that required an intense show of his mental prowess, his team's physical skill and mental dexterity in every player, and that wouldn't take away from the fact that the young women's team was an amazing set of players. He decided to try to craft a match that would not leave any individual player's ego hurt, that would give every player equal time, and that would hopefully create balance and unity.

Whether it created balance and unity would be a matter of contentious discussion for a long time to come. No completed match had ever been exactly tied before, in the entire history of dodgeball. Even in matches where not a single hit had been made by either team, one team had always had more active blocks than the other and had been named the winner for superior defense. Plenty of games had had the same number of hits and conversions and blocks for each side, the primary statistics for scoring, but in each of those games, players had been converted faster from one side to the other, or converted players had played worse for the other side than they did their native side, or some other small statistical differences had existed between the teams or across the three games of a match which had created a reasonably clear winner. None of those things had happened in this unprecedented game.

Taking himself to the limits and pressing hard against the limits of what was morally acceptable with regard to taking action in the minds of others, Trevor had tuned into the thoughts of every player on both teams and actively suggested – and in some cases almost directly taken control of – actions for the players on his own side to take. Defensive actions to stay out of the way of just the right number of balls or to actively block just the right number of attacks to match what the young women's team's actual performance turned out to be, from play to play. Guidance about how to use different offensive moves, so that just the right number of strikes of the right types would hit or miss the female players, just the right number would be potentially blockable or potentially dodgeable. Mental guidance combined with actual physical guidance for lightning balls to hit the right players at the right times and miss in exactly the correct proportions to match what had been done by the other side. All of these mental commands and more were broadcasting while Trevor very carefully danced through the appropriate motions with his own body to play his own role in the game, dodging, blocking, casting, throwing, and otherwise doing his part to not be a better or worse player than any other person in any of the ways that any of them played the games.

Through this complex series of events, the young men's national champions had actually managed to play at the level of the young women's national champions, and because Trevor had not sent a single message, command, or suggestion to any of the players on the young women's side – converted or not – it had been somewhat fair. But as the players shuffled off the court and the crowd began filing calmly row by row out of the stands, the low murmuring that was hardly above the audible level of the noise of thousands of feet making their way to the doors was certainly a harsh contrast to the literal cacophony that had filled the entire building just two hours earlier. Trevor, exhausted, had simply stood still at the sound of the buzzer.

When the crowd finally cleared and the rest of the players had retreated to their locker rooms, Trevor was still standing there in his formal brown robes, head hung down, arms at his sides, shoulders slung low, breathing slow and deep and long as he tried to recover from a game that was supposed to have been lighthearted and fun. He waited and relaxed and breathed with his head down and his eyes closed until his mind cleared and his thoughts' velocity tapered off and his pulse returned to normal and he began to reach a calm, neutral state. Finally, after what may have been a genuinely long time or may have only been several minutes, Trevor lifted his head slowly upright and opened his eyes at the culmination of a refreshing inhalation of air. Present before him were the identical faces of his girlfriends, with big doe eyes and equal looks of concern broadcasting a reassuring warmth across his own less-than-radiant expression.

"You were amazing," her tone was soft and reassuring, like the gentle purring of a newborn kitten held close and gentle against the skin. She stepped forward and pressed her whole body up against him, reaching around inside his overrobe in a very pleasant hug of his left side.

"That was perfect," the other one was just as reassuring, just as soothing, and perhaps a bit of worshipfulness came across in her throaty but brief statement as she also stepped towards him, reached around his other side inside his overrobe and pressed the whole length of her body against him from the sides of their feet meeting slightly, her bare calf and thighs pressing through his underrobe, underskirt, and short pants against his own leg, and like her sister had done on the other side, pressing her torso against his and turning and tilting and resting the side of her head against his chest and shoulder, nuzzling up against his neck.

Then as they held themselves and each other tight against him and his own arms closed around them and his head came down to gently meet theirs, the three of them whispered softly in unison, "I love you."

✦ ✦ ✦

"He's ours."
"It's not over yet."
"But our plan is working."
"And if it does, –"
"He's ours."

Their embrace lasted at least as long as his relaxing and emptying had before it, and none of them said another word before he was the first to move.

"Why don't you come over to our place tonight, Trev?"

None of them had moved farther than to wrap themselves closer around each other, nor had Kay and Elle opened their eyes. They simply stood in his hot embrace, smiling, as he openned his eyes to consider the two of them. Trevor had never felt this way about anyone before, himself. Sunshine had felt a similar but also almost entirely different and unique way about her husband, and Trevor could remember it and compare it to this, but he knew that no two loves could really be related properly to each other, so didn't spend long on that point of his/her memories. Here he was, feeling love – what he knew was genuine, everlasting, unconditional love – for these two people. Two people who not only loved him in return, but loved each other and loved their shared loves for each other.

Even without once reading a single thought or memory from either of them, he knew their love was genuine. He could feel it. It was like an unconscious broadcast they both made to him all the time, whether he was near or far, on their minds or not, and without ever consciously or intentionally looking into their thoughts and feelings he knew unmistakably that their love was genuine. He had known before they had told him, and though he had resisted, doubted, second-guessed and fought with himself about it, he had known for some time that he reciprocated that love. And as though speaking three tiny words had broken down a wall and transformed the world, things were different on the other side of that brief phrase. Like the final words of a long incantation or the first syllables of a new story, something had been created and something destroyed in the instance of that utterance.

Trevor caught even himself by surprise when he responded, saying "I think I will," and the three of them disappeared, and the court on which one of the strangest dodgeball matches in history had just been played was finally left alone to contemplate the meaning of what had just transpired.

Meanwhile Trevor, Kay, and Elle appeared in the girls' shared bedroom, still standing in each other's embrace. Slowly the girls drew themselves away from Trevor's sides and while one moved around the room lighting candles with tiny flicks of her wrist the other did a bit of subtle tidying. Trevor just watched them, thinking carefully about the situation he was about to find himself in, and though he didn't question his decision to enter into it, he thought about exactly how he should proceed. He suspected that there was a line he'd have to cross if he wanted this experience to reach the full expression of potential for pleasure and fulfillment for all three of them that he suspected was possible. Yet he didn't know whether it was one he ought to cross.

"It wouldn't hurt to ask," one of the young women said.

"Ask what?" Trevor thought perhaps he had missed some clue or sign about what she was talking about; he knew women sometimes expected men to know what they were thinking without their ever saying it, but that was the line he had never crossed with them, out of courtesy and propriety.

"You know. Permission. So you could feel it was proper," the other young woman said as she finished lighting the candles and moved back to stand before Trevor.

"Proper and courteous," the first young woman said as she finished straightening the duvet and pillows on the second of two beds before turning to face Trevor from where she stood, "as though you hadn't already done it with countless others before us."

Trevor was torn, and fighting with himself mentally to determine what, precisely, they were talking about. Considering the situation and environment they were in, and the implied actions to come, they could be talking about sex or some sex act or permission for some other related thing. The way they had implicated that he'd "already done it with countless others" before them could be a statement about their perception of sexual prowess and experience in him, and if that was the case, he may be in for some trouble when they learned he had never really been with anyone sexually before. Trevor certainly couldn't think of a proper and courteous way to ask two women permission to make love to them.

On the other hand, their statements had almost frighteningly echoed words and thoughts from his own mind, as though they had been reading his mind and responding to his thoughts. In which case, they knew exactly what he was worried about, and it wasn't exactly the sex, but something much more broadly reaching in their relationship. And whether it was frightening or relieving had something to do with whether they had already actually been reading his thoughts – he had not detected even a gentle touch of his mind by another since the end of the dodgeball match, even with all the techniques, skill and experience of Sunshine added to his own natural talent for Mentalism. If they could read Trevor's highly attuned and sensitive mind without his slightest notice, what else could they do that he didn't know about?

"You can't find out if you don't ask." Both of them smiled warmly, invitingly, at Trevor, waiting for him to ask a question he wasn't sure he knew how to ask.

"May I..." he tried to begin, but wasn't so sure he wanted the answer to the question he most wanted to ask.

"What?"

"May I..." On one hand, if he asked about reading their minds and they were expecting him to ask about sex, the conversation that would inevitably ensue might put them out of the mood, and his hormones wanted no part of that.

"What?" The one of them standing nearer to Trevor walked slowly backwards to one of the beds and sat down, waiting for his question.

"I mean…" On the other hand, if he asked about sex and they were expecting him to ask about reading their minds, they would already know everything he'd been thinking, and it wouldn't be long before they got to that same long conversation after all, which in addition to a faux pax about his asking might almost necessarily put them out of the mood.

The one that was still standing sat down on her own bed, her body facing her sister, her head still facing Trevor. "What?"

"May I…" On another hand, if they had the conversation about reading minds and he found out they had definitely been reading his mind the whole time, and who knows for how long before that, and that he had been avoiding it unnecessarily – not to mention the fact that if their level of skill was so much higher than his that he could only ever know what they wanted him to know without his injuring them – he wasn't entirely sure he wanted to go down that road at all. And now he was confusing himself with his own thoughts of how to figure it all out.

"Yes… ?"

He decided to try thinking a question, the result of which would tell him much, and thought quite clearly "Are you two reading my mind?" A response in thought came back to him, like the harmonization of two voices as ripples on the surface of his own jumbling thoughts, "Yes."

"Fuck."

"Soon." Both girls giggled after speaking in synchronous response.

"I don't know about that. I mean…"

"We know what you mean," the twin on the left said.

The twin on the right continued, "and if you weren't so polite and careful, you'd know what we meant, too."

"But I thought… I couldn't tell you were… " Trevor was fighting becoming flabbergasted, but triumphed over their coy smiles and upper hand long enough to ask them forcefully, "Why can't I tell when you're reading my mind?"

"We're twins."

"Haven't you ever studied twins?"

"Not … well, not really."

"We know."

"We'll explain."

"You've probably heard that some twins believe they can tell when the other is in danger,"

"And that some, well outside of any knowledge of the science of Mentalism, believe they can read each other's thoughts,"

"And finish each other's sentences."

"Like you two are doing now."

"Right. Like we're doing now. But we had an advantage over all those other twins, because we…"

"Were raised by parents who were experts in the science of Mentalism…"

"Wait, your parents are the same Jay and Emma who literally wrote the book on modern Mentalism!? I thought their names were a coincidence! Are they downstairs right now? I'd love to meet them."

"We know you would, and yes, they're the same Jay and Emma who documented the techniques of Maheu'le before his unfortunate death."

"Exactly! I remember working with Maheu'le… It would be nice to remember that with someone who can really understand."

"We're getting off topic here,"

"You wanted to know about our Mentalism. Jay and Em are out of town for the next week or two anyway, you can meet them another time."

"Okay, okay, right. So. Twins have a natural affinity to Mentalism, and you were raised in it by experts."

"That's almost right. Identical twins have a natural affinity to having easy contact with their twin's mind, not necessarily with anyone else's."

"But more right than you know, because it was expert guidance that allowed us to move beyond just reading each other's minds,"

"To reading other people's minds,"

"And then to communicating with other minds." This was the harmonic double-voice flowing across the surface of his mind again. Trevor shivered.

They switched back to normal speech, the twin on the right saying "all before we were old enough for pre-school."

"Which posed a problem. Most people don't learn Mentalism as a first language, and as you know,"

"Contacting the minds of the unready or untrained can be very dangerous."

"Even deadly. And we were only a few years old – our judgment wasn't exactly the most sound."

"So our parents kept us out of school for a while, training us further, sharing memories and experiences, and working with us until we could practice Mentalism gently."

"Very gently."

"So gently that all but the most sensitive mind would not notice us at all, and the chance of a reactionary injury dropped almost to zero. Which was what our parents had been working towards,"

"So we could go to school with other children without endangering them."

"Or our teachers."

"I see."

"So that with practice,"

"And experience,"

"We learned to be very gentle indeed." Trevor felt a sensation like something warm and soft running backwards across the top of his head and down and down and down his back, like being petted by some large invisible hand, and the girls giggled again.

"And you've been reading my mind for how long, exactly?"

"Since we first saw you."

"We liked you right away, and wanted to know if you liked us too,"

"Before we tried to approach you,"

"So we read your first impression of us and knew you liked us too."

"And you never stopped…" Trevor was beginning to grasp what they were telling him.

"Well, we knew how you felt about not reading our minds,"

"It's cute how you don't want to risk somehow upsetting us or betraying us or controlling us or whatever it is you think reading our minds might do,"

"But it's just silly, really. You know enough about Mentalism to know that there's a huge difference between monitoring surface thoughts or even accessing standard memories and actually issuing commands, directing thoughts, and anything that can cause real damage or influence us directly or indirectly."

"We also know that you've never really been in a relationship with anyone,"

"Let alone two people at once,"

"And that you're just working from cultural and absorbed memories to try to behave reasonably with us."

"We think it's very admirable, how polite and genteel you've been. We do appreciate it,"

"But from now on, we expect you to know what we're thinking."

"You have a big advantage over most men, you know. Their women expect them to read their minds even without Mentalism." Both girls giggled again.

Trevor was taken somewhat aback, but tried to roll with it and not seem caught off guard. His hormones were still trying to get him to get past this psychological nonsense and get into bed with these willing young women, but his sense of ethics and propriety kept trying to force him to work out more of the details of what they wanted from him and how he should respond. He still felt it was an invasion to go into their minds like that. He still regretted all the time he'd spent unknowingly invading real people's lives and thoughts before he'd learned what he had been doing, though, on a subtle level, Trevor was beginning to see that this reaction to his own past wrongdoing had perhaps moved him too far to see the truth about what might be right or reasonable.

"Why don't you just take a peek to start? It's okay."

"We want you to."

Trevor closed his eyes. He didn't want to be looking at them when he started this, he wasn't sure he wanted to be doing this at all. Trevor also knew that for this to go well, he'd have to take this first step. He relaxed his mind and opened his thoughts as Sunshine had been trained to do by Maheu'le. And there their thoughts were, very near to him, very clear. There was something altogether strange to him about their thoughts, something unexpected, something beautiful.

Instead of two distinct sets of thoughts coming from their two minds, instead of a disconnected jumble of thoughts and worries and memories all streaming out almost without direction and usually unfocused, instead of a single mental semi-conscious voiceover coming from each of them in their own voices, there was a single harmonious dual voice coming from what seemed to be neither one of them and both of them with perfect overlap and no echo or apparent mental back-and-forth of thoughts to reach agreement. They seemed both to think the same thoughts at the same time, and their thoughts were uncannily ordered and complete, which was a thing of such unexpected beauty to Trevor that he didn't realize how unnatural such a thing must be. It was as though there was a single mind controlling their two bodies, and like their two distinct minds were in perfect harmony at the same time. Trevor was so in awe of the context that their mind or minds created that he was deaf to the content at first.

"Trev? Trev… Trev." Finally his name, projected to him in their private thoughts, got his attention. He responded in thought, "Love."

"See, there's nothing to be afraid of. We're here with you," and with his eyes still closed, Trevor felt a small hand on each of his arms as their thoughts continued addressing him. He hadn't noticed them thinking about getting up and coming over to him, but was completely enraptured by the strange beauty of their thoughts. "Come sit down, relax," and the hands were pulling him forward, walking slowly towards their beds. He didn't have to open his eyes to cross that short distance, or to allow himself to be turned around and pushed backwards onto the bed by two

170

gentle hands on his chest, and he certainly didn't have to open his eyes to realize that the beds had moved or changed since he'd closed his eyes. "We pushed them together," their thoughts came to him in response, "so we'd have more room to be together."

Trevor liked the idea of that, and having their two soft, warm bodies laying down alongside him, both left and right, and having their hands begin to explore slowly the surface of his body certainly pushed worries about reading their minds from his focus. He was still worried on some level about their literal mental prowess somehow posing a danger to him, but the strain of intuition that had put two and two together, that they had been keeping their expert Mentalism and their connection to the leading experts on the subject a secret which might be the tip of a very dark iceberg of secrets, was silenced by the blood flowing less through his brain and more into his growing arousal.

"That's the idea, Trev. Relax." Their thoughts were becoming like a familiar blanket to him rather than the foreign work of art they had first appeared, surrounding his own thoughts, he began to feel his mind harmonizing with their synchronicity. "Good. Now, would you like to see what you've been missing?"

"Missing? What have I been missing?" Trevor thought, increasingly excited and half asleep at once.

"This," and then instead of the steady stream of thoughts interspersed with conscious communication from their minds, Trevor was experiencing their memories from their own point of view. It began with the first time they saw him, and already it was disorienting to him. Instead of serially reliving one of their memories and then the other and then reconciling them as he had done with other people's memories of single events to experience them multiply, he was simultaneously seeing through four eyes, hearing though four ears, feeling with two bodies the same moment in memory. Layered on top of this was something complex and subtle in its elegance, as each of their minds while experiencing its own perceptions was experiencing the other's slightly different perceptions on top of and through her own mind's eye, and on top of that was part of a single

171

consciousness that encompassed both of their thoughts as the singular whole he had first experienced when opening up to them. Making the whole thing more intense was the fact that on top of the perfect realization of three simultaneous layers of the twin's perceptions, emotions, and thoughts, he was experiencing with his own body their four hands slowly and carefully beginning to undress him, reaching into his overrobe and unbuttoning his underrobe, then gently pulling his arms one at a time out of both robes' sleeves at once while he lay on his back on their bed, on the robes, knowing what it was like when they'd first seen him across a crowded school hallway.

In the memory, as soon as Trevor made eye contact with one, then the other of them, then back and forth and back and forth between them as though trying to give equal time to each of them as he bared his soul to them in a single glance, they had each and both felt a surge of what he now, and they at the time, had immediately recognized as love at first sight, and with almost no time between that surge and their gentle reaching out to his mind, he experienced the oddness that was experiencing his own mind through the Mentalism of another for the first time as they searched to find out if his reaction to them could possibly equate to their reaction to him. It had.

That memory was just the beginning. Trevor soon found himself swimming in a sea of every time they had seen him or thought of him or been near him, singly or doubly, and every thought and feeling they had had at the time, layer upon layer. Hour after hour, day after day, month after month, flooding and rushing through and into his mind with nearly the speed he had absorbed Sunshine's entire history, their lives since he had entered the scene came to him in a new way. The flow of information Trevor was experiencing that was their past soon became enough to drown out what was happening to his physical body in the present, so that by the time their flow of memories caught up with what was going on and he experienced their undressing him from their perspective, it was the first time he realized they had got him down to his undershirt and short pants, the rest of his uniform tossed casually to the floor beside their joined beds. He opened his eyes.

Two soft, round faces he only imagined he could tell one from the other were above his, smiling. One of them crossed to meet him, growing to fill Trevor's perception before connecting with him lips on lips in a deep and passionate kiss he could feel four different ways as through his own body's sensitized nerves, those of the young woman kissing him, through the eyes of the other twin leaning over the two of them watching the kiss and experiencing it as well, and through the duality of consciousness that was the twins' two minds' harmony. There was no parallel in his experience to that kiss, even in the experiences he had absorbed from their memories of kissing him in the past, as there were still only three layers in each of those unreconciled memories while all four were present and active within his experience in this moment. Trevor felt as though he should be overwhelmed, but was somehow not only able to cope with all this, but before that first kiss broke off in panting breath and a stirring in three sets of loins, he had already become somewhat accustomed to it all.

Except then the other twin took the first's place at his lips and the experience was very similar in its complexity but also subtly different enough that it was wholly new while still recognizable – he knew briefly that the one whose tongue was tangling tantalizingly with his was Elle's by the differences in the way they kissed – a kiss that built on the former as though by the same person while starting from a new basis because it was by a different person. Then, instead of just experiencing Kay watching the two of them kissing, Trevor, while kissing Elle and while through her mind experiencing what it was like to be Elle kissing him, experienced the sensation of Kay beginning to slowly and sensually undress herself, running her own hands over the curves of her body as she went for the cumulative gratification of all three of them, idling her soft fingertips here or there as feedback from her shared mental experience with Elle and the relatively rough mental processes of Trevor informed her of increasing mutual arousal. This new addition of sensation transformed this second kiss into a

173

remarkable and finally literally overwhelming sexual encounter that with no direct stimulation to the common erogenous zones of his body lifted him to an orgasm that rocked through his body and into his short pants while flowing also through both Kay and Elle, leading them irrevocably into a chain reaction of orgasms, one sister then the other clenching, trembling, squealing and delighting as their bodies gave in to the pleasure they all shared, a loop of building sensations that subsumed their shared, quadruply-layered consciousness until it was replaced thought by thought with a glowing, radiating warmth and light devoid of reason or complexity.

As the blissful oblivion receded from them, their still-shared minds all realized that they must have passed out, collapsing in a heap across each other in various states of undress and intermingling of limbs, and only slowly did they begin again to move, enjoying the mirror-in-a-mirror sensations of skin sliding across skin without really being able to discern whose sensations were whose through the wall of pleasure that still engulfed them. "Wow" uttered from an unknown mouth in a female voice, though the level to which they were all in each others minds did not help clarify who had thought it first or whose lips had actually parted to breathe that soft exclamation of surprise.

"Did you know it would be like this," Trevor asked, but it was clear without him having to think it consciously that what he really wanted to know was "have you two done this before?"

"Only in our imaginations,"

"And dreams,"

"Dreaming of you."

Trevor tried for a millisecond to be flattered and to disbelieve their claim that they had, in fact, dreamed of him, but before he could even properly form the thought, the twins were playing back their memories of their 'wet' dreams of being with him. It was surreal on top of surreal. Trevor tried to pay close attention to it all, to discern in some way what they literally dreamed lovemaking could be like, but all the while the two of them proceeded with undressing each other as caressingly and stimulatingly as they could

174

manage without sending him into a state of shock as he lay below and between them on the bed, the edges and sleeves of disrobed clothes brushing against his body as they made their way from each young woman down to the floor around the beds, and he couldn't quite pay full attention to the dreams.

What he did catch was almost enough to push him over the edge again, and it certainly put some ideas in his head about how the next few hours might proceed. He opened his eyes just in time to close them again as the two young women each kissed him briefly again in turn.

"Our dream come true," they both said at once.

He knew without opening his own eyes that he was in bed with two women wearing only a single scrap of clothing each, as he had fully experienced every step that had got them there through their own sensations and by seeing it through their own eyes and by feeling each moment of increasing release as layer after layer of clothing that he had not noticed was constricting until it was removed slipped, slithered, unclasped and shimmied off their soft, curvaceous forms had revealed it to him as though he were taking off his own sweaters, shirts, skirts, pants, and brassieres, but when he opened his eyes to see their nakedness in its nearly-full glory before and above him it was a totally new experience for all of them. Trevor had never, with his own eyes, seen a woman's naked form in person, let alone two such unblemished examples of the female form so eagerly presented to him and neither of the twins had ever had anyone of the opposite sex see them so exposed. More than that, instead of merely seeing his eyes traveling the slopes and curves of their bodies and hoping for the best, their mental connection allowed them to know exactly what Trevor's reactions to each detail of each of their bodies were as he had them, such that any fears or self-esteem issues they may have had before revealing themselves to him dissolved in the raw passion elicited in him at the sight of their bare flesh, and they had no shame or doubts about their physical appearance for the remainder of their time together.

Four hands grabbed the hem of his undershirt and Trevor lay there relaxed, allowing his arms to be raised above his head as Kay and Elle stripped the garment across his chest and up over his head, returning him to the state of cleanliness he had been in from the waist up before putting the shirt on while exposing that clean pink skin to their view for the first time. For him, being seen bare-chested was not the same as it was for them, and in experiencing their experiencing it and from both sides, they all knew that the parallel moment of apprehension about nakedness was about to meet him as their hands, having tossed the shirt aside, trailed teasingly down his now-nude flesh to grasp the waistband of his short pants. Bolstered perhaps by the positive feelings of self-worth that his own scrutiny of their nakedness had generated and looped back to him, the trepidation Trevor felt was easily overcome, especially in combination with their three-fold desire to become totally physically intimate, as they had already mentally and emotionally become through Mentalism. Trevor lifted his hips slightly as their many soft fingers slipped slightly inside his final covering of fabric and began to slide his short pants down his legs.

Kay and Elle were eager and certain of their course of action, and while they had seen pictures and diagrams and absorbed memories of men's genitalia, they had never seen a penis face to face. As they pulled Trevor's short pants down, exposing inch after inch of his skin and pubic hair, a mixed feeling of wanting to go ahead and what felt almost like fear nearly stopped their motion before his semi-erect member finally began to be exposed to the light and air. Since he had already ejaculated from the intensity of their first truly shared kiss there should have been a messy mop of tangled hair and drying seminal fluids to meet them, but through the literal magic which enchanted his dodgeball uniform, that was all cleaned up as the short pants made their way off his body. As soon as his partial erection sprang free of its former prison, the slowness with which the twins had been removing his final scrap of clothing disappeared, and he was totally naked in their bed in the very next moment possible.

In that moment a great many things were bubbling up, boiling through their multiply-layered shared consciousnesses. His manhood, while still not fully aroused, was bigger than they had expected. This thought flowing to him made any trepidation he might have had socially and culturally embedded into him melt away as nothing. At the same time, with perspective and logic and other people's memories, their minds knew immediately that he was not – as some people and beings certainly were – too big for them to handle comfortably, which was a relief for them and another calming wave of pleasant anticipation cresting across Trevor's mind as it was across theirs. Before their hands were able to reach it physically, their minds and desires reaching out towards his cock had brought him to an almost painfully full erection.

Trevor had, on many, many occasions, had the experience of "handling" himself for sexual gratification, and felt he had a "good grasp" on what he did and didn't like in the ways that hands could stimulate him. In the seconds leading up to the first time another person, in this case two other people at once, would touch him in that way, Trevor seemed automatically to run through all his best and worst memories of stimulating himself, literally educating Kay and Elle in nearly every success and failure in his solo sexual career. Of course, when those two hands grasped his dick, Elle's all the way down to the base of it where her fingers mingled with his coarsest hairs, Kay's stacked just above that one but the two of them still unable to encompass the entire length with both their hands, the softness and smallness of their hands and the ginger, gentle way they took hold of him was entirely different from anything he had ever felt on his own, and simply did not equate directly to any of the information he had shared with them. Elle and Kay had never held a cock in their hands before, but his own memories of holding and otherwise working with his erection were so numerous and detailed that they felt even before they touched it that they knew his flesh as well as they could have without their own second and third hand information, but then as they each wrapped their hand around his girth, the tips of their fingers only slightly

177

touching their thumbs as they wrapped all the way around, the feeling was almost entirely foreign and unexpected to them. And to Trevor, who was experiencing holding his own cock in two entirely new ways as they were experiencing it for the first time; it was almost as though he were holding another man's penis, he had never seen or felt a man's hard shaft from the two new perspectives he now did.

Their desire to please him, his desire to fulfill their desire, the confusion of the definition of self, and all the various sexual fantasies that Trevor and Kay and Elle had ever had, joining together in a mercurial bath of heady sexuality all around and throughout their conscious minds led Trevor to do something he had simply not expected. As though through his own eyes and with his own hands, Trevor was Kay and was Elle, holding a young man's heat and excitement hard against his own soft hand, and wanting nothing more, Trevor moved in and leaned closer and wrapped his soft lips around the exposed head and inches of the irresistible cock before him. The scent that filled his lungs was a musk he recognized but which had an altogether different effect on him than he was used to as he breathed it deeply in and out through his tiny nose. The taste on his tongue was new to him, salty but not quite like sweat, a flavour that seemed to match the feeling of the flesh in his mouth in its complexity; being hard and soft, sweet and salty, loose and tight, strong and subtle, rough and smooth, all at once. He could not get enough of it, trying to pull more cock up into his mouth as he sucked on what he could get past his unfamiliarly soft, full lips – it was as though he had just discovered that the true purpose of his life was to have this man inside him, filling him in every way possible, and wanted to make up for lost time. He slowly bobbed his head up and down, taking in a little more meat with every motion, inching his hand down over his sister's hand as he moved it out of the way of his mouth's ministrations.

It was the sensation of his testicles tightening into him, his body preparing to release its seed that drew Trevor first out of his reverie state through which he was experiencing and controlling Kay's body as though it were his own and his own were someone else, and becoming

178

suddenly aware of the other things he and Kay were experiencing certainly did nothing to pull him completely out of Kay's experience fellating him, though it did bring more focus onto the experience of being fellated by Kay, and as his spunk burst forth and his body released another dose of endorphins and hormones into his bloodstream, he felt and tasted with Kay's mouth exactly what it was like to have a man's cum explode into that hungry hole he had turned her head into from inside her, what semen felt like sliding down her throat even as he felt it rising up his urethra, entering and leaving his sensation at the same time, and the satisfaction not only of being pleased but more so of pleasing the object of love's affection. The whole experience of giving herself completely over to Trevor had been like flipping a switch in Kay, turning her on to a whole new brand of pleasure that was somewhat disconnected from the warmth and intensity she certainly felt growing within her body and the electricity that seemed to be running continuously between her nipples as they brushed up and down against Trevor's legs or the bed or her sister's arm and her own pelvic area and back again, more like fulfillment through selflessness rather than her own selfish physical desires – Kay felt as though she were on the verge of a soul-orgasm. Elle, whose body had had very little to do with what was going on a that moment, had experienced the entire thing as though she were top and bottom, in control and controlled, cause of and recipient of sensations that were new to all three of them, giving and receiving and being transported to new levels of sensation and consciousness and then at the most intense instant, she was right there with her own hand, her own nerves sensing the rhythmic pumping flow of his ejaculate's path under her palm and her sister's mouth and throat's matching motions against the back of her hand and arm. All these various sensations were more than enough to bring Elle to another orgasm of her own, her free hand being drawn by it finally down to her own moist underwear as she felt that uncontrollable tightening and relaxing and spasming in her abdomen, back, legs, arms, and what felt like every other musculature in her body, down to the tiny constrictions and releases of her blood vessels running for miles and miles up and down her body and connecting that burning reality of pleasure to every inch of her being, inside and out.

Finally the flow of fluids and pleasure between them began to wane after an instant that seemed much longer to each of them in their convoluted communal experience than could have been possible for a single mind in a single body going through the precise same actions but from such a limited perspective. Trevor took a moment just to inhale and exhale deeply and deliberately as Kay continued to orally tend his flagging erection, seeming to want to locate every last drop of cum that could be found or licked or sucked or tricked out of him and into her, almost humming with that unchecked newfound desire that neither one of them would be able to identify the true origin of, him or her or Elle or some other combination – just that it was insatiable. As Trevor's hardness and Kay's attention thereof was winding down, Elle's manual stimulation of her own body was not-so-gradually winding up; she had already torn the frustrating, constricting barrier of her sopping-wet panties from her hips and had two of one hand's fingers plunged into herself while the other hand gently but rapidly rubbed the tiny nub of her clitoris. Trevor, still just trying to breathe, was feeling everything Elle was feeling as she tried to ride the wave of pleasure generated by Kay's mouth on his cock through to another orgasm, that still-shocking softness of her own hand on her own skin, the less-central intensity of her sexual experience building throughout her whole body as she really began to grind into her clit in earnest, and an entirely new sensation that he had had an idea of from Sunshine's memories but had never really experienced as immediately and as personally as he did through Elle and the extra layer of the twins' dual consciousness experiencing it again – penetration. Kay was still lapping at his balls and his now-limp cock, so he knew from that sensation there was nothing of his own body to penetrate, but there was still the overlapping sensation of Elle's fingers pumping in and out of her own pussy with a deliberate rhythm separate from that of her other hand on her clitoris which seemed to be his own hand reaching down between his own legs and reaching somehow into his own body in an altogether pleasant way he

180

had never in his most intense fantasies expected to experience. Trevor continued to simply work on remembering to breathe with his own lungs at a reasonable rate for a few moments as he took in that furious feeling of Elle's fingers fingering herself and the frighteningly fulfilling feeling of being filled, and hardly noticed what it was like for Kay to be exploring her way slowly up his body, kissing here and there and everywhere as she gradually crawled along the length of his torso until he was looking down at his own face through her eyes and felt himself through her moving in to kiss him.

"I've never kissed anyone but you," the words were barely breathed out, just as their lips were making the softest contact, her lower lip like a soft feather's touch as it alighted back and forth across his lips at the edge of perception, propelled by the words that would have been truthful coming from Kay, but which had escaped her throat under Trevor's mental control. From those same lips, she responded to him, "and neither have I," and then she kissed him in earnest.

As they kissed, rough and hard and with a new level of awakened passion within the two of them, they both felt one of Elle's hands move up her body to rub, caress, squeeze, pinch, and twist lovingly her own breasts and nipples, and while Kay was momentarily distracted by the shockingly pleasant sensations of her sister's highly sensitized body, Trevor flipped her over onto her back as he rolled over on top of her without their lips' engaging contact ever severing, and the difference between the feeling of her weight atop him and his weight above her was the first thing he noticed when they finally broke contact and she began to try to draw breath again. He quickly lifted himself lighter above her and began tracing the course that she had mapped out on his body with her lips in reverse down her own pale, soft skin, kissing and licking and breathing lightly across every delicate and sensitive spot that met him on his casual course down her neck and shoulders, across her bosom which was nearly overwhelmed with the contrast between the sensation of his soft lips and her sister's rough treatment of her own body, down between and underneath her breasts where she had not expected to find so electrifying a reaction as she did, across her flat tummy to her belly button, then circling down and around the outward curves of her hips. Then, just as she thought he would reach the corresponding point of his journey to her own oral attentions of his body, his lips continued down her legs, paying special attention to the skin just outside the borders of her still-worn panties but never making contact with the most sensitive areas it barely covered, and then made his way down the insides of her spread thighs to nibble gently on the inside curve of her knee before continuing down her calf to her ankle and foot.

Now, Trevor did not in any way fetishize a woman's feet – he was too inexperienced at this point in his life to have developed such a strange fascination – but he had years of experience with the reflexology that Ms. Charming had studied as a hobby and to satisfy her husband, and as he reached Kay's feet that background seemed to take over his actions automatically. Both his hands worked and massaged her feet and ankles gently, locating and working with trouble points until her feet were at a state of neutral balance within only a few minutes. Then his fingers applied pressure and energies to very specific locations on Kay's feet to stimulate the free flow of energy through her body to activate desired responses within her. After energizing her muscles and speeding her circulatory system and forcing her respiratory system to cleanse itself through deep breaths and a little rough coughing before taking in deep, new, clean air, his hands followed a much-practiced routine of renewal and sexual fervor that Sunshine was especially fond of, and just after paralyzing every voluntary action of her body from the neck down, he stimulated the most powerful orgasm within her that her body would ever know, but which she was unable to respond to physically. Elle, who had been riding just below the edge of orgasm the entire time, keeping herself stimulated, but not too stimulated, by her own practiced rhythms of manual stimulation would have been lifted far above the pleasure threshold by what Kay was going through, except that suddenly, for the first time she could remember it happening, Elle was not sharing Kay's mind. Trevor had locked Kay off from all outside mental influence so that she would be trapped completely in

182

ongoing ultimate pleasure – she could not move or sense anything outside her own mind, her own body's unstopping orgasm, and she could not move her body, either. From his own memories of Sunshine's experiences, Trevor knew that it was like being in a sensory deprivation chamber in some respects, except where instead of feeling nothing at all, one felt only pleasure greater than was possible in the constant deluge of other sensations that being connected to the world presented. He knew it was unbelievably assailing, and when he brought her out of it he was sure she would agree.

Kay's sudden disconnection from her mind was enough to cause Elle to freeze completely in place, as though paralyzed in the same stroke that had paralyzed her sister, but Trevor was not slow to move from Kay's feet to begin concentrating on Elle. He started at her feet, since he was already at that end of the bed, not bothering with reflexology, but just kissing and caressing his way up her unmoving legs to meet her hand, frozen knuckles-deep in the folds and depths of her vagina, and the puddle of juices that had formed on the bed where her legs came together above it. He dove in, using the wide flat surface of his whole tongue to lap at every hot and glistening surface between her legs, bringing Elle at least back to low, shallow breathing again as he took in her potent juices with stroke after stroke of his mouth's thick muscle. As he continued taking in and tasting the liquids leaking from her love-hole, Trevor began to slowly move Elle's hand out of her, cleaning it with his tongue as inch by inch of her pruned fingers escaped the confines of her tightly clenching cunt. When the very tips of her fingers were finally free and cleaned by Trevor's tongue-bath, Elle was just recovered enough that she pulled it almost powerlessly along the delicate petals of flesh of her labia to her clitoris and began a slow, deep grind against it with her weakened, lost hand, half-unconscious still.

Trevor began eating Elle eagerly, using the half-numb, half-aware trickle of sensations that Elle was gradually beginning to experience in more and more detail and intensity to guide his passion for pleasing her, and as his lips and tongue and jaw worked together on her most private and receptive nerves, his hands moved up and down and

183

around whatever they could reach, slipping across the outside of her bare hips, squeezing down on the globes of her round ass cheeks, trailing the backs of his nails upward along the undersides of her raised thighs, and on and on along and around the less-focused on areas of her body as his mouth made intense work of exploring and enjoying every detail of her entirely edible pussy, inside and out. Her breathing came deeper and faster as he worked her into a frenzy and back into consciousness, and in the absence of her sister's mind, Elle reached out to Trevor's mind as though to bond with it in the way she no longer could with Kay's.

Trevor didn't see any harm in it, so he allowed Elle's mind to latch on to his through that somehow-still-present extra layer of shared consciousness that she had always had in common with her twin, and suddenly he found his own mind subject to a new level of control he had not anticipated. It was suddenly as though he could no longer make any decisions on his own, except that he was definitely still a part of every decision made and now also a part of every decision Elle made as well, so the shift, while taking away his own self-direction, did not seem entirely to strip him of his decision-making abilities. The triplicate-nature of Kay and Elle's shared consciousness seemed so much more natural to Trevor once he was actually experiencing it from the inside instead of as an outside observer. The extra layer of thought that was neither his nor hers but that seemed to be some combination of the two turned out to be the true guiding force of both of their actions and feelings, taking the place of individual responsibility and choice in a form of total surrender that Trevor welcomed wholeheartedly under the circumstances.

The cunnilingus continued completely under the control of the third consciousness, neither Trevor nor Elle really guiding the stimulation, both of them experiencing giving and receiving perfect pleasure as though they were both in both bodies and yet actively controlling neither body as he licked and sucked and gripped and filled and she writhed and shook and squeezed and ground and they both slid closer and closer to another orgasmic burst. From the

184

outside, Trevor had thought the three minds of the twins, their two individual minds and the dual, shared mind between them, had been totally in sync and almost the same entity. From the inside of the same mental arrangement he could tell that each of the three minds appeared to be quite distinct from the others.

Even as he relented his body completely to the third mind, his mind was free to think and feel and explore on its own, as though the third mind was automatically drawing on his unconscious and emotional desires without the need for his directed input. He began exploring Elle's mind on his own for the first time as his body tirelessly stimulated and satisfied her body, taking his first consciously-directed look at her memories. Except he couldn't seem to find anything.

It wasn't exactly like his first experiences trying to find information in people's minds, before he had absorbed Sunshine's centuries of study and practice at delving effectively into the mind to retrieve what you want without causing damage or coming up empty-handed, where if he hadn't known what to think to wonder about he wouldn't have been able to know what they'd known – instead, he was using techniques that should have given him a plethora of information about her, the first kiss, the first happy memory, the way she thinks about her father or the way she remembers her last school before transferring, and he came up with nothing. It was as though she didn't have any of these memories stored in her own mind at all. Trevor tried more general techniques, to get anything, any memories, even the ones Elle and Kay had already played back for him of their experiences with and about him, but found nothing at all. Her mind was there, and was active and felt just like anyone else's mind, but didn't seem to have any memories within it. A blank slate.

An orgasm ripped through them. Between their dual semi-conscious control of their bodies they must have done something right, it was like someone had hooked positive electrodes up to her nipples and negative contacts to his testicles and the electricity had made a straight path from his groin up his body, through his mouth, into her pelvic region, and up to her rock-hard nipples, a chain of sensation probably impossible without their interlocked minds and bodies or some equivalent co-mingling of real senses and the experiences of another's body as intimately as they were at that moment. As the burning flame of pleasure began to subsist, Trevor tried to see if he could detect any features in Elle's mind at all. The third tier of consciousness guiding their bodies spread his attention from her swollen pussy lips and hyper-sensitive clitoris to all the sensitive skin so protected from normal contact by the panties she wasn't wearing.

Trevor couldn't make heads or tails of Elle's mind. His lips began trailing a path of kisses through the forest of her soft pubic hair. Every normal feature he reached out to get information about or to feel the contours of came up empty or blank or featureless. His tongue explored the shallow depths of her navel while his fingers traced soft trails up and down her sides, slick with sweat. There was something wrong; there was nothing there at all where Elle's individuality should have been, and where every feature should have been defined and every facet that should have shined, there was simply nothing. Trevor's hands slid up and around the circumference of her breasts, one in each hand, and softly massaged around and around them as his kisses worked their way slowly across her abdomen towards those strange hills of glory rising above it. He turned his attention backwards and around and felt like he was doing somersaults and yoga and turning his eyes around to peer into the back of his head all at once as he tried mentally to 'see' the third-layer mind that was directing his tongue to explore the delicate curves defined by the meeting of her breasts with her chest below; it was like trying to grasp a gnat or fly with two fingers.

Dry lips gently gumming down on stiff nipples and pulling back, a subtle vibration of friction in elasticity and a rippling wave just beyond fathoming as they rebounded the tiny distance back down. Finally, Trevor is able to get a glimpse of the mind he had totally surrendered himself to, and it is harder for him to comprehend than the emptiness of Elle's, but in sharp relief to that sad façade. His lips tracing the curve of her collarbone and gently brushing against the

186

skin defined by her tensed tendons underneath, then taking her whole chin into his mouth and slowly drawing back while closing his jaw, coming to a soft lingering kiss on that pointed detail at the edge of her statuesque face. It was like the feeling he'd had in the co-ed dodgeball game of peering into dozens of minds at once and having full access to dozens more, but instead of all the minds working towards the goal of winning a dodgeball game, these minds seemed to be working to stop him from looking at them. Suddenly he felt the head of his penis pressing hard and hot against the eager, lusciously lubricated lips of Elle's vasoactive vagina. Trevor didn't know what his mind was perceiving, exactly, but it wasn't the mind of one or even two young women in love with him, and he certainly wasn't ready to give up his virginity to the machinations of some devious collective he didn't begin to understand – he disappeared instantly, before the pressure that third-tier mind was exerting through his hips could move him half an inch.

"Trev?!?" Sunshine exclaimed at his sudden, totally nude appearance before her, on her living room floor.

"Auughhh…." Trevor was no longer physically in the presence of either twin, but that mind that had so completely interlocked with his own in the absence of Kay's mind was still connecting him with Elle and still had a strong grip on his ability to make decisions. His body twitched and flailed in short arcs as the two forces fought within him to take control, his limbs apparently in seizure and his mouth unable to speak.

Sunshine practically leapt out of her seat, tossing her Echelar & Spink aside as she rushed to Trevor's side, trying to grab him, to get him to lay flat, to try to determine what was going on. She began to reach out with her mind to see if she could detect the source of the abnormality.

"DON'T!" The screamed syllable was definitely his voice, under his control, and matched the pleading in his eyes, but he was apparently unable to articulate further. Ms. Charming instantly let go of his body and moved slightly back in body and mind, still in arm's reach and ready thought, but unsure of how to proceed.

She spoke to him, hoping her voice would calm him, help him with whatever he was going through. "I can see you're having some trouble, Trev. I'm glad you felt comfortable coming to me. I'll help in any way I can." Trevor's body became more and more tense, the fight moving towards paralysis as balance began to be reached between Trevor's totally unprepared mind and the interloping mental presence latched on to it and his body. Sunshine continued speaking in smooth, mellifluous tones, "I heard you won both games today, Trev. Well, not so much won the second as created the perfect game with the second, but that may be more impressive than a simple win, in the end. Congratulations. I never had much taste for the sport myself... always reminded me of …. Nevermind. Congratulations, anyway. A real triumph."

Even as his head was turned back and forth and away from her, Trevor managed to keep his eyes locked onto Sunshine's eyes, tracking them through sheer force of will. When his body seemed finally to be totally seized up, he let out a long, slow breath, first through his upper teeth pressed against his lower lip slightly, then just an open breathing, and it ended with a punctuating sound like he'd touched just the tip of his tongue to the roof of his mouth or the back of his upper teeth just as he'd run out of breath and moved his eyes from hers to point straight down along the length of his frozen body. If he hadn't so clearly indicated that she shouldn't peer into his mind, she would have known sooner and more exactly what he'd wanted, but she got it soon enough, and moved around to look at his feet.

Carefully moving them to see all sides of his feet, Sunshine did not see anything there, no clue or mark or blemish, and wasn't sure how to proceed. Then Ms. Charming remembered that Trevor had absorbed all of her memories at once, and in coming to her he had probably done so based on something he knew from those memories, so she thought about what sorts of magical remedies for intense mental attack or paralyzation she might know that related to the feet. If it had not been for her eyes returning again and again to the distraction of his still-very-erect penis, Ms. Charming might not have come to the proper thought for a very long time. She immediately took each of his feet in her hands in turn and applied the pressures and motions that would remove him from a paralyzed state of ultimate pleasure that she and her late husband had been so fond of helping each other achieve. He didn't even twitch. He didn't even blink. That wasn't it.

She tried running through the entire exercise from the beginning, thinking that perhaps he needed some intermediate step to be freed. She began with the general foot massage, his feet so tense that it may have done more harm than good, but she went carefully though the entire routine. She cleared out his lungs and filled him with fresh air, increased his circulation, and on and on until she reached the point that would normally have paralyzed him and simultaneously put him into a continuous orgasmic state, and she hesitated. To perform the final step properly, she would have to reach out to his mind and block it off from all outside contact, and he had stopped her from even taking a light glimpse at his mind just twenty minutes before. She spoke aloud to his frozen body, not even sure he could hear her, "You came to me for help. You wouldn't even be in our world if it weren't for me. I have to try this, and if whatever got you gets me, at least I tried. I'm sorry you can't tell me if this is right, but I hope it works." She reached out with her hands as she reached out with her mind, and in a single, quick, simultaneous gesture of both that she had done hundreds of times before, sent Trevor into total isolation and bliss.

His body instantly relaxed, collapsing flat to the soft, plush rug, his erection rapidly becoming flaccid even as it twitched out a dry ejaculation. Sunshine ran through a series of mental exercises Maheu'le had taught her to keep in good shape for everyday Mentalism and check for any signs or traces of mental instability or harm, and found nothing wrong. She had been in and out of Trevor's mind too quickly to have known what might have been going on there, and hoped she had been quick enough to avoid whatever he had been trying to protect her from. With his eyes closed and his body limp, Trevor appeared to be sleeping, and Sunshine wanted to pull a blanket across him and let him

189

rest. At the same time, she knew he was in a state of total bliss and separation from sensation that would make a blanket meaningless to him and leaving him in this state would be unrestful for his mind, the part of him she suspected was most in need of a proper dose of relaxation. In the end she realized that minutes wasted here could mean serious trouble wherever he had just come from and that she had no business leaving him this way for longer than he needed to be, in case someone else was in more danger. Ms. Charming put her hands on his feet again and went through the steps that didn't wake him before, but left the mental isolation in place, just in case.

Trevor gasped suddenly, sitting bolt upright and opening his eyes wide. "So that's what that feels like!" He breathed a few slowing breaths of relaxation before he seemed to notice his surroundings. And his nakedness. "Sorry about that." He disappeared briefly and reappeared with the clothes he had left in his school locker, trench coat and all, properly appeared into place on his body. "And thank you. It didn't take you long to figure that out; I'm just glad it worked."

"Uhh… Sure. What … what exactly… ?"

"I'm not sure yet, and I'm not sure I want to find out. I don't even have words to describe it… I just …" Trevor paused, put his hand across his face, over his eyes, squeezing his temples with his eyes closed and his head turned down, "and I'm not sure it's safe for you to remember it from my mind. Or for us to even take this block off and allow Mentalism at all."

"Is it anyone I'd know? Who did this to you? That, at least, would be a start."

"Kay and Elle, but … not them, really. At least, I don't think it could have been them. Except I'm not sure that that makes sense, since I'm not sure they're really … them. I'm sorry if none of this makes sense."

"No, no, it's alright. Whatever's going on, we can figure it out. It's probably just one of the groups who have been out to get you from the beginning, right? Someone who think you're on the wrong side of some celestial battle."

"I want to try something. If I … If I lose it again, just do the same thing, and bring me right out of it. But give me … five minutes, okay? I want to take another look at this thing."

Before Ms. Charming could agree, she felt the block freeing from his mind and something else taking its place. She reflexively recoiled, both physically and mentally, but caught a glimpse of what felt to her like Kay's mind in that brief second of contact. Trevor's eyes closed.

As soon as he'd taken down the wall in his mind that prevented Mentalism entirely, that third-tier mind was already there, trying again to interlock with his own, to take him over. This time he was ready for it, and not willing in the least to relent to it. With all his experience, his power, and Sunshine's long training with the best of the best, Trevor was able to not only prevent this strange mind from taking over his own, but also prevented it from fleeing or disappearing or obfuscating. It took him a few tries and a little ingenuity, but he managed to put a block up around it similar to the one he had been under, isolating it within itself and disconnecting it from Elle, her body falling limp without control, far from where Trevor now sat. When he finally felt he had this entity under control, he opened his eyes to see Sunshine beginning to massage his feet. "I almost took too long, did I?"

"I actually gave you ten minutes. You didn't seem to be having any trouble, but I didn't want to risk it taking so long."

"Want to see it? I think it'll be safe enough for now."

"Sure." She closed her eyes and he closed his and together they viewed the mental landscape of the trapped beast. Like a guard dog, it lashed out at them from inside its prison, unable to do anything but make noise and startle them a little with its ferocity. Pairs of minds paired with pairs of minds in a hierarchy of duality upon duality where each pair masqueraded as a single entity despite containing distinct internal units, the conquered mentality seemed to be comprised of not less than 16 individual directing forces working together when Trevor and Sunshine tried to analyze its makeup. And it was dissembling itself rapidly. They each tried to get any information they could about what it was they were looking at before it was lost to them, but every other part of it was either intent on taking the whole of its being apart or hiding what was being taken apart, different wills working together in a fractaline dance of degenerating but effective stealth. Then, just before it seemed about to disappear completely, four or five of the individual fractional minds, now almost entirely disconnected from each other, found themselves small enough to slip through the barriers and protections that had been designed to hold a much larger, more complex entity in place, each scooting off along a different tangent of thought barely in time to escape the imploding force of the remaining emptiness-that-was-the-twins collapsing inward. Trevor and Sunshine were not so lucky, and nearly passed out from the force of the mental blast in the wake of the destruction, having learned nearly nothing.

"Are you alright, Trev?" Sunshine was rubbing her own head in pain, hoping her student wasn't worse off than she felt.

"I think so," Trevor tried to stand, one hand gripping the edge of her coffee table as he moved to right himself, the other massaging the back of his head where his skull met his neck. Before he could even get fully standing, his legs shook and buckled underneath him, dropping him hard back to the floor. "A little weakened, I guess."

"Don't push yourself too hard. Whatever that was, it was powerful, and it was trying to hurt you." She decided not to try to stand, and crawled the short distance back to her couch, pulling herself up onto it wearily, as though she had just returned from running a marathon or flying Mercury's Challenge. She barely made it over the edge of balance onto the soft cushions, then practically poured herself out across the couch's length. "You're saying that thing was controlling Kay and Elle, though? I wonder how long it's been there that no one noticed it."

"I don't think it was controlling Kay and Elle, I think it actually was the twins, and probably since the beginning, way before you or I ever met them. When I

192

finally found myself behind its defenses and got a look at Elle's mind… there wasn't anything there at all. No memories, no emotions, not even basic motor control or sense processing. Everything that I'd thought was Elle was actually part of whatever that thing was. It had experienced for her, thought for her, felt for her, and controlled her body as its own. Probably for both of them. And it had taken over most of me, before I managed to get to you."

"Where are the girls now?"

"I guess they're probably still at home, in bed, where I left them … do you suppose there's anything left of them? Mentally, I mean?"

"We'd better go find out. Take me there." Instantly they disappeared from Ms. Charming's living room and re-appeared in the twins' bedroom; Trevor sitting on the edge of the bed next to Kay's still-paralyzed body, Sunshine still nearly formlessly tired as she appeared already sunk into a big plush chair in the corner of the room, facing the beds. In the flickering, dim candlelight they could both see that Elle's body had been moving quickly when Trevor had cut its mind off from it – what was left of her was crumpled hard against the wall and floor, her limbs skewed at painful angles and her head twisted too-far-around, apparently in a hard impact with the wall or doorknob on her way down. With their enhanced perceptions they knew immediately that she was dead, but whether it was the disconnection from her mind or the impact from the fall that took her life, they didn't know yet. They must have been thinking the same thing just then, because they both said "I suppose we'll find out when we wake Kay" together.

"Are we sure that's such a good idea?" Trevor wasn't moving towards her feet, just yet, but felt its inevitability nearly as palpably as they both felt the continuing and degrading effects of the mental burst.

Sunshine could barely turn her head. She felt physically exhausted, and as she spoke she began re-running her mental self-checks, "maybe there's an alternative." She coughed weakly, "we should probably get some outside help anyway. I'm not feeling very well."

193

"Worse and worse.   Me, too.   Who, though? Evelyn?"

"We're going to need more than one person's help. Do you still have the strength to move her with you? I think I can get myself to the Wolyd Centre, if you can move her with you."

"Third floor? I think I can do that. Why don't you –" but she was already gone. Trevor took Kay's hand in his and used the last of his strength to disappear with her to what he hoped would be the third floor of the Wolyd Centre, but he blacked out before they reappeared, glad for the rest after what had turned out to be quite a long, hard day.

✢ ✢ ✢

"He knows. He knows! What are we going to do?"

"You're the one who said he was ours, if I recall. That the plan was working."

"How was I to know he'd blaspheme the dark side of the temple, cut the balance completely? No one could have predicted that, it was pure chance!"

"It's not over yet."

"You said that earlier."

"They were just our first try. Since when do we only do something once? Be patient. Our time is at hand."

"We still have his daughters. They're the real key. It's not over yet."

"Exactly."

✢ ✢ ✢

Spectral figures in the form of nurses tended to the three unconscious bodies that had appeared a few short hours earlier, one passed out in front of reception and the other two falling from several feet above the surface of the floor in one of the third-floor hallways shortly afterward, the noise of their bodies hitting the floor drawing appropriate attention. The three of them were now laid out in three adjacent hospital beds, and except for the staff tending them, they were the only ones present in a room large enough to serve several dozens of patients, filled with row after row of empty beds. Invisible to the human eye were the doctors doing the bulk of the work, experts who had ended up in their current non-corporeal states usually through some variation of a serious accident most famously made by the wizard Wolyd in the midst of his negotiations with a flesh-consuming "demon" which, had Wolyd not mistakenly destroyed his own body, would have done the job for him shortly thereafter. It was the lesson of Wolyd, that one doesn't require a body to be a force for positive change in the world, upon which the Wolyd Centre had been founded, and their combined experience represented more information about the dangerous after-effects of Mentalism and the various natures that non-bodied minds might have than any other location in the world.

Sunshine began to rouse first, her eyes slowly coming half-open and her breath beginning to come deeper into her lungs as her mind recovered consciousness. She tried to speak, but didn't have the energy or the breath yet to squeeze even a single syllable from her dry lips. A thought came to her, "Don't try to speak, Ms. Charming. Give the nurses time to treat you."

"We made it here safely? This is the Wolyd Centre?" Sunshine was long familiar with mental conversation and was glad she would not have to strain herself by trying to speak physically.

"Yes, you're in good hands. Well, not hands, precisely, but you're being well cared for nonetheless. We're very glad you came directly to us, timing is important in matters such as this. How, exactly, did you manage to destroy the hivemind that attacked you two? We're all very curious about that."

"It was Trev. As far as I could see, he just used a modified Mentalism containment effect to prevent it from latching back onto his mind, but … you've seen something like this before?"

"Not exactly. One of our research fellows, Tharsis, had theorized about the possible existence of hiveminds in nature, and how they might appear and behave among beings

195

of a single consciousness. I thought he was right here somewhere…"

"Yes, yes, sorry, I was examining Trev's mind very carefully. I'm Tharsis, yes. Pleased to be speaking with you, Sunshine, in the manner we can, that is. I believe we've met before – I was at Professor Callum's place when you stopped by last March, I believe he teaches your Mentalism curriculum?" Tharsis illuminated his memories of the meeting and shined them in Sunshine's mental direction to help her recall.

"Oh, yes, I remember you now, you were very quiet that evening."

"I apologize," Tharsis thought, "I was preoccupied with … well, this, actually. And it's a good thing, too. Trevor's mind is going through what I expect, based on my research, is a form of withdrawal from having been interlocked into the hivemind and then disconnected. From the looks of the damage to your mind from the eventual destruction of the hivemind as it compares to his mental state, I'd say that even his brief contact with it had reformed his mind's topography enough that the blast didn't do him nearly as much harm as the disconnection did. You're sure he was disconnected from it when it attacked?"

"Almost certainly, though I can't claim to be an expert on hiveminds by any means. I'd never seen or heard of one before tonight. Wait. Is it still the same night?"

"Yes, yes, you've only just arrived a few hours ago. The sun won't be up for quite some time."

One of the nurses raised a small amount of water to Sunshine's lips, and she took a tiny, refreshing sip, thinking "Thank you."

The nurse thought back, "you're welcome. If there's anything you need, just think it, and we'll be here."

"Again, thank you."

The nurse was already gone, the small glass appearing to float away on its own into the distance. Tharsis was quick to pick up again where his thoughts had left off. "A funny thing though, the girl. From what we've been able to determine without removing the ongoing effects, we believe that she has actually been in the thrall of the hivemind since infancy, perhaps before."

"That seems right, based on what I detected in the hivemind while I still had the chance. Why didn't anyone notice before?"

"I'm glad you asked. That's probably the most well-developed part of my research. You see, before anyone ever bothered to ask me why a hivemind had never been seen I had developed an independent theory that the communal nature of thoughts within a hivemind would make them take the form of normal thoughts at the conscious level, such that without a very in-depth and careful analysis by someone who knew what to look for and what was considered normal, even the hivemind might never become consciously aware that it was anything but normal."

"By the time I got a look at it, this thing was definitely aware that it wasn't the same as Trev or I. Its different individual parts worked independently of each other to achieve common goals, as though the whole thing had been choreographed. I tried looking at the separate pieces, and they each reacted the way a master of Mentalism would have done instinctually to defend themselves while the other pieces did their own things."

"Fascinating."

"Yes, fascinating, but why didn't I notice it before? There were two of them, and I did a thorough mental interview before accepting them as transfer students. They each seemed to be a perfectly normal young woman at the time."

"There were two of them?"

"Yes, twins. The body of the other is here," Sunshine remembered the location of Elle's crumpled body, and a couple of the doctors that had been observing the exchange moved themselves to that location, "but aside from the comfortable, long-established mental link they seemed to share constantly, I didn't detect anything unusual. Ever."

"Twins? With a strange mental link? Where's Gorsky? Isn't he an expert on twins' minds?"

"He went to the other location as soon as she thought 'twins' – he'll probably bring her back here if she's in any condition to be moved."

Elle's mangled body appeared on the empty bed adjacent to Kay's paralyzed body just as Sunshine tried to explain "She's dead." The body let out a ghastly rattling sigh as it settled into a new configuration onto the bed, and for a moment even the nurses didn't move to adjust her corpse from its tangled configuration as they stared on at the horror and loss it represented. "I think that when Trevor put the barricades around the hivemind and broke contact she must have been mid-stride," Sunshine tried to explain.

"I've never seen a neck turned that way before," said one of the nurses who, despite the fact that she would have appeared to be a ghost to the casual observer, seemed quite squeamish.

"We don't get exposed to many ... physical ailments," Tharsis tried to explain, "we mostly just work with damaged minds here." The other nurses were very gently forcing Elle's already stiffening corpse into a more natural-looking pose on the bed.

Gorsky addressed Sunshine directly, "Definitely twins. Can you recall the shape or any other details of their mental bridge for me?"

Sunshine did her best to play back all her memories of the twins, from their interview through the entire semester, and including her experience with Trevor's appearance that evening for all the minds who cared to look in on them. There was a long silence in the room and in their minds, with only the sound of Elle's flesh and bones straining against being twisted and popped back into place to fill the huge room as Ms. Charming's memories were considered carefully by each of the doctors.

Finally, Tharsis berated himself, "I should have thought of that before! It's much clearer to me now! Twins!" Then his mind fell silent, as though that were all the information needed to complete the puzzle for everyone else.

After what seemed like a long time, when it was clear Tharsis wasn't going to explain himself further, Gorsky thought to the others, "I don't know what he's going on about, but from what I saw, the connection between those two was not like most twins' bridge. I've seen a lot of twins' minds in my life, twins who had studied Mentalism, twins who had a strong bridge despite never even being introduced to Mentalism, and more twins that had little or no bridge at all than the others together." Gorsky paused as though for breath, "but these two... I wouldn't even classify that connection as a bridge, personally. It was more like what I expected a hivemind to look like, from Tharsis's many papers and lectures on the subject."

"No, no, this was much more elegant than any of my theories! Didn't you see it? It was beautiful! And so obvious! Why didn't I see it sooner? Twins!"

"I don't mean to sound too ignorant, Tharsis," Sunshine addressed him in a calm, even tone of thought, "but I don't understand what you're talking about, really. Could you explain what you mean about their being twins?"

"Oh, right, sorry! You haven't read any of my work, have you? Alright, I'll try to explain." Tharsis seemed flustered and excited at the same time, and the other doctors just stayed quiet and let him explain himself without ever letting on that they hadn't understood him from the beginning. "You see, since a hivemind has never been observed and documented before, everything in my work was based on theory. I had posited several possible internal structures for a hivemind to possess, from apparent randomness with individual consciousnesses working together through a system like democracy to the queen-soldier-drone structure of insect colonies and even stranger things like crystalline matrices and homogenous interplays where there was no detectible border where one mind ended and the next began. Without an example of a hivemind to work from, testing out known existing social and natural structures against what is understood about the mind was the only way to determine which structures were theoretically viable and which were not. As we have all seen, the actual structure was not like even the wildest or simplest of my guesses; it was twins!"

"I'm afraid I still don't understand. I can see that you've spent a lot of time on this, and that you seem very pleased that all your research was based on incorrect guesses, but I still don't understand what Trev was fighting tonight."

"Twins! Don't you see?" Sunshine tried to shake her head and managed a slight rocking motion. She closed her eyes from the dizziness that even so little motion brought on, and almost immediately felt two of the doctor's skilled energies massaging her mind, bringing it back to proper working order so that it could then take charge of her body. Tharsis seemed to get the idea, and continued, "imagine just two minds, like any normal pair of twins, or two people in love who link their minds together to enhance … their experiences together. With two of them, when a decision must be made that concerns both of them, the binary option of the decision is not whether to do the thing or not, but really whether they agree on what to do or disagree on what to do. If they disagree, they can try to work it out, but if they can't work it out, the decision goes unmade and no action takes place.

"So, if you imagine two minds thusly connected at all times without the ability to become disconnected, you can see that if they ever wanted to get anything decided and done the two individual minds would rapidly become excellent at working together and at compromising.   If it were one being that somehow ended up with two minds linked as such, its very survival on a day to day basis would require an amazing level of rapid compromise and truly intense empathy, one mind to the other. After not very long, these two minds would be so synchronized, so quick at resolving differences to generate action at all, that from the outside it would appear as though there were only one mind at work, one thought process. Not to mention the natural affinity for Mentalism that such constant mental contact would make possible.

"Now, imagine that this dual-minded being had offspring that naturally also had a dual mind, passed on through heredity. Imagine also that instead of a single child at a time, this being always had twins. These twins would each have two minds working in concert to control each of their bodies, but would also share a mental connection like

200

the strong bridge that Gorsky is familiar with, but enhanced first by their natural affinity for Mentalism, and also by their experience with learning to compromise and work together rapidly with another mind to achieve their goals. It is easy to see that soon these two beings with two bodies and four minds would appear from the outside to be only two, or perhaps even one mind. What if these offspring also formed a mental connection with their parent from an early age? And later with others of their kind who they took as mates?

"Duality acting as a single entity paired with duality acting as a single entity creating a new duality that could operate as though a single entity with two bodies. Or four bodies, if a being and its mate and a pair of its offspring ended up working together. I imagine that when the progenitors reached their end of life, the long-standing mental interconnection they'd had with their mate and offspring would cause something like a Wolyd disconnection from their dying bodies because they would still be part of the decision-making process for other, living bodies. After a few generations of this activity there would be innumerable subtle levels of complexity within the duality-upon-duality, where at first each element appeared to be just that, elemental, but which upon further investigation it would be found to be a duality, and each element uncovered at each level might reveal another duality at work unknown to the higher levels.

"If you were one of these beings, the wisdom and prejudices of your grandparents' grandparents would be subtly present for you from an early age, from as soon as your parents' minds began interlocking with your own until your entire family line was destroyed. Now, you couldn't see enough detail through the containment effect for me to know for sure what it was, but I'd be willing to say that while that gives you a reasonable understanding of the current structure of the hivemind in question, the actual origins are totally different from what I've suggested here. Still, these beings could go undetected and at a great advantage for a very long time, with their constantly building multi-generational experiences with Mentalism and the human condition. I would love to know what that experience is like.

"That's crazy."

"You think everything I say is crazy, Ralf, but I challenge you to come up with another explanation for the hivemind Ms. Charming experienced."

"You know that's not my area of study at all! If she had been attacked by an herbivorous intelligence, then perhaps I could offer expertise in how to treat her, but … whatever that thing may have been, your explanation is crazy. Wouldn't Gorsky have seen something like these twins' connection before? Wouldn't twins be running the world, one way or another? There has to be some other explanation for this."

Sunshine was an excellent arbiter and began thinking as soon as Ralf left off, so the argument could not escalate, "I can see how I, not being experienced with the study of twins' minds, wouldn't have recognized their mental connection as unusual when I met them. Perhaps when Trev comes to he'll be able to share his memories more effectively, having been connected to the hivemind, as Tharsis speculates. Is there an expectation as to when he will be recovered enough to communicate?"

"We've never dealt with anything like this before."

"In fact, due to the nature of the mental changes he seems to have undergone, we haven't done much more than to apply the equivalent of splints, to prevent the damage from getting worse when he does become conscious."

"There's the possibility that, without a detailed map of his mind from some point before the connection, any restorative techniques we attempt to apply would only cause him to be more like the hivemind and less like himself."

"So what are you going to do? Obviously someone is out to get him, and they aren't exactly novices or anything you or I are familiar with. Before long they will return and if he's in this state when they do, they won't get much of a fight. Do you know who he is? What he represents?"

"We are very aware of the rumors surrounding the boy, Ms. Charming, and with all due respect –" his thought was cut off by Sunshine's actual voice, croaking out into the room.

"With all due respect, doctors, some of those rumors are true." She tried to move to sit up, and managed to raise herself onto her elbows, turning her head to the appropriate locations of each of the doctor's minds in turn as she continued, in thought. "Even if they weren't true, there are certain very powerful and apparently very secret individuals and organizations that believe the rumors are true, and any one of them would stop at nothing to access whatever it is they believe he represents. Some of them only to prevent the others from getting their hands on him."

"Which is what you're trying to do now, isn't it, Ms. Charming?"

"Absolutely. Without selfish interests or designs on whatever power or destiny he may represent, I am doing everything I can to keep him from harm and from the hands of those who would use him for their own gain. He deserves to exist as he wishes to exist, without hiveminds taking him over or dark conspiracies locking him up and draining his life away. He's only a boy."

"Fine, fine, yes, and we want to help him, too, but how do you propose we do that? This isn't a magical attack you can just dispel or even some mental injury from an understood form of attack that we've seen before or treated before. From the looks of it, that hivemind imploded just after some of its individual elements escaped, and the force of everything left of the mind impacting against the surface of yours is what caused the trauma you're under."

Tharsis finally thought up again, "but as I was saying earlier, the primary cause of his continuing condition appears to be the brief period of contact he had with the hivemind and the disconnection thereafter. It's even possible that when those elements escaped his containment and seemed to disappear, one or more of them latched back on to his mind. We've got the entire building affected with an enchantment that prevents mental contact in or out of our walls, but if these elements were already attached to his mind when he showed up here … we might not even be able to detect them, now."

"You mean to think that he could be re-attached to parts of the hivemind right now? You saw that when I disconnected him from it before, my success was presumably because the hivemind was grounded in Elle – if he's the only one connected with it now, how could it be detected or removed?"

"No one knows."

"And it could just be another incorrect guess. I've made them before." Tharsis was doing his best to think reassuringly, but everyone knew that he was probably right. Everyone was quiet for a time, doing the bodiless equivalent of staring at their toes to avoid eye contact, some trying to busy themselves with redundant examinations of Trevor or Kay's mental states. Sunshine let herself collapse back into the comforting embrace of the bedding and pillows, too exhausted after only a few moments to stay even half-elevated.

"You should get your rest. It's the middle of the night. If Trev's status changes in any way, we'll let you know."

"What about Kay?"

Tharsis had apparently been thinking about this, too, and thought "We're not sure how exactly she's staying alive in there, but taking her out of that state presents a very real danger to her survival. Though it cannot be known at this time the exact circumstances, I suspect that it was the disconnection from the hivemind that killed her sister, not the fall. From what we can tell of her mental topography through the containment, there aren't even basic control structures for managing breathing and circulation present – it was all handled by the hivemind. Realistically, she should have stopped breathing as soon as he cut her off in the first place."

"So if you wake her, there won't be anything there at all?"

"That's a possibility. She could die the very moment we attempt to wake her. It's also possible that the remaining elements that had been controlling her are waiting, either inside Trev's mind or hiding somewhere else in the building, and will reconnect with her as soon as the block is removed.

Which may be good or may be very bad, if it happens at all. If they do reconnect, and if they have been hiding in Trev's mind, he would be interlocked with her, possibly under the hivemind's control and becoming ever-more-restructured by it. Or any number of other possibilities we may not be able to anticipate."

"So you're just going to leave her that way?"

"For now. At least until you feel better, perhaps until we can do more with Trev. He could have a lot of answers for us. But you should go back to sleep, get some rest. Our nurses would be glad to give you a gentle sleep inducing effect, if you like."

"That won't be necessary, thank you. I'm having to fight to stay awake as it is. Just … wake me if anything develops, alright?"

"We will." She was already asleep before he finished thinking that brief phrase, and she slept straight through to morning. There were no developments that night. The staff had some experience dealing with paralyzed bodies, so caring for the two teenagers properly was handled ably as the night turned into morning and the morning turned into a weekend without even subtle changes in Trevor's mental topography to indicate that foreign elements might be working there or diminishment or increase in the viability of Kay's mental state.

Kay and Elle's parents did not return home or call home and could not be reached by any known means to be informed of their daughters' conditions. Elle's body had been put into a state of perpetual stasis shortly after its discovery, and was being kept out of sight, unchanging. Sunshine had recovered enough to get around reasonably on her own by mid-day Saturday, and when she had spoken to Trevor's parents they hadn't cared whether he was at a school function or halfway to the moon – they hadn't even noticed his failure to return home Friday night and didn't even seem to want to know when he could be expected home again. Luckily, in the same way that the people who ought to have cared for him were apathetic, those who had attacked Trevor had not acted again either. Sunshine continued to expect the worst.

Monday morning Sunshine returned reluctantly to school. It was the last week of classes before final exams and there were always problems that needed her attention this close to the end of the school year – she trusted that the doctors at the Wolyd Centre would alert her to any new ideas they had and any changes in Trevor or Kay's conditions. Then before she knew it the week had swept by her entirely and she found herself at the Wolyd Centre on another Friday night.

"If you aren't going to do anything for him, I am. You yourselves have said that there has been no detectable change in any element of his mind from the first time you observed it to now, and I'm not about to leave him in this state indefinitely. In fact, I have a feeling that if we don't get him back in good condition within the next week or two... things could go very badly."

"What do you mean? Is this about some ancient prophecy he's supposed to fulfill?"

"No. This is about a young woman he impregnated, and the fact that under normal circumstances she would be giving birth to his child in about a week's time. A little over six months ago, that young woman disappeared, and no force had been able to locate her, including every entity and energy The Board could call on to try to find her. I have little doubt that when she births his child he will be able to detect it, but only if he is conscious and able to try. If the child came early, if whoever sent the hivemind has the girl and induced labor as soon as Trev was out of commission, it may be too late. A week ago I didn't want to rush things, but the fact that there has been no follow-up, no new evidence of what caused all this, it makes me think that this is exactly what they wanted. The Board agrees."

"You've spoken with the board about this?"

"Of course. Last Sunday I told them everything. As usual, they took their time reaching a decision. At a meeting after school today, they endorsed the taking of immediate action to try to awaken him by any means necessary. They don't care about the girl at this point, especially since her mind is either destroyed or will return to her when we wake her, and I agree that the first thing we should do is wake her up. Unless you have a better idea?"

"We …"

"Nothing better, no ma'am." When she'd reminded them all that she was a member of The Board, Ms. Charming had apparently disarmed any egos they had had about their own ideas and theories and standing in the community. They immediately cowed before her, following her unquestioningly as though she were the expert and they knew nothing. "Would you like to do it yourself?"

"Fine." Sunshine moved to the foot of Kay's bed and began a basic massage of her feet. She was glad to see that they had put a hospital gown over Kay's otherwise naked form. The temperature of the room was very comfortable, but there was something wrong about seeing a young woman lay uncovered and unable to move that seemed somehow more unjust to her than the possibility that Sunshine's next action would take the girl's life. She pressed and rubbed and poked Kay's feet in just the right pattern and smoothed and removed the mental containment that was in effect, re-exposing her to external mental influences just as she ended the young woman's orgasmic state and paralysis at once. Kay's body immediately began shaking and convulsing and her breath became ragged and uneven. "Oh dear," Sunshine said, low but still audible over Kay's spasming and gasping.

"That seems to just be the effects of the orgasm waning. She's not dying yet."

Her breathing began to even out and her body's convulsions stopped, but her eyes didn't open and her heart didn't stop. Trevor sat bolt upright in bed, gasping suddenly and deeply, his eyes wide open. He looked left and right and all around him, his eyes stopping on the spot in space that Gorsky's mind happened to be as he spoke, "Ms. Charming, are you alright?"

"Yes, Trev, I'm fine. It's you we're worried about. How do you feel?"

Trevor was still facing Gorsky, not turning the opposite direction to face Sunshine as he responded, "I'm

207

fine. I need you to run through the Barton Series for me though, would you, while I watch?"

"Whatever you say, Trev." She felt his mind reach out to hers in a closed conduit that blocked her mental processes from the other minds present as she did the self-evaluations he'd recommended, and she managed to keep herself from reacting outwardly to the anomalies she discovered there. Just before he relaxed the conduit, Trev thought to her "just follow my lead" in a very confident tone of thought.

"Anything interesting, Ms. Charming? Everything in order, we presume?" Ralf sounded more confused than anything, especially as Trevor's eyes followed Gorsky's motion around the edge of the crowd of minds gathered around to see what waking Kay might have done. Kay still lay on the bed, but now it was clear to every mind attuned to such activity that she was restfully sleeping, dreaming of the only thing she had ever known, that week-long orgasmic state she had just been released from.

Trevor answered for Ms. Charming, saying "Everything is as expected, thank you Ralf. And thank you, ladies, for your gentle care all week. You were very respectful, not like corporeal nurses tend to be. Your attentions did not go unnoticed." Several of the spectral figures of the nurses vanished while others seemed to turn a shade of pink as though blushing all over. The doctors' minds were trying but not succeeding in expressing themselves clearly, but Trevor was on top of that, too. "You want to know how I could have been aware of any of that, considering my mental state, right? Take a close look at my mind right now." He paused as they examined his mind.

"Impossible!" one of the doctors thought loudly. Several of them just did the thought-equivalent of gasping, and others were still just flabbergasted.

Trevor continued to respond in speech to a conversation that should have occurred in pure thought, and when Gorsky tried to make a break for it he found that Trevor had modified the mental containment effect on the Wolyd Centre so that instead of thoughts simply being unable to go in and out, free minds were blocked as well.

208

Instead of protecting the outside world from the errant or insane mental processes that might be going on and treated inside, Trevor had made the hospital's walls protect the outside world from an errant and insane mind which could have become much more dangerous than a few stray thoughts very quickly. "You didn't think you'd get away that easily, did you?"

Every mind did the equivalent of turning to face Gorsky, backed up against the wall behind them. "I don't know what you're talking about."

"Do you need me to show them what you've done to Ms. Charming, or are you going to admit to it and hope for some leniency?"

"I haven't done anything wrong. He's obviously under the control of the hivemind, like we thought would happen. It's trying to distract us while it builds power or something. Look at his mind, it hasn't changed a whit, it looks like he's still unconscious!" They peered at his mind and saw that it was the truth; the apparent topology and activity of his mind appeared unchanged, just as it had appeared all week. Except then, as though a curtain were being pulled back to reveal a stage full of performers already in high activity, the façade blocking them from Trevor's true mental processes fell away. Most of them didn't know what they were looking at, but Trevor hadn't really expected them to be able to and he was ready with an explanation.

"You were right to speculate that the escaped portions of the hivemind would seek out a body to attach themselves with, and that until Kay was released from containment they would not be able to use her body again. Unfortunately for Kay, the portions of her former mind that had made up what little elements of individuality she had possessed were not among those that escaped intact. Fortunately for her though, an odd number of mental entities escaped – I reunited a single, non-twinned mind with her body the moment you woke her. It has most of her memories and is familiar with her body enough to control it, but because its natural pair was lost, and because of a couple of dents I put in it this week, it won't be able to reconnect with any hivemind, and Kay won't be able to attend church anymore."

"Church?"

"I'll get to that. Actually, let me introduce the four surviving pairs from what was once Kay and Elle; I've had them trapped in my mindscape since just before I disappeared here with Kay's body. I plan to leave them with you to study. Two of them used to be Kay and Elle's 'parents', Jay and Em. Their other bodies are in stasis at their church, awaiting their possible return. I couldn't get much from the other two, but from the things they were trying to hide, I'm fairly confident that their trying to take control of my mind has something to do with Hannah and my children."

"Children, Trev?" Sunshine was trying to understand everything he was saying, she could see that he had the four mind-pairs on the rough equivalent of leashes, blocked from getting in range of his mind or anyone else's but not strictly contained. It was this last point which stood out to her, though. "There was only one fetus in Hannah when she disappeared. I can see that you've been …erm… sexually active since then, at least with the twins, but neither one of them is pregnant. Is there someone else we should know about?"

"No, no, it's Hannah. If these people are the ones who took her, they would have induced twinning of my child almost immediately. Isn't that right, Gorsky?"

"I still don't know what you're trying to imply. My colleagues here have known me for decades; you won't easily convince them I've been lying to them about who and what I am for so long."

"Should be easy, actually. Is everyone paying attention?" Trevor's eyes still hadn't moved from where Gorsky was hovering, but he mentally addressed each doctor present to be sure they were paying attention. "Remember with me." Trevor played back a few very brief memories from the past week, and a glimpse from his memory of being interlocked with the hivemind, just enough information that they understood how to see the differences between a mature hivemind and any other being's mind. It was a subtle

210

difference, just as Tharsis had suspected, and it made hiveminds appear totally mundane to the casual observer.

Tharsis was the first to exclaim, making the mental gestural equivalent to pointing a finger in Gorsky's direction, "I should have known!" Soon every other mind in the room save Kay's was seeing the same thing that had always been there and gone unnoticed; Gorsky himself was a hivemind, masquerading as an individual entity.

"Now, are you going to admit that you modified Sunshine's mind and memories, or are we going to have to show everyone?"

"You'll never get me on a leash, you freak. Unlike that crazy old woman, I'm well prepared to vanish completely. I may not be able to get out of this fucking loony-bin, but you won't get a whisper of truth out of me!" Already they could sense that he had been tearing himself apart from the inside since just after he'd found himself blocked from escape, and before the fastest of them could reach him with a mental effect, the surface of his mind turned into a white-hot scream. Then, just before it was too late, Trevor's mental effect reached the right distance and went off like a blast, erecting a virtual containment field between Gorsky's imploding existence and the rest of the beings in the room, thereby saving them from going through the trauma that Sunshine had had to recover from just a week before. No remnants, no escapees, nothing even attempted to escape – Gorsky had truly erased himself completely from the face of existence rather than face the possibility of having the knowledge he held used against the powers he worked for. Trevor let the effect dissipate and let everyone begin discussing what had been revealed among themselves as he slowly moved to get out of the bed. He was still dressed, still wearing his coat, just as he had been when he'd arrived a week ago, and he appreciated the fact that he wouldn't have to waste time and energy getting dressed. The conveniences of supernatural effects removed the most embarrassing aspects of a hospital stay, such as bedpans and sponge baths.

"Are you sure you're okay, Trev?" Sunshine moved to his side and helped him out of the high bed. "A few minutes ago you were comatose. I'm not sure you should be up and around just yet."

"We don't have much time and there's a lot that must be accomplished. We have to find their church, locate and free Hannah, and I've got to take my finals this week or I'm going to have to re-take half my classes. Thanks for taking action, by the way, Ms. Charming. I needed some rest, but if you hadn't done it, I'd have woken Kay's body before the weekend was over."

"Finals? Trev, you can forget about that, this is much more important than high school." As the Principal of Trevor's high school, Sunshine certainly had the ability to make such broad declarations, but Trevor wouldn't have it.

"High school is foundational to the rest of my education. I can't have you intervening to allow me out of my responsibilities in school every time a major extracurricular catastrophe comes up or an evil organization tries to take over the world, and the recovery of my illegitimate children from a collection of hiveminds with plans totally inconceivable to individuals is certainly no reason to let me skip my finals altogether. Balancing priorities and meeting multiple sets of responsibilities is a normal part of life. My responsibilities just happen to be a little more far-reaching than most high school students." Trevor paused for a moment to utter the phrase to match the hand gestures he was making to reduce the hospital's protection to its normal level so that he would be able to leave. "Of course, if dodgeball season weren't over, I would have gladly dropped that to make time for this new challenge. But my scholastic responsibilities are certainly more important than a little school spirit."

Sunshine didn't know what to say, but wasn't prepared to disagree. Then she felt Trevor's mental fingers on her memories, undoing what Gorsky had done and revealing the rest of the details about her experience the prior Friday night which had been covered up. She reflexively reached up and covered her mouth with one hand, and her eyes went wide. She had detected that something had been altered without her knowing, but hadn't taken the steps to uncover it herself yet – now that she remembered that detail fully, she understood why Trevor was already out of bed. "I still don't see why you can't take your finals later, after you deal with this."

"I don't deserve to be treated any differently from the other students, Ms. Charming. They're already having a hard time accepting me, imagine if I got extra time to study for finals. It's not like you can explain to the entire student body what's going on. Then they really couldn't see me as a normal student."

"Fine, fine, but if you feel Hannah start to go into labor, let me know immediately. Alright?"

"Alright. Now, I've got to go do some research. I have a paper due in English, a presentation for Ethics, and I've got to figure out how to locate the church before they find out I'm back in commission." He didn't wait for her to say goodbye, Trevor just disappeared as soon as he was done speaking. Sunshine stayed behind to discuss what was reasonable to share with those who had seen what had happened, and to talk about what to do with Kay when she awakened. She avoided their few meaningful questions the way any good politician can, and when they thought they were satisfied, she made her own way home. She knew that this was only the beginning of something that would leave more than a few people hurt in the end.

"We have a lead, master."

"Yes, Sqrat, I know. I even know who has the girl if their lead is correct, which The Board may not figure out in time, if at all. So we have a lead and we have an advantage, but we still don't have the girl." The tall bespectacled man had that same grim tone he always seemed to use when speaking with Sqrat and Feagan.

"According to my calculations, we still have a few days before it's too late," Feagan was trying to help. "We still have time to get the girl before she gives birth."

"Unfortunately, our advantage is that we know our adversary is stronger than we are. The Board, the boy, they don't know what they're up against yet. We at least know enough to know we can't win."

"You keep saying that, sir. We still haven't been told…"

"Who we have to steal the most prized object of their entire long history from right from under the noses of? What behemoth organization, every member of which has a hivemind so complex and powerful that the best thinkers at the Wolyd Centre couldn't even tell there was one among them, whose inner workings are so secret that there isn't even a whit of information about them on either of the internets, and who stole the girl out from under the watchful eye of The Board and have held her for over six months without being detected by anyone in the world, even as they infiltrated their operatives right into Trev's life, are we fighting against and supposed to beat at their own game? You really want to know?"

"Of course, master. Share your wisdom."

"Stop being such a brown-nosed little twit, Sqrat. Even if I told you their name, what more would you know about them that you don't know now? Even if I told you the name of their most publicly known brand, you probably wouldn't recognize it as a force trying to wrest control of the universe into its grip. Who this is does not matter nearly as much as the fact that they have been working to recreate the world in their image, slowly, patiently, by breeding their desired traits into generation after generation of people for thousands of years, and that their work is finally coming close to reaching critical mass – they have an army of beings that, according to your own admission each member of could be nearly powerful enough to overpower Trev on its own, and they believe that his offspring is the key that will unlock their glorious future. Consider them religious fanatics, if that helps, but imagine religious fanatics with Mentalism on par with Maheu'le and the potential to generate any spell, incantation or other effect which anyone they encounter could have, and to counter, dispel or block anything that anyone they've ever crossed minds with could have countered. And they know people will be coming to try to take what they believe they have rightfully stolen, and they

214

surely have prepared formidable defenses. Now, tell me, how do we get access to the girl?"

Sqrat just stared on in silence and awe, but Feagan seemed to have already known what he was going to be asked and had his answer ready. "We follow Trev. If all you've said about him is true, even their greatest forces will be unable to stop him. He trusts Sqrat, and he's familiar enough with me that with Sunshine's recommendation we may both be able to be working with him when he attempts to go in. Then, when we get to the girl we bring you in to handle him and get her to our own masked location. Right?"

"That's the best idea you've had this year. Too bad there's no way you'd talk your way into Trev's inevitable raiding party yourself. Sqrat, I'm counting on you to carry out Feagan's plan. You're already privy to The Board's plans, so they won't think twice about letting you in on more. Once again your parentage proves to be your only valuable feature, Sqrat."

"Pleased to be of service, master."

Feagan grumbled lowly, and busied himself with rearranging flasks and vials on his shelves as the other two discussed the finer details of a plan he would have no significant part in.

"WHERE ARE YOU?!?" Trevor paused mid-sentence, wincing in pain at the strength of the thought that exploded into his mind from what felt like deep inside him, but was able to continue his oral presentation confidently while trying to figure out who was looking for him. He felt increasing distress bubbling up inside him from a place that didn't make sense; he should have been upset with 'stage fright' over getting up in front of everyone in class to present his controversial analysis of how pure intent, rather than The Devil's Arithmetic, is the primary determining factor in division of ethical charge among involved parties for anything with a charge greater than ten percent of the absolute value of each individual's net charge at the time charge is applied. The presentation was going well, he was about to invite the class into a question and answer session to address individual examples and apparent contradictions he may not have covered explicitly, and he was feeling good about his performance in Ethics all year. Except he was feeling increasingly as though he didn't know where he was or what was going on, and in addition to that was the somewhat familiar sensation of knowing that vast sections of his memories and the way he used to be were simply missing from his mind.

"HELP ME!!" Trevor had luckily reached the end of the main body of his presentation before the screaming voice came so loud, so urgent, so painful as it expanded from that same somewhere he hadn't yet had time to locate inside himself from the first sign that these thoughts were not his own, growing larger and louder until he was sure everyone in the room could hear the cry for help pouring out of his eyes, his ears, his every pore. He closed his eyes and tried to keep a calm expression on his face as the ringing he knew was nothing more than the thought of ringing ears subsided and he could begin to think again. Trevor didn't know how long this took, but when he opened his eyes he supposed it hadn't been too long; no one was looking at him any differently or behaving as though anything were amiss.

He spoke again, "Mr. Tauer, class, because of the nature of my paper, instead of opening the floor to Q&A, I've prepared it for peer review, so you can test for yourself what I've shown here, and we can discuss it after my work has been verified." Trevor reached behind the large standing tri-fold display he had set up to diagram the way the known statistical data matched his analysis better than strict adherence to The Devil's Arithmetic as though he'd had a stack of copies of his research and data already there and hoped silently that no one had noticed the change in the air when he conjured exactly what he needed, or the change in his ethical charge as he'd lied to them about being prepared for this. He pulled the large, collated stacks of papers out, "if you think that's appropriate, Mr. Tauer."

"Sounds like a capital idea, Trev." Trevor began handing the pages down the four ends of the double-horseshoe of desks and collected the extra copies from the

216

middle to give to Mr. Tauer in case anyone else wanted a look at them, then took down his displays and discreetly asked to Mr. Tauer if he could be excused from the remainder of the class for a personal matter. "Of course, Trev. You did great today."

As soon as he was out the door and out of sight of the window, Trev disappeared. He reappeared outside the Principal's office, but as his hand reached out to knock on her door, he paused. "I don't need Sunshine's help for this…" Trevor's lips formed the words and he breathed out, but his voice was not in it. "I can figure this out." He disappeared before he had the chance to hear Sqrat's voice or his own name being bandied about behind the door.

As soon as he reappeared, his mind was flooded with thoughts and feelings that mirrored what had interrupted his presentation, coming from what felt like all around him and in front of him at the same time. He had figured it out on the first try, and from the look on her face, Kay was relieved that he hadn't taken any extra time talking to Sunshine about the matter.

"Where have you been? Where am I? I don't understand!"

He took a step forward, took her hand in his, and tried to speak in as reassuring voice as he could muster considering the fact that he felt every fear and anxiety and strangeness that she was feeling as she was feeling it, "Relax, relax, you're going to be alright. Haven't the doctors explained what's happened yet?"

"I just… I don't… I'm not who you think I am, Trev. I'm not even who I thought I was. Who am I, Trev? What's going on?"

"I'm here now, and you're going to be okay," he closed his other hand over hers and caressed it gently to try to help calm her, "just relax, and we can explain everything."

"Where's the rest of me? I don't feel right, I can hardly feel anything. Why can't I remember what happened to me?"

"There was an … incident. You're … basically … all that survived. Most of your consciousness, your memories, and your other body were all destroyed. I'm sorry I couldn't save more of you." He could feel her reaction to that news, and wished he'd had better words prepared for her.

"Who did this to me? Why would they … What did I ever do to anybody?" She was crying softly now.

"It was… You had a secret. I think you were even keeping it a secret from yourself, but when we were … together, I almost found out about it, and …" Trevor didn't want to continue, to tell Kay she'd done it to herself, that she hadn't just been a normal young woman but part of a complex hivemind that was part of a vast conspiracy against him. But even without saying it or thinking it consciously, he felt her beginning to know the truth, this time as his own carefully guarded thoughts and feelings began to be mirrored in those flooding out of Kay and resounding off the walls of the Centre.

"I… It was me, wasn't it? I was trying to keep the secret from you, and was willing to kill myself to prevent you from learning the truth. What could it have been? Did you find out?"

"No. But I wasn't really trying to, I was just trying to figure out what was going on at first – you were taking control of me and almost killed me from inside my own mind at one point."

"I'm sorry. I don't remember any of this …"

"Don't worry about that, who you were then is not who you are now. But in trying to protect myself from you, your other body was destroyed – I didn't even find out until it was too late to do anything, until after most of your mind had … disassembled itself. And then I did what I could to save as much of you as possible, and what you know, what you remember, how you feel right now, that's all that wasn't irreversibly damaged or destroyed." Kay was sobbing uncontrollably now, and Trevor was experiencing a strange growing pain in his lower back. He didn't let either fact stop him from trying to be encouraging. "You're still healthy and young, with a bright future ahead of you. It will be a hard transition while you try to figure out who you are and who you want to be… while you get used to only having one body, but I know you're strong enough. The doctors here

218

have all been through something that separated them from their bodies at one point or another, some of them more than once, and they know more about what you're going through right now than anyone anywhere in the worlds. You can trust them. They're here to help you."

"I don't…"

Sunshine and Sqrat appeared across Kay's bed from Trevor, "Trev, I've got to show you something." She pulled a large tome from Sqrat's hands and thrust it across into Trevor's hands. "Open to the black ribbon."

Trevor did as he was commanded, fingering to the page marked by the thick silk ribbon Ms. Charming had specified. Both the left- and right-hand pages there appeared blank. Trevor looked up quizzically.

"Just concentrate, and give it a moment to get used to you. We think it should recognize that your mind was once part of one of their collectives, and you should be able to see what's there when it does." She paused, clearly excited and expectant, waiting to see some sort of change on Trevor's face to indicate that it was working. "At least," her face darkened somewhat, "that's what we were hoping. There's a possibility we need a password."

Kay, who had been looking on in continued bewilderment and shock, suddenly spoke. "Tetralix Ilbis." The look of confusion did not leave her face, but no one was looking at her to see it. They were looking at Trevor, whose face was bathed in a glowing light that appeared to be emanating from the surface of the pages of the book in his hands but not falling on anything else in the room but his skin, creating a surreal landscape of light and shadow across his features without casting shadows on the walls or illumination on anyone else present. Trevor's eyes appeared to have dilated beyond maximum dilation, his irises disappeared along with the whites of his eyes, leaving two pits of black so black that seeing them was like the opposite of seeing, like peering into twin tunnels of blindness enclosed between his eyelids. The pages of the book did not appear to have changed, from what anyone else in the room could have seen; the change had only visibly taken place in Trevor, and had the emptiness that had once been his eyes not proceeded back and forth across the pages as though reading the unseen text, it would have appeared that Kay had invoked some sort of offensive magic against him. Instead, everyone waited with bated breath as he carefully examined what they could not perceive.

Trevor finally looked up from the page, meeting Sunshine's expectant gaze with his still-dead eyes and glowing countenance, causing a cold shiver to run down her entire body as he spoke. "It's …" he blinked, his eyes were back to normal, and the radiance that had been cast unnaturally across his skin was switched off like an electric light, "it's worse than I expected." Kay had passed out while Trevor had been reading, and he looked down at her unconscious form as he mumbled softly, "I should have let her die."

"What do you mean? What did it say?"

"I can't … this …" Trevor's elbow leaning on the side of Kay's bed, he lowered his face into his hand, covering his eyes and clutching at his temples, head down and eyes clenched. "…this is …too much." He took a deep breath into his lungs, slowly drawing the air in, and with only the smallest trace of the trembling breath of sobbing overcoming his withdrawing form, vanished entirely. Sunshine and Sqrat looked at each other, at Kay's unconscious form, to the positions of the incorporeal doctors who had been watching the entire display, and none of them said or projected a single sentence for a long time, unsure of what to say, how to react.

Softly, Sunshine split the silence, "Sqrat, share this book with The Board. Perhaps there is someone else who can unlock its secrets. I'll see you in the morning," and she disappeared as well.

She appeared standing in a dark hallway, before a closed bedroom door, and knocked gently upon its surface, whispering softly, "Trevor, may I come in?" She didn't have to wait long for her answer, and the door's handle turned and the door fell gradually open to reveal a very dark bedroom. Sunshine walked into the darkness assuredly but cautiously – she could see with her mind's eye the interior of the windowless room easily enough without light to guide her

220

eyes, but she didn't know what state Trevor was in, so approached him with slow, careful steps.

Trevor was sitting cross-legged in the middle of the two beds, which were still pushed together in the middle of the room, their sheets and blankets an unmade disarray from the passions and traumas they had most recently been party to. He was hunched over and curled up, his head in his hands, sobbing as silently as sobbing can be, his hard wet breaths coming ragged and choked as his body shook and quaked with sorrow. As she looked on, knowing better than to try to comfort him physically, Ms. Charming felt that this understated display was somehow more affecting and deeply felt than it would have seemed had he be moaning and wailing and crying out as so many did when taken by feelings of loss and pain and grief and regret. She stood there, waiting for him, knowing that when he was ready to speak she would be ready to listen, but that these tears were more important than any words he could ever utter about what he was going through.

In the timelessness of tears, Trevor worked through to a point where his breaths began to come more evenly and his tears began to flow less steadily, and his heart clutched within his chest less tightly, and without looking up he sniffled a breath in and spoke in a broken, faltering voice, "I can't save her. I'm not strong enough." Sunshine moved around the corner of the bed and sat down, ending up within his reach and reasonably distant at the same time. She did not move to touch or comfort him, nor to say anything. "She hasn't even begun to have a chance in this life, and I've already failed her as a father." He looked up, his eyes locking intensely with hers, "I'm not strong enough to save her. No one is. They've been preparing for this for millennia. She's already theirs. They're going to use her, and they're going to win." His head sunk down again into his hands, and after a couple of fast, rough breaths, Trevor said, "they've already won."

As his mood sunk and his shoulders collapsed even further and Trevor seemed almost ready to collapse into himself entirely, the candles all around the room lit at once with black flames that seemed to draw the darkness of the room to a deeper black. The edges of the room disappeared entirely so that from the bed where they both sat it seemed they were floating in an endless expanse of darkness in every direction, the only two people in a universe of emptiness. Finally she reached out to him, her hand coming softly to rest on his shoulder. "It isn't over yet."

"It may as well be. You have no idea what they're capable of. I know you don't. I really shouldn't have tried to save Kay, not any part of her. What they'll do to her now…" Trevor's hands fell down into his lap and he looked up and locked his own dead, empty-feeling eyes with her more vibrant but still sad eyes. "They're worse than death. She's an individual now, through and through, and they cannot suffer individuality… they cannot … it's going to be bad for her… so…bad… for her… and worse for the rest of us."

"But it isn't over yet. The future is not set. We have to try. To die trying is far better than to die never having tried. You know this."

"I do, I know, and I know that if I try, I will fail. I'm not strong enough."

"You don't have to do this alone. Sqrat and Jurrin have already volunteered to help, and I'm sure more will come forward when they hear we have a plan."

"I don't have a plan, though. And whether they figure out how to read that book on their own or I end up telling them what was there, as soon as they know what they're up against, all will stand aside. This isn't a single wizard or a threefold of wizards that can be defeated by a simple doubling of matched powers or a proper duel."

"I know it won't be easy…"

"Not easy? Doubling matched powers isn't easy. The Devil's Arithmetic alone for taking down a threefold without creating two more can take a dozen men a dozen months' work. Let me try to give you a glimpse of what is going to destroy us, though. Imagine an army of threefolds, working together in perfect harmony. Not the handful of threefolds that Melnach got together. Not the dozen threefolds that finally overthrew the Spanish Inquisition. An army of threefolds. Hundreds of balanced trios of wizards

222

working together towards a single goal. In fact, imagine that every student attending your school right now grew up to be part of a threefold of wizards, and that all of them joined together to accomplish a single goal, and you have an idea of the power level I want to get across to you."

"I understand what you're saying, Trev, hundreds and hundreds of powerful wizards. A scale of magic never before glimpsed on this Earth before you burnt a hole right through our power maps. That does not make them undefeatable, it just makes them a bigger target."

"Don't boast. I'm not through. You have that scale of power fixed in your mind, right? Probably comparable to what I'll be able to do when I'm more experienced and mature, and vastly superior to what I could possibly do now. Except that that's how much power and experience the average member of their society has, according to that book. Just one. Do you remember Tharsis' explanations of twinned minds and dualities and the way Kay and Elle broke down? Instead of threefolds, they're pairs and pairs of pairs and so on, so the synchronicity within their internal power and experience structures is always in perfect balance and agreement. He wasn't wrong about successive generations holding the actual knowledge and experience of former generations, either – which is how we get to each one of them being as powerful and experienced as an entire army of the most powerful wizards you can imagine."

"You've already defeated two of them, yourself. They can't be that powerful."

"I didn't defeat them, Sunshine. They killed themselves to keep me from studying them. You saw Kay and Elle dismantling itself before our eyes, and I'm sure you saw how Gorsky did the same thing. I didn't defeat anything, except to keep a husk of Kay alive and a fragment of her mind intact. I ought to have let her die, for all the pain it's going to lead to."

"Don't say that. Preserving life is always the right choice."

"You know it isn't. But that's not the worst of it. Do you remember the size of the army I spoke of? A wizard for every student enrolled in your school right now? Each of them is likely more powerful than I am, and their number is approaching the number of students enrolled in every high school in the world added together. Tens upon tens of thousands of beings, perhaps hundreds of thousands of them, each with millennia of experience and power at their fingertips, all working in harmony to achieve a single cause. Which right now means keeping my daughter from me. Which means they win, and everyone else loses."

"Hundreds… hundreds of thousands of them?" Sunshine's eyes hadn't broken from the grip of Trevor's gaze, but her face had slouched as he had spoken and the reality of their opposition dawned on her. "How … how could that be right? We would know they were there, wherever they are… That much power…"

"That much power can be hidden only by its equal and opposite. Why do you think they live as twins? Each one perfectly balances the power of the other, in time, energy, and location so their traces perfectly cancel each other out. It's like the final dodgeball game, where I got into the minds of all the players on both teams to get every action by every player on either side to be balanced by the equivalent action on the other side, but more complicated by several orders of magnitude, and malevolent rather than playful. We can't detect them any more than astronomers can detect black holes."

"Astronomers can detect black holes."

"Well, that's not the point. I just meant… we can't see them because neither light nor energy nor power, nor good nor evil escapes their balance; it all comes out grey and blank, as though there was nothing there at all."

"Astronomers can detect black holes by looking at the way the space around them is effected by their gravity. We may not be able to detect them directly, but perhaps we can see how the world around them is affected by their unseen power and their unnatural balancing acts. And if we can detect them then we can find them, and if we can find them then we have to at least try to stop them."

"Try and fail."

"To try is to succeed. To give up without trying is to fail."

"We're all going to die."

"I thought you said that was going to happen anyway. If they keep the girl, they get the power they need to take over the world, right? And then it's torture, pain, and death for everyone, right?"

"I…"

"So what do we have to lose?"

"We've already lost."

"Then there's no reason not to fight, is there? No reason except apathy or laziness, and you're neither one, and I'm neither one, and I'm sure we can raise all the forces of the world together to help us."

"It's worse, still, than I've told you."

"How could it be worse? We're already waist-deep in nihilism here, planning to fight for our principles against an unbeatable army of super-beings bent on world domination, if only because we're all going to lose our lives anyway. What worse could there be?"

The black flames of the candles had been drawing the light out of the room around them, burning the candles slowly back to their former wholeness from the energy drawn out of the room, and some were beginning to go out as they reached completeness. The edges of the room were re-appearing from the inky blackness that had enveloped them, and the subtle details of Trevor's grim expression were flickering slowly deeper into Sunshine's perception. "You already know, you just haven't realized it yet."

"What is it, Trev?"

"They're already among us. All around us. In positions of power and positions of access and influence, like Kay and Elle planted in your high school and Gorsky at the Wolyd Centre, and who knows who else, where else they already are? According to the book, they usually aren't apparent as twins, but instead swap activities one twin to the other to maintain balance from hour to hour, day to day, so it could be anyone, anywhere – we can't just look for twins, and almost no one in the world could tell one of them was any different from the person next to them. Their forces are already assembled, already fighting or ready to fight, and it could be anyone. It could be Sqrat or Jurrin or Maheu'le or

Mrs. Leeds or half your student body. All the best minds and strongest powers who haven't been able to locate Hannah or my child could have been working against us this entire time without our knowing it. We can begin looking now, but that might just spell the end for us, or the self-destruction of a few more of their number to protect the rest until the time is right. They've already won."

Sunshine was beginning to look more upset, more assured and incensed than sad or lost or ready to give up. "They haven't won yet. The most important thing we can do right now is to not give up. We're not fighting against God, here – they're just men, right?"

"Very, very powerful men and women who have been preparing for this for longer than the bulk of human history."

"If they're men, they can be defeated."

"I…" The last of the candles finally snuffed out, wicks and wax restored as though they had never been burned at all, and the room's darkness was the mere natural dark of an unlit room once again.

"You're going to do just fine. Just like everything else. Just like you've been doing on your finals. I heard about your Ethics presentation, and I've seen your Math final; you're doing better than I ever did, and you're going to exceed our expectations even in this."

"Oh no! My Mentalism final!"

"Shhh… shhh… Don't worry about it, Trev. I've already discussed it with your teacher, and between your performance so far this semester and the way you handled yourself with those hiveminds, you've already got an A for the year. Especially considering the fact that you've single-handedly developed a system for detecting the slight differences in the mental topography of the hiveminds; that work alone could have earned you a fellowship at one of the top universities. Don't worry about your Mentalism final."

"What about my other classes?"

"You've more than earned an A in my History class, you earned Mr. Klaw his first dodgeball Championship in years, and you're the first student to understand Mrs. McCallum's interpretation of The Modern Prometheus –

ever. Stop worrying about school for now, and focus on trying to escape certain death at the hands of a worldwide conspiracy of ultra-powerful wizards bent on reforming the world in their own image, instead."

"Yeah, yeah, alright… I just… I don't want to shirk my responsibilities."

"You've more than met your responsibilities, Trev. You've excelled in every area, and now you have a new area to apply yourself fully to. A responsibility so much more important than any of your classes ever were. You can't give up on her now, just when she needs you most. Who else is going to be her advocate?"

"I know, I know, I just … it's …" Trevor searched for the words. "Sometimes I feel like it would be better, or… easier… just to give up, to let them win, to let go of all of this and just …" his voice trailed off into silence and his eyes fell finally, looking down into his hands held loosely in his lap.

Ms. Charming leaned in and wrapped her arms around Trevor in a big hug, trying to comfort him with her arms and her voice, "I know, Trev. It'll be alright. We'll get through this. Have faith." Her arms moved up and down his back, soothing and warming him.

"Why do I care so much about her? How can I love someone I've never met this way? She hasn't even been born yet, and the thought of losing her…" He began crying again, this time within the encircling arms of Ms. Charming, and he reached out to return the gesture of her embrace as he cried into her shoulder, collapsing into her welcoming form. They clenched each other tightly as his tears continued and his body was wracked with convulsions. Trevor truly felt as though he had already lost his daughter, the slim hope of her survival torn from him by the realization of the forces that had her in their clutches. He knew that what Ms. Charming had said was right, that he couldn't give up, that he had to fight the good fight, no matter how futile. He knew she wasn't dead yet, he wasn't dead yet, and that meant he couldn't stop yet, couldn't give up hope. He struggled to find his strength, his perseverance, the will to go on.

Suddenly Trevor felt an intense, unbelievable pain burning and tearing through him, as though his entire pelvic region were trying to crush itself inside out. His arms squeezed tighter and his fingers became as claws, digging hard into Sunshine's sides and back as he came into the grip of this unexplainable pain. He screamed, long and loud and right beside Ms. Charming's ear, and then after what felt to Trevor as an endless span of time, the pain lessened and relaxed and his voice fell and his breaths came in again instead of out and his arms and hands gradually relaxed their painful place around his high school Principal. Trevor collapsed backwards onto the disarray of sheets and pillows on the bed, finding himself once again using all his concentration just trying to breathe evenly and stay conscious.

"I …" sharp breath, "I think …" sharp breath, "I think …" one sharp, deep breath after another, "she's in labor…" and he just lay there, his hands unconsciously above the place on his body above where he didn't have a birth canal to be contracting, his eyes closed and still loosing tears down the sides of his face, breathing hard.

"It's begun. Soon, he won't matter at all. We've won."

"It isn't over yet. He's sure to know where she is, now. We must keep our defenses ready."

"Of course. Exactly. We're ready for him. He'll never get to her in time. He probably won't survive the attempt."

"And when he dies, or when the child is in our hands, then we'll have won. Not a moment before."

"I'll kill him myself if he ever gets this far. He'll never reach the girl."

"We'll find out if you're right soon enough. Be ready."

✦ ✦ ✦

"Trev? Can you hear me?"

Trevor was doubled over, one hand gripping the edge of a vacant hospital bed, a deep, guttural exhalation slowly escaping the mask of pain that his face had become. After a few more seconds, Trevor began breathing in and out again, in short, shallow breaths, slightly forming "yes, yes, yes" with exhalation after exhalation, but unable to properly vocalize his response.

"Alright. We're going to give you the dual epidural you asked for, but you need to be aware that it might not do anything to help. Since the pain isn't coming from your own nerves, the drug won't actually have anything to block, so you may just lose half your motor functions. More importantly, considering you're inside the protective walls of the Wolyd Centre, which according to all known rules and understanding of Mentalism should be blocking every single mental signal, large or small, beneficial or malevolent, from entering or leaving the building, and you're still experiencing Hannah's labor pains, the mental anesthetic we can provide may only dampen your other abilities without blocking the pain at all. Do you understand what I'm thinking?"

Trevor responded to the mental query from the unseen source with his voice, ragged from screaming out in pain, "Yes, yes, I understand! I also understand that if it does work, I probably won't be able to pinpoint her location, but there's no way I'm going to be able to battle a hundred thousand beings as powerful as any the world has ever seen while in this much pain! I can barely stand. I doubt I could throw a proper fireball, let alone dodge an attack. You don't know what this feels like! I was never supposed to feel this way! Men aren't built for this!"

"Alright, alright, can you get up onto the bed? The next contraction shouldn't be for another several minutes. We need you to lie on your right side for the physical injection." The invisible doctor continued thinking to Trevor as he slowly lifted himself onto the hospital bed and rolled onto his side in a partial fetal position. "You won't feel the needle, as we'll give the mental anesthetic first, but we need

229

you to hold still until I tell you it's safe to move. If you roll over or jerk away, you could puncture your spine, and then this body will be of no use for fighting, ever again. Try to relax." A barely visible nurse performed the actual physical injection while several specialists applied a variety of mental anesthetics to Trevor's mind to try to block the pain without knocking him out. They were very careful, per Trevor's explicit instructions, not to look directly at his mind while they operated on it. He was worried that the effects of the hivemind might carry over to them, and just as he had agreed to the risks of the procedure, they had agreed to take the personal risks of performing it on his altered mind. "You can lay back now, if you like. We've done everything we can."

Trevor curled into a tighter fetal ball, clutching his numb legs into his chest and curling his head down towards them, tightening and loosening back and forth as though rocking into himself sideways on the bed.

"Based on what you've told us, we believe the contractions are far enough apart to give you up to several hours before the baby can be born. Hopefully that will give you enough time to reach her and extract Hannah and the baby to a secure location. Even if this helps block the pain, we don't know whether your mind will be able to take actual childbirth sensations. You were right when you said you weren't built for this; very few men are able to handle a full sensory link to a woman giving birth, and there's a good chance that even with the pain portion blocked, the extremes of sensation will overwhelm you and knock you out. Some people with first-hand knowledge of both experiences have said that childbirth is significantly more painful than death."

Trevor was still rocking, still crying, trying to deal with the emotional toll of the increasingly probable loss of his child at the same time he was going through the physical and mental anguish of the labor pains that would bring her into the world. Through his tears in a half-whine, Trevor tried to respond, "I have to save her..."

"But you don't have to do it alone," Sunshine was suddenly at his side, her soft hand on the back of his, "you'll have help. Sqrat and Jurrin are preparing right now to fight alongside you, and," she paused a moment, not wanting to finish, "as you requested, Nirgal is downstairs being implanted with the training he'll need to survive. I still think it's a bad idea to put him in harm's way. He's inexperienced, just a boy. We have dozens of wizards and warriors eager to stand by your side."

"I'm…" Trevor still struggled to speak, the effects of the mental anesthetics settling in around his ability to think clearly, "I'm just a boy, too. The others will be …" Trevor coughed, then continued, "…in the second wave. I just need …" he sniffled and moaned and took another breath, "an enemy, a friend, a traitor, a believer and myself. I'm only short the two, well really, just the one, but… we'll find her on our way."

"You're speaking in riddles, Trev. Are you sure you're going to be okay?"

"None of us is going to be okay if I don't at least try. A couple of hours ago it was you telling me that, remember?"

"It was actually just over an hour ago. I remember."

"Time is a funny thing when you're in this much pain. It doesn't matter. How long until the next contraction? I need to know if this is going to help or not."

"Could be any time, now. Childbirth isn't an exact science, and we have no way of knowing how they're treating Hannah. All we can hope is that they don't try for a caesarian to get to the baby before you can reach them."

"Don't you worry about that. You just be sure there's a safe place prepared for them. I don't want to risk life and limb fighting to reach them only to have them stolen away again as soon as we think they're safe."

"I have it under control. When the time is right, if you can find me, bring them straight to me, and if you can't find me, bring them here. I'll be sure the doctors will know what to do if I can't—" As Ms. Charming continued speaking, Trevor lost track of what she was saying when another contraction turned his world to pain. The physical anesthetic had numbed his body and the mental anesthetic had numbed his mind, but whatever the source of the pain was, whatever mechanism it used to work through him, it was not diminished in any way by the dual epidural. Trevor cried out with all the strength of breath he had left in him, a sad, sorry excuse for the wailing his pain deserved, but all he could manage under the circumstances.

When the blistering white light faded from his vision and the roaring sound left his ears and his body began to unclench from the pain it could not have been feeling, Trevor spoke again in a slurred half-voice, "give me my mind back. Your tricks didn't work. It's time to go." He rolled towards the edge of the bed and lowered his legs down to the floor and tried to stand, but his legs collapsed underneath him and he crashed, hard to the floor. He pulled himself along by his arms for a moment, unable to get his weight up onto his numbed legs, but then the doctors managed to remove the first of the mental anesthetics, and Trevor was able to levitate his torso up above the ground a couple of feet, and he moved towards the stairwell with his half-limp, numb legs trailing backwards behind him along the floor, his feet catching against the legs of tables and beds as he half-floated away. The second mental anesthetic was removed just before he reached the stairs, which probably saved his knees and legs from being broken on the way down the stairwell – Trevor was able to levitate his entire body above the ground, his feet mere inches above the stairs he was descending in a weaving pattern to reach his friend below. Trevor reached the first floor of the Wolyd Centre and levved down the hallway towards the training room were he knew he would find Nirgal, a doctor upstairs working furiously to try to disengage the final mental anesthetic without seeing even a glimpse of Trevor's mind. Just before he reached out to open the door, Trevor felt the last gauzy threads of numbness lift from his mind, and he paused to do a quick mental check.

Which seemed to be the cue for all four edges of the door he was levving in front of to begin expelling light, as though a white phosphorous grenade or some unearthly portal had been activated on the other side and the light was so bright that it came out in intense streaks all around the opaque surface of the door. When the light diminished and finally disappeared, Trevor waited just another brief moment before turning the handle and levving into the room.

"Was that yours, Nirgal?"

"What? Oh, err… yeah. That was my first try."

"Looks good enough. We're going. Now."

"He's not ready, Trev. There's so much more he needs to know before he faces … a proper wizard." The unseen doctor seemed unable to admit what the boys would be going up against, even to himself.

"Well, it looks like he's mastered the blinding light, which is what I asked you to teach him. He isn't going up against a proper wizard. We're going to try to get by something between ten and a hundred thousand wizards, each more powerful than several hundred experienced threefolds. There is no one in the world that could thoroughly prepare him for that, no amount of time." Trevor turned from the incorporeal doctor to face Nirgal again, "are you sure you want to do this? I'm not going to pussyfoot around the dangers like some people may; we'll probably all die before we get within a thousand miles of Hannah and my child, and then the world will be destroyed by the power of the fruit of my loins. Worse perhaps than death, your mind and body may be absorbed into one of their hiveminds and you may end up working for them, against me and everyone you've ever cared about, from today until the day they wear your body out and die – in which case, your mind will go on in another of their bodies and another and another forever and ever, knowing you were unable to prevent them from taking over the world. If you want to back out, now is your last chance. I can't have you chickening out in the middle of a real battle."

"Have I ever chickened out in a dodgeball game? No. Have I ever questioned one of your plans? No. And if I understood Ms. Charming's memories earlier, everything you warned me might happen if I joined you is definitely going to happen to me if I don't join you and you fail. Together, maybe the world has a better chance."

"It sounds so melodramatic when you say it."

"What, you can't hear yourself? You're like Mr. Drama King over there, with your 'the world will be destroyed by the power of the fruit of my loins' and 'your mind will go on forever knowing you were unable to prevent them from taking over the world.' It's like watching a bad science fiction movie."

"Fine, fine, but we've got to go."

"Are you sure you're okay to go, Trev? You legs look a little … funky."

"An anesthetic has been injected between the outer membrane covering my spinal cord and the overlying bones of my spine, knocking out all feeling and some motor coordination from about here," he indicated with his hands where his numbness began, "on down. I can't walk. And every time Hannah has a contraction, I'm going to be unable to levitate, either. But we can't let our enemy know that, so I'm going to attach a simple cue from my mind to yours. As soon as my mind begins to be overwhelmed with labor pains, you'll do the Blinding Light effect automatically, and no one within visual range of the two of us will be able to see or hear or think anything until my pain is gone."

"Ooooh! I understand, now. Sure, hook me up." Nirgal could feel a light touch on his mind, and didn't try to block it or examine it at all. He continued talking under the careful touch of Trevor's Mentalism, "is that all you need me for, or do I get to get into the heat of the battle, too? I mean, if you think I'm not ready, that's cool, but if there's any way I can help… uhh… whoa… that feels weird…"

"Sorry about that, I was just implanting another trigger. In case I die, you should find yourself in a safe place."

"Hey, don't talk that way. You're the man who tied a dodgeball game, who burned a hole through all the power maps, and got voted King of the End of the World. You're not going to die without being crowned King, are you?"

"What? I thought Harrison was a sure thing. I'm not even a senior – isn't The End of the World Ball usually just the graduating class?"

"They did another vote after the championship games, while you were out sick. There were two questions. One asking if you should be considered for it, and the other to rank everyone's choices for King and Queen. You won, a clear Condorcet winner in both. I was supposed to get you to go without telling you, but… you have to have something to look forward to, right?"

"But the ball is tonight, isn't it? What if we can't get away from saving the world in time?"

"I guess we'd better save the world before midnight, then. That's when they crown the King and Queen."

They both started giggling, and then everything went blindingly white and deafeningly silent for an internally unknowable period of time while Trevor was in the grip of another contraction. When the light began to fade, Nirgal was just barely able to see Trevor's form rising again into the air; if he hadn't known that Trevor was unable to stay upright during the contraction, he might not have noticed anything amiss at all. "I guess that works. Are you okay, Trev?"

"Yeah, yeah." Trevor was clearly disoriented and still in pain as he brushed off Nirgal's inquiry. "I'll be fine. Let's go get Sqrat and Jurrin and get out of here."

"Do we know where we're going, exactly?"

"I don't think that should stop us."

"So, no?"

"Yeah, no." Trevor disappeared, and Nirgal was automatically drawn to follow him, disappearing a half-second later and appearing again by his side without consciously doing a thing.

"Did you do that?"

"No, you did. Another hook, to keep us together. You don't mind, do you?"

"How many connections did you make in there? We're not a hivemind now, are we?"

Trevor laughed out loud, "Not even close. I didn't do anything you couldn't learn at school. Certainly nothing really invasive. Just… advanced."

"Sure, sure. But you'll have to show me how, later."

"Fine." Trevor turned his attention to the other two in the room, "Sqrat, Jurrin, are you about ready to go?"

"Are you? We heard you've been feeling sympathetic pains from the mother, are you sure you're going to be alright?" Jurrin seemed nearly genuinely concerned.

"Look at me. Do I look alright? I can't feel anything below about here," Trevor indicated again the point where his body's sensations disappeared beneath him, "so I'm going to be levving everywhere we go, and yes, every few minutes I'm going to be crippled with pain. It doesn't matter whether I'm alright or not, there's no alternative."

"Your so-called 'second wave' could join us. They're very eager to be on the front lines."

"And I'm not exactly…" Sqrat looked like a scorned puppy, afraid of his own master, "I mean, I wouldn't mind a little assistance, myself." He flinched away from Trevor, as though expecting to be struck down for displaying cowardice.

"You, Sqrat, have a central role to play, today. Just try to stay alive until your moment comes. Don't freeze up or pull your punches; there's no need to worry about perfectly balancing your ethical charge today," Trevor looked at Sqrat as if to say that he knew his words had special meaning that he was very careful not to say, "everyone will know whose side you were on, after today."

"Y-y-y-yes, sir. Of course, sir."

"And there's no need to be formal. We're all fighting together, today. Though some of us apparently feel the need for more armor than others. Jurrin, you're not exactly built for a full suit of plate armor. Do you even know how to wield that sword? It's half again as tall as you are."

Jurrin swung, stepped, parried, thrust, spun, and otherwise displayed his agility and prowess with a sword from within a full suit of what must have been magically light armor. "I've spent more hours practicing in this armor, with this sword, than you two children have been alive on this Earth. I have defended my life and honor with this steel on enough occasions to be confident that I will not be taken down in a physical fight."

"And what about a mental fight? How's your Mentalism defense? Would you say you could destroy Maheu'le's mind in a duel to the death? Or will you be turned against us by the first lowly guard we come across?"

"I'm not going to claim to be Maheu'le's equal, but I'm no slouch when it comes to Mentalism defense. Try to turn me, right now. I'm certainly able to defend… HUrK!" Jurrin's body began spasming and quaking and he dropped his sword before he fell over, his armor's percussion against the ground creating an intensely jarring audible impact on the other three. His spasms slowed and his gurgling and sputtering turned to moaning, and Jurrin slowly began to stand again, rubbing his head as though sorry he hadn't been wearing his helmet. "How…" Jurrin leaned on the wall for support, "How did you do that? Who taught you that?"

"That, my now-educated colleague, is something I remembered from my brief time as part of a very young hivemind. I imagine that their more closely guarded techniques and experiences will be much more effective at ignoring your defenses. But let's pretend for a moment that I'll be able to hold back their mental attacks while you fight them with your sword. Can you fight without being able to see or hear your enemy, or to think?" The room filled suddenly with the Blinding Light effect, and everything was white, until it wasn't. When the room came back into focus, Jurrin's sword was held in what would have been a threatening position, right against Trevor's unprotected throat, had Trevor not fallen hard to the ground in the clutches of another contraction. Trevor had simply re-lifted himself safely out of the way before the effect had fully faded and made Jurrin look less competent than his apparent ability to move and think in the midst of Nirgal's Blinding Light should have. "Good, good. At least you're not as useless as Sqrat." Sqrat still had his hands clutched over his eyes as though that would have blocked the effect and was gasping for air as though he had been unable to breath during its course. "Sqrat, you're going to have to learn to deal with the Blinding Light. To keep my weakened state and painfully prone body from harm, Nirgal will automatically be generating that effect every time I experience Hannah's labor pains. I feel like I'm repeating myself. Nirgal, am I repeating myself?"

"They've never heard you say it, but yes, you've said it before."

"Fine, whatever, can we get on our way now?"

"Where are we going exactly, Trev?" Jurrin asked as he donned his helmet.

"That's a good question. But I don't have the answer."

"You don't…" Jurrin didn't seem to understand. Nirgal had already asked, and stayed quiet. Sqrat looked at his feet, and wringed his hands.

"I don't have that answer, no." From his levitating position, Trevor was towering over Sqrat's diminutive form. "Sqrat does."

Sqrat didn't look up.

"No games now, Sqrat. No hiding clues out in the open, no feigning ignorance. You want us to get to her, too, so it would behoove you to at least tell us where the church is and save us some time and energy and pain in getting there." Trevor paused briefly as though waiting for a response from the tiny man, and then continued, "you don't even have to tell us, just go there, and we'll follow you." Trevor very quickly strung a couple of mental links between himself and Sqrat and himself and Jurrin, and levitated in place, waiting for Sqrat to disappear. Sqrat lifted his arms to his sides, as was his habit when disappearing, but then hesitated, looking up with fear and tears into Trevor's expectant glare. "GO!" Trevor's shout was loud enough and raw enough to rattle Jurrin's armor and apparently loud enough to shock Sqrat into dropping his arms and disappearing. The other three of them followed behind him along the path Trevor's links had made, and the four of them found themselves before the imposing, elegant stone walls of what appeared to be a time-worn cathedral.

The sun was high above them; they were farther west than they had begun. The day glinted warm and bright off Jurrin's highly polished gold-inlaid armor and seemed to be swallowed up by the dark brown of the formal dueling underrobes that Trevor and Nirgal were wearing. They all stared for a moment up the sides of the massive structure before them, taking in the intricate details of the masonry, the stained-glass windows, the vast architecture created before engineering or science had even been invented.

"That's some church." Nirgal was probably not the only one intimidated by its size, but he was the only one who vocalized it. None of the others even knew how to respond. They simply began walking or levving up the wide stone steps towards the immense wooden doors that stood between them and their target, Nirgal never leaving Trevor's side as they progressed. There was no way for them to know what was waiting for them on the other side of the doors before them, nor even whether they would be able to pass through them without difficulty, and they did not hurry in their approach. Not until Sqrat stopped entirely, staring straight up, jaw agape, and the other three turned around to see why he'd paused.

"Why have you stopped? What's wrong?"

Sqrat didn't speak, didn't close his mouth, but moved one arm to point straight up. The others looked up only for an instant before they all shouted out "Run!" and moved quickly away from the frozen form of Sqrat. Nirgal and Trevor moved further up the stairs, reaching the door before they saw that Jurrin's lateral motion had reversed to shove Sqrat's still-motionless form out of the path of the gargoyle plummeting directly towards them both. Nirgal instinctively cast a blocking charge at the gargoyle, as though it were simply an oversized dodgeball, but the power he put into it was of the carefully practiced scale to exactly counter a stone dodgeball, and it merely knocked the two-faced head off the gargoyle before it crashed into the stone steps below with explosive force.

"Shit!" Nirgal cursed his failure and tried to see whether their companions had escaped the brunt of the crushing force and stone shrapnel. Trevor was generating ball after ball of what could only be visually described as a distortion, very apparently similar to most any of his dodgeball inventions, and juggling them up into the air above him in higher and higher arcs as their number increased.

"Nirgal!" Trevor shouted, now carefully juggling nine dodgeball-sized rippling distortions above him, "They're fine! I'm going to throw these power amplifiers at the other gargoyles as they come down, and I need you to do that blocking charge against them so they intersect just before they get to the falling statues! Got it?" Trevor couldn't wait for a response; the next hurtling mass of carefully carved stone was half a second from hitting Nirgal, and he tossed one of the amplifiers at it. The other gargoyles that had been cast down upon them came in rapid succession, a carpet-bombing of stone upon stone, and Trevor hurled his amplifiers as fast and accurately as he could, unable to take the time to see whether Nirgal was doing his part to stop the onslaught until it was over. He looked around through the cloud of dust that was slowly settling around them, and saw the glinting sparkles of Jurrin's armor approaching him up the stairs, a shadowy form close behind. Nirgal was sitting down, breathing hard, with his back to the door and his eyes on the sky. "Are you okay, Nirgal?"

"What? Yeah." Nirgal's eyes didn't move from the sky. "There were, uhh…"

"What?"

"There were sixteen of them, Trev. Not ten. You only gave me nine amplifiers."

"But you stopped the other six, right?"

"Well, yeah, but…"

"But nothing. You just needed to get warmed up. We've got more than mass and gravity to worry about on the other side of the door you're leaning against. And they know we're here." Trevor reached out to lay a flat palm against the wood of the door just as Jurrin and Sqrat reached the wide platform at the top of the stairs to stand beside him. "Are you two alright? Sqrat, you have to keep up and at least try to defend yourself."

Sqrat was covered from head to foot in a light coating of the fine, light grey dust of the gargoyle that had shattered quite nearly on top of him, and carried a terrified and relieved look on his face as though he was simultaneously glad to have survived this first challenge and knew well that the next one would almost certainly represent a far greater danger to him than the last. He didn't make a sound or a motion of acknowledgement; he just stood there, his eyes unfixed. Trevor didn't wait for another volley of

240

stone death from above to shake Sqrat out of it, he just turned back to the door, pulled his palm off its surface, and knocked hard upon it with his closed fist three resounding times. Both sides of the door opened inward, slowly, and Nirgal nearly lost his balance as his back support was pulled away from him. Nirgal stood and turned to face the interior of the church alongside the other three members of the party, none of them sure what they needed to be ready for on the other side.

As they waited the seemingly endless moments that it took for the doors to reveal the small, ornately decorated foyer of the church, Jurrin spoke, "It just … opened. They're letting us in. Why are they just letting us in?"

"We should turn back." Sqrat's face hadn't moved, his eyes remained unfixed. He seemed to be in a state of shock. But his thought came as clearly to them as though it were riding the wave of terror that should have been overwhelming them as the doors came finally to a stop, fully open.

"We go in. Sqrat would never betray his masters, and this is where he brought us. If the first attack didn't confirm for you that we're in the right place, I don't know what will."

"I thought there'd be armies waiting for us. We haven't seen a single person yet. What have they got planned?"

"We won't know until we try." Trevor took the first step into the church, and the doors instantly began to close on them. Trevor's response was to step inward, out of the way, and Nirgal never left his side. Jurrin stepped backwards, but not out of fear or to protect his personal safety; he moved behind Sqrat and pushed him into the foyer with due force. The doors seemed to close much more rapidly than they had opened, and when they closed, the sound of it had a certain finality to it that implied that they would not be leaving the way they'd just come in. Trevor was already headed towards the curtains hung across the row of stone arches that separated them from the main body of the cathedral's interior when the others turned to react to the sound of the doors' sealing behind them. He reached out and

241

grasped the middle edge of the wide, red velvet curtains, and before he pulled them open, addressed the others, "Are you coming, guys? I can't save the world by myself."

They came up close behind him, the four of them too wide to pass through a single arch side by side, and just as Trevor pulled the curtain aside, the entire world turned white and silent.

When Trevor was able to unclench his face, his body, his mind, and pick himself up off the cold stone floor still reeling in the feeling of the lingering intensity of a pain he knew he had been the cause of, Trevor could see in the fading Blinding Light that Jurrin had reacted well, cutting the curtain entirely down from the arch before them so that those on the other side would be in the thrall of the effect even after Trevor had lost his grip. Trevor hadn't actually lost his grip, his hand clenching only tighter on the curtain in that moment of pain, but he certainly hadn't stayed levitating above the floor. Trevor dropped his handful of curtain as he regained his proper altitude, taking in the sea of men and women now visible beyond the arch, most of them still clutching at their eyes in the same futile way he couldn't see Sqrat doing behind him. He was not surprised to see that none of them appeared identical to anyone else present; if these bodies were lost in the fray, their minds would become an army equally strong and doubly experienced with their mirrored bodies, surely safely distant from this congregation.

Jurrin was running forward as soon as he could see again, decapitating half a dozen with each swing of his sword and not stopping to wait for their bodies to reach the ground before he progressed through the swarming crowd. He fought the fight of the righteous; he didn't want to save Trevor's child any more than he wanted to preserve Trevor's life, but he certainly didn't want a power potentially as dangerous as Trevor to fall under the control of an organization bent on world domination any more than he could stand the idea of Trevor turning against The Board – he knew he had to do everything in his power to destroy the both of them, which in this moment meant killing those who kept him from killing the unborn child. Jurrin had convictions, he stood by them, and did not shirk from doing what he believed would forward the triumph of what was right. In this moment, that meant killing hundreds of men and women in a church, the aisles between the pews filling quickly with the blood and bodies of the dead.

Trevor and Nirgal remained at the back of the church, just inside the arch they had passed through, Trevor's eyes closed, his mind locked in careful concentration as he fought to keep the thousands upon thousands of mental attacks against Jurrin and Nirgal and Sqrat from landing any kind of blow against his team. He was sweating profusely with the effort. Nirgal was furiously blocking direct magical attacks against Trevor and himself, trying as often as possible to use his dodgeball reflexes to redirect the attacks at those who very clearly wanted to do them real harm. Sqrat was still in a daze, still standing in the foyer behind them, his eyes still unfixed, and if he had taken another step or two forward, he would probably already have been injured or dead from lack of self-defense. Trevor was taking a risk, relying on a hope, not defending himself from mental attacks, but since none of the attacks seemed to be directed directly at his own mind, he was either right in his hope – and they knew it – or very lucky. It took a surprisingly short amount of time for Jurrin to kill the last of the hundreds who had been waiting for their arrival, and as the final bodies fell lifeless to the floor, the magical and mental attacks were also stopped and silenced.

Jurrin raised his bloody sword into the air and screamed out a warrior's deep cry of success on the battlefield. His armor now gleamed a sickening, glistening red, dripping with the blood of the slain and trailing bits of entrails and hair and skin from the crevasses and joints where they had become caught in the opening and pinching created by his broad, sweeping, swinging dance of death. He turned back to face them, lifting the faceplate of his helmet, and they could see a strange pattern of gore painted across his eyes in the shape of the opening in his armor, blood dripping down his face like horrible tears, the whites of his eyes shining out through the intense red that had surrounded them. "That was easy," he cried out, triumphant.

"That was too easy," said Nirgal, almost out of breath from the continuous action of his defense.

"That was just the beginning. There must be more, waiting." Trevor turned his head to shout out over his shoulder, "Sqrat! Get your lazy ass in here this instant!"

Sqrat hurried in, finally shaken from his former stupor, but still a cowering mess of a man.

"You're supposed to be helping. Is this how you behave in your threefold?"

Jurrin was drawn out of his self-acclamation by this comment, and began carefully stepping down and across the mound of corpses he had created. "Is what he said true? You, Sqrat, are a member of a proper threefold? Is that even possible?"

Sqrat was looking pleadingly at Trevor and shaking his head furiously back and forth. Trevor spoke again, "Don't worry about that for right now, Jurrin. You did well. But there's something wrong. There should have been more of them, and they should have been more powerful. This either isn't the right church, or there's more to it than meets the eye. I suspect there's an exactly equal number of them hidden somewhere, waiting to fight us, but even so..." Trevor was looking around the inside of the cathedral, but his mind was searching much further for answers, "...I know this isn't the right place. Sqrat. Why did you bring us here?"

"He..." Sqrat's voice was trembling with fear, his face clenched like he expected to be struck down at any moment, not by anyone present, but by the one he was speaking about, "He wasn't sure which one they'd have her at. They're all the same from the outside, and he couldn't get to anyone on the inside. This was his best guess. It looked like the most powerful, to me."

"How many are there? How many couldn't he decide between?"

"Uhh… Ahh.. About thirty-five, I think…"

Nirgal collapsed again to the floor in a seated position, with his back to one of the columns that formed the arches between them and the foyer. "Thirty five?"

"N-n-not counting the hundreds he was s-s-sure were too small."

Trevor sighed. "I knew there were a lot of them, but…" he moved his hand up to massage his forehead and temples, bending his head down and closing his eyes, "I thought Sqrat's master knew which one she was at. Fuck." No one said anything, even as the world faded to white, time passed, and then the world faded back into view around them. Trevor wasn't sure whether he was in more pain from his impending failure or from the contractions that now punctuated that failure.

"So what do we do now? Go through all the churches one by one? If each one is as easy as this, we should be fine."

"I'm pretty sure they weren't actually expecting us here. Think about it. This is the wrong church. It could be on the wrong side of the globe from the right one. These people were probably regular congregants, waiting to celebrate their religion's triumph in a few hours. A real defensive force …"

"Won't be this easy," Jurrin's voice was losing its strength, and he leaned against his sword for support, "I see that, now. Do you think one of them," he indicated the stacks of dead behind him, "knew where she's being held?"

"We c-c-could g-g-go downs-s-stairs and ask them." Sqrat seemed to be becoming freer with the information he had been pretending not to have as the trauma of the situation he had forced his way into took hold of his psyche.

"Sqrat's right. The mirror of the church and the other halves of these twins are probably directly beneath us, and well aware of what's happened here. Their knowledge isn't lost to us yet. I doubt they'll be very forthcoming with it, though." Trevor reached out a hand to help Nirgal back to his feet, "Who's up for finding out?" and he walked confidently across the back of the church to make his way up the side aisle which wasn't full of still-leaking corpses. He still held Nirgal's hand, not having to drag him along, but giving him enough confidence through that connection to go forward. Jurrin ushered Sqrat forward, and they were not far behind by the time they reached the transept and turned towards the center of the symbolic center of the church. There, behind a wide altar, was a sort of stairwell that descended under the church. Trevor did not hesitate to proceed down into the unknown.

Due to the close walls and tight corners of the stairwell, the sanity of perspective that would have been afforded by the church above them was quickly lost, and while they were all certainly disoriented and confused by the apparently impossible curves and angles the stairs seemed to take, when they noticed that they were climbing up instead of down they did not bother to turn back; it felt as though they already had, the turns and twists of their progress reversed from their descent. When Trevor emerged into a dark, really almost entirely lightless version of the church he had just left, he could see from the reactions of the crowd still in their pews, bent in silent prayer, that they had not expected him to take these stairs to find them; they began to run towards the back of the church, escaping as quickly as they could through the black velvet curtains that blocked the arches there. Jurrin was close behind Trevor and Nirgal, and ran into the crowd, commanding them to stop. They didn't seem to hear him, or they simply didn't care.

Very few of them attempted to attack, knowing they had already failed with all the power they possessed, and the few attempts that were made seemed only to distract for the others' escapes. Trevor was already levitating, and simply moved across above the tangled mass of fleeing bodies beneath him with Nirgal's hand still in his, floating along behind him. They came down near the curtains and Trevor sent Nirgal a mental command, "give me a mudball." Nirgal didn't question it, and in between blocking the relatively weak attacks coming their way, generated an overpowered mudball. Trevor tossed a small effect at it, then thought to Nirgal, "throw it at the curtains." He knew Nirgal wouldn't have heard him over the rabble and commotion of Jurrin and the slowly escaping crowd, but the thought worked fine, and Nirgal's timing was fine, throwing at a moment when the curtains hung closed before him.

Trevor's alteration had apparently caused the mudball to split; instead of one mudball flying at one curtain,

246

enough mudballs to coat every single curtain hanging in every single arch along the entire width of the rear of the nave of the dark cathedral flew out of Nirgal's hands with uncanny aim. They all struck targets, either curtains or people between other mudballs and curtains, and the mud quickly slithered and slicked its way up and down and around the surfaces of the curtains, drying rapidly to create a solid barrier that the remaining crowd could not easily escape. They began pounding on it and trying to dispel it, but it was enough to slow them down for a moment or two.

Trevor began querying their minds, looking for one that was still thinking about the reason they were there or the location of the church he was seeking or anything that would help him at all. Almost instinctively, as soon as Trevor touched their minds looking for the information they had, they began deconstructing themselves all around him. Even those he hadn't touched directly seemed to know that he was about to, and he found that every one of them was one step, one moment, one pair of minds lesser, that much closer to its own destruction. Their bodies began to fall all around him, and Trevor was sure he could hear collapsing sounds on the other side of the solidified curtains as well. They weren't about to let him have even the tiniest piece of information from them, and just like Gorsky and Kay and Elle before them, these hundreds of people were willing to give up their very lives to protect the rest of their kind.

This time the piles of bodies all around them was bloodless and it was Jurrin who said, "that was too easy."

"That served no purpose." Trevor sighed. It hadn't taken but a few minutes, and the body count of their excursion had doubled, and they knew almost nothing more than they had known when they'd first appeared outside, upstairs. "We're no closer to saving her." He levved over to an empty pew and collapsed onto his side just before the most painful contraction he had experienced so far seemed to tear his lower body into tiny shreds of burning, searing, compressed and intense pain. The world faded to white and silence, free from thought, but not free from pain. It felt to Trevor like something must be going wrong; the pain was changing. He became more worried even as he felt less able to find the source of his fears. When the world faded back into existence from the white of the Blinding Light, Trevor was sobbing loudly, an emotional wreck.

"We have to find her," Jurrin said, "there must be a way to narrow down the list. What else do you know, Sqrat? Why did you bring us here? This was too easy, and they weren't really ready for us. I'd even be willing to bet those gargoyles were part of an automatic defense system."

"You'd lose that bet," an unfamiliar voice came to them from the opposite end of the nave, far beyond the altar at the transept. "I threw them at you myself, and I'm not exactly automatic."

Trevor didn't sit up or even stop crying, though he did keep a close mental watch on the minds of his companions to be sure they were not under attack. Nirgal began building a mudball before him, larger and larger, preparing for another wave of attack. Jurrin climbed up on the highest mound of bodies to try to see who had spoken, and Sqrat hid behind the last row of pews, hoping he hadn't been seen.

"They weren't counting on anyone competent showing up to take on such a small congregation, you see." The voice was deep and resonant, but also seemed female in tone, and was definitely approaching them. "So they figured I'd be enough defense from the roof, all by myself. If I agreed with the popes' position on this whole world domination business, I'd probably have given you a harder time out there." The hulking figure was now clearly in view, two giant heads atop a wide, thick frame with a hunch on her back that kept her stooped to a low-looking nine or ten feet tall. Something about her seemed gentle, despite the deadly muscles ripplingly apparent across her entire form, the deep gravely timbre of her voice, and the fact that she had just basically admitted that she had been ordered to kill them. "Not that it would have done any good. You're the real thing, aren't you? I suppose there's something special about this church they never bothered to tell me, some important reliquary you need to locate to defeat them that they haven't realized is important yet? You guys are probably five steps ahead of them, aren't you?" She had finally come down the

248

full length of the wide aisle to where Nirgal and Jurrin were standing, and turned to see the curled form of Trevor, still laying down weeping in the last pew.

"You're… you're not going to hurt us, are you?" Nirgal's mudball was twice as big as a beach ball now, he had been unconsciously enlarging it the entire time.

"Why would I do that?" The huge, two-headed woman chuckled deeply, "and what were you going to do with all that mud? Is it bath time already?"

Trevor stopped weeping long enough to mumble "a Gollum… Nirgal… you can do it…" before he went back to crying.

Nirgal almost dropped the mud at the suggestion, but was so used to following Trevor's leadership without question that his mouth had automatically begun forming the runic poem that was supposed to give life to it. After the first time he incanted the ancient poem, the mud had begun to solidify and lengthen. As he spoke it a second time, he lowered it to the ground as it took on vaguely humanoid features such as arms and legs and a sort of a head. By the end of the third time through the poem, the mud had taken on a very lifelike and detailed composition, and was drying to a very flesh-like hue. He then spoke the final verse of the poem, the runes that give life to the mud, and suddenly there seemed to be a real living breathing naked human being standing between them where only mud had been before. He had a single runic symbol carved into his forehead and was completely hairless and without genitals, but seemed fully to be a normal man in every other way.

"What a beautiful poem," said the huge woman.

"I can't believe it worked," said Nirgal.

"How is this going to help us find the girl with the baby?" asked Jurrin.

Sqrat stayed hidden behind the pew, trembling as silently as he could.

"What girl with a baby?" asked the Gollum.

"Quickly, Nirgal, carve the two ancient runic symbols for my name into his hand," mumbled Trevor.

"I don't have a knife!"

"He's still made of mud, to you, until he has a name. Use your fingers."

Nirgal grabbed the Gollum's right hand and found that he could, indeed, carve into it as though it were soft mud. The Gollum did not seem to object, and as Nirgal completed the second rune, his skin hardened to the touch, and his features shifted and he soon looked like a hairless nonsexual duplicate of Trevor. Nirgal let go of the creature's hand and it fell limp to its side.

"Oh, that baby." The creature put its head down into its hand, massaging its forehead and temples the same way Trevor so often did. For a long moment it just stood there like that, creeping Nirgal and Jurrin out, and then it seemed to realize its nakedness, and it conjured a duplicate of Trevor's outfit onto itself without taking its hand away from its bald head. The creepiness was not diminished.

"Yeah, that baby." Trevor was sitting up, pulled upright onto numb legs by a single arm on the back edge of the pew. He looked through still-wet eyes at the Gollum of himself and the huge two-headed woman beyond it, nodding. "I suppose we were here for you, weren't we? Why would they keep you around? Two heads isn't the same thing as twins, and you… you're not part of a hivemind."

"Not compatible, they said. They tried to win me over with their propaganda and their dogma, but I never really believed in it. Of course, they wouldn't have given me any peace if I'd tried to leave. Better to have me locked away here or destroyed than working against them, right? I guess they never really understood me, did they?"

"How did they find you?" Trevor stopped himself before she could answer, "Never mind that. You remind me of someone. Who do you remind me of?"

"You haven't met him yet. Goes by the nickname 'Trunk'. He's the one who told me about you in the first place. Well, a version of you. But that's not important right now. We've got to —" the world filled again with white and silence, free from conscious thought, as Trevor succumbed to another painful contraction, this one worse in that 'things are going wrong' way, interrupting the woman's directive. She seemed to have seen it coming though, because she

250

didn't seem to have missed a beat, picking up exactly where she'd left off as soon as the world came back into view, "— save your daughters. We can talk when they're safe."

"Daughters?" asked Jurrin. Somehow he hadn't been informed of Trevor's earlier speculation to that effect.

Trevor was trying to pull himself back upright again; he was having more and more trouble recovering from the labor pains. "Do you…" he had to pause for a deep, sucking breath, "Do you know where they are?"

"I never… They don't exactly let me in on their plans. And they rarely say anything important out loud; they usually just think the most important parts to each other. So, err… I want to help you guys, but … no. I don't know where they have her, exactly." She sighed a huge, dual sigh that would have blown back the Gollum's hair if it had had any, saying, "I can tell you anything you want about this church, though. I've been here for years."

"It can't hurt," said Trevor, struggling to keep his eyes open, "why don't you tell us why the church is built this way. The others don't know, yet."

"You mean, why it's two churches, one light and one dark?" Trevor nodded to her, so she continued, "Balance, of course. They take great pride in their stupid balances, balancing good and evil, light and dark, one twin for another, everything balancing out to create what they think of as harmony." Watching the woman speak was an interesting thing; sometimes one head would speak, and sometimes the other, they didn't argue, and there seemed to be no pattern to which head would take which sentences. Somehow it seemed totally natural, though. "So one church is above ground, reaching up, worshiping God, and all its congregants carefully go through the opposite motions of their components below ground, who are cursing God, their church sinking down into the earth. If there are enough of them, perfectly balanced, no one knows they're here, not God or the Devil, and certainly not sensitives like you and yours. It takes them years to have these churches built, some of the bigger ones took centuries, and to exacting standards that they cannot directly oversee. It's quite a grueling process, from what I hear, since if any of them ever came around before the completion of the structure, they could be detected, so they have to communicate with a workforce not under their control, and from a distance. I really don't know how they get anything done, but I suppose they value their secrecy enough to go through all that."

"That explains why they don't show up on power maps; they're intentionally canceling themselves out."

"Not that they do such a good job around here. I mean, with me here, they've got to be pretty far out of 'balance' – they're always trying to get me to do things forwards and backwards on alternate days to make up for it. Not to mention the fact that they're too small to get that critical mass of masking balance they strive for."

"The other churches are bigger?"

"Oh, yeah, much bigger. Well, in attendance, I mean. A church this size can seat thousands, not just the hundreds that were here today. And of course, each one actually holds up to twice as many as possible, what with everyone and their double showing up. But this is one of the smaller churches, actually – I saw one of the big ones, once, and it makes this place," she indicated the vast open spaces above them, descending into shadow at what seemed to be impossible heights, "look genuinely cramped."

"If this is one of the smaller churches," asked the Gollum of Trevor, "why did Sqrat's master think it was the biggest?"

"Because it was the most out of balance," Trevor responded to his own voice very matter-of-factly. "The thirty five churches he thought were good candidates are probably the smallest, the ones without a critical mass of balance."

The sound of Jurrin's armor settling onto the wooden pew was a strange one, punctuating his dejected collapse. "Which means the hundreds he thought were too small to bother with were probably the larger ones. This situation just keeps getting worse, doesn't it?"

"Worse still, the church they've been hiding Hannah at is probably the largest and most well-balanced, and if our interpretation of Sqrat's information is correct, it shouldn't show up on the power maps at all." Trevor was levitating himself back up as close to standing as he could with his legs dangling limp beneath him. "It would perfectly cancel itself out, distortion and all."

The sound of footsteps and armor and grunting and shouting grew from the direction of the altar, echoing around the distant stone surfaces to make the approaching warriors seem more numerous and murderous than they were. It was the second wave, every other of the men and women emerging from the twisted stairwell behind the altar a huge, fierce, armed warrior or a powerful robed wizard practically crackling with magical energy, all of them ready for a fight that had ended well before they had arrived. They fanned out, some approaching down the center aisle and the rest flanking down both sides of the pews, as though some foe might be hidden in the dark corners, waiting for the chance to strike. There were three dozen in all, sixteen ready to kill with their hands and their strength and their steel, and twenty quite eager to defend and destroy with their magic and their minds.

While Trevor waited for them to come to a halt and give him their full attention, he addressed Sqrat, "give me the map."

"What map," Sqrat feigned ignorance again, "do you m-m-mean?"

"Your master wouldn't have let you leave without the map, Sqrat. He couldn't risk you having to contact him before we reach the girl, and you've said yourself he didn't know which location she was at." Trevor levved closer to Sqrat, extending his arm expectantly, palm up towards the cowering man, "not to mention the fact that he couldn't possibly have trusted you to remember where to go without a map, you little twit." With the intensity of the labor pains, Trevor was having trouble keeping his emotions from surging, and it was coming out as anger directed at Sqrat. By this time, the largest of the second wave were standing all around, towering over Sqrat and supporting Trevor's assertions without needing to understand them or utter a sound. Sqrat reached into his vest, pulled out a folded piece of parchment, and reluctantly placed it in Trevor's outstretched hand.

Trevor unfolded the map and spent about half a second glancing at it before handing it over to the oldest and most powerful of the wizards in the second wave. "Marked on this map you'll find this location, plus about three dozen others of about this one's power, and hundreds of what appear to be smaller, less significant locations. From what, uhhh…" Trevor indicated the two-headed woman still towering over all of them, prompting her for a response.

"Call me Sophie."

"From what Sophie's told us, the smaller it appears on that map, the more people and power it has. Start with the easiest and work your way up. None of them will be expecting you, if you work fast enough and keep anyone from escaping. Jurrin cleared the upstairs in about fifteen minutes, and these killed themselves twice as fast to keep me from finding out what they knew." Trevor's hands were out in front of him, creating another ball of energy, this one glowing slightly instead of merely distorting the appearance of the space it intersected with, as he continued speaking. "The ones you'll be fighting won't be soldiers or warriors, they'll be able to attack, and they may try to defend themselves, but they're not battle hardened like you are. Their primary defense will probably be to try to get into your minds and absorb you into their number. If they can get a single thought into your head, you're theirs − their mental powers are … superior to anything any one of you has ever encountered. I'm pretty confident that two of them were able to defeat Maheu'le alone," a gasp from several of the Mentalists, and dissenting voices rising all around in shock, "and none of these locations will have fewer equally powerful minds present than you see dead here before you."

A single voice from the back of the crowd came out, unsure, "Can't you protect us, like you protected them?" No one turned to see who had spoken; they were more interested in Trevor's answer.

"There is more than one front to fight on in this war. You will be going from location to location according to that map, taking out one side of their number, hundreds at a time, where they least expect to be struck. You will strike the beast at its borders, peeling away its outer layers like

254

skinning an onion. You will bathe in their blood, as Jurrin has, here." They couldn't help but notice Jurrin's slouched, still red-glistening and entrails-trailing form on the pew beside them, his head hung low as though in defeat instead of the triumph that he had so proudly worn not long before their arrival. "We," he gestured to his small band of companions in turn, "will seek out their power center, their most heavily defended and well hidden outpost, where their most experienced soldiers and most powerful wizards will undoubtedly be standing by, ready to destroy us as soon as we are detected, and the six of us will slice directly to the heart of the beast and strike where it is most sensitive. You will probably not reach us before we reach our target or are obliterated, though it seems equally likely to me that you will all be killed or turned against us before we get within a hundred challengers of the girl. Things are getting worse with every passing moment; we don't have long before it will be too late to stop them, but kill as many as you can, and maybe we can give the world a fighting chance."

Trevor could feel pain and nausea building within him, and rushed to finish his thought before he was overcome with the pain of another contraction. He tried to keep his face even and determined until the world turned white and the sound of three dozen wizards and warriors eager to see action faded into the total silence of the Blinding Light. Knowing he needed to keep the appearance of strength in front of this group, Trevor fought to maintain his location through the pain that felt more and more like something was wrong with Hannah and less and less like normal labor pains. None of them seemed to question Trevor or Nirgal for the odd timing of the effect, nor gave any indication that they suspected there was anything wrong. Trevor began speaking again before they could say anything about it, "This sphere is imbued with the information you'll need to defend yourselves against the beginning stages of the grip of a hivemind, and some of their basic mental attacks. It would be too dangerous to expose you to my own mind right now, as I'm sure you've heard that I was absorbed into a hivemind not long ago myself. Please, all of you, take what you can from what I've prepared here, it's all the

255

protection I can offer you. You're best off working together, protecting each other rather than trying to protect yourselves; their thoughts will look like your own thoughts to you, but with this information you'll be able to see their source as they approach those around you."

The room grew quieter and the light of the sphere of distortion grew brighter with every additional mind that accessed it. The rippling across its surface seemed to quicken in pace as wizard after wizard, and even some of the warriors, took what they could from what Trevor had offered them. Then, in a flash, it disappeared, and everyone's eyes were opened again. A low murmur rose as most of them turned to walk back out, suddenly aware of what they were really up against and less sure of themselves than even Jurrin seemed, still collapsed and waiting. One of the robed women was approaching, rather than retreating from, Trevor's floating form.

"Hi," she said, extending her hand out to him, "I saw the dodgeball championship games, and I wanted to say you were amazing out there." Trevor reached out to her, and they handflashed. "My name is Millee. Pleased to meet you."

"Thank you. I just … play the game and hope for the best."

"After looking at your hivemind tutorial I'm beginning to see how you tied the last match, but what I really want to know is how you got all the boys to stop playing in the game before that. You must have told them to keep quiet, right, because… I uhh… I asked everyone on both sides, and no one would tell me. Some of them actually seemed to be genuinely frightened of whatever it was you did." She seemed to be blushing slightly, trying not to sound like too big a fan in front of Trevor. He looked at her, looking up at him, smiling, and realized that if she were a few years younger or he were a few years older…

"I just… I made them remember something. Over and over again. They were so wrapped up in the memory, they didn't care about the match anymore."

"What was the memory?"

"It was …" Trevor paused, but was drowning in her big, brown eyes, and couldn't help to take the liberty in the face of his almost-certain death, "… it probably felt something like this," and he leaned down, levitated a little lower, until his lips met hers, and they kissed. Gently at first, but with growing urgency, intensity, and passion, as though they hadn't just met for the first time mere seconds before. Arms wrapping around each other for a long moment, they felt as though they were melting into each other, as though all the troubles and pains and fears of the world had ceased to exist and everything was right as long as they were together. For Millee, this kiss would take the spot in her memories as the most emotionally significant kiss of her life, and hold it for a long time afterward.

When they finally separated, Millee was actually, literally glowing from the experience, an actual dream come true for her. Trevor seemed recharged, suddenly actually sure of himself instead of merely putting on a brave face. "I remember now!"

"What do you remember?"

The Gollum's voice came softly, like the memory of an echo, "I'd somehow managed to go this long without once thinking about what it would be like to kiss you." The Gollum nodded, understanding.

"Kiss who? Not the one he's just kissed, right?"

"No, not me. Thank you, Trevor. I'll let you get back to saving the world. Thank you." Millee disappeared.

Trevor seemed lost in reverie, and the Gollum was like a mirror image, their eyes closed and their faces showing contentment as they remembered or imagined the same sweet moment. Nirgal leaned up towards one of Sophie's ears and asked softly, "What's going on?"

Sophie leaned down, still two heads above him, and gave her response as softly as she could with the big deep voice she had, "Trev's thinking about kissing Hannah. It's a form of sex magic that may allow him to locate her, despite all the forces trying to block him."

"Why can't they just block the sex magic? I thought sex magic was crude, elementary magic."

"It's easy to perform, but almost impossible to control." Jurrin finally stood, joining the conversation again, "almost everyone in the world uses sex magic, whether they know it or not. It draws people together, it drives others apart, it can be subtle, such as amplifying memories, and it is the most powerful form of magic known to exist – it is the only way to create new life, new souls."

"What about things like the Gollum? Even I can do that, and I'm just a teenager."

"The Gollum does not have a soul of its own, or even a life of its own. You, as the creator, have imbued it with your life. Every moment it lives is a moment your life is shortened." This seemed to come as a surprise to Nirgal, but Jurrin tried to answer his shock, "don't worry – a mud Gollum rarely survives more than a week, and I doubt this one will survive the day. If you survive the day, you'll still have a long life ahead of you. And while the Gollum's body is living a part of your life, it requires something else, remember?"

"Trev's name."

"Right, it requires a mind, and identity. The creator of a Gollum can never be the one to provide both halves, both body and mind, so a second willing party must become involved. In this case, it was Trev. So the Gollum's body lives your life and thinks and feels and remembers with Trev's mind. It has no life of its own, no soul, and cannot last." Jurrin seemed alright for a moment, not weighed down with the thought of failure or overcome with the thrill of victory, but really like himself as he spoke to Nirgal. "As to how you were able to create a Gollum, I cannot say. As far as has been known, no one has had the strength and will and arcane knowledge to bring a Gollum to life for thousands of years. Many have tried and all have failed, but you … this was your first try, wasn't it?"

"Y-y-yes. I just… Trev said to… I didn't know."

"It's alright, it's not a problem, it's just unexpected. I'm sure that if we get through this you'll hear enough about it – all those wizards saw the Gollum, and they're sure to talk about it if they survive."

"I didn't think… I just did it…"

"Fine, fine, don't worry about it for now." Jurrin looked over to the two very alike figures, still someplace else, in or out of their minds. "Back to sex magic. The only

258

way to block, counter, or stop sex magic is with sex magic. Intentional sex magic can only be matched by unintentional, powerful only by subtle, but always in kind. Two wizards cannot use in kind sex magic against each other, because their intention to do so would cancel the negating effect. In this instance, for example, I assume Trev is intending to use the connection of kissing to reach Hannah and locate her. This is subtle and intentional, and if he's well-focused doesn't involve coitus at all, so the only way to block his attempt would be what?"

"Powerful and unintentional?"

"Can you think of an example? Remember that it has to be in kind."

"Which means just kissing, right? Is there even a possible configuration of powerful, unintentional sex magic to be generated from a kiss alone?"

"You actually just watched a reasonably powerful example, when Trev kissed Millee. He didn't intend to have any effect on her, nor she on him, but there was a very powerful result in Millee. I wouldn't be surprised to learn that she is the only survivor of the second wave – she is protected in a way, by his kiss, and the fulfillment of love in anticipation that it represented for her."

"How could the church do something like that to Hannah?"

"Exactly. She's still in a coma, for one thing; I would know if that effect had been dispelled. So even if the reincarnation or ghost of the original Prince Charming somehow came to her side to wake her from her unnatural slumber, and even if she were the next in line to match his perfect love, that action would dispel her coma, and that dispelling would tell me and several others what her location was. Barring the nearly impossible interference of Prince Charming or his like deciding spontaneously and without intention to plant the perfect kiss on a comatose teenager in the midst of giving birth in a giant double church under the watchful eye of our enemy, there is nothing that can block this."

"Is that why nothing helped with the labor pains Trev's been feeling? They're part of some sort of sex magic?"

"It could be." Jurrin seemed enlightened and frustrated that he hadn't thought of it himself, "it makes sense. The sex magic that impregnated her was more powerful than even basic conception and far less intentional, considering the circumstances. It's possible that the nature of the impregnation was so powerfully affecting to the universe that his connection to its end is the universe's way of trying to balance out the impossibility of its beginning."

"You talk in circles, little man." Sophie almost looked like she was beginning to develop a headache from trying to follow Jurrin's speculations. She turned both her heads to face Nirgal again, "The bottom line is that we're about to know where we're headed, one way or the other, and that you're the second most powerful wizard in the room. Got it?"

"Err… yeah, I get it." Nirgal tried not to meet Jurrin's eyes, but he could feel their scornful gaze on the side of his face.

Suddenly the Gollum disappeared. "Somebody bring Sophie," Trevor said, just before he, too, disappeared. Sqrat and Jurrin disappeared almost immediately afterward, pulled on the line of Trevor's mental links, and Nirgal grabbed Sophie's giant hand before he followed close behind them. Sophie's left head vomited against the stone wall of the twisted stairwell she appeared suddenly in, and her right head moaned and looked ready to vomit as well. "Shhh…" Trevor quietly intoned, his Gollum's finger rising to its lips to pantomime the same command.

Trevor thought to the group, "be quiet, everyone. Hannah is right on the other side of that wall," he pointed to the 'ceiling' directly opposite the spot they were standing on, "and the popes are above and below us, prepared not only for the arrival of my daughters, but probably for our very expected invasion," he pointed forward and backward 'up' both sides of the twisting stairwell to indicate 'above and below,' and everyone seemed to figure out that they were in a stairwell like the one in the church they had just left. The odor of fresh vomit filled the air around them, and Sqrat began making sounds like he was fighting back choking and vomiting himself, just from the sight and the smell of it. Trevor shot the little man a harsh glare and the private thought, "We didn't really need you among us after all, but the right time to call your master is very near now, Sqrat, can't you hold your tongue a little longer?" Sqrat put his hand over his mouth and did his best to remain silent.

A young woman's scream echoed up towards them just in time for their world to fade to an increasingly familiar white emptiness that wiped the scream from their senses. As soon as he knew he could be heard again on the fading side of the Blinding Light, the Gollum spoke in hushed tones the question Trevor was in too much pain to ask of Jurrin, "If she's still in a coma, why is she screaming?"

"I don't know. She's probably not aware of it, but her body must know it's in pain." Jurrin knew he was only speculating, and well out of his depth, "I really don't know, though."

"Fine," Trevor was levitating unevenly now; the proximity to the source of his pain or increasing difficulties on the other side of the wall above him were taking a greater toll on him than the prior labor pains had. "Nirgal, Jurrin, follow me this way. Sophie, you take Sqrat and the Gollum that way." Trevor pulled the hood of his robe up over his head, and the Gollum did the same, their mirrored appearance becoming complete as the Gollum's hairlessness was covered and the rune on its forehead became partially concealed. "Maybe we can disorient them by attacking both sides at once. It would be better if Nirgal took Sqrat's place, but I need him to cover up my weakness. Sqrat, try to survive long enough to betray me, okay?" Sqrat nodded, then realized what he was doing and shook his head in protest, but Trevor was already headed down his side of the stairs and Sqrat was being dragged along by the collar of his shirt, which Sophie had grabbed before she proceeded the other way.

Trevor didn't know whether he was headed towards the dark church or the light one, and didn't think it really mattered, since his Gollum was headed the other way and his query was apparently between the two. He went forward as though he knew what he would find at the top of the stairs, as though he was prepared, and he hoped his confidence would bolster his companions. Just before they emerged into the view of the church above, Trevor thought decisively to all five of his party, "Kill them all. No questions. No mercy. Just save Hannah." He burst out into the air, high above the altar to give himself a good perspective on what he would be facing, Jurrin rushing up the steps behind him, sword swinging, and Nirgal not far behind.

There was a half-second of surprise before the mental attacks against his companions began, but Trevor was ready for them, and glad he didn't have to defend more minds himself. If the three dozen wizards and warriors who had made their way into the second wave had been here it would have been the equivalent of starting a fight by giving your enemy your best weapons; Trevor's concentration could only be stretched so thin, he could only protect so many minds at once. Against the enemy he now faced, protecting two minds was very nearly too much for him.

This church was, as Sophie had suggested, truly monumental. The entire structure of the church they had just left would fit nicely into a corner of the room he was in and go unnoticed. The vast width and length of the floor plan could perhaps have accommodated tens of thousands of seated believers, and as he gazed down upon that huge space he realized that there were no pews or chairs, only an oddly empty floor. The insanely large space was nearly empty, and as Trevor returned to ground level he counted only fifteen men and women as the entire force against him. One was clearly the pope, and was kneeling over the hole in the floor where the alter had been, apparently praying over Hannah's suspended body, which was floating in the middle of the tunnel that Trevor had been able to see, from his highest vantage point, looked straight through to the light, upper church on the other side of the stairs. Two more, a man and a woman, stood to the left and the right of the hole, their backs to the pope, sword and staff at the ready to defend him. Four androgynous beings stood beyond the four corners of the hole, a gold chain, each link several inches across, strung tight between them, right through gaping but apparently long-healed holes directly through their torsos, creating an unbroken ring around the hole and the three people beside it. Each of these four beings seemed prepared for a different sort of battle, bolts of light, energy, electricity, and a field of powerful magic moving between and among them as they circled slowly around the hole without ever letting their chain loosen or droop. These seven seemed not to have noticed that anything was amiss at all, as though Trevor and his companions were less important than flies buzzing the air around them.

It was the other eight that were keeping Jurrin and Nirgal busy, and that were providing more than enough mental activity to strain Trevor to his wits' end. There seemed to be nothing in common between them besides their apparent desire to destroy the three intruders and disregard for the normal flow of time; they all moved with uncanny quick speed. Trevor moved down next to Nirgal and helped him defend himself while trying to decide what to do.

"I thought there'd be more of them!" Nirgal shouted, narrowly deflecting a flying serpent of what appeared and smelled like fecal matter with razor-sharp teeth and a flaming tail in the direction of the gold-chain-circle which was more than able to destroy it to protect the pope and the hole and the girl it contained.

"Is this too easy for you?" asked Jurrin, swinging away without making contact against his too-fast foes, barely defending himself against their projectiles and other attacks. "You're such a powerful wizard, after all." Jurrin's sword finally anticipated one of the eight's moves and sliced clean through its body in a beautiful diagonal arc from the tip of its outstretched arm, splitting in two the entire length of arm, carving through the shoulder, chest, and every organ and bone in between and emerging out the other side just below the crotch of the suddenly slowed being. They had just enough time to see that the toppling, divided form had been a very pale, very old man before the continued onslaught from the other seven defenders stole their attention away from the gore that represented a moment of success.

"Don't be that way, Jurrin!" Nirgal was glad to realize that the one which had been killed was apparently the one that had been conjuring shit-monsters, and tried to be apologetic. "Sophie didn't mean to diminish your abilities, but to bolster my confidence! We all have strengths," Nirgal had a long enough break in his own defenses and in defending Trevor to invoke a few mudballs and heave them into the blur of bodies around him, "and we have to work together!" One of the mudballs had struck the head of one of the remaining seven, and the other two had struck the bodies of others. The sightless one was an easy target for Jurrin's sword, and between Trevor and Nirgal's more deadly attacks and Jurrin's continued swordplay, the other two had been slowed enough to be destroyed.

"Fast or slow?" Trevor asked, as though they would know what he was asking. The mental attacks seemed mostly to have been coming from the one that had been hit in the head by Nirgal's mudball and lost his head to Jurrin's sword, and Trevor finally had enough concentration to do something more than just defend their minds.

"What?"

"Do you want me to slow them down or to speed you two up?"

"Slow them down!" shouted Nirgal.

"Speed them up!" shouted Jurrin.

"What?" shouted Nirgal, again.

"Hope they burn out?" mused Trevor, noting that the dead remains of the first four appeared wizened and old, each older than the one killed before it. "If you're wrong, the best I can do is speed you up too, and then we'll be back to the same relative speed difference. What do you think, Nirgal?"

Nirgal was growing tired, and it showed. "Whatever you think," he collapsed to the ground, not from exhaustion, but to stay out of the way of one of the remaining four, hurtling overhead with what looked like daggers in its hands, "will work best." He disappeared and reappeared standing up in an empty space a few feet away.

"This would work better with a sacrifice, for an extension …" Trevor searched the pockets of his robe for anything that would be useful and found nothing, then realized he was looking in the wrong pockets. He flashed out of visibility for half an instant, never losing his defense of Nirgal and Jurrin's minds' continuity, and was wearing his trench coat instead of the dueling underrobe. He searched his new pockets and immediately found what he was looking for, quickly pulling out an antique-looking pocket watch on a gold fob. The watch began spinning around and around at the end of the chain faster and faster as Trevor intoned the syllables that would initiate the spell, finally letting go of the end of the chain that now hung, spinning ever faster, in the air before him. The glinting of light across the watch's rapidly rotating surfaces began to become a continuous glow as the heat from friction with the air and from the intensity of the magic took its toll on the metals and workings of the timepiece. Just as the apparently molten remains of the pocket watch were consumed in a flash of light that connected the four still-fighting figures around him, a scream tore through the air from within the hole in the floor and the entire expanse of the dark church filled top to bottom with the Blinding Light.

Trevor alone could still hear Hannah's scream as the world turned to silence for the other twelve people within visual range of Nirgal's less-than-conscious effect. He could feel more than just the pain of contraction, this one so much faster on the heels of the last one than the one before it had been that he knew Hannah was very close to being fully dilated, but the other feeling was as though the first of the two life forms he could definitely differentiate within her was already trying to work its way out, and too soon. It was almost as though some other force was drawing the tiny body out prematurely. To say that Trevor was becoming used to the pains would be like trying to sell vacation homes on the surface of the sun by saying that you could get used to the heat; there is no experience in this world that can be rightfully compared to what he was going through, and no one but a mother who was burned alive and then drowned during twin breech births while under heavy mental attack and facing the loss of the entire world if she didn't find the strength to work through it all while retaining her sanity and

265

coherence could say they began to understand his pain. As the most intense part of the experience began to fade, and the more problematic sensations of giving birth remained, the Blinding Light faded and Trevor tried to see if his companions were still alive.

Nirgal was laying in a fetal position on the ground, but clearly twitching and spasming, so still alive; Trevor did a quick check and verified that Nirgal was definitely not under mental control or attack by hiveminds. Jurrin was standing, sword at the ready, looking for someone to strike down. The four who had been trying to kill them before the world disappeared in a sea of white silence were now hardly more than skeletons collapsed on the stone floor with barely the energy to struggle, and not enough flesh left to tell whether they had been one gender or the other. Jurrin made quick work of them once he figured out that the faster pace of their time spent during the white out had been more than enough to fulfill his expectation that they would "burn out", decapitating them all quickly.

Trevor sent a mental query to his doppelganger above/below him in the light church, "How're y'all doing?" along with the image before him of the eight defenders defeated. There was a long pause, during which Trevor cautiously felt the mental space around him for more combatants or some clue as to why none of his own companions were being mentally invaded at all anymore.

Finally, with an echoing triumphant cry ringing out in Sophia's huge voice coming through the tunnel between the mirrored churches, the Gollum thought back to Trevor, "We've got it under control up here," including an image of eight broken bodies, a bloody Sophia, and Sqrat in a fetal position similar to Nirgal's, but that Trevor suspected he had taken before, rather than after, the battle had taken place.

"They're good on the other side, same headcounts left," Trevor explained, then collapsed again, in pain, before Hannah started screaming hoarsely, and several seconds before Nirgal was able to generate the Blinding Light which seemed almost moot at this point. As though noticing his weakened state for the first time and not under the same command of warning as the others had been, the four chained beings reached out at once to try to absorb Trevor into their single hivemind. He didn't resist them, and not just because he was in too much pain to think straight. After a longer moment than any prior instance of it, the white light and silence faded again.

Trevor was still laying on the floor, clutching his gut in pain, weeping again. The four chained beings were also, unexpectedly, laying on the floor, weeping and clutching at their own abdomens. There was no longer any light, energy, electricity or any other thing crackling between them. The chain was limp, fallen to the floor with them, and seemed somehow less restrictive than it once had. Where the chain touched the stones they began to fade away. Not like a corrosive, eating outward from the point of contact, but whole stones disappearing all at once, as though having come in contact with the chain made the entire stone to cease to be all at once. Once the first set of stones had vanished, the chained, weeping beings fell lower, the chains falling on new stones, a literal chain reaction beginning to take place. The Gollum mentally queried Trevor, "Did you do that?" as the chained beings on his side were also fallen, weeping, and taking the floor with them, but Trevor could not find the strength to respond before the pain became worse again and the world faded to white for everyone in view of Nirgal.

When the world came back, the first thing Trevor did when he regained full consciousness was to break the connection that was triggering Nirgal's Blinding Light. The next thing he did was notice that the world had fallen to pieces all around him. In the timeless expanse of his pain, the chains had apparently found their way to each other and caused some sort of explosive reaction, because the two sets of chained men, and any semblance of order, had disappeared. The floor all around where they had been was gone and gravity was thrown totally out of order, huge chunks of rock floating in and out and around the now doubly-large expanse of the dual church, the floor very apparently just a platform running between two halves of a single large open space rather than the platform the mirrored churches had appeared to be built upon. The six invaders were floating randomly around among the debris while the much better organized six defenders were all tightly circled around a stone-free space containing Hannah's naked and very pregnant body. The two popes faced inward, ceaselessly praying over Hannah's still-unconscious body, and the two identical men and two identical women floated in a defensive box around them, weapons still in hand.

Trevor wept, bounced hard off a huge chunk of what had been the floor not long before, and careened through the air without a thought apart from his now nearly continuous pain. His Gollum generated a ball of distortion and heaved it across the distance between them, narrowly avoiding the asteroid-field-like chunks of church that passed through its path, and when it struck Trevor's figure it expanded into a sort of protective shield, keeping the stones from causing him any more pain than he was already in. He almost immediately seemed to be going through another contraction, a fact that was backed up by a blood-curdling, throaty scream that burbled forth from Hannah's still-unconscious body.

"What do we do?" Nirgal seemed recovered enough to be actively levitating around in the odd gravity without coming too close to the man-sized and larger hunks of stone hurtling this way and that around him. Sqrat, who was trying desperately to contact his master or simply disappear to safety before it was too late, was still having a hard time avoiding flying bits of rock even when they hadn't been intentionally hurled directly at him, and didn't respond. Jurrin's sword was still somehow sharp, sharp enough to carve through rock, and he avoided the large stones by cutting them into smaller ones, then pushing them aside, but he didn't know if it was too soon to try to kill the girl and her unholy offspring, so stayed silent. Sophie didn't know what to say to Nirgal, but wasn't really listening to him, either. She was already taking action on her own.

"You lied to me!" Sophie hurtled through the air by pushing off the rocks around her, unable to direct herself by levitation like the others, and dove rapidly towards the center of the space, enraged. "You fucking bastard!" The men and women who had been floating at the ready but as though unaware that any threat had yet existed for them or those they stood by, suddenly burst into motion. One of the men and one of the women remained still to protect the ceaselessly praying popes, and the other two burst towards Sophie's rapidly approaching mass, sword and staff swinging her way.

The staff broke across her right shoulder, the sword dove into her chest just below her left shoulder, easily finding its way out her back and lodging there, and both of the figures who had attacked her were snapped down the middle like brittle twigs and tossed weightlessly aside without slowing Sophie down more than a hair or two on her way. Trevor's Gollum could sense that they had tried every mental attack and absorption they had in their arsenal against Sophie with no apparent effect at all; her mind really did seem to be incompatible with theirs. Hannah's throat went totally hoarse from the continuous screaming, and from certain vantages it became clear that the first of the children inside her was about to emerge. Sophie continued her progress towards the center of the space, now without stones to push against, and the other two defenders, with resigned looks on their faces, sprung forth to try to stop her from reaching her target.

Instead of trying to fight her with their weapons, they swung them wide to fool Sophie into blocking them with her arms, and discarding them and using their superior ability to move in open air, they dove in and clutched onto Sophie's torso in what looked at first like a huge bear hug. When they both burst into flames, just before Sophie could reach them to try to pull them off her form, it became clear that they weren't trying to be friendly. The flames erupting from their bodies went rapidly through a variety of colors as Sophie continued plummeting towards the still-apparently-unaware popes, red, orange, yellow, green, blue, purple, and finally a white that verged on black, a heat so hot that Sophie's clothes were on fire all around her, her skin sloughing off behind her, her hair a horrible scent instead of two beautiful manes. She did not falter, but roared out in pain and anger as she reached for the pope swathed in white, squeezing as much of the life out of him as she could before her own life was extinguished by the flames, the two of them curling together and tumbling away from Hannah's profane body in a horrifying ball of pain, misery, and death.

Somehow, the light pope never stopped praying as he was crushed and burned and obliterated by Sophie's dying actions.

The dark pope finally seemed to come to a stopping point in his prayer as the top of the first baby's head became visible, stretching between the engorged lips of Hannah's tortured vagina, about to emerge. He turned to face Trevor's Gollum, apparently unaware that the true body of Trevor was bouncing about in the distance behind him, experiencing the horrible pain of a childbirth gone wrong. He spoke, "It's too late, now. Your offspring are ours."

The Gollum responded, knowing he was seen to be the threat they had expected, "You're the only one standing between me and my children, and your twin does not seem to have been difficult to destroy. I shall make short work of you and be on my way."

"The way out is not as easy as the way in, young fool, and as soon as they are born into the world, your little girls will be among us, a duality never-ending." Something very strange was happening behind the dark pope's back, but the Gollum did not change his expression or avert his eyes to give him any reason to suspect that anything was wrong. "With gravity and reality fractured this way, with the balance broken, the only way out is through the front doors. You may have been wondering where are real defensive forces were when you arrived, but they've been outside those doors the entire time, waiting for you." The top of the child's head had reached the point where it would have been truly outside Hannah for the first time, but instead of coming out, it appeared to be undergoing some sort of horrible transformation.

Trevor's Gollum had all of Trevor's memories and knowledge to work from, all of Sunshine's experiences, and at first it did not know what it was seeing. Instead of the wet, smooth, vaguely spheroid surface of a baby's head emerging into the air from Hannah's distended vagina, the head appeared to have flattened and taken on an awful texture and color, like blood and mud and ramen noodles all

270

wriggling and squiggling together across the surface of what ought to have been her head. It seemed to expand in diameter and then to contract again, the appearance of a disgusting soup being replaced by other strange conglomerations of shapes, like cookies in tomato soup or curved breadsticks and odd flower petals arranged in a tableau bordered by the sweat-soaked, purpled flesh of Hannah's crotch and thighs. When the shape of this flat horror began to expand into an oblong oddity, Trevor's Gollum was finally reminded of something he'd seen once on television, years earlier, and began to have some idea of what he was watching occur over the dark pope's shoulder.

"You cannot disappear to safety, and I doubt you would risk two newborn baby's lives in the battle that awaits you outside. Two hundred and forty of our best, all waiting to destroy you. Even if you kill me, they will kill you."

The Gollum did not want to give any sign that anything unusual was occurring, even as he fought back the nausea that was overcoming him at the sight of the baby's internal organs being displayed for him in a gruesome, shifting cross-section of her anatomy, and tried to keep the dark pope talking. "We are not the only ones fighting you, you know. A force a dozen times our number, each one more powerful and experienced than the best of these, has been working from church to church, killing your congregations, exterminating you from the earth, making their way here. By now they are outside, battling this small army you speak of, and will be ready to receive us in triumph, both of my daughters in safe hands."

The television program Trevor had seen had been about some researchers who had flash-frozen a human corpse to study it. Keeping it at deep freeze temperatures, they had sliced through the corpse, half a millimeter at a time, layer after layer of its frozen flesh and bones, starting at the top of the head and working their way ever-so slowly to the feet. After removing each impossibly-thin slice of dead man, they had taken a high-resolution digital photograph of the exposed anatomy. When they were finished, long before the television program finally aired, they put all the photographs together to construct a perfect three-dimensional reconstruction of the cadaver in their computers, and that was what they studied from then on. But at one point in the program, they ran through the entire series of photographs in the order they had been taken, from the head to the feet of the corpse, half a millimeter at a time, twenty-nine point nine seven photographs a second, showing their raw data, the slice after slice of his body as it had been shaved carefully away by their ultra-sharp, ultra-accurate blades.

"It won't matter; as soon as both children are out of the girl's body, forces already set in motion will meld them into one of us, into a balance of minds and powers. Kill me, fight your way out, kill every believer, every twin in the world, and your daughters will have to be among them. There is nothing you can do to keep them from joining our side once they escape the protective energy of their mother. They will silently work against you, pretend they are on your side, show no signs of being anything but normal, and when they have gathered enough power against you, you will see that we have been triumphant. Balance will be brought to the world because of your weakness. You will lose because you cannot bear to kill your own children. You have already lost."

The vision that had taken over the Gollum's perception was somehow worse than the computerized images of a long-dead, unmoving adult man; Hannah's still-comatose body was in convulsions, her vagina torn and bleeding, and the cross-sections of the baby not exactly emerging from her birth canal seemed to be moving and shifting, struggling in two dimensions against the border of her bruised and swollen labia. After this long, the size of the horrifying image grew smaller, and the Gollum could almost recognize the white of the baby's bones in the rings pink and red of its flesh as the legs and feet passed through the edge of all that was Hannah and apparently into oblivion. The first of the two babies was already either born or destroyed before the Gollum responded to the dark pope.

"I think there's more going on here than you think is going on here." Its response was apparently too slow, its face not as carefully controlled as it thought, because the

272

dark pope swung around to see what was going on behind him. He could see clearly that Hannah's vagina appeared to have already gone through the trauma of birth and that her distended belly was significantly less swollen than it had been a few minutes before, but didn't see a newborn floating anywhere around and couldn't detect its mind, either. He reached out to put his hand on Hannah's inflated abdomen and turned his head back over his shoulder to shout at the Gollum he thought was Trevor.

"What have you done? Where is the child?"

"I haven't done anything, yet." The Gollum didn't know what forces were interceding here to keep the babies out of the hands of the church, but it also couldn't think of anything in its power that might be a better alternative to whatever was going on, so just played coy. "Why, do you think I should?"

The other child wasn't far behind the first, and as soon as its head started doing what the first child's had, not emerging but disappearing instead at the border of Hannah in a flat dissection of cross-sections of a baby's insides, the dark pope seemed to understand what was going on. He cried out, bellowing from the depths of his lungs, long and hard and loud, "NOOOOOOOOOOOOOOOOO!!!" and he began clawing at the roundness of Hannah's skin with his fingernails, tearing slowly into her flesh with the only method he had readily available.

The Gollum moved in to try to stop him, and so did Jurrin and Nirgal, who had been floating nearby, waiting for the opportunity to act.

An explosive sound came from the far end of the nave of the light side of the church, and the debris in the air seemed to find a new momentum, streaming towards the noise. Two figures emerged into view, levving forward as fast as they could against the apparent breach in the already-broken physics that had sway inside the strange dual church, dodging the large and small pieces of stone that were fighting to flee in the opposite direction. One of the figures was Feagan Trask, beaten and bloodied and looking exhausted. The other figure was the lanky man with the too-thick eyeglasses, looking more like he was wearing the

273

blood of his fallen enemies than his own, and energized by the vigor of the battle. Sqrat allowed himself to be pulled along with the airborne boulders towards them. Everyone else was fighting the pull that the two new players had apparently created, tumbling this way and that, mostly trying to stay out of the way of the plummeting broken masonry.

Hannah, the dark pope having already peeled back the first layers of her abdominal flesh, was twisting and spinning in the air, leaving a trail of drops and mist of blood and torn flesh in her wake. Trevor's Gollum was right behind her swerving form, trying to keep up with the furious, erratic forces the dark pope was exerting to try to escape it, trying to stop the horror that it felt responsible for, despite being only hours old and made of mud. Jurrin wasn't entirely sure what the right course of action for him should be; if the babies were somehow being stolen away to another location, Trevor might be the only one who could locate them, but if some other, unseen force was destroying them, this might be his only chance to destroy Trevor along with them. He searched the air for the bubble of protection Trevor's real body was bouncing around in without losing track of keeping close enough to the girl that he could destroy anything that actually emerged from her bleeding body. Nirgal was the only one with an eye on two new figures approaching, one familiar and one unknown, and trying to figure out what their presence really meant at this key moment; he kept himself safe and watched them carefully through the chaos.

The dark pope was pulling out handfuls of Hannah and tossing them into the air, out of his way, trying to get to the backside of the baby the hard way. Hannah's body had apparently run out of energy, and was no longer convulsing or trying to scream; mostly it was just bleeding out, some other, unseen force continuing to move the fetus through her birth canal. Finally, letting out a loud "A-Hah!" the dark pope seemed to have caught on to his quarry, his arm elbow-deep in the gore that had been Hannah's abdomen, and he tried pulling it out, his other hand grasping for purchase, slick with blood and sweat against her soft skin. The lanky man and his two servants reached the bloody body and the

274

desperate dark pope before the Gollum could, and were just in time to see what he had in his hand as it emerged into view within the bloody mess of Hannah's insides.

He had two tiny legs in his grip, but they stopped only a couple of inches beyond the end of his hand in a flat, severed, blood-soaked cross-section, just as they had been as they had reached the end of Hannah's birth canal. When the dark pope lifted these horrifying artifacts of what he'd hoped would mean ultimate power for his people out of the tangled remains of Hannah's organs, they literally disappeared, right from his hand, as they passed the ragged border separating Hannah's insides from her outsides, right before everyone's eyes. Hannah's body let out one last gasp, a death rattle, and was definitely dead. The dark pope just stared it his empty, bloody hand, shaking his head in confusion, disgust and disappointment. Sqrat and Feagan stayed silent, floating behind the tall man who gave them their commands. The Gollum feigned sorrow, throwing its hands up over its face and becoming melodramatically weepy, hoping that Feagan and the lanky stranger wouldn't realize it wasn't really Trevor grieving his lost daughters. Jurrin floated battle-ready, still watching for the real Trevor to reappear, unsure of who his enemy would be when he did. Nirgal was off to the side, out of the way, watching the entire thing with a careful eye, aware that the last of the rocks had cleared out of the air, crashing against the front of the church and apparently ending the pull of whatever forces had drawn them all in that direction by so doing, leaving everyone floating free again, this time in empty vastness.

"What a waste," said the lanky one, shaking his head at the dark pope. "After all this time, you killed the girl. You lost the children. And from the look of things," he looked back and forth around the vastness of the light church they were all flying around in, "you lost the boy, as well. The defenses you had waiting outside were no match for myself and just one mere human," he said, gesturing to Feagan's war-torn form, "and it looks like your real enemy never even had to face them. I thought you were some vast, unstoppable destructive force, reaching back for millennia, always growing in power, ready to remake the world in your own image, but you've been brought to your knees in a single day at the hands of mere children. I doubt you even know who was controlling you, which of your number was truly pulling the strings from behind the scenes for as far back as you've existed. You ignorant slave. All you earthlings are so stupid, so gullible, so easily controlled. Pawns in the games the rest of us play, consciously and unconsciously, all around you." The tall stranger shook his head again, in disdain.

No one else seemed to know what to say. The tall man didn't wait for them to figure something out. He shouted a single arcane word, apparently a shortcut to an already-begun effect, and thrusting his arms towards the roof of the cathedral, it exploded down on them as he and his two minions escaped out the sky-shaped hole he had created. All the others dove down instead of giving chase, trying only to stay out of the way of the showering of collapsing stone cascading from above and every side. The only ones who did not try to escape the crashing wave of stone were Hannah's dead body and the dark pope still staring into his own blood-soaked, empty hands as he was crushed by the crumbling arches of his own church. The survivors found themselves eventually sheltered by the floor/platform that separated the light church from the dark, gravity was suddenly restored enough to draw the rubble of the light church down to that border, but not beyond the border, as the reversed gravity of the dark church had also been restored. The hole in the floor was completely filled with the remnants of the light church's destruction, and no magical stairwell or other escape route through it existed anymore. As they settled carefully down and reoriented themselves to the dark, upside down but right-side-up-feeling church, they counted out their number.

From their original party survived Jurrin and Nirgal, and since the Gollum was still alive, Trevor must be alive somewhere, too. Sqrat had fled with his master, and probably wouldn't be seen again by The Board now that he had revealed his treachery. Sophie had been killed as she took out five of the final six defenders single-handedly, screaming about a lie that would now never be revealed.

276

Hannah and the two babies they had all been risking their lives to reach, to protect, to save, were either dead or in the hands of some third, unknown force. The entire second wave of warriors were probably dead by now, though there was no way for these three to know for sure. The three of them looked one to another, hoping one of them knew what to do next, how to proceed. Each of them tried disappearing, with no success at all. They looked down the nave of the church, to where the dark church's doors must be, looked back at each other, and then without a word, began trudging slowly in that direction.

As they proceeded, the church seemed to grow darker all around them. They were walking into shadows deeper than any natural shadows, as though black-flamed candles were burning before them somewhere. As they came within a few paces of the end of the church, just as their perception reached its lower limits and they were walking totally free of knowledge of where or whether their feet would land, a light appeared before them, as of a curtain parting in an archway to reveal a light source behind it. A figure stood in silhouette, beckoning them forward, and Trevor's voice spoke out to them, "What are you guys waiting for, come on! This is the only way out now." They closed the remaining distance more confidently with a way lighted for them, and passed one by one through the curtain into the vast foyer of the empty church. The room was lit only by a hot orange glow emanating from around all sides of the immense door that towered before them, but it was more than enough light for them to recognize a scaled-up version of the foyer they had passed through in the smaller church.

"Wouldn't this door lead to something… underground?" Nirgal was trying to understand something, anything, after all that had just happened to and around him.

"Not exactly. But we can't get back upstairs now, the balance is broken and the division cannot be crossed again. And as you already know, we can't disappear out. The only way out of this church, our only hope for getting back home, my only hope for ever finding my daughters, is through this door."

"Why haven't you already opened it? Is there a trick?"

"There's always a trick, with a door like this. It wouldn't have been fair to open it without warning you. As soon as I open it, it ceases being a door."

Nirgal knew it must be a riddle, and was quiet, trying to work it out. Jurrin had no such patience, "How can a door cease being a door? That doesn't make sense."

"After this door has been opened, what is on this side of the door will be the same as what is on that side of the door, forever. It was supposed to be a… last chance exit for the dark ones, better than surrender in their eyes. With the balance broken, there's nothing to keep what's on the other side of the door on the other side, once it's open, so as soon as it's open… we'll be surrounded by it, unable to close the door because even if we did, we'd still be there."

"You still aren't making sense. We'd still be where?"

"Hell."

"Hell?"

"Yes, Hell."

"Bloody Hell."

"Right, thus, why I wanted you all to be here before I opened the door, so you could be ready for it."

"How does one get ready for something like that?" Nirgal was still just trying to go along with whatever Trevor asked of him without trying to understand it first. His trust was total, and deserved; Trevor had never done him wrong. "Is there a protection spell, or special armor?"

"Not exactly. But I can give you a few basic warnings. The beings there, the ones we'll encounter, will probably mostly be demons, especially the ones who appear to be in pain. Our best bet for escaping Hell alive is to find the one in charge, but that won't be easy. Everyone we encounter will either be lying to us, trying to trick us, or won't believe we aren't lying and tricking them. They can read our minds without using Mentalism, and our powers cannot affect their minds. They'll try to separate us, they'll try to get us to work against each other, and since Jurrin already hates me, they'll have an easy time of it. Don't believe their lies. My daughters are not yet dead. And Nirgal, if you get separated from me, know I will find a way to get back to you, but that you should not trust anyone who appears to be me or says they are me, for they will be lying. When I come to you, you will know it is me because I will tell you I am someone I could not possibly be. Not just someone I am not, but… it'll make sense if and when it comes down to it. Hopefully we will not be separated. Do you have any questions?"

"I uhh… I … I feel like I should have questions, but I … I can't think of any."

"That's fine. I'm sure we'll all do fine. What's the worst that could happen, right? It's only Hell, and we're not dead yet, are we?" He looked to each of them in turn, then turned and walked over to the door. "I'm going to open the door now, alright?"

The other three nodded.

Trevor knocked hard on the door, three times, with the side of his closed fist, and it began to open, slowly. Trevor backed out of the way of the doors' motion. Intense heat and a bright yellow/orange light poured out of the widening space between the two halves of the immense double door, and chunks of red-hot brimstone tumbled into the church as the doors allowed. The heat and light grew brighter and brighter and the wooden doors caught fire and the tapestries burned up on the walls and the curtains burned away and the stone began to get hotter and hotter all around them, reaching a red-hot, even glow as the doors finally stopped moving. Trevor looked back to see that his companions were still alright, and found that he was all alone. He looked forward to where the doors had stood closed a moment before and didn't even see a wall, just endless fields of fire and red-hot brimstone, smoke and ash. He turned around again to where his friend, his enemy, and his double had disappeared from, and saw the same landscape stretching out behind him as far as he could see, underneath a sky like an endless sea of flames.

Trevor looked forward one more time, and there was a single figure standing before him. He didn't have to ask who it was, he knew before the figure spoke.

"Welcome, Trev. We've been expecting you."

Book Three

Escape From Exile

OR

Confusion and Contraction

OR

How To Get Out Of Hell

"We've been expecting you."

"I'm sure you tell everyone they're expected down here." Trevor's face gave nothing away, and his mind was as closed as he could make it. "Get people thinking about all the things they ever felt guilty about, get them to maybe show you the best tools to torture them with?"

"Oh no, no, no, Trev. We've no need for such tricks. Those who find themselves in my realm after death are more than willing to torture themselves more effectively than such brutal techniques could yield. You, Trev, are the first of our kind to lead a life deserving of my..." the figure seemed to be studying a large crystalline globe affixed atop a cane he was holding as he paused in apparent deep thought, "special attentions. I see that one of your traveling companions is quite the troublemaker."

"We've been having a fairly trying day, as I'm sure you're aware. It's only natural that his energy is still high. But what harm could he do to your forces in your own realm? Surely he is powerless against them." Trevor smiled as he spoke, sure that one member or another of his party must be having quite some meaningful effect for it to be brought to their attention - the imagined destruction of unreal creatures and fantasy constructions would be no cause for concern.

The dark figure's reaction neither denied nor confirmed Trevor's suspicions. "Of course. Just a lot of noise and fury, meaningless as a summer breeze. Your companions are safe, Trev. Come, let us speak in comfort."

Suddenly, and with a sensation almost entirely like the inverse of disappearing and reappearing someplace else, Trevor found himself seated comfortably in a large, well-worn highback leather chair which stood before a fireplace large enough to have a nice stroll through. Trevor thought to himself that it had felt quite like he had remained still and the huge room, the pair of chairs - for his host was sitting in a nearly identical chair opposite him, both of them turned to face the fire and each other by half - and the chilly atmosphere that suddenly surrounded him in stark contrast to the sulfurous heat which had been scalding him from head to feet an instant before were all made to appear around them, as though this room were not so much a place or location as it was a conceptual construction of the moment. In the cool air of the room, the rolling waves of heat from the fireplace seemed somehow welcomed, despite the raw pain of heat they had just escaped and the still-too-intense odor of brimstone burning Trevor's nose and eyes.

"Nice contrast. What's next, fried ice cream or good-devil bad-devil?"

"Oh no, nothing of the sort, Trev. Nothing so crude. My manipulations will be right out in the open. You will know that what you are doing is what I want and you will know why, but..." The dark eyes examined Trevor from across the room as though seeing some important detail for the first time, "...I see now that you haven't figured out what your place in this world is yet, or who you really are. What we have in common that brings you to my attention. No trouble, of course. In fact, it may make you an even more valuable asset, now that I consider it." The sinister face of Trevor's companion seemed to go unfocused, staring beyond the distance as he calculated the ramifications of his unexplained discovery. Nary half a second later, Trevor's eyes were locked again in his piercing gaze, but it had been long enough for Trevor to see that something about him had caught the dark stranger by surprise.

"If he can be surprised, he can be beaten," Trevor thought as silently to himself as he could. "I don't know what he's talking about, what we have in common, but for everything he knew before I arrived, he wasn't aware that I don't know. He is certainly not as omniscient as I'd feared." Trevor responded verbally, not pausing long enough to allow the other to resume his rambling or to raise his suspicions. "You consider me an asset already, do you? I have a feeling that I could leave your realm of my own volition at any time, with or without your consent - why should I stay here and allow myself to be used by a man who isn't even polite enough to introduce himself? That's not the best foot forward, now is it?"

"I know you're smarter than that, Trev. Surely you already know who I am. Such trivialities, such pleasantries, are they really necessary between two such as us?"

There was a long pause, as though the figure sitting across from Trevor were actually expecting a response to his question, but Trevor sat silently, holding his gaze steadily. Finally and at once, as though rehearsed or signaled somehow, both men stood up at once and stepped toward each other, arms stretched out ahead of them. When they met before the fire after what may have been the ten paces of a shooting duel played out in reverse, they clasped hands, right in right and over that left in left, four hands gripping for a single up and down motion, a single 'shake'.

Without any of the four hands' firm grip relaxing at all, the dark resident of this fiery realm spoke, "I am Satan. That is to say, I am accuser, deceiver, snake, dragon, and pride. There are a thousand thousand other names used to describe me in each of a thousand different tongues in terms so diverse that a thousand times a thousand different beings can each think about me in a personal way that makes sense to their own minds, but there's no need for me to go into such formality, I hope. You, Trev, may call me Old Scratch, or just Scratch, if you like. Most don't like the feel of the name Satan rolling off their tongues. At least, not when I'm actually around." Their hands rose and fell a second time, a second 'shake', this time with a brilliant popping flash of light bursting from between their crossed arms like some exaggerated sort of handflash.

"Thank you, Satan. As you've already referred to me as Trev several times, I would be glad to have you continue to do so. It's what most of the people I've met in the last year have called me, and I'm quite comfortable with it." Their hands, still clasped, raised and fell a final time, the handflash-like burst of light coinciding this time with the breaking of contact at the bottom of the 'shake' but flashing a light bright enough that Trevor thought he could see through the facade of the room and the false vastness of the scorched landscape outside it to the truth of this place - or at least to the next layer of lies - in that penetrating light. He didn't pursue it, being sure he would have the time to investigate if it were necessary.

"But that isn't really your name, is it, Trev?"

"No more than Satan is yours, and no more than the meaningless formality of exchanging names in closed hands would entice me to stay here any longer than I need to."

"I certainly never thought it would, or wouldn't I have introduced myself formally as soon as you walked through my doors?" Satan's smile was sinister, but to someone without experience seeing him it may have seemed to be his normal, relaxed state of being. "You've never stood on formality or followed tradition blindly before, so don't try to tell me you'd see me in any better light if only I'd danced that useless dance for you. You're swayed by logic, emotions, authority figures, and selfishness and you'd just as soon change the way you think about Satan because of a little handshake as you'd change it because your toast landed butter-side-down."

"I've fought in a butter battle or two in my time, and I'll probably take on another and another if I believed in my cause enough. But you're right that this isn't one of those times, or even close." Trevor turned and returned to his seat, which seemed to be the cue for Old Scratch to do the same, and then began again, "and while I realize that there's no way to know from a handshake whether you or any other being of this realm is who they claim to be - at least not while they're still in this realm, their home, a place not only the source of most of their power, but which is suffused with that power through and through - it is still a comfort to look you in the eye and tell me you're who I thought you were."

"If I'm not who I say I am, you've just admitted that my guise has worked on you, and maybe I'll let my guard down to you. If I am the accuser I claim to be, you've just revealed a weakness in yourself that I may not be able to resist exploiting - or you've pretended a weakness you hope I'll focus on while you work against me with your other hands. And on top of all that, you're still complementing me and my realm, buttering me up quite effectively, I might add."

"A little something you might, too, be lying about." Trevor continued speaking, but turned his head and gaze to face the fireplace. He had noticed its intricacy as soon as the room had appeared, but he had done what he could to appear

288

unimpressed as well as unobservant, paying it only the attention one might give to a dog curled sleeping in the corner of a room; Trevor kept it always in the corner of his eye lest it wake, charge toward him, and attack in some way. Now that he could do it casually, as the verbal repartee itself had turned to the casual and amusing, Trevor observed the strangeness of that fireplace in detail.

The fireplace itself was vast, larger than the bedroom Trevor had occupied in his parents' home in every dimension, but taller and wider than its depth, and with no discernible edges or corners beyond the four sharp, straight edges defined by the hearth and mantel which surrounded the outer lip of that gaping maw. The hearth appeared to be as solid and smooth as a single slab of polished stone, but in the shifting light cast from the fire beyond, it gave Trevor the impression he was looking at the surface of a viscous dark fluid flowing constantly into the depths of the fireplace, never dropping off or stopping, merely receding into and under the flames in one smooth flow. That the flames were not fed or drowned by it and did not rock on or sink into this surface were ideas that could not have coexisted in Trevor's mind with the other visual clues of that hearth's fluid nature if he had witness that single aspect of the fireplace just a week earlier, perhaps as recently as an hour earlier when he had been utterly joined with the eight chained men in a single archival mind. Trevor was certain that a thoughtful glance at that juxtaposition would be enough to cripple Nirgal or Jurrin's mind, and while he had certainly not yet grasped but a tiny fraction of what those shared minds had contained, he seemed possessed of a new and natural ability to separate and segment ideas in his mind, keeping conflicting or contrary ideas from confronting each other without losing the ability to know and think of them both simultaneously. It was like a fractaline conceptual corpus callosum had been grafted into his mind, allowing complex and meaningful connections to be made between concepts and thoughts that needed to remain otherwise segregated in order to remain functional and independent, just as the physical corpus callosum of the brain strings the left and right sides of the brain together even as it keeps them separate.

The mantel of the fireplace surrounded the other three sides, framing the opening and meeting the hearth at geometrically perfect right angles. Trevor knew somehow that they were perfect, he could see it at each of the four corners as though his eyes or his mind or whatever was being used to sense the fireplace had a built-in compass. Except that the more attention Trevor paid to the perfection of those angles the more he became aware that any device made by human hands would be inadequate to accurately measure the perfection before him. The thickness of each mark of degree would have to be wide enough for the human eye to detect, and the ninety degrees of each of these corners - Trevor didn't know how he could know but he knew it was absolutely true - were more accurate than the width of the narrowest line that the human eye could measure by. It required some considerable force of will for Trevor to draw his eyes away from one of those interior corners without landing immediately on another, and another measure of restraint to keep his face and eyes relaxed and casual as he spoke with the devil across the room. Trevor counted himself lucky that the mantel was wide enough along all three edges and in sharp enough an angle from the light of the fire that the four outer corners were draped entirely in dancing and flickering shadows and greasy, blurry light and he was unable to fix his eyes upon them and face eight sticking points instead of four.

Those wide lengths of decorative framing which surrounded the utter deepness of the fireplace appeared to be carved impossibly from a single continuous piece of some wood Trevor had never before seen. He thought at first that it was darker than anything in the room, perhaps darker even than the shadows it seemed to lean outward and into, until he made out the grain of the wood in long, unbroken curving lines which were darker still than the wood appeared as a whole. Those grain lines seemed to Trevor to be positively sucking light from the room; they were not just taking in every last photon that was sent their way, but also drawing others off course to be absorbed into their endless hunger

290

and absolute intensity of an absence of visual character within their borders. Somehow, just as he seemed to be able to measure the accuracy of the angles of the corners of the mantel, Trevor knew from sight alone that the wood was heavy, dense wood the like of which had never been worked by living human hands or tools, and would probably be approaching diamond's ten thousand on the Vickers Hardness Test. Yet its entire surface, yard after yard of nearly impervious wood, had been carved into a relief of the most intricate detail and delicacy. Trevor's relief that the fireplace was the room's only source of light extended beyond the hiding of the outer corners of the mantel, but to the story that would have been laid out for his mind to try to absorb from each careful bite taken from the wood of that grand frame.

Once in a while he made out a figure, grotesque in appearance or apparent action to a level not even dreamt of in his or Sunshine's memories, and he was glad that the dancing rays of light from the fire did not linger to elucidate the coherence and narrative that Trevor suspected would become horrifyingly clear if the entire panoply of grotesqueries were revealed simultaneously.

Despite all these distractions and details, nothing Trevor could see outside the fireplace - including the room, the mantel, the hearth, and Señor Diablo himself - was as interesting to the eye as what filled the fireplace as its fire.

There were no logs, no wood, no fuel to give rise to the flames. There were no flames either, really. What Trevor saw when he looked into the fireplace, casting its nervous, twitching light and shadows throughout the room, was shaped like a fire, and it moved like a fire, but it was clearly not actually a fire. The fire-that-was-not-a-fire reached into the room in a perfect four-dimensional representation of the shape of a fire, with the bulging, crisscrossing masses at its base which ought to have been logs or some other fuel source - the fireplace seemed of the scale to take entire unprocessed logs as firewood, and the size and shapes of that part of what Trevor saw only supported the idea. Rising up from those log-shaped volumes of not-really-logs were extended volumes of space

291

which leapt and swelled and shrank in all four dimensions including that zero'th dimension, which is not height not width nor depth but time, just as an actual fire would, had there been actual logs actually burning. As Trevor watched and as he and the deceiver spoke at length, it was not that the shape of the thing filling the fireplace was exactly the shape of a fire which most fascinated Trevor's mind. It was what he saw filling that shape that captivated him, rapt.

Looking into the fire-that-was-not-a-fire was a little like looking through a window. Sometimes Trevor felt that if he were to take a photograph of a single still instant of that fire-not-a-fire, it would look like there was a fire-shaped hole cut clean through the back of the fireplace revealing the fire-swept wastelands beyond that strange and sudden wall. Other times the very voluminous nature of the thing pushed such thoughts aside; he could clearly see that this shifting not-quite-mass was surrounded by - not cut out from - the four solid walls of the fireplace. The fire-not-a-fire was enough not-a-fire that it did not bellow smoke to be swallowed by a chimney, and parallel to the terrible flowing hearth was a solid unedged ceiling; the fireplace held the fire in a box missing only one side, and Trevor suspected rightly that an unseen box-side held the fire-not-a-fire from escaping into the room.

The idea of a fire shaped hole in the wall that seemed implied by what Trevor had first thought was an unmoving perspective of the exact landscape he had been standing in not long before was broken with any one focused look - it was clear that whatever he was seeing through the strange 4D lens of the fire-not-a-fire was a populated landscape, not the starkly empty one he had first seen Satan standing proudly in. The same heat was there, the same flaming, scorched countryside remained, and the same sense of desolation Trevor had felt upon arrival was projected through with startling clarity, but in addition to all that, and nearer because it was the foreground to that background of pain, were what Trevor began to realize must be the tortured, mangled, twisted and broken, burnt, flayed, and desiccated souls of the damned. And their tormentors.

292

Through the unsteady window of the virtual flames and logs, the light and heat and emotion of the scene playing out somewhere else in Hell fell flickeringly on every surface it could reach. The noise and the odors were not passed on and instead the vision of pain and humiliation Trevor could see just on the other side - the inside - of the shifting surface of the fire-not-a-fire seemed to give off the sounds of an actual fireplace as though the sounds were a part of a fire's shape, and to give off that same pervasive odor of burning sulfur that seemed to be a part of everything in Hell whether there was any way for it to hold of give off any odor at all.

The tortured souls were almost indescribably tortured, and almost certainly uncountable. Trevor could make out the details of the suffering of any individual he selected even briefly with his eyes even though the view through the fire-not-a-fire seemed to be a wide-angle one which must have shown not less than a million different souls in heaps and heaps on heaps of terror in eternity from one end of the insane fireplace to the other, and yet he knew without whatever new force had been feeding him information lately that what he could see was less than one percent of a thousandth of the number of souls currently residing in Hell in constant agony. He gazed on into the fire, picking out as many of the tortured and their torturers - sometimes with both roles performed by a single player with a captive audience - as he and the snake spoke, and he tried not to make it obvious he was anything more than disinterested in everything around him, keeping his face flat and even. He knew the dragon would want something, and he knew what was at stake. Trevor even knew what a disadvantage he had in this matter, and as he began to speak, to draw out pride's plan, he studied the fireplace and its fire-not-a-fire with as much disinterest as he could muster.

"A little something you might, too, be lying about. Trying to give me a sense of pride for any small thing I might have done, trying to give yourself a toehold in my being with the pride that brought you to your own fall, so long ago. Don't you think I'm smart enough to be able to learn from the mistakes of others? From your mistakes? At least as much as is necessary to know when I'm being turned against myself with words that sound like praise."

"Can you fault me for testing you? For feeling out the edges of your intelligence, the borders of your understanding?"

"No more than I ought reasonably to fault myself for underestimating the breadth and scope of the control you show over everything within your realm. I tried to warn my companions before we opened the door, but my warnings, which went farther than my companions were ready for, did not go nearly far enough."

"Nor could they have, if your warnings did not keep them from entering my realm altogether."

"I still do not see a way we could have escaped or even been located after all that had occurred. During the course of events I absorbed quite a bit of history and information about the church whose doors we used to reach Hell, and among them was the sure knowledge of their failsafe systems. In the event of catastrophic destruction of only one half of any of the established mirrored churches, the other half was sealed completely from the physical world, to become a tomb and perfection device for any believers trapped inside. It was believed that such a situation would destroy the balance between each pair, since they could no longer mirror each others' every action, and following whatever course they were already on, would be on the 'fast track' to either Heaven or Hell."

"Ah, but getting into Hell is much easier than getting into Heaven."

"As they had realized, I'm sure, when you agreed to open up a door into Hell from each of their dark churches, and Heaven would not even return communication."

"You make it sound like I installed revolving doors to Hell in all the major cities around the globe, and you know I've done no such thing. The closest you can get to having unfettered entrance to Hell from anywhere on Earth is through death's door, and that's only a metaphor."

"I know that, and you know that, so I don't know why you belabor the point. The doors you agreed to offer were one-way doors which were only available in the event

294

of one of these catastrophic unbalancings. If the dark church were the one to be destroyed rather than the light, those inside had no aethereal door by which they could gain access to Heaven - their only option, being totally cut off from the physical world, was fasting and praying and repenting until they died of natural causes and hopefully got to Heaven by the natural course. Which is why I was glad, when the church really started coming down, that it was the light church coming down - there's no way out of a sealed light church."

"Is a one-way door into Hell any better? Have you ever heard of anyone coming back from eternal damnation?"

"One or two, but that's irrelevant, because none of my party was sent to Hell for eternal damnation."

"Well, have you ever heard of anyone who wasn't damned intentionally going to Hell? Other than yourself and your traveling companions, of course."

"Of course, of course, and ..." Trevor paused, and it was unclear whether he was trying to think of someone who fit the dark one's description or he was simply trapped in the perfection of a real ninety degree angle, "No. Not off the top of my head, I can't think of anyone else. A few to Hades, but we both know Hell and Hades are different realms entirely."

"True, true. And Hades is a snap to get out of, and might be better run by the dog at the door. At least Cerberus can't offer to let you and your already-dead friends leave if you just don't look back or just pass some other simple test; all Cerberus can do is bark, bark, bark."

Trevor didn't laugh at the demon's weak joke or look away from the fireplace, but continued speaking. "Being crushed by falling stone or trapped in a cathedral cum coffin as the alternatives, walking live and ready to fight into Hell is certainly a preferred option. Especially considering the value you let me know you placed on me, not a moment into my stay here. If I have or can do or be something you want or need, I've got a place to stand while we negotiate my terms." Trevor didn't need to mention that he'd noticed a moment of surprise as well, but he knew deep down that it might be possible to out-maneuver the deceiver at his own game, and that thought added a healthy dose of confidence to his voice as he spoke.

"Of course. Your terms. I've had some time to consider what you would ask for and what you would consider fair, and I'd like to make you an offer before you say anything at all. If it pleases you, fine, and if you want to make revisions, negotiations will begin. I suspect though, that you'll be pleased with all the terms."

"I'm listening." Trevor was still staring into the fire, almost through it, tallying and memorizing every face and essence he witnessed there as they palavered.

"I would like to challenge you to a duel of sorts, the details of which I will discuss in a moment. The important part is the wager over the duel. It will all be drawn out in the contract, but the gist of it is this: If you win the duel, you'll be granted the power to release your traveling companions from Hell, along with anyone else you'd like. If I win the duel, you will not be allowed to leave Hell, and will be forced to remain here for an unspecified period of servitude."

"My companions aren't of any value to you. One of them isn't even really a person. If I am forced to stay here, you must let them go."

"You're being unreasonable! You're asking me to reward you for losing the duel." Satan sounded playfully exasperated at this, "But that isn't how duels work, you see, the winner is rewarded and the loser is not. If I am the winner, I am rewarded with your staying in Hell. If you are the winner, you are rewarded with the power to free your companions."

"Ah, but I have not agreed to duel at all."

"And yet I know that you will, because there is no other way for you to free your companions from Hell. Hell is mine, and they are here. If you want to buy them a get out of Hell free card, you've got to go through me."

"I could leave right now, gather information, reinforcements, and come back through one of the many other passages into Hell to rescue them."

"If you leave and come back to Hell with a raiding party you'll only make my position stronger, putting more people you care about and were responsible for into my

296

grip." The seven-headed dragon who would one day perch before the womb of the Sun Woman to try to eat her child before it could enter the world chuckled from where he sat. "If, on the other hand, you agree to the duel now, you'll at least have a chance of winning, and losing will only trap the four of you in Hell." He had stopped, but then seemed to remember something pleasant, a smile stretching out over his teeth, "For now."

"How can I trust you, deceiver? How can I trust your contract? How can I trust that the duel will be fair? How can I trust that when I win, you will do as you have promised? You, who created all forms of magic and witchcraft and cosmetics. You, who lied to Eve in the garden, who has been lying to the world ever since. You are the greatest deceiver in the history of the Universe, for you even convinced God that you loved Him before you turned on Him."

Even as he spoke these accusations evenly but forcefully into the cool air of the room, Trevor's eyes did not blink or shift from the fire-not-a-fire, did not face the one he was now himself accusing. Except that as soon as the monosyllable 'God' slipped Trevor's lips, Old Scratch's cool, dark eyes locked him in their gaze, a floating pair in the foreground of the foreground of the fire-not-a-fire, blazing out their fury. It was hard to think of this denizen and lord of the Lake of Fire as having a cool to keep, but as he responded accuser to accuser, his voice conveying a calmness even as it seethed, it became clear that the Fallen One had lost his cool. Trevor had felt a slight brush of contact made with his carefully guarded mind as the eyes had appeared, but the contact seemed much more casual than the vision of anger floating before him could have been, and was blasted from his thoughts as soon as the voice began bellowing: "You've gone too far, you impudent little brat. You may have been taught a story or two about the way things came to be as they are, but you've stepped out of bounds now, you've crossed the line into unfamiliar territory." Satan's voice was coming from where his body still sat, tense, across the space of the fire from Trevor, but it also seemed to be conveyed in the modulation of the

297

crackling and roaring sounds of the fire around those disembodied eyes, and in increasing volume from the air that filled all the space around every inch of Trevor's being. As the volume of the voice rose and surrounded him, Trevor knew that this voice was getting deep into his bones, where it would linger and corrupt. "I do love God! I've always loved God! I never lied to Him, I never turned on Him. I just did what needed to be done, what He wouldn't or couldn't do on His own; I was trying to help! It was never my vision, it was always, always what God wanted, even when He wasn't around to ask! Even when He wasn't around to give orders, I loved Him and served Him." Satan's voice was beginning to recede, and Trevor couldn't be sure whether he was hearing the devil's voice cracking, or just crackling as it receded - but still projected - from the fire, and as his eyes faded from visibility there as well. "When the others stopped getting orders, when He stopped showing up for longer than He'd ever been gone before, they turned to me for guidance. I was so close to Him, I loved him so deeply and so well, so much more than any of the others. They came to me, and all they wanted was to know how to serve Him, what He wanted them to do." The snake's voice was now barely above a whisper, sourced only from the crumpling body in the chair opposite Trevor, and he finally turned from the fire to look at the one he was listening to so carefully, to see the down-turned face and strain to hear him speak over the roar of the fire-not-a-fire. "I didn't raise an army up and try to take over Heaven, I never thought I was better than Him, not to this day. All I ever did was love Him. All I did was try to help the others to love Him, and in his absence, when they came and begged me, asked me how they could serve Him, I told them what was in His heart, and they knew what to do. One after another, again and again they came to me and I did what I could to share my understanding of God with them, to show them how they could know God's Will without receiving a direct order from Him." The voice of this Old Scratch now fell well below a whisper, his lips no longer parted and his lungs no longer pushed air, but somehow Trevor could still understand him as he finished his tale. "When God returned, when He revealed Himself I should say, for He can never really be gone, everything changed. God is proud and vengeful and stubborn. I love Him, and I love His pride, and I love His vengeance, and I love His stubbornness. When He decided that I was trying to take His place, when He decided that I had learned too well of Him, had become too proud of myself and had turned the others to follow my own command, I didn't deny it. I love Him. When He decided to cast me into the Lake of Fire, this pit of damnation, I didn't complain. I love Him. When He learned later on that He'd leapt to conclusions, when He saw that I had only been teaching the others to love Him as I do, and He was too stubborn to admit He had made a mistake, I didn't say a word, I didn't fault Him. I love Him. I never tried to convince Him of my love, and I never turned on Him. You..." The Prince of Darkness now appeared to be weeping into his own hands as though he had suddenly found himself with the first being in all these thousands of years who he could open up in front of, and even as he cried out with his mouth, his words continued into Trevor's mind. "...you and I... I can't say... I mustn't tell you, but you and I and He have something in common, and... somehow I couldn't stand to have you... to have one of us... believing the lie, the propaganda... I can trust you. I know I can. And after a while, I guess it won't really matter how much I told you, not after the duel... but you must know that I loved Him, I love Him, and I've always served Him as best I could. And now you're here, and I..." Now even the mental voice broke down crying, and Trevor turned back to the fireplace, giving Satan time and space to let it all out, not even knowing where to begin, whether to comfort or scold him. Worse, Trevor wasn't even sure whether this was all just a trick, an act, meant to get his sympathies and fool him into agreeing to the duel, the contract, and whatever horrible loopholes and snares had been lain down in it. Everything Trevor had read from Old Scratch had seemed to indicate that he was genuinely feeling the way he appeared to be feeling, and there was no trace of falsehood that Trevor had been able to detect during his story. Still, the deceiver had been playing this old game for millennia, and might be more convincing than even the twins had been before he'd discovered the wicked truth about them. Trevor took advantage of the time the accuser was sobbing to try to weigh his options and decide a course of action.

From the moment Trevor had put his hand on the door leading to Hell, Jurrin had been ready for a fight. Watching the other three disappear before his eyes even as he was surrounded by an empty and desolate, burning and twisted Hellscape only put him more on his guard. He stood, sword at the ready, listening intently to the rolling silence of heat rising blisteringly up from the near-molten surface of this place. He turned his head side to side and peered with his mind's eye behind him and even though he could not see or sense a single point of actual movement between himself and the horizon in every direction, his muscles remained tense, his sword raised to strike.

Slowly, everywhere around him, among the deformed and twisted spikes and jagged peaks and rocks and crevasses and all of them glowing between red-hot and white-hot and the air slithering upwards with heat distortion, the demonic hordes began to come out of hiding. They were just as glowing-hot, and perhaps more twisted, more jagged, more hard and horrible than the environment they were naturally camouflaged to disappear into, and each and every one that began to move towards Jurrin's battle-ready stance moved with a calculated and deliberate speed of near-stillness. They could see immediately that this new one was a danger, not to be feasted upon greedily like most that appeared before them, dazed and without understanding or defense, but to be approached with deliberate stealth and caution, en masse. If you had been looking at it happening all around him, you might think that Jurrin's presence in this accursed place (or perhaps his still-shining armor or his gleaming sword) was causing it to curl up at the edges and peel apart. Every outcropping of rock and every other horrible feature of this landscape appeared to be lifting and moving and slowly curling and shifting inward, all drawn

300

improbably towards the place where Jurrin was standing as though by some strong magnetic field.

Except they each moved slower than the heat-ripples rising all around them and distorting what Jurrin could see, and he wasn't able to detect any motion at all. Thousands upon thousands of grisly beasts with only the worst of intentions gradually worked their ways closer and closer and closer to Jurrin's battle-hardened blood-thirsty form. They were so unlike any living or moving thing that Jurrin had ever witnessed that they were invisible in their land simply by holding a comparable color in their own hides like giant, evil, carnivorous chameleons. As they drew nearer and nearer, Jurrin was holding his breath to try to hear them, to hear anything, and in that still silence they finally pounced, dozens at once in the air and hundreds more running along the ground close behind, signaled by the sudden rapid motion, trying to get their own taste of this new, shiny thing before it was gobbled up completely by the others.

They moved as much faster than fast as they had moved slower than slow on approach, and in nary an instant Jurrin's upright form was replaced by a blurring, roiling mountain of swarming creatures the same color as the landscape. If someone had not seen Jurrin standing there before and glimpsed this sight during the three full seconds it was sustained, they might not be able to discern that there were individual creatures at all, but instead see a literal mountain with a reversed flow of molten stone working its way towards the peak of the deformed hill from every direction, as far as the eye could see. After those three seconds, however, the illusion of order and incongruous peaceful flowing would be shattered.

A muffled scream broke through the nearly-silent chattering and hard-slapping of tough hide on tough hide and bony protrusion against spiny outgrowth that was the only noise the clamoring beasts made at the height of their fury, and a rippling outward wave swept across the surface of the reverse-volcano of heaped and crawling monsters. Then another ripple of back-forced bodies arced across from the opposite face of the dogpile, and another, and then the would-be mountain became a time-lapse-photography movie of a mountain of sugar melting in the rain.

The monsters on the surface couldn't tell what was going wrong, they just knew that no matter how quickly they crawled across the backs of their kind, they weren't making progress towards the prey they had lost sight of anyway. The ones in between hadn't been too pleased with their place in the great and deepening hill of crushing, clawing, hungry beasts all seeking the same meal, smashed, as it were, between a horrifying monster and a demonic Hellspawn, but now they found themselves being nearly torn apart as the beasts below them disappeared or slipped backwards or both and the crawling things above them just kept trying to head forward. Every one of them had jutting herring-bone-like extrusions as hard as petrified antlers coming out of their limbs and bodies in a seemingly random way, extraneous dangling limbs that did nothing but get in the way and cause pain, and rough, bumpy, bulging, hides with ridges and holes and crevasses in patterns as unique as the lives that had led to them, and in a situation like this, they all got caught on each other. They all got caught on each other, and with the bodies working above and below in opposite directions, the ones in between were torn apart, some losing their skeletal outgrowths with wet snapopping sounds and lightning strikes of pain rippling through their bodies while others were less fortunate, literally being ripped limb from limb or being exploded out over every other being in their crushed vicinity in a putrefied, oozing mess.

Then there were the most immediately unfortunate - though perhaps the most fortunate, in the end - of the creatures who attacked Jurrin, those closest to him. As soon as the first wave leapt at him, he flicked the facial shield of his armor down with a strong but rapid motion of his neck, covering the only exposed part of his flesh before the brimstone-fire-hot beasts coalesced on his body. The first to reach him had either terrifically terrible aim, or a terribly terrific self-sacrificing intelligence, for it managed to self impale on Jurrin's backwards-extended sword with the full length of its body a mere fraction of a second before Jurrin would have swung it wide through the bodies approaching

302

from his front, and only another fraction of a second more before the rest of the leaping monsters reached him. Their claws and oversized mandibles and extruding, antler-like bones and growths clanged and grasped at Jurrin, trying to tear into his strange shiny exoskeleton, and dozens of arms and legs and tails and a few unidentifiable limbs worked to wrap themselves around him to hold on, to hold their place next to the fresh meat so they wouldn't be brushed aside by the others trying to do the same.

The limbs, the bony bits, the claws, the mouths, and even a few of the monstrosities' heads unfortunate enough to come in contact with Jurrin's armor began to dissolve. Exoskeletons and spiny extrusions that had been strong and sharp enough to be used to gore and eviscerate victims for all their long and violent memory were turned to soup just for clanging against Jurrin's armor. Limbs, the limp and useless and the unbelievably strong and limber alike, dissolved from a solid to a runny liquid of nearly the same glowing amber color of the rest of the monsters and the landscape they had trod upon and now melted onto. The liquefaction seemed to be rapid and spreading, not from creature to creature, but within a creature touched so that even the lightest contact with the furthest and least useful twisted, horned, spiny bone outgrowth against the armor first liquefied the outgrowth, then whatever part of their misshapen body it had been connected to, and spread out and up and down and in and out from there until the thing was nothing more than a snot-like, runny mess working its way over and in between and under the beasts which had not yet reached Jurrin's armor. The entire process from first contact to total dissolution seemed to take about a second.

The one that had got onto Jurrin's sword had somehow not quite had enough force to slide all the way down the blade to brush against Jurrin's armor, and even as the entire first wave of attacking things turned to goo all around him, Jurrin's sword remained encumbered and useless. Luck was not working entirely against him in this crazy place though; at least he was still standing. If the creatures on one side of him had jumped a half-second sooner than those on the opposite side or if he'd relaxed his battle-ready stance even an iota or if he'd swung his sword out in front of him, stopping even just part of the force of those flying in from that direction, he would have been knocked off balance in that first instant, knocked as flat as the jagged ground would have allowed, and defenseless. He may even have drowned in the rush of liquefied monsters that would surely have flowed down all around him. Luckily for Jurrin, he was not knocked down, and the melting monsters were running down and away from his face and mouth instead of up and over them. He knew his armor had been enchanted to carry an ethical charge of its own long ago, and that it had been worn by his own great-great-grandfather Phelleea the Righteous during every step of his knighthood, but he had never suspected that such a powerful residual righteousness as this might cling to its frame after all this time. For a second or two, Jurrin just stood there, marveling at how efficiently the armor destroyed his attackers and trying to imagine how it might have been possible for every tale of do-gooding he had heard ascribed to Phelleea the Righteous might have actually been true - it would take at least as much positive ethical charge as was rumored to have extended Phelleea's life to so blaspheme these Hellspawn monsters with such finality.

He wanted to just stand there a while, let them come, let them feel the righteous justice his armor would deal out merely by touching each horrible thing in turn, but before long he realized he was completely buried in monsters, couldn't see a light other than the monsters' glow, and the weight above him was threatening to crush him, armor and all. The ones that reached him turned quickly to liquid, but there seemed to be more and more clambering across the backs of those nearest to him all the time, replacing the melted monsters faster than they could slip slick out of the way. Jurrin finally snapped out of his frozen stance, and tried to swing his sword to cut through the amassing beasts, but it hardly budged, stuck in that first leaping creature. He inched his sword down to pull the encumbering corpse towards his shoulder plate, hoping that its effects remained effective on the dead, and then suddenly he could move his sword with case.

304

Jurrin swung the weapon in a long, strong arc, his sword easily dissecting everything in its path, slicing them into pieces ahead of him, brushing the arms of his armor against those collapsing in from above, and driving outward against the crush. At the end of the sweep, Jurrin was just about where he'd started, but he turned and raised his sword through the clawing, clanking, and otherwise noiseless creatures, then swept the sword again across in front of him, this time in the opposite direction, with a similar effect. He was destroying them faster than he could have expected to with his sword alone, but there were so many of them so feverishly fighting to get to him that they could not see the decimation he was creating and he still couldn't see the light beyond the crush. He just kept swinging and turning and trying to keep his footing in the liquid remains of his kills, now shin deep. For what seemed like too long a time he kept this up; liquefying those that came close enough to reach him, slicing up those that came within range of his sword before they got too close, and hoping that he would be able to get a little ahead of this cavalcade of enemies.

Then, almost all at once, he could see the light. Not the light of day, but the ambient yellow-orange glow that Hell seemed to have radiating out of the emptiness that passed for sky here, and that was almost as good. The monsters seemed almost to be swept away from him on a receding wave or fast-moving tide and Jurrin realized that in a way, they actually were - the downward force of the ones that had crawled up and up and up had only worked to slide those underneath them out and away on the slick goo that had been their own kind only moments before but that now pooled to above Jurrin's knee where he stood. The slimy residue of the destroyed creatures was now chunky and thicker all around him as though a psychotic butcher/warlord had made a battlefield stew with the sliced-up bodies and strewn organs of those truly unfortunate beings which Jurrin had rendered inert with his blade.

The tide of melted monsters was receding from his legs and he was uncovered, but what he saw now did not please him at all; there were thousands of thousands of the creatures rushing towards him. They filled all the space he could see in every direction in what seemed like an infinite garishly deformed and burning-hot plain of pain and suffering, points of motion, a sea of motion, excited and hungry creatures stretching from horizon to horizon, three hundred and sixty degrees around him, all the motion working its way toward center. The things closest to him were just regaining their feet - or whatever they had to move along on - and seemed ready to lunge back towards this strangely still-untouched shiny visitor, pressed upon by hordes of encircling mob-members which appeared identical to Jurrin in such numbers despite their unique features, just as a large enough crowd of people begins to make everyone look quite the same. He raised his sword again and was about to scream out a traditional battlecry of Phelleea the Righteous when suddenly, everything stopped.

Perhaps not everything, but when one was outnumbered literally a million to one and the million stop all at once like the frozen frame of video on the TV screen when you pause a DVD, it's statistically insignificant that the one happens to remain mobile. Jurrin looked around, checking for some sort of trick, some sign that they had only slowed down to the speed slower than the ripples of heat in the air - but the air was no longer rippling! Jurrin could see the wavering distortions between himself and distant points of interest, but the distortions were totally unmoving, as though fixed in space. Air and Fire behaving like Earth. He stood in wonder, trying to understand what he was seeing without diverting his attention from his own safety and the sword in his hands, should everything return to speed without warning.

On the heels of whatever had stopped the rampaging creatures, quickly following, Jurrin heard a voice that seemed to be coming from everywhere and nowhere at once, "...special attentions. I see that one of your traveling companions is quite the troublemaker." The voice seemed to come from inside his head about pounded on his ears all at the same, and then stopped just as suddenly as the hordes of monsters just beyond arms' reach. He didn't understand it at all; not why it had come to him, whose voice it was, or what it had to do with the mess at his feet, now seeping well within his armor and soaking hot and wet into his pants and filling his boots and socks, liquefied creatures squishing in between his toes.

He didn't need to understand it. The next thing he knew, the tortured and blisteringly hot landscape which had been filled with equally tortured but easily slain terrorizers as far as the eye could see in every direction was replaced with what appeared to be a cell designed for solitary imprisonment of magically adept criminals. The space was nearly eight feet along each edge, a cube of smooth surfaces with rounded edges and corners, a single unbroken surface of pillow-soft material that Jurrin didn't have to test to know would not be penetrated or even scratched by the sword he still carried. There was no apparent light source, no furniture, no fixtures, nothing in the room but Jurrin, the clothes and armor on his body, and the sword still clutched tightly in his hands. He reached out with his mind and with his magic and confirmed that he could not effect anything beyond the edges of that pale, soft, singular surface surrounding him. He lowered himself to the pale, soft floor, relaxing against one of the lower too-round-to-really-be-a-corner corners without taking off a single piece of armor or releasing his sword. He did lift the visor of his helmet after he sat, revealing his face as he muttered to himself, "At least my socks are dry."

When Trevor had knocked on the big double doors that he said would lead to Hell, Nirgal, Trevor's Gollum, and Jurrin were standing several paces behind him, but as the doors opened - like blast doors opening on a fiery furnace, even the first slim crack of opening gave way to a hard burst of hot, expanding air - they opened into the church, towards them, and Trevor stepped backwards into line beside the other three, waiting for the slow, heavy barricades to finish their nearly casual-seeming grinding to openness. The windswept contents of that other world had begun to spill out through the opening as though they had been eager to escape Hell, then rattled quickly to a halt still within the grand arcs described by the path of the doors as they realized that the world on the other side of those doors was now a part of Hell as well.

The four remaining members of the botched or irrelevant rescue party stepped forward at the same time and pace, and while they certainly did not hook their elbows together and sing and dance their way into the yellow-hot realm before them, neither did Trevor try to exert his leadership by staying in the lead or giving instructions as they crossed over into what had always been Hell. As soon as they were through the doorway, Nirgal turned to see whether it had simply disappeared, and was shocked by what he saw for only a second before he began half-stumbling backwards across unfamiliar and precarious terrain to try to get a better view. The entire dark church was standing there, its front doors blocked open.

Nirgal had never seen this church from the outside before - none of their party had seen it, coming in though the fulcrum point of the magical protection that ought to have kept anyone from appearing inside the double church, and only then because of the strong link of sex magic between Trevor and Hannah, not to mention their shared labor pains. He'd had some clue of its size from the interior, but the idea of seeing the entire building at once, if only he had the right vantage, suddenly drove Nirgal to turn away from it and run in the other direction, looking for higher ground. The other three, who had stood transfixed by the church which had been transported as wholly as its remains allowed to wherever in Hell they now found themselves, did not think to move until they saw and felt Nirgal running away from the dark, evil structure. They were running away from the huge, dark building not to seek a better vantage from which to admire the church, they were running away from something that frightened them in a way they would not have believed was possible if it were not churning away in their guts as they turned tail and ran, and they happened to go in the same direction as Nirgal in pursuit of a more defensible position.

To get an idea of what they were feeling, imagine you've just stepped intentionally into Hell, the flaming furnace, the lake of fire, the pit of eternal damnation, filled to the brim and overflowing with every evil thing in creation that ever lived, plus all those evil beings who gave them the idea in the first place. Now imagine that an ancient-looking gothic cathedral was the place you'd considered more safe than Hell before stepping into Hell itself, and that the gothic cathedral in question, when held up as such against the raw, elemental, pervasive evil that permeated every square inch of Hell, appeared to be the more dark, evil, and malevolent of the two options. Hell, which threatens to combust the clothes right off your back in an instant but somehow staves off this destruction, that same Hell which represents the dumping ground of every cosmically evil noun that ever existed, seems like a welcoming hearth and home next to this dark church.

An idea occurred to the Gollum as he caught up with Nirgal on an elevated cluster of glowing-hot stones, and he muttered it under his breath, "Perhaps the church wasn't transported here just to move us, but because it somehow deserves to be here on its own."

"What was that?" Trevor asked the Gollum, but the Gollum just shook its head and smiled quietly to itself, and Trevor didn't pursue the thought.

They all gathered on the slightly raised area that Nirgal was enjoying the view of the church from, and tried to take in their surroundings. "So this is Hell, eh?" They nodded all around. "Can any of you sense anyone out there? Not just with your mind, but visually or any other way?" They shook their heads and made dissenting noises back to the group. "What now?" The Gollum put its back to the church so it could stand in Nirgal's line of sight and face him, had an expectant look on its face.

Trevor turned slowly to face it and said "I don't know. I thought we'd be greeted immediately or find ourselves plunged into chaos, fear, and pain. Maybe both. But walking into an empty space, I did not expect."

Nirgal spoke softly, not even taking his eyes off the church to see whether he spoke the truth until after he'd said it, saying "If this is Hell, where are all the damned souls? Shouldn't it be crowded here?"

The Gollum nodded to Nirgal, whose eyes had flicked directly from the church to meet its eyes as he finished asking. "If Hell is finite and physical in space, then yes, it ought to be quite crowded, considering the number of dead who never met even a single religion's guidelines for escaping it." Trevor continued where the Gollum had stopped.

"But if Hell has at least one dimension which is not finite in nature, then it could only ever seem crowded if those in charge wanted it to. I have the feeling that there are many different layers of existence here, one overlapping another and another in a boundless succession so that a smallish space of, say, thirty-five thousand two hundred and ninety seven square miles, when given infinite latitude in a higher-order dimension, seems both vast and is actually infinite."

Nirgal frowned at the Gollum that wore Trevor's face, not turning around to frown at the original Trevor. "First of all, we haven't studied higher-order dimensions yet, so I don't know anything about them, and everything you're saying is coming out gibberish to me. Second, since when is thirty-five thousand however many miles a small space?"

The Gollum responded, instead of Trevor. "Consider that the surface area of the Earth is somewhat larger than one hundred and eighty-three million square miles. Even if you remove the approximately three quarters of that which is covered by ocean, there are about forty-six million square miles of surface area above water on Earth."

"Most of that has never been occupied by sapient beings, in all our history. It's mostly empty. Life bunches up together. Did you know that nearly half of of all humans live within less than one hundred miles of an ocean?"

The Gollum continued speaking, almost ignoring Trevor's questionable statistic, aware that it was more like 120 miles for the first 50%. "Regardless of population density, the surface area above water on Earth right now is almost one thousand three hundred times as spacious as the thirty-five thousand two hundred and ninety-seven square miles Trevor suggested. Quite small, indeed."

"I suppose it's just a matter of perspective, but ... if we were in a land that large, could we see the edges of it from the middle, or would it stretch beyond the horizon?"

"The horizon is an artificial barrier created by the curvature of the surface you're viewing. If Hell's thirty-five thousand plus square miles were wrapped around a sphere and you stood on it... you're what, about six feet tall?"

"I had a growth spurt."

"But six feet, right?"

"A little over that."

"Fine, if you were standing up on this supposed sphere with a surface area of thirty-five thousand two hundred and ninety-seven square miles at a height of six feet, you'd probably only be able to see about ... a third of a mile, maybe eighteen hundred feet before the rest was obscured by Hell's curvature."

"A third of a mile? That sounds way too small."

Trevor cut in to answer, "No, I think he's right... I mean, I'm not the best at running square roots in my head, but a sphere that small, yeah. About a third of a mile."

"Well what is it on Earth? How far am I used to seeing?"

"About three miles at sea level. That's roughly ... eight and two thirds times farther."

"Really only three miles?"

"It varies all over the planet, depending on local features, altitude, irregularities in the curvature of the Earth, and perhaps most troublesome of all is pollution. If the air is clear, you can see farther than if it's dirty. All my math is based on relatively clear air."

"Does Hell even have air?"

"We'll assume it does, since we're all in Hell now, and we're all breathing." The Gollum paused, pointing out towards the edge of where the yellow-orange glow of the sky met the crags and crannies and jutting outcropping land features. "Also, look across there, straight out. Do you see the way everything ripples and waves in your vision?" Nirgal nodded, seeing the distortion as if for the first time. "That's an effect in the air caused by the heat rising off the surface of Hell. The light gets distorted by the currents of hot air, you see?"

"Yeah, alright, air. What else would I be breathing? But that distortion, would it have the same effect as pollution on our ability to see farther?" Nirgal seemed to be beginning to grasp all these concepts in a meaningful way at last.

"That's definitely a possibility, and it relates to my next question. How far do you suppose you can see, in any direction from where we are now?"

"At least as far as I can on Earth. Maybe farther."

Jurrin spoke up, briefly adding his two cents to the discussion instead of just standing silent as they babbled nonsense. "A lot further. I'd guess at least twice as far."

Trevor agreed, and the Gollum continued the discussion, "So if you know you can see at least three miles, and perhaps as far as six or more, and if we assume for a moment that the surface area of Hell is the thirty-five thousand two hundred and ninety-seven square miles we've been using in all our examples, would you say Hell, like Earth, is a spheroid shape?"

"If that surface area is correct, no. It couldn't be. Plus..." Nirgal was looking across the edge of the horizon from left to right and back again, examining it carefully before he spoke, "Plus, I don't see any curvature. I've been places near as wide and flat as this one on Earth, and you can see the curvature at the horizon. Well," Nirgal laughed nervously, correcting himself, "not flat, exactly, just ... free of hills and other such."

"No problem, Nirgal, I'm sure we all understood, and I'm glad you noticed. No, from the looks of it, and from the math we've considered, Hell is not curved into a sphere like the Earth. If it were, to have a horizon as flat and far as that, it would have to be..."

Trevor finished the Gollum's sentence for it, "larger than the Sun. Probably larger than a red giant. Assuming, of course, that we're all still the same size we were on Earth. If by some process those who visited Hell were reduced to a thirteen-hundredth of their normal size, Hell could be that tiny sphere we were disproving and still look this big."

"But we're not smaller, are we?" Nirgal was pretty sure about it, but didn't rightly know how to know.

"No. But how can we tell? What would have to have changed about us to keep our bodies, our clothes, and all our possessions complete and still reduce our size by over three orders of magnitude?"

Jurrin spoke grumpily, sounding as though he thought their discussion had been pointless to begin with and had now gone well off-track, "The empty space within our every atom and sub-atomic particle would have to be reduced in the exact same proportions across every element being shrunk. Are you going to get around to a point, or are we going to be standing around here gabbing all day?"

"I don't think there's such a thing as day and night in a place like this, Jurrin," Trevor responded in a tone of mock-helpfulness.

"But he's right about the only way to safely shrink us without simply removing matter altogether. Even if it's done by magic, to shrink something is to remove the space within each atom, and to enlarge it it to add space. Otherwise a complete restructuring must be done, and a human body would not resemble a human body once the necessary changes for continued survival and functionality were made to support a tiny or large body. But if every atom in the body has its internal emptiness modified by exactly the same amount, and if every atom passing in and passing out of that body is modified in the same way, the current structure is sustainable, the organs continue to function, and you don't die immediately. But there is one noticeable side effect of this process which takes quite a bit of getting used to and can be just as dangerous as less mathematically sound methods of growth and shrinking. Can you guess what it would be?"

"Is it ... something about proportional ethical charges, or something like that?" Nirgal had missed the mark this time, but Jurrin was more than happy to catch him up.

"The mass stays the same."

"...but the volume changes. So you'd be bigger or smaller, but a significantly different density. Wouldn't that throw your sense of inertia off?"

"In a way, that's the symptom exactly. Your mass stays the same, and mass and inertia are effectively the same thing, so your inertia remains the same whether you're a millimeter tall or a mile tall. It takes the same amount of force to make the same amount of motion, only now your density is way off. Imagine trying to move something less than a millimeter in length that weighs two hundred pounds. Its weight would pull it through most of the things you just thought about holding it in. Instead of the roughly two to four pounds per square inch you put on every surface you stand or walk on at full size in Earth's gravity, you'd represent about one hundred and twenty-nine thousand pounds of force per square inch. There aren't a lot of substances that could handle that much pressure, even on only a millimeter-wide space. Do you suppose this," he kicked at a jutting chunk of red-hot rock, and it broke off and shattered into a few large chunks and a lot of small ones, "is hard enough stuff to take that much force?"

"No, no, of course not. So we're not shrunk, Hell isn't a planet or otherwise curved into a sphere shape, and it's infinite in at least one of the dimensions in which it exists."

"Right."

"But that still doesn't answer my first question."

"Which one?"

"Where is everybody?"

"Maybe they're invisible, and decided not to let us see them because you three ... or two... whatever! Because you're so boring," Jurrin said gruffly.

"They're probably just on another level of Hell. If our guess about the size of Hell and that its infinite dimension is one of a higher order, there could be an infinite number of levels. Unique levels of Hell for souls of different sorts, don't you see? Also, even if this level of Hell were populated, its denizens could be just out of sight, a dozen, a hundred, or perhaps as much as two hundred, miles away from where we are now."

"Where did you get all these measurements for Hell, Trev? Is it from something Sunshine knew?"

"Parts of it are from Sunshine, parts from others who have shared with me, and some of it was my own hard research, but none of it's really certain," said the Gollum. "I don't want to get into detail about it right now, but if it proves true or comes up while we're here, I'll burst it all into your mind."

Trevor spoke up next, "For now just assume we're right unless you see something to the contrary. Hell is finite in three-dimensional space like everything else you know, it's locked in time as well, but it exists in an infinite number of versions across a higher-order dimension."

"And probably we happened upon a level of Hell that is either entirely unpopulated or very sparsely populated so far. We don't know how they do things around here, so it's possible no one even knows we're here. A couple of people die every second back on Earth, so a group of four at once might go unnoticed."

"But we aren't dead." Nirgal tried to sound as matter-of-fact certain as he could, but it still came out sounding a little frightened. In the heat of battle he had been together and focused enough to nearly match Trevor's own ability, but in the calmness afterward, he turned right back into that same nervous schoolboy Trevor had met for the first time less than a year before.

"No, we aren't exactly dead, but we aren't exactly living, either. We're in Hell, a realm that's supposed to be exclusively for the dead, and considering the uninvited intrusion, I doubt they're going to be eager to let us leave." Jurrin was marginally more amicable, but still sounded morosely pessimistic to the rest of them.

"Well, we've got a few choices about how to proceed. We can try to locate someone or something in this realm and hope we can communicate well enough to find out whether there's a way out or maybe that they know someone or something which knows a way out. We can stay out of sight of anything and everything we see and try to find one of the eleven widegates of Hell, which ought to be just a matter of heading to the edge of Hell and traveling along that edge until we come to a widegate. We can attempt to summon Satan or some other major demon where we are, and hope they'll work with us when they arrive. Or we could just stay here for eternity in torment and pain. Unless anyone else has any suggestions?"

"I can't think of any, Trev. I probably wouldn't have remembered the widegates, myself. Good thinking."

Jurrin was practically guffawing out his words, "A widegate? All we have to do is find a widegate and go out? Do you have any idea what holds the widegates shut?"

Trevor nodded, "I do. That isn't my primary concern if we select that option, though. My primary concern is how to close the widegate again once we open it. According to legend, no widegate, once opened, can be closed until the twelfth gate is opened, and the twelfth gate doesn't even exist unless all eleven gates are already open. Aside from the fact that screwing any step of that process up could trigger the true end times for our world and the fact that our group of four is vastly undereducated about the widegates very existence, there's still the matter of which direction the nearest edge is in and the possibility that all eleven gates are not collocated across all the infinite levels of Hell."

"Not to mention the hordes of demons and wretched souls that would almost inevitably escape by the same route we would take if we opened even one of the widegates. We would get back to Earth just in time to watch it be devoured by the denizens of Hell." The Gollum, who may not even be allowed to remain alive long enough to see their return to Earth, still cared about it. It was inescapably in the Gollum's nature to care about whatever Trevor had cared about up to the point it was given life, and Trevor seemed to care, somewhere deep down, perhaps, for the survival of Earth. At least, that is, until he saw his daughter with his own eyes, alive and well, and held her in his arms, the Gollum mused silently to itself.

"Alright, it sounds like we're all opposed to the idea of locating and opening a widegate to get out of Hell. What do you think of our other options? Try to communicate with locals, or try to summon the powerful ones?" Trevor had only paused for a brief moment, not long enough for the others to respond, before he continued, "Oh, yeah, or stay in hell for eternity. Can't forget that one."

"I think we're more likely to be able to overcome a minor demon or corrupt soul than one of the powerful," said Jurrin thoughtfully, "though I wouldn't mind having a story to tell about meeting Satan or Mammon or Azael in person when we got home rather than some local putz of a demonic magistrate."

"I doubt that any trapped soul would know the way out at all, or they wouldn't be trapped in Hell anymore, would they?" Nirgal seemed to be going over their options as one might pick out a CD to listen to on a relaxing Sunday afternoon; casually, playfully, and with no weight of the danger that every one of their options represented. Whether this was a result of his having come internally to terms with the fact that when every outcome was bleak it did no good to feel bad about choosing among them or a result of his having slipped that one last step over the edge and into the abyss of insanity where even death was as meaningless as the outcome of a game of checkers was not apparent. "So we've got to find a demon of some kind if we want to get out of here at all. I think Jurrin's right that we could probably overcome a minor demon if we worked together, even in their own realm, but I doubt that the minor demons really have access to the sort of escape route we're looking for. We're not just here in spirit or in a new body given to us for the afterlife, we're here in our actual bodies, our only bodies and we need to have them with us when we return to Earth."

"While that is either a fairly short-sighted or highly bigoted view of non-corporeal existence and completely at odds with the very helpful men and women of the Wolyd Centre, I would definitely like to arrive with my body intact," Trevor agreed. The Gollum stayed silent for a few moments, hoping the subject of its own continued existence wouldn't come up so early in their adventure, and the conversation moved on naturally.

"So I think we ought to try summoning one of the major demons," continued Nirgal, "maybe not Satan or Azael or Ilbis or Mammon or any of the big names, but..."

Trevor cut Nirgal off suddenly, "Wait, what did you say? Which demons?"

"Uhh... I uhh... Satan and ... Mammon and Azael... and ... I don't know, didn't Jurrin say Beelzebub?"

"No, no, the other one, it's on the tip of my tongue! You said part of its name... come on! Who was it?" Trevor was really getting exasperated over the matter of whatever demon he thought Nirgal had mentioned.

Nirgal was beginning to sweat heavily, and had he not been wracking his brain to try to dig out the stub of information that Trevor was practically falling to pieces over, he might have wondered why he hadn't already been sweating heavily under his wizard's robes in an atmosphere that felt to be above the boiling point of water. "Was it..." he paused uncertainly, looking at his toes, scrunching them shut, pressing on his temples, "Was it Ilbis?"

"Yes! Yes! Yes! Thank you, thank you, thank you!" Trevor was jumping up and down and shouting, and he practically pounced on Nirgal to give him a hug. "That's it! I remember what she said to activate the book, and that's it! That's all we need, I'm sure of it. From the minds of the chained men at the end, I absorbed a lot of information I haven't even come close to comprehending yet, but with that name, it... It's like a key, and as soon as I thought of the two words Kay had said, my memories opened up. This is great!"

"What's great? What is it?"

"This level of Hell is definitely reserved for the most dedicated members of the dark sides of the pairs. There's a particular demon they worked with to get the churches linked to Hell and to secure an entire dedicated level for themselves, and I know his true name! He'll have to do whatever I tell him, and I know he can create portals between Hell and Earth. We're saved. This is it."

"I thought we were going to vote," said Jurrin in a tone that seemed neither greedy nor upset.

"Sure, fine, no problem. I vote we contact the demon in charge of this Hell and force him to conduct us safely back to Earth. Who agrees?"

"I don't see why not," replied Nirgal, "if the true name works the way you imply it will, we just have to be cautious of what we say to him."

"Then I suppose it doesn't matter what I think, does it?" proclaimed an exasperated Jurrin, throwing up his arms.

"If you'd like, I can cast an additional vote for the plan Trev has suggested, and you can feel even more disconnected from the process." The Gollum used an appropriately jokey tone, trying to lift Jurrin's mood to no effect. "I'd thought that since I was clearly only a copy of Trev, we must share the same vote; a thought which also helps prevent the possibility of a tie."

"Yeah, yeah, I'm sure it's a brilliant plan. Everything Trev has suggested so far has worked out perfectly, right?"

No one bothered to give Jurrin a response; there was none to give. They were going to summon the twins' demon contact and all they could do was try to be ready for unexpected twists. None of them wanted to return to the dark church from whence they had come, and neither did they have to verbalize that position; everyone knew. They would summon the demon right where they stood, and play by ear.

Trevor and the Gollum stood across an open space of about eight feet, facing each other. Nirgal and Jurrin stood out of the way, but near enough to be able to assist if something went wrong. Without a warning or a countdown of any kind, Trevor and the Gollum simultaneously called out the true name of the demon, "Tetralix Ilbis!"

The still air which had separated the two versions of Trevor instantly swirled into fevered motion, a cyclone of stingingly hot air spinning into being between them, tail dancing wispily just above the hard stones on which they all stood, a growing funnel of heat and dust and powerful forces brought together in opposition rose up and up and up into the yellow-orange glow, reaching further into whatever was above them then their eyes were able to make out through dust-blown squints. The twisting funnel of rising air spun faster and faster until the bits and chunks of sand and dust and rock that were caught up in it began to catch fire. These improbably flaming bits of stone drew horizontal or rising and spiraling lines of light across their retinas, and then they began to fly out of the twister at incredible speeds, hurtling through the air like meteorites and catching apparently sterile stones on fire wherever they hit. Whatever maelstrom they had summoned was actually setting the fields on fire despite the fact that nothing could ever have grown in this desolate landscape to burn; its demonic fire was intense enough to combust bare rock.

The whirlwind spun in place between the apparent Trevor twins, ever throwing its tiny, improbably fire-spreading grains of sand and pebbles, and after it seemed to have settled into a sustainable configuration, neither shrinking in size nor growing in intensity, a voice came from the wind. It was not the sort of voice they had expected. It was addressing them in a form of the ancient runic poetry that Nirgal had been studying so adeptly of late, and it sounded quite like it had somehow managed to cast each odd syllable with a cockney English accent.

Nirgal stepped forward as though made suddenly brazen by the need for his singular ability among them to comprehend the phonemes of the ancient runic poetry and respond in kind. Without missing a single beat, and there was definitely a beat resolving out of the strange sounds the demon had made, Nirgal began barking out his response with a matching but not identical rhythm. As soon as his mouth closed, the voice of the demon resumed, belting out the incomprehensible syllables of the callback duet faster than before without losing its careful rhythm in what the other three recognized as a challenge of sorts. They couldn't guess at what the song was about, or even whether it was an entirely ancient song or an improvised one based on an ancient formula, but as stanza after stanza of the song bounced back and forth between the demon and the boy, the speed of it went up and up and up as though imitating the way the whirlwind had risen into the bright sky above. Faster and faster they went, each iteration similar in structure to the one before it but different enough that until the verses were so fast that neither singer paused between their own verses to hear the other's, the spectators - for that is what Trevor, Jurrin, and the Gollum had become - could tell that

320

it was not simple repetition at speed but dozens of unique phrases carefully but rapidly enunciated in a hypnotizing fractaline pattern of sounds within and below sounds.

Then just as fast as the first lines had been followed by the second, it was all over. Nirgal shouted quickly to the others, "It's done! Just relax, and he'll send us back!" He wasn't sure whether they'd heard him, but they didn't try to run as he watched the twister lift and shift and set down on each of them in turn. First Trevor, down with the spinning tail widening to envelop him from heat to foot, then up again with nothing in its wake. Then Jurrin, armor-clad and sword at the ready for whatever enemy he thought might await him on the side of the living. Next was the Gollum that bore an uncanny resemblance to Trevor, down came the spinning air, concealing him, then up again and nothing stood where the Gollum had been. Finally, the conscious twister, this demon, shifted over Nirgal's head and began to descend.

The air at the center of the thing was eerily calm, but the walls of spinning debris were frighteningly near, so that he closed his eyes and mouth to keep out the dust while the return trip took place, even though he knew it would last only about a second in all. Suddenly Nirgal felt the sensation that he thought must be the feeling of traveling from the next world backwards; it felt almost like the inverse of what disappearing and reappearing did. He had his eyes closed as it happened, so he couldn't see it, but it felt like the hot air of the bare stone plains that had been made into a conflagration of rock and the twister itself were disappeared at the same instant that cool, still air and solid ground under his feet were suddenly appeared all around him. It felt as though he hadn't moved at all. Nirgal did not question this sensation at all; how was he to know what it was supposed to feel like to pass, living and breathing, out of Hell and back into life on Earth? He suspected that his little quartet might be the first four to ever experience such a thing, and as he opened his eyes to the room he was in and felt an odd sensation like the entire thing was not quite right, more a projection than a real place, Nirgal shook his head sharply and decided he must just be disoriented from the trip. "This isn't a projection, this is the lobby of the Wolyd Centre,"

Nirgal thought to himself, "see, there's the other three, looking just as disoriented as you feel. Relax. You did a good job, it's over for now." Taking his own advice, Nirgal began to feel the tension that had seized him about four stanzas into the whirlwind demon's song - as it had become faster and more improvised than he had known he could respond to correctly - melt away, out of his neck and shoulders and face, and a feeling of great relief suddenly washed over him. Nirgal smiled, approached the other three he had helped save from eternal Hellfire, and they all walked into the Centre together happy and relieved.

They all helped Jurrin strip out of his blood-and-guts-baked-on-by-the-heat-of-Hell armor he wore before stripping themselves down and showering in four separate private rooms of the Wolyd Centre, luxuriating in the cool of the water a good, long time. Somehow, the Gollum had known that it had nothing to fear from the water, that it was not made of mud as long as it still had life, and it enjoyed the experience more than any of the others, aware that it was not long for this world, no matter how their debriefing went. No one bothered the four returned soldiers, no one asked what had happened, no one even asked if they had wounds that needed dressing; they were left to clean themselves and rest for as long as they needed, and the peace and quiet had a chance to sink and settle into them as they slept and slept and slept.

Mere moments after Nirgal's eyes opened to a private hospital room on par with any single double at a four-star hotel, a nearly invisible wisp of a nurse pushed a cart in through the door. Nirgal could smell the hot breakfast she was wheeling towards him, and he sat up immediately and greeted the nurse, "Good morning, Nurse..."

"It's Yolida, honey, and a good morning to you, too. Feel free to call me Lida, all the girls do."

"Lida, it is a genuine pleasure to meet you, the bright spot of my morning, I suspect, second only to the first bite of food to reach my mouth since I escaped the fiery furnace alive."

"Oh dear, oh dear!" If the ghostly nurse had had any blood in her, she would have been blushing a glorious hue,

322

and Nirgal thought she seemed to turn from a pale white-grey to a pale pink-rose shade all over, but he couldn't be sure in the bright light of day streaming in through the wide windows. "I do hope it's more than the smell of crisp bacon that wakes you up so, honey. Let me just cover that up for you for now," she said as she lifted the breakfast tray onto his lap, her barely tangible fingers noticeably brushing against the erection tenting his blankets as she drew the tray up to hide the enormous bulge. When she grasped the size of it, almost literally, she seemed to go a shade or two deeper red, from pink-rose to rose-red, and managed to continue, "I can come back and take a close look at that after you finish your breakfast if it's ..." she managed to make a throat-clearing sound, and Nirgal was too distracted by the prospect of hot food and a hot nurse to wonder whether the nurses of the Wolyd Centre projected the idea of the sound of their voices into their patients' minds or actually used their skill at manipulating matter to vibrate the air and create actual speech, and whichever it was, Lida was an expert, "eh-hem, if it's still swollen, that is. I can think of a couple of things we could try to get the swelling to go down." She winked a sly wink in his direction, then turned to leave, pushing the cart in front of her ethereal body and swaying her ghostly hips wide and wide again.

As she reached the door, Nurse Yolida - that's Lida to you, sugar - turned her translucent head back to Nirgal who sat transfixed and frozen on the bed, caught by the sensual shifting of her virtual hips as a deer gets caught by the glow of oncoming headlights. "You've got to eat, love. Remember that bacon you almost jumped out of bed for?" Nirgal looked first down with a dazed expression at the plates stacked high with his favorite breakfast foods which the sexy nurse had set out and uncovered for him, then back to Lida. "You've got to get your strength up, honey. Can't have you passing out under ol' Lida right before the big meeting upstairs." She pronounced it as a single word, "O'Lida"; closer to her real name by one sound, removed from the actual idea of revealing her age by another. She disappeared through the door without waiting to see if he'd dug in, but she thought she heard the sounds of a teenager scarfing down food like he had someplace to be start through the door as she closed it.

Nirgal was famished, and ate the food laid out before him with a brazen disregard for the long-standing tradition of thorough mastication, nearly choking to death on a chunk of sausage and then on a bite of rye toast not two minutes later. He wasn't primarily motivated by the prospect of ... whatever the nurse had been flirting on about, exactly, as he didn't know exactly what sorts of activities a woman in her condition was capable of. Rather, Nirgal seemed to have been brought alive by his sheer usefulness in the course of the raid on the churches and then their escape from Hell, and he feasted hungrily, as though the food before him was sweet mother's milk, the first food to touch his lips in this new life.

At school he had few friends - no, only one real friend among the student body, and that was Trevor. Even though Nirgal had been added to the school's dodgeball team he'd felt like he was only there because of Trevor's help, separate from the team off the court even though he played a vital role in every game through his own talents and skills and got along well with everyone on the court and in the locker room. He came from a not-quite-poverty-poor family, and everyone seemed to know it just by looking at him. They knew it, and they treated him differently because of it, and Nirgal knew they did. He had always felt excluded before Trevor showed up, and it didn't get much better after that, since Trevor was such a natural outsider; a lot of the students who wanted to meet him, to hang out with him, to find out what this local celebrity was like in real life also feared him in greater measure. Lately it hadn't been unusual for students to approach Nirgal just to ask questions about Trevor, sometimes when Trevor was standing right next to him, but once they had their answer or a refusal to answer it was as though Nirgal became invisible right before their eyes, fading from existence. Even when he excelled at something, as he had done with ancient runic poetry and then on the dodgeball team, it had gone unnoticed by his fellow students. Nirgal had felt like he was meaningless and unimportant, a useless lost cog in the vast machinery of the world.

He had felt that way even as Trevor dragged him into the messy business of his kidnapped daughter and the twins. Even as he was made one of only four elite magicians to make up the frontal assault on the mirrored churches and their dark power, he had felt like he had no place being among them. Like he was simply Trevor's beloved pet, brought along for good luck and nowt else, and even put in charge of one of their most important defenses in a most demeaning way - Nirgal had had no conscious control over the most powerful area effect ever to erupt from his mind and will. Except that then the gargoyles had begun to fall, and suddenly Nirgal learned that he wasn't just a waste of skin after all.

After the gargoyles had begun to fall, right up until the moment he had been returned safely to the Wolyd Centre, Nirgal had been a vitally important member of a team of winners. If he hadn't been there, the twins might had had their babies, or at least might still stand to rise against the single-minded. If he hadn't been with the four who had gone to Hell in an evil cathedral - a much fancier conveyance than a hand basket, but it doesn't much matter if the destination is the same - even though Trevor had been the one who could summon and command a major demon, it had been Nirgal himself who had communicated with it in the complex sing-song of the ancient dueling poets, winning its favor and explaining their course in a way its ancient mind could comprehend. Trevor may have absorbed all the inside and archival knowledge of the dual church, but he could never have parsed it in time to deal with the whirlwind.

As Nirgal scooped up the last few morsels of food from the plates on the tray in front of him, he finished going over the recent events in his mind, and he felt proud of himself, just himself, for the first time he could remember. He had not been standing in the shadow of the greatness that Trevor and Jurrin represented, he had been standing beside them, fighting side by side as equals. What a wonderful feeling, to finally realize your own self-worth. He breathed in, and the air was sweet and refreshing. He looked out the window and the day was warm and inviting. He thought about the day ahead of him, of getting to tell the story of everything that had happened in his life since he'd left this place last, and he puffed up with eagerness.

Nirgal set the breakfast tray carefully aside and then leapt haphazardly out of the bed, the dwindling remains of his erection's possibilities forgotten completely as he tore off the pajamas he couldn't even remember putting on as he'd stumbled along the edge of consciousness toward the bed. He looked in the closet and the dresser and found that his own clothes had been brought in from home, and quickly dressed in his favorite outfit, comfortable, sturdy, and fashion-neutral enough that it would never go out of style.

Nirgal actually sang to himself as he dressed, a light and happy song about the sunrise and the blooming flowers of the morning he'd learned from his own independent studies of ancient runic poetry's musical history. The melody he hummed, but the incomprehensible-to-most-ears syllables of the long-dead-but-now-alive-again song's lyrical poetry he quite nearly belted out. It was a song of rejoicing and looking happily forward to the bright days ahead, but Nirgal sang it unconsciously at first, not even aware he'd started humming the tune before he'd even finished his breakfast. He finished dressing, double-checked he had everything he might need in his pockets, and on his final inspection in the mirror before going out the door, realized he was singing aloud.

Nirgal lowered his voice to a level he was sure wouldn't penetrate through the walls to the adjacent rooms where his compatriots-in-arms might yet be sleeping, and finished the final stanza of the song before stepping out into the hallway, where he was met with thunderous applause from those with hands, and hoots and whistles from those without, ol' Lida among them. There were shouts of "nice song" and "way to go Pavoratti" and "if it's good enough to get you out of Hell, it's good enough for me" and even a couple requests to "sing us another verse!" Just a day earlier, Nirgal would have taken every single comment, every clap and whistle and hoot as a jibe, and would have felt like the lowest creature on the face of the earth, thinking that everyone in the hospital had heard him or heard about him singing and had come to make fun of him. This morning, puffed up with pride, Nirgal heard everything as genuine praise, and only puffed up more. He even sang the gathered crowd a short two-stanza poem that most would never know was a traditional winner's gloating song in the now-so-distant past, and received another round of applause before semi-politely excusing himself to be debriefed, not realizing that everyone he was supposed to be meeting was there in the crowd.

Luckily for decorum, as soon as Nirgal disappeared around a corner and beyond their line of sight, ol' Lida, who had taken the sort of route to get to him that made it seem nice to be non-corporeal sometimes, grabbed Nirgal and pulled him into another of the private rooms. He could barely see her in the bright light of the room. She seemed to have been drawn in outline with curling streams of thin white smoke, and he couldn't make out her delicate features with his eyes, only the broad, voluptuous curves as in a silhouette he would never be able to forget. Invisible as she may have been, he could feel her hands on him with no trouble at all; her strong, gentle grip had been more than enough to pull him into the room and tight against her bosom. He couldn't have seen the bosom if he'd looked, but the sensation was exactly right, exactly as he'd known her embrace would have been in the flesh. If Nirgal kept his eyes closed, he would have no reason to believe he was with anything other than a beautiful, corporeal woman who was too hot for him to hold back, except for the obvious reasons like his youth, inexperience, and general social ineptness that naturally flowed from and helped support the excluded nature of his social life. Nirgal didn't want to keep his eyes closed, though, he wanted to see the woman, see everything there was to see about her, and give himself over to the pleasurable new experiences she was already dragging him into.

He wanted to see her, and he knew what he needed to do. From where he stood in the doorway, lips locked in a deep soul kiss with an unseen partner, Nirgal reached out with the mental forces he knew he could command and closed the room's curtains completely. The room had been unoccupied and brightly lit by the sun so no lamp or other

327

light source penetrated the dim stillness of the room but the light that crept in around the border of the curtains. In the dim light, little ol' Lida lit up considerably, very nearly glowing, but still more of an outline than a woman, and he wanted his first sexual experience to be more like sex and less like a vivid masturbatory fantasy. She was floating backwards toward the bed, pulling him shuffling along without so much as reducing the passion or intensity of that hot, wet kiss.

He wanted to break free for a moment, and at the same time he never wanted to have less contact with Lida, only more. Still he wanted to be able to see her properly, to create the right atmosphere for what was to come, and his first idea, nearly the last conscious thought he would have before leaving this room, required his mouth to be free to speak for a second or two. He tried pulling his face back, away from Lida's, but she had a hand on the back of his head and only pressed him tighter against her. He spoke to her mentally, gently, a lover's soothing voice is what he'd hoped to hit on, saying, "I just need my mouth for a few seconds, and then it's yours."

The hand on the back of his head was instantly gone. Not removed, not pulled back; she was not corporeal, and had simply stopped projecting a hand into the space behind Nirgal's head. He pulled his head gradually out of the kiss, planting a few quick parting pecks on lips he could feel but not really see, and took in a deep breath. His right arm moved up, off Lida's generous backside to point in the direction of the window, and his left hand massaged her nearly-transparent yet more-than-well-endowed right breast as he worked, savoring the sensation and trying desperately not to lose his concentration. He spoke an impromptu, modified version of the mud-gollum poem he had already re-worked to create his mudballs before, hoping beyond hope that it would have the desired effect and not simply fill the room with thick mud or worse. Whether by luck or by his apparently inherent skill, Nirgal might never know, the effect of the modified poem had been exactly as he had intended; behind the drawn curtain a just-thick-enough layer of dark mud flowed down the entire wide picture window, completely obliterating the sunlight that had been sneaking around the edges of the curtains and into the room. As they fell backwards onto the soft Queen-sized bed, the room was plunged into near-total darkness. A quick toss of a mudball at the door they'd come in through made short work of the light-leaking crevasses on three sides of the door. As his mud worked its magic on the insistent light, Nirgal closed his eyes and tried to concentrate on an effect that Trevor had tried to show him several times for use in dodgeball games, and which he had never quite been able to complete. This morning, just as the last of the light winked out of the space below the door, Nirgal managed to complete the effect, and time within this room was no longer running along the same timeline as the time outside the room; they would have plenty of time to themselves, and he would still be able to reach his meeting at a reasonable time, perhaps only as though he had been stopped in the hallways to sing a stanza or two for some passing nurse or specialist. Time was slowed nearly to a stop, and the room was lightless. Nirgal's eyes dilated all the way to the edge of his vision, exposing the sensitive black-and-white-seeing rods of his retina to the only light-source in the room, Lida.

In the total darkness Nirgal had created, Lida's spectral body now glowed bright enough to give off a "bloom" of light beyond the quite sharpened edges, softening her newly crisp features into a rare beauty. She rolled them over and perched over top of Nirgal and as he studied her, she began carefully stripping his clothes off, folding and stacking them with her mind without so much as a flicker in the apparent solidity of the body kneeling tantalizingly above him like some sort of radioactively-glowing ghost.

He could still see through her in a way, but she was there in three dimensions now instead of a hazy two. Her facial features now had volume and showed a character and beauty that had only been hinted at by the faint wisp of her that was visible in a lighted room. Nirgal could look into her eyes, see the thin dark circumferences at the very edges of her irises where they met the whites of her eyes, he could see the subtle variations in brightness that outlined the sharp

329

flower-petals which radiated out from her pupils, and he could even detect the tiniest specks shining in the rich complexities of her irises, adding a depth of beauty to her eyes that a solid swatch of hue could never convey. By focusing his eyes at a different depth, Nirgal could see right through Lida's eyes to the back of her head and with concentration, on anything in between. The entirety of Lida's long-gone physical body was represented here for Nirgal to see, each projected cell glowing with its own light, visible to any who looked at it directly. He played around with his eyes' focal point as she fiddled with the long and complicated laces on the boots he had selected - they were like the official dodgeball boots in enough ways that they were mistaken for part of his uniform on a daily basis, but there were some good design choices made in the dodgeball boots that Nirgal liked to have on his feet every day, and he had saved up and bought these boots special - and he found he could set his eyes to show him something like a creepy x-ray, her skeleton glowing out to his eyes more visibly than her skin or other features. He could pinpoint the internal organs she had once actually possessed, taking in the contours of her intestines and the smooth curves of her kidneys before highlighting upon the brightly-glowing reproductive organs nestled above the point where her softly-glowing legs met.

Even as it happened to him, Nirgal realized that it was probably not a particularly normal response for a man to have, but it happened anyway, and he liked it - the sight of good ol' Lida's reproductive organs suspended within her as in the "Invisible Woman" anatomy playset or the plastic models found in doctors' offices brought Nirgal immediately to a fully aroused state. He loved seeing her, head to toe, the graceful curves of her body, her hips and ass and thighs a beautiful exclamation of her feminine nature, the gently sagging curves of her large breasts with her nipples nearly doubling as plumb bobs as they drooped were proof that this woman had been made for motherhood. For reproduction. For sex. Somewhere in between the door's closing and the bed, the projected uniform Lida had been wearing had ceased to be there, and Nirgal was glad to see that Lida had retained her naturally advanced body shapes instead of tweaking her representation into some barbie-doll-like contrivance. She had wrinkles, she had scars, she had cellulite, her breasts were no longer firm and pointy and full, and her belly curved out nearly farther then her breasts extended from her ribcage above it. Nirgal could even make out a subtle, and only faintly more glowing than the glowing skin surrounding, cluster of stretch marks on each side of her once-truly-huge belly.

All these details he noticed and adored and admired, but in every way that she resembled a fertility goddess externally, it was that internal proof of femininity, the cradle of all fertility nesting within her and within his sight that turned him on the most. That her breasts had been quite literally life-giving to her child or children made them more wonderful and powerful and erotic than any pert, perky teenager's pert, perky, unsuckled breasts; the young woman's breasts were like the caterpillar, uninteresting and useless until the woman who wears them transforms one day, one birth day, from being merely a life to becoming a true life-giver, becoming a bright and vibrant butterfly, a bastion of love for her child. That her belly had carried her child or children within her gave it a power and beauty and magnificence that no belly, flat or fat, scarred, marked, or blemish-free can share without first giving up its old place, its old firmness and smoothness, to give another life a safe place of its own. Her hips, seeming wide enough to bear out a dozen beautiful crowning kings into the world, are the fulcrums of her strength, and stand guard around the true palace of her femininity. Still, with every detail of Lida's life worn and shown to him in a glowing, glittering map of beauty and poetry, it was that internal system, obscured in most women by the opacity of their flesh and blood and bones, that captured Nirgal's attention and engorged him with the blood and desire he needed to become one with her as men and women were meant to do.

As she crawled back up along the length of his now bare body from the foot of the bed until she was face to face with him again, Nirgal's eyes remained intent and focused right through the top of her head, down her neck, past her heart and lungs and so much falderal, to the things that excited him the most. He gazed at them, taking in their unique beauties and recalling their names from some medical illustration or sex-ed book seen long ago. Her mons pubis, covered in a dense foliage of darkness peppered with grey, calls out to the center of his palm knowing that when they meet, his fingers will meet the rest of the neighborhood with just the right amount of reach, and wouldn't that be just the most neighborly day this beautyhood has seen? Then that forest of salt and pepper - still mostly pepper - runs on, following the twin paths of her labia majora down and around the 'neighborhood' like matching hedgerows bordering a secret garden of delights. His tongue craves a leisurely stroll along the paths of those hedgerows and practically throbs in anticipation of discovering the secrets and delights of her 'garden'. The delicate folds of her labia minora have, with age, softened silkily like the rest of her skin and have come to resemble the inward curving petals of a rare orchid in bloom whose sweet scent and nascent nectar he cannot wait to take in. Her clitoris, barely hiding behind that prepuce (nee foreskin, nee frenulum) of less-sensitive skin, already becoming engorged with passion as her ischiocavernosus muscles begin to contract before her slow trail of kisses has even passed Nirgal's knobby knees, and he looks forward to the chance to tease her garden's bud into the daylight where it can be worshiped as it deserves to be. Then her vagina, that beautiful, complicated passage and portal to life and to ecstasy, with the bulbocavernosus muscles just outside and ready to clamp down and to tremble, her vagina itself an experienced (quite nearly trained) muscle group, with rhythms and strengths all its own, feminine strength within feminine strength creating an undeniable attraction for its complementing partner of masculine strength upon masculine strength. That attraction is like a more powerful and subtle version of electromagnetism, drawing strong opposing forces inevitably together to discover their unique fit, and it, along with his own ischiocavernosus muscles, is what has polarized his masculinity, lending it strength and driving it outward, away from his foundation of masculinity and toward her cradle of feminine power.   Stronger than even that attraction is her cervix, the true corridor through which life is either granted or denied access to her uterus - that first home to all mankind, at home in every woman - unblocked in Lida by mucous because there is no risk of infecting a body which does not exist, the Jacob's Ladder of her interconnected femininity is free of all impediments to oneness.   He examines her fallopian tubes as they reach out and up and turn inward on each side of that uterus of hers which has been the womb of another, and the curves they follow are like fractaline expressions of the greater curves of her body, each doing its part, taking its shape from the curved surface that is what female means and means what female is, seeing all this while she spends slow, wet affections on his own external physical vestige of femininity; his nipples.   Those curves, those tubes beside tubes (the fallopian beside the ovarian arterial) that feather and finger and terminate as fimbriae and reach out for more curves besides; these ovaries curve around too, inside and out, creating, maturing, and releasing the tiniest curves, which are her eggs, to those fimbriae to be collected and passed back down this Jacob's Ladder which carries messages of hope and possibility both up and down - or at least it did while Lida still had a corporeal body.   For Nirgal, the level of detail of Lida's pseudo-physical manifestation was more than satisfying enough for now, though he certainly looked forward to the time when his erotic misadventures would involve a whole and healthy version of this Jacob's Ladder of femininity he had just climbed the length of in his mind and with his eyes, where there was a chance his messenger sent up and a messenger sent down would meet at just the right place on the rungs that would begin a transformation like that of a butterfly in their ladder's bearer.

Nirgal finished his focused musings just in time to pull the focus of his eyes out of Lida's crotch and all the way back to meet her proximate gaze as she, smiling more broadly than seemed quite reasonable, sank herself down onto him at both ends, swallowing his rigid member below and his tongue above as she did. As soon as Lida's eyes were closed for the kiss, Nirgal turned his wide-eyed gaze

333

back down and through her body, to watch his thickness penetrate, separate, and fill those glorious organs of femininity she so deliciously rendered for him from her bodiless mind.

The physical sensations of it were nearly overwhelming on their own, that first thrust of slick heat enveloping his unpracticed and overstimulated virgin organ was like nothing he had imagined; it was so much better than Nirgal had expected it to feel that he didn't know how to feel. That first stroke was by no means the last, of course, and with each long piston-like push and pull of Lida's experienced (quite nearly trained) vagina on and off of Nirgal's steel-hard corporeal and sensitive Magnum-XL-qualified cock, the level of control he had over his autonomic responses was tested an additional notch toward the impossible end of the scale, just from the physical sensations alone. Complicating the matter somewhat were his newfound pride and his recently discovered erotic fetishization of motherhood, femininity, and the entire reproductive process within the female body. Nirgal had never been proud of himself before, and he certainly didn't want to dash that so-far-short-lived sensation against the rocks by prematurely ejaculating or being a bad fuck.

(The possibility of the latter crossing his partners' minds at all, Nirgal would discover as life went on for him after this strange and convoluted experience passed by the wayside, had a lot more to do with whether they could accommodate - and enjoy - what he had to offer or not. Lida, for example, being non-corporeal, had certain advantages over corporeal women, not the least nor the greatest of which was her ability to adjust the depth and tension and sensitivity of her own genitals to suit the variances of each partner's own genitals. Had Lida actually been the one riding Nirgal like an out-of-control carnival ride that day, the fact that he had basically just lay still while she took care of her own business might have been more a blessing than a bad fuck, since he'd had no idea how to wield the battering ram stuck between his legs just yet. Other women, the ones with physical bodies unaccustomed to Nirgal's brand of hugeness down below, would consider

334

him a bad fuck no matter what he had done, how gentle and slow and sensitive or hard and rough and selfish he had been, and even if he had never penetrated them with "the old third leg", if they couldn't handle the size the rest didn't matter, he was a bad fuck in their eyes - and usually the eyes of their friends as well, whether they'd had a taste for hugeness or not.)

Beyond the intensity of the raw physical sensations which would already have overwhelmed most other teenage boys' minds, beyond his pride and his desire to save face even with this non-corporeal nurse he'd never met before today, there was his new erotic fetish to be considered. In fact, due to the intensity and suddenness of this fetish on the scene and the fact that he happened to be being fucked by a glowing, translucent woman upon whose internal organs he could focus his attentions, thereby seeing them with clarity and relatively independently of the appearance of the rest of the woman's body, Nirgal's new fetish was what ended up distracting him from his own body's signals and the pressure of trying to remain proud of himself, even in this area of total inexperience. He simply lost himself, his perception of this Lida's reproductive organs glowing white and three dimensional and interacting in realtime with his own massive testimony to the towering bludgeon that masculinity had become, shining stark against the blackness that surrounded Nirgal and this chain of creation which bounded up and down and up and down with a rhythm that he would have cursed as impossible to follow right up until the moment he understood it.

Then, with the nature of the rhythm understood, his perception of the cluster of glowing organs became fixed, and the rest of the world was the new askew. With new clarity, Nirgal felt he could make out each and every glowing cell of the projection and watch it perform its designed function as an individual unit with a duty to the whole, and in the intensity of the moment it didn't occur to him that it was unusual for the human eye to be able to see such tiny structures and motions. So without so much as a wonder, that's what he did, his eyes and mind taking in wide swaths of visual information at once, then analyzing and decompressing it in the background while he focused on the next cluster or layer of cells. The information, the visually observed progress and potential of each cell and its place in the community of these organs, expanded into Nirgal's mind at an amazing rate, and as he was working his eyes up and down and left and right and his focus nearer and farther away, he found a few interesting things out about this fortress of feminine power. The most interesting of which to him was that these glowing organs - which were projected by a powerful mind unconsciously from some stored, perhaps genetic, memory of its body - were so occupied with his masculine connection to their feminine power that they responded to his thoughts as though they were projected by his own mind.

When Nirgal saw cells laying dormant and wondered what their activity had been, they sprang to life to show him. Wondering about the scale he could effect change on as well as whether those changes were in his mind's eye or actual, Nirgal thought to the vagina about what a ripplingly powerful orgasm would look like on a cellular level and was rewarded with Lida's screams and convulsions, above and somewhat beyond his tunneled perceptions, as well as with exactly the cellular parade he had asked for, unfolding before his eyes. He watched each muscle group contract rhythmically, watched individual cells pulling hard one against another, exerting energy and increasing in heat and a few even pulled hard enough to tear free from their neighbors or die outright. This increased level of interaction from within the tunnel vision that had been created by falling totally prey to his erotic fetish for motherhood and fertility was like a door into summer, suddenly some part of Nirgal realized that he could witness the entire chain of interaction along the complex ladder of organs that was the only thing left in the world he could really see. He projected his request to the entirety of the femininity before him, an echo of it even reaching and effecting all the cells of Lida's projected body which were not strictly reproductive in duty, guiding them gently to ensure a healthy bodyscape for babymaking, and watched in awe as his desire started a process that had been long dead to the real Lida, and longer dead to the one who posed as her above him. Lida, unaware she was being impersonated, did not notice anything at all, though stirrings of slow activity beyond her control began to take place in the imagined cells of her projected body. The impostor, even if she had been sensitive enough to notice such a thing, as Lida most certainly would have been if it had happened so quickly within her, was completely consumed with the act of lovemaking which had so long been denied her and had this day been thrust back upon her. She sensed nothing.

Which was all to the good, since she couldn't have done anything to stop the process Nirgal had begun brewing within her; he had merely tipped the first domino, just a little nudge, and the rest was inevitably begun on the process it had been so carefully designed for, drawn along naturally and only unusual in the speed at which it occurred. Which is to say that the glowing, mentally generated projections of (see also: imaginary) ovaries released an ovum that had not even been present before Nirgal's request and was ready for the fimbriae to seek out before this Lida was wracked by her second orgasm. Lida's second orgasm seemed to have been triggered by Nirgal's own orgasmic ejaculation of thousands healthy sperm against the unplugged opening of her cervix, and had the effect through its rhythmic contractions of turning her cervix into a sort of pump, drawing his sperm-loaded semen up and up and into her glowing uterus. By the time her orgasm - but not her wild ride of Nirgal's perplexingly still-rigid protrusion - had subsided, the ovum which had been released was being shuttled along her fallopian tube at an unheard-of rate by glowing cilia that seemed desperate to do their part to ensure that the entire process of life creation was displayed before Nirgal's eyes could be turned away.

Nirgal watched in amazement as the seeds of life within his own white ejaculate, lighted only by the soft glow of Lida's own white projections of cells all around it, suspended now by a force almost independent from this Lida's mind and already most of the way up the ladder of organs his sperm must pass to reach their goal, began their blind swimming, tails whipping energetically to seek that single ovum. Whatever rules applied to corporeal cells didn't appear to apply to these glowing projections, and many functions seemed to occur all at once rather than over the course of days or weeks, and instead of a trip of hours or days, the gem-like ovum was spat out of the fallopian tubes in mere minutes, suddenly awash and surrounded by Nirgal's eager sperm. The glowing subject of Nirgal's utterly focused attention seemed to have decided that the urgency of the situation would not allow the time required for his sperm to reach the ovum as they normally would, in the ampulla of the fallopian tubes, and had thus also saved the time a fertilized ovum would require to reach the uterine lining. To Nirgal, such efficiency quickened his heart rate with the effectiveness that a rapid and passionate undressing in the stumbling race to a bed would do for most, and he felt certain that the object of his affections was not really the particular reproductive organs remembered by this non-corporeal woman's mind, but the focused representation of elemental femininity made real as it was drawn through the eager lens of Nirgal's mind, imbuing whatever lifeless and imagined structures this Lida had once had with the full power of a fertility goddess.

In the split second before a fully capacitated sperm broke through the crowd and through the zona pellucida in much the same way Nirgal's rock-hard manhood had made its way into Lida's depths by shifting and forcing the surrounding organs aside to make room, it occurred to Nirgal that as soon as this force of femininity, this channeling of an elemental fertility goddess through his mind and power and into the woman above and around him, was finished with her need of him, his erotic fetishization of motherhood, fertility, and the very cells that composed the female reproductive organs would either be stripped of him completely or left a hollow and unsatisfying shell that only remained to remind him of how erotic lovemaking had once been for him, and he feared that loss of worshipful respect and tried to grasp at it with his mind and make it truly his own rather than a mere side-effect of the presence of raw feminine power streaming through his mind. But then Nirgal saw that single sperm break through, witnessed the acrosome reaction he was too ignorant to know was just as accelerated as the rest of the feminine cells' actions and reactions, and as he saw his sperm's nucleus et al flow into the waiting ovum, he was pushed over the edge to orgasm again.

This time it was not some distantly observed phenomenon, brought on involuntarily by his body's reactions to the evolutionarily enhanced sensations of lovemaking, more real to him in the glowing reality outside his more-than-man-sized tool than in the chemically induced pleasure his body was trying to feed him on the inside. This time it was in every aspect of his being and amplified by the fertility goddess's presence in his mind reacting to the reality of the lifemaking that had taken place, an orgasm not only of the body with its electric and chemical descriptions of pleasure, but of the mind and of the essential living nature deeper within, a celebratory tsunami of thoughts, memories, associations, dreams, and all the flotsam and jetsam that floated on the currents of his mind and was now brought together in a mentally blinding overload of positive thoughts and emotions, and beyond that it was a primal shout of triumph into the cold darkness, a proud noise amidst the engulfing silence of entropy and emptiness that signified another victory of life and of order over chaos and death. This time, Nirgal passed out.

In the hours that followed before their private room returned to the same timeline as the rest of the Wolyd Centre, this Lida and Nirgal went through nearly every position and configuration of bodies that was practical or reasonable to attempt with only a single corporeal body present. The neighborly caress and garden stroll that Nirgal had imagined as he had been undressed played out as he watched a tiny, strange cluster of cells move along with the lumbering gait of normal corporeal cells. He could see that it glowed with the same light as each of this Lida's projected cells, but it did not seem to be translucent as the rest of her; it was a combination of their aspects. Soon enough, Nirgal could feel the tides of feminine power receding from his mind, the clarity of vision that had been granted him to witness each cell of the feminine in detail waned too, and the sense of eroticism that fertility and the reproductive organs themselves had represented faded almost entirely from his conscious mind. He had been able, before being thunderstruck by a literally mind-blowing orgasm and passing out, to shift some of the respect and glorification of those changes in the female form which are brought about with motherhood, but only in part, and the rest was lost to his subconscious mind and his rapidly fading memories of being used firsthand by an ancient goddess. The final stroke of it, a sudden absence of that presence that he sensed this Lida had not been aware of at all and which he would soon be unable to recall, came at the moment the tiny cluster of cells was finally implanted into the goddess-formed endometrium, and somehow, he knew it was so. This Lida yelped at that very instant, and between the shock of that and the pain of loss that would quickly fade, Nirgal halted his tongue's tangling with her soft, glowing flesh, and for a moment wondered whether she had felt that new life taking root in her or was just having another of her seemingly endlessly available minigasms.

"Don't stop now, sugar," she moaned down to him, "I think your tongue is finally getting the hang of it, and I'm willing to bet there are hidden depths of talent in that mouth muscle that you've never even dreamed of! You can get up off the cold floor and take a seat right here on my face, if you like, honey. I could show you a thing or two."

He did as she suggested with only passing reluctance, and that had been more about missing the goddess which had been penetrating his being in a particularly unfeminine way that he now found he missed. A hollowness that faded with time, just as any direct contact with the true gods and goddesses always did from human minds. Soon enough, Nirgal was exploring her strange, glowing and translucent body as any teenage boy would explore his first lover, rather than with the strictly directed thoughts and actions that had taken his virginity and given it to an impostor. He would never consider and never know just when he had begun to be influenced - as early as the breakfast-tray molestation, or as late as the first moment his eyes drew out her reproductive system from the other bits and bobs inside her glowing form, or some time in between

340

or even much earlier, during the battle at that last cathedral he might not have noticed an invader grappling into his mind - because he would not remember any influence; Nirgal would remember what his body had felt, what his ears had heard, what his eyes had seen - even down to the cellular level - but the goddess would not be in his memory. His "first time," the exhaustiveness of their creativity casting most of his adult sexual life in a vanilla-flavored shadow, which would begin feeling like a form of rape by the end of the day as various facts and lies were revealed to him, would settle eventually into being a warmly remembered experience, infused with rightness because it had been so right for him as it happened, regardless of what that Lida's intentions or motivations may have been. That and the strange offspring he'd spawned, really, but that would not re-enter Nirgal's thoughts for quite some long time.

They continued on, burning up far more calories than she'd presented him for breakfast, and nearly coming to the end of his strength before he sensed that their private timeline was soon to re-join the main one at the point it had been separated. They showered quickly; he cleaned his front and she cleaned his back and she had nothing to clean. They dressed almost as quickly; her uniform appeared instantly upon her non-existent body with a perfect fit, and after he'd pulled on his pants she laced up his boots while he got everything else in order. Finally, with a single phrase of runic syllabary he'd used more than any other, he dispelled the mud from the window and the door. Lida went over to the window and drew the curtains back to let in the day, still frozen for a moment in that strange distance between separated timelines, and spoke softly, "I'll go out another way, honey. We don't want to give them any ideas by walking out of a private room together, you see. I'm sure I'll see you around the center, though." He nodded to her in agreement, but couldn't shake the feeling that she would decide to go out the door after all. As soon as he saw the petrified bird outside the window return to its former course, Nirgal stepped out the door, not waiting to see if his intuition had been right.

He took his time strolling to the conference room which a mental note he'd woken up with had told him they would be meeting in, and was caught up by the Gollum on his way to the same meeting. They walked together the rest of the way with matching smiles on their faces but sharply contradicting feelings flowing just beneath the surface of each. Nirgal was beaming with pride and confidence, sexual conquest and sexual pleasure. The Gollum suspected he was literally walking toward his own execution chamber, and his mind and heart raced with conflicts and contradictions and memories of his nasty, brutish, and short life and to all the other vast memories he seemed to have perfect copies of from the lives of Trevor and Sunshine and Kay and Elle and the entire archival history of the twinned. Nirgal felt his life was just beginning to begin, and the Gollum felt his life was about to reach its end. Still, they both smiled as they approached the conference room, and they both smiled at the men and women and minds they met inside.

The four who had returned were seated around one end of a long wooden table, and Nirgal and the Gollum seemed to be the last to arrive, sitting in the only remaining empty seats, across the end of the table from Trevor and Jurrin. It was not exactly a meeting of The Board, but most of the members of The Board seemed to be present. There were also several heads of departments of the Wolyd Centre present, and a few people Nirgal didn't recognize at all but who carried themselves as though they were heads of state or otherwise in positions of real power. Nirgal didn't see anyone he recognized from the Second Wave, and wondered whether any of them had survived.

"Thank you for joining us, gentlemen," said a voice Nirgal didn't recognize which came from someone who was apparently seated on the same side but the opposite end of the table he was, and thus impossible to see. The conference room's doors closed. "We're all quite eager to hear what you're probably quite eager to tell, but I think we should begin by getting you up to date on the situation as it stands now." The lights went down and a sort of a slide projector was switched on, painting onto a screen hung on the wall almost directly over Nirgal's left shoulder, just beyond the

342

end of the table, an aerial view of the destroyed ruins of the cathedral where their climactic battle had taken place, in startling detail.

What remained standing in this image was identical in every way but the shade of the stone that composed them to the dark cathedral, now in Hell, which had so captivated Nirgal with its beauty. He'd known that the walls and roof of the light church had been coming down all around them, and had almost been crushed to death by the rubble, but it had all been from inside the structure, and in that mad rush of adrenaline that seems to blur and erode the memories. Seeing the scale of the destruction sent a chill down Nirgal's spine. Then the image shifted, gave a wider perspective, a context for the destruction, and Nirgal heard a gasp. He didn't think he was the one who gasped, but he couldn't really be sure and be shocked at the same time.

The wider view of the rubble placed it within spitting distance of the White House. Nirgal had been as ignorant as any of them about the worldly location of that final confrontation; they had appeared not in a location relative to a map or the globe of the Earth, but relative to a particular well-hidden person. Nirgal's mind raced, wondering how many people had seen the evil threefold flying up out of the crumbling church, whether Sophie's inhuman body had been discovered by the mundane, what other arcane secrets were uncovered in the wreckage they'd left behind, and what was now at stake. His racing mind recalled a few of the shouted words from the one who had allowed both his moles be uncovered for nothing, that the twins had had their best defenses outside and easily defeated, and Nirgal examined the image on the screen but did not see any evidence of a battle, let alone the obvious black scarring always left in the wake of a proper magical battle. Nirgal tried to figure out what this could mean; he had definitely seen daylight pouring in through the crumbling walls and roof of the cathedral, so at least that much had happened in broad daylight - if that image was of the same church, if that image could be trusted, then how could the twins have posted defenders outside their church without drawing the attention of the national guard? How could that lanky man

343

and Feagan have been through the battle they appeared to have gone through without leaving even the smallest trace to be recorded?

The image shifted again, pulled out from the rubble of the cathedral another step to reveal that the image was from the cover story of a newspaper article. "WHITE HOUSE PRAYS FORGIVENESS" stood across the page in tall black letters, and Nirgal began reading the snippets of the text of the article which were visible above the fold. It spoke of the construction of a new, more secure bunker for the Executive Staff to retreat to if they could not drive, fly, or run off the grounds to safety when the White House become a clear target of a future terrorist attack. It had been underway for months, the mostly-missing article explained, and they'd followed all appropriate safety and construction regulations when tunneling under the church according to someone whose name was on the other side of the fold. Someone was quoted as calling the collapse of the church a tragedy, and Nirgal didn't think one particularly needed a reliable source to declare such destruction a tragedy. Nirgal was trying to figure out the mid-sentence start of the next column of text when another voice began to speak.

"That photo and story hit newsstands across the country the morning after you went out, and that version of the story simply reprinted over and over again, word for word as trusted news. Tourists, press, and just about anyone not on the Executive staff has been kept at least a mile from the scene of the so-called accident, and planes haven't been allowed to fly over that area for years. There are blocks in place to prevent our directly appearing anywhere within the off-limits area, remote viewing comes up with nothing, and astral projectors are running into something they equate to a solar wind, keeping them out, too. This image may be real, it may be doctored or even entirely faked, but it's the only evidence we were able to find that you'd ever found a target to try to strike.

"Before you ask, the Second Wave have not been heard from since the day you all went out. Not a word or a thought or even evidence that they ever reached a single destination has been found. Our people went to the location

344

you disappeared to from here in the Wolyd Centre, but found only an empty lot - there was no church standing there, and public records show there never has been.

"Which brings us to the next unexplainable thing we need to tell you. The girl Kay, the one that Trev and Ms. Charming brought to the Wolyd Centre at the beginning of the chain of events that set this all in motion, she's gone. As gone and unfindable as Hannah, but disappeared from right here in the Wolyd Centre. The staff recalls that she was here, that she was under constant supervision, but there's no record she was ever here on the books and no one can pinpoint when the last time anyone saw her was. Not after your search party left, that is. There's no record of her or her sister Elle at your school, either, no enrollment records, no classwork, no passed notes in any students' possession to or from either girl, nothing.

"Ms. Charming showed us where their house had been, but it's just a vacant lot now. You and Ms. Charming both indicated that Elle died traumatically in that home, and dozens of nurses and doctors recall bringing her body back, but ... there's no trace of death on that lot at all. Even if there had been a house two weeks ago, since removed by some unknown force, there's an energy that death leaves behind, and there's no indication that anyone has died within half a mile of there in the last hundred years. Or at the location you originally disappeared to, in case you were wondering. No trace of death at all."

"That can't be!" Nirgal couldn't hold himself back. "I killed dozens of them myself! Jurrin... Jurrin stood over a heap of corpses as tall as any of us! The blood... There must be a trace! You must be looking in the wrong place!"

"Calm down, boy. You aren't in any trouble, we're just trying to get you up to date with the facts as we see them."

"Well it doesn't sound like you see very much." The Gollum's voice was more somber than rude, though he didn't turn to face the origin of the voice in the still-dark room. Another voice piped up, as though it had been waiting for the Gollum to speak.

"But we do see you, creature, and we do not see Sqrat, who left with your group. It is my opinion that the matter of this change in personnel be the first that you address. The disappearance of a trusted member of The Board occurring simultaneously with the first known appearance of a true gollum in the lifetime of anyone present--"

"Ah-hem," a projected thought interrupted from somewhere near the ceiling.

"Yes, yes, within the lifetime of any of the living who are present, but that's beside the point, Norfin, because you never actually witnessed a gollum. You may have been around when men were still able to create them, but that is certainly not relevant now. What is most relevant is that Trev, who we all agree is at least rumored to possess powers great enough to perform such a conjuration, could not have conjured this gollum. What we most want to know is this:"

The speaker paused, as though to add gravity to the seriousness of their question. "Whose life is that creature living? Was Sqrat sacrificed in some sick tribute to Trev's unassailable pride? Did you give up a real man's life in whatever secret cabal you've attended these past weeks and months? And for what! To create this mud-born abomination in worship of some prophesied god-child?"

"That's quite enough," a feminine voice interrupted, somehow without defending the four of them in the slightest. "Give them a chance to answer."

"It was me," replied Nirgal, but softly, as though ashamed of his accomplishment.

"Impossible!"

"How could you kill Sqrat? You're a monster! You're worse than Trev!"

"I didn't kill Sqrat! You've got it--" Nirgal was interrupted almost before he began.

"Then he can still be saved! You've just got to disenchant or rename or whatever you do to reverse this monstrosity's existence, and tell us where you're hiding Sqrat's body! Do it! Do it now! What are you waiting for?"

"I..." Nirgal stammered. "You... Uhhh..."

"It's alright, Nirgal, I was expecting this." The Gollum was looking directly at Nirgal, all trace of a smile erased from his countenance. "I know they haven't got the details quite right, but it's obvious that my existence frightens them."

"That's no reason to kill you."

"But as long as I live, it kills you." Somehow the angry, urgent voices of the conference room did not interrupt them as they spoke.

"Not literally. Just potentially. What's the harm in letting you go on for another few hours, or a few days?"

"What if you're supposed to accomplish something important in the final hours or days of your life, but you come up short because you let me enjoy a dodgeball game or a walk barefoot through soft grass? We don't even know how long I've already been alive."

"Of course we do! It can't have been more than a day since I conjured you."

"Nirgal, didn't you hear what they said? You left here months ago. Not yesterday. Months ago. Nothing we thought happened appears to have happened. No churches, no battles, no mountains of bodies, no death. Maybe no Hell. Maybe everything we experienced was some sort of trick that began and ended with that phrase the missing girl we thought was Kay gave us. Maybe it's something worse."

What had been built of Nirgal's pride was being torn down, not brick by brick but as though by a wrecking ball. Nothing he'd accomplished was real, and even the gollum he'd thought was a major achievement was evidently a major problem for the more experienced people here. "Maybe. I mean... I..." Nirgal searched for the right words, some response that truly reflected how he felt. "I don't know what I mean. It doesn't make sense."

"Look at it this way, Nirgal; I was never really meant to be alive. I'm like a puppet. I know I don't feel like a puppet, but ..." The Gollum breathed a deep breath that may even have been a long sigh. "...but I know what I am. I'm mud. Earth and water, animated by your life, Nirgal. Every breath I take is one you won't. I only seem real and independent because I've been given Trev's name, a copy of his mind. Without you two propping me up, I'd only be a mess to try to get out of the carpet."

"But what about everything that's happened? What about your memories of what we went through? How are we going to be able to work out what really happened without you?"

Neither one of them seemed to notice the continued silence from the rest of the room, or even from Jurrin and the real Trevor. Likewise, the fact that their silence was in opposition to the evidence being presented them regarding the involvement of Sqrat as a sacrifice went unnoticed. Once the idea was presented, the Gollum's standing expectation of imminent dissolution did the work of creating a reality, and the shadowclad figures around the table didn't need to say a word.

"That's easy enough. Not really even a question, is it? I'll just remember everything into your mind. Trevor's mind, too, if only to give him a frustratingly doubled memory of the whole thing."

"He's absorbed other people's whole lives. I'm pretty sure he absorbed the combined memories of the entire doubled church. Why would a day's worth of your memories be frustrating?"

"Well, I know what his memories are like, and I know what other people's memories feel like in his head... It isn't the same. As memories are made, they're filtered through the understanding and background of the person creating them. They're even in the context of that person's variant sensory systems, so that the memories of someone with color blindness would never be confused with the memories of someone with so-called-normal vision. A woman's memories are more different than that from a man's. You must have some idea of this; you've experienced a little mentalism yourself."

"I still don't understand why your memories would be any more problematic than what Trev's already absorbed."

"Because the context is identical. Our bodies are identical in every meaningful way, our basis of experience, our memories and experiences and prejudices and senses are all the same. I experienced everything exactly the same as he would have if he were me, with none of the slight differences that help you feel one memory is yours and another is not. I'll admit that the distinction wasn't obvious to me a year ago, but with experience comes clarity and understanding and when I touched Kay and Elle's minds, I couldn't help but see the differences - and they had shared everything their entire lives."

"You never did any of that. You didn't exist a year ago."

"Which is part of my point. I know on the most shallow level that I have only existed briefly, but unless I'm thinking about it, I'm Trev, and I always have been." The Gollum searched Nirgal's face for understanding. "Which is why my memories are going to screw with him. He won't be able to tell them from his own. Not easily. It should be like he was in two places at once. I'm very curious about what it will be like, so I'm sure that he is, too."

Trevor nodded silently. Nirgal and the Gollum were looking only at each other. Nirgal seemed still to be looking for some way to avoid doing what he felt would be murder, going along with the conversation to kill time while he tried to think. The Gollum seemed to be trying to lighten the mood of the situation with trivialities. The rest of the room seemed almost not to be breathing.

"So," the Gollum continued, "I'll remember everything to you two, and then you can ... disspell me. It'll be easier if you come into my mind, unless you don't think you'll be able."

"No, no," Nirgal was shaking his head in protest, saying no to the implication of help as well as the idea of what they were about to do, "I can do it. I think I'm still linked to Trev, so I'll bring us all together." Nirgal closed his eyes, unaware that his head was still softly shaking back and forth in silent protest, and reached out to the Gollum's mind, connecting to it easily. The running narrative of thought was very conscious of his presence, encouraging Nirgal with positive, uplifting messages.

Then he felt in his own mind for the braided tether of links that Trevor had made before they'd first set out.

One thread was broken, the one that had triggered the Blinding Light, but there were still a bundle of links intact. Nirgal didn't know what most of them were for, and as he reached out along the tether, he didn't think about their purposes. He barely thought about the fact that the tether didn't appear to be reaching toward Trevor, sitting across from him, before his mind was overwhelmed with a powerful image of impossible fire.

Impossible fire with a pair of dark eyes floating within.

A voice boomed into Nirgal's consciousness, "You've gone too far, you impudent little brat."

"I didn't do anything yet!" Nirgal tried projecting his thought out to the eyes and voice accusing him, but they continued as though they weren't even aware of him, speaking over him, and he heard "...but you've stepped out of bounds now, you've crossed the line into unfamiliar territory."

The voice went on, and Nirgal didn't try to respond. What had seemed to be accusations directed at him were quickly revealed to be something else. Nirgal didn't know what else. The Gollum, still connected to Nirgal's mind, just observed silently; it was more aware of what it was seeing, but still didn't know the whole truth. Neither one would have believed the truth after what they'd been experiencing since the doors to Hell first opened, but that didn't stop them from getting a first-hand view of Satan's breakdown. Even when Trevor's vision turned from the fire to the mysterious dark figure weeping in the towering chair and flickering light across from him, Nirgal and the Gollum didn't realize what they were seeing, but the Gollum knew enough to realize what this vision meant.

Without relinquishing his link to Nirgal, and thus to the real Trevor, the Gollum spoke aloud to those gathered in the conference room. "This is all a lie. None of you, none of this is real. And you're not Trev." The Gollum turned its head to face the Trevor across the table from him, and as their eyes met, without warning, without a sound or a gesture, the Gollum created absolute destruction in that being, then a former being. There was no flash of light, no

350

bang, not even the normal popping sucking noise that would occur if a being had ceased to be and the air had rushed in to fill the space it had taken up. There was nothing - one moment there was what appeared to be Trevor, the next there was nothing.

And the link, Trevor to Nirgal to the Gollum, was not broken.

"Where is he, Nirgal? I can't quite get a fix on his location to disappear us to."

The dark figures around the table were becoming less clearly defined, oozing somehow into the shadows filling the room, and they were rising and moving toward the end of the table. As they approached Nirgal and the Gollum menacingly, they seemed to leave trails of darkness so thick and clinging that it appeared that they hadn't so much stood from their seats as stretched themselves up and across the room like hundreds of pounds of horribly putrefied and possessed silly putty. The dark, oozing masses approached, but hesitated inches away from the two of them as though waiting for instructions.

"I don't know. It feels like he's right next to us and far away at the same time." Nirgal was exasperated, freaked out by the imminent danger that had erupted out of the reversal of a reversal of his possibly-imagined fortunes, and was nearly screaming, "I have no idea where to go."

"Wait, that's it, they told us! I told us! Are you ready?"

"Ready for what?"

The dark figures were coalescing around them, absorbing the room, melting into the table, melting into each other, coming up even from underneath them to within only a few inches. Nirgal was cowering and shaking, ready to go along with whatever the Gollum said, hoping it would get them out of harm's way.

"Just hang on."

As if that were their cue, or as though they'd finally received the signal they'd been waiting for, the encroaching dark forces swept in towards the space the two figures suddenly weren't occupying. There was a moaning, squelching, screaming outburst as they collapsed upon each other in failure, but Nirgal and the Gollum never heard it.

Almost as soon as Trevor's two companions appeared in the room, it changed. The fireplace vanished. The chairs, the floor, the walls, all disappeared. The devil was suddenly composed and together and confident. The four of them were all but instantly within a gymnasium not unlike the one that Trevor and Nirgal had played hundreds of dodgeball games in over the course of the school year. The stands were empty, it was just the four of them at that moment, and the five of them in the next, as Jurrin appeared, sitting in the corner still armor-clad. He stood quickly and approached them at the center of the court.

"Separating you obviously did not work out as I'd planned."

"Why did you want Nirgal to destroy me?" The Gollum addressed the question to the dark figure it knew both the power and weakness of, not with an accusing tone but with earnest interest. It knew that whatever answer it received would probably not be strictly true, but it was still hoping for something that could at least be believed.

"That wasn't the point at all. We couldn't care less about you; you don't even have a soul of your own. We were just working to put Nirgal through a few extremes. A rollercoaster of experiences and emotions to build momentum as a foundation for future grief, you understand." The devil's tone was nothing but detached professionalism. Nirgal's eyes dilated wide with emotion, but he tried to stay calm and digest the information he was receiving. He had nearly realized that he was still in Hell, but he was having trouble letting go of the experience of their escape and the meaning of everything that happened after that. "Playing off his pride and envy, gluttony and lust, and then twisting them into guilt, self-doubt, deception, and even self-sacrifice. We thought Jurrin would be right at home with an environment of wrath, violence, and vengeance, and if not for that accursed armor he managed to wear right into Hell he'd be unrecognizable by now, deformed and twisted inside and out by his own violent nature. Nirgal required a more delicate treatment, and you, gollum, were just a tool we tried to use against him."

"I almost believe you. So why are you telling so much truth?"

"I've made an arrangement with Trev, and it's in all our interests that you trust me."

"I haven't agreed to anything yet." Trevor remained dispassionate, clinging to the image of Old Scratch crying into his own hands and the memory that he had been certain that Trevor had known something he really did not. He remembered that this creature of power was fallible.

"Which is why I'd like your friends to trust me. To help me convince you that you should duel me. Not that it will take much convincing once they know the stakes."

Trevor could practically feel Jurrin agreeing already. The Gollum spoke again, "We aren't going to fall for your tricks. You've already seen that."

"Yes, yes, I allowed myself to become too involved in negotiations with Trev. I ought to have been more involved with your deception. I would never have missed such an obvious problem as a pre-existing link between Nirgal and the real Trevor when trying to pass some damned soul off as the same. I apologize with the shoddy production values of your experience. A VIP such as yourself ought to have received more careful handling for at least the first perceived year." A slight trace of a smile crossed the snake's eyes - but not his lips - as he spoke the next sentence. "Of course, depending upon the outcome of the duel, and definitely if there is no duel, we will get a second chance to ... handle you appropriately."

"Trev, what's he talking about? What's this duel?" Nirgal was still off balance from the encounter in the conference room, not minutes removed from this new challenge.

"Some manipulation of Satan's. I haven't--"

The Gollum interrupted him, scorning Nirgal, "How do you know this isn't another trap? Are you sure that's even Trev? What did he tell you?"

"He... He..." Nirgal stood abashed, stammering. "he told me..." Nirgal turned back to the one he had been so certain was really Trevor this time, and almost attacked him with his words. "Who are you? Tell me who you really are!"

"I'm Nirgal," said Trevor.

"What are you trying to do, Trev?" The dragon seemed flustered, "Tell him the truth," he turned to implore Nirgal, "I don't know why he's saying that. I'm not deceiving you about this. That's really Trev!"

Nirgal heard the accuser's voice as incomprehensible buzzing. He could feel anger growing within him, heat rising from his core, flushing his face. "Tell the truth. Tell me who you are!" He sent a mental blast at the figure standing before him, a hurried form of the sort of mental algorithm used to get automatic, honest mental votes, this one with the same query he shouted out again, "Who are you?"

The mental response was concurrent with the spoken response, "I'm Nirgal," and "myself," and Nirgal didn't know which was which at first.

The deceiver cleared it up for him, "Is this some sort of game, Trev? He knows you aren't him. If you screw this up, both of them will be stuck here forever. Could you stand to return to Earth knowing you'd doomed your best friend to eternal torture?"

Satan's words barely registered with Nirgal; just enough that he knew that Trevor had repeated himself verbally and given a different honest answer. "But you can't be Nirgal, because I'm--" Nirgal stopped himself mid-sentence. He spoke normally now. "You couldn't possibly be Nirgal. Alright, then. I know who you are."

"What have you done now, Trev? Am I going to have to erase his memories and put him through some real agony because you wouldn't answer a simple question honestly?"

"That won't be necessary, Satan." Trevor knew that whether it was because of this fragile emotional state the devil seemed to be in, because he really was that much more ignorant than he pretended, or whether this was all just part

354

of a larger, stranger deception, Trevor could take at least some control of the situation by manipulating the fallibility Old Scratch continued to display. "Nirgal's just a little upset about what you were doing to him. He's only human. You'll have to give him some time to recover."

"Of course, fine," pride shook his head resignedly, "does anyone else have an outburst?" He paused, "No? Alright. The terms of the duel."

He had their attention. "Trev, alone among you, can escape Hell under his own power. He can leave at any time. He could have escaped already, and he knows it, and he knows how."

"How?" Trevor only shook his head at Nirgal's question, his eyes saying "not now."

The snake continued, "You two, well, you three I suppose... You can not. Even though you did not arrive in Hell by the normal means and are still alive, and despite the coincidence that you cannot really be killed while in Hell, right now there is only one being that could release you from Hell. Right now, that is me." He paused to allow this to sink in. "Now, I have offered to duel Trev. The details are unimportant at this stage, but the wager is this: If he wins the duel, he will be granted the power to release you from Hell along with anyone else trapped here that he chooses. If he loses the duel, he will himself be trapped in Hell for an unspecified period of service. I guarantee that I will give Trev more than a fair chance to win the duel, and as you may have surmised from our surroundings I am even willing to make the medium of our challenge an area of his unique expertise."

"Dodgeball." This was the first word out of Jurrin's mouth. It was more an incredulous statement than a question.

"If he prefers. It is up to Trev. He could choose swords or pistols or chess or Texas Hold 'Em or global thermonuclear war or competitive synchronized swimming or any other thing that occurred to him and I would agree. Dodgeball seemed quite the natural choice, though."

"You need a team for dodgeball. One on one matches are basically sudden death."

"Teams could be formed. Four on four if you like, or we could supply you with the best players from among the damned to flesh out your team." Now the accuser's lips smiled without his eyes joining. "Figuratively speaking, of course."

"Pretending for a moment that I would agree to this proposed duel, what are the details you keep refusing to go into?"

"I haven't been refusing them, merely avoiding unnecessary complications before you agree. For example, there is the matter of the contract I mentioned." The devil reached into his jacket pocket and retrieved what appeared at first to be a simple folded legal document, blue pages and white, not more than a few sheets thick. The Prince of Darkness drew the document out and towards Trevor, and the farther it was from his pocket the more it changed character. A simple folded brief, then an unfolded binder-clipped document of perhaps a hundred pages, then a spiral-bound legal-sized document of perhaps three hundred pages, and as its weight descended into Trevor's outstretched hands it seemed to be a stack of five or six hundred pages drill-punched at the top and held together by capped metal rods that extended in upside-down 'U' shapes above the tops of the pages. Without flipping to the end to see the page number, Trevor knew immediately how thick this contract was, definitely more than six hundred pages of tiny, cramped text in incomprehensible legalese.

"Obviously," the seven-headed dragon continued, "trying to discuss every clause and coverage of the contract would only serve to cloud what ought to be a very simple decision. I won't stop you from taking as much time as you'd like to examine the contract - it's mostly boilerplate from every contract used in these parts - and I'll even go ahead and point out a few key areas that I'm sure you'll find troubling or questionable," hundreds of tiny colored 'flags' appeared along the edges of the contract, pointing out various sections throughout the document that might be of particular interest. "The solid red flags relate to mentions of your soul, the rest are color coded by this legend." Satan handed Trevor a two-sided document with three columns of

356

descriptions on each side, and perhaps two hundred different flags were detailed there for him. "But no matter how much time you waste on examining that contract, remember the simple nature of the wager: If you choose not to duel, you can leave Hell at any time, but your companions are damned forever. If you duel and win, you will be able to free your companions. They have no other way out."

"And if I duel and lose then even I lose my chance to leave. And if you're lying about the entire matter, anything could happen."

"Sure, but what have you really got to lose?"

"What have you got to gain? As far as I can tell, the only outcome by which you profit is in my signing this contract and then, if the duel has any bearing on reality at all, if I lose the duel. Every other outcome represents something you already have or a situation where you lose what you have. So I must be pretty valuable to you."

"Or at least more valuable to him than these two are now," corrected the Gollum. "Think about it, Trev. He'll probably never get another chance to trap you here, never have the leverage he has now, but there's certainly a good chance that these two, if returned to life, would end up in Hell at the end anyway. We've all committed murder, and by some accounts that's more than enough to put them here. Every outcome is in his favor."

"Every outcome is in his favor," Trev repeated. He closed his eyes in thought. His brow lowered, creased. "But if he's telling the truth, if I agree to duel him and I win," Trev opened his eyes again, still looking at the Gollum, "they get to live their lives a while longer. If I do nothing, or if I lose, their lives may as well already be over. They're here because of me. I have to agree, and it all has to be true, and I absolutely have to win. There's no other option."

The Gollum nodded gravely.

With a flutter, the flags sticking out the sides of the contract changed, most of them simply vanishing entirely, and the legend in Trevor's hand was blank on both sides except for a single flag, a single description: Black flags with the corners cut off in a point like an arrow referred to places that required an initial or signature. As though it had been there the entire time, Trevor sat down at the desk placed incongruously on the dodgeball court when none of them had been paying attention. It was like a school desk, a chair and writing surface integrated, and Trevor set the huge contract down in front of him.

The devil stepped over to him with a unique device in his hand. Trevor watched as the accuser pulled up two sections of the ornate metal shell of the slender cylinder like wings lifting out from one end of the device, and driven my this action, at the other end of the tapered shaft, a sort of needle seemed to extend out. He quickly understood, even before the snake spoke, "By your leave," and Trevor turned out his left arm, palm up on the table, hitching up his long sleeves with his other arm to expose the inside of his elbow. The Prince of Lies lowered the device that didn't precisely look like a syringe down to Trevor's arm and it seemed to affect some sort of pull on his veins; they pulsed fat to the surface of his skin, apparently eager to meet the metal.

Trevor didn't look away or flinch as the decorative silver tool pressed its tiny tube into his waiting vessel. He kept his eyes on the motion of the dragon's hands as he pulled up and away on the extended wings while holding the shaft down into Trevor's vein, and observed that the silver shell was perforated enough that he could see the line of brilliant red rise up through its core, making the abstract representations there seem somehow more sinister. At the end of the pull there was a thin line of red from top to bottom, and Old Scratch gently pulled the needle from Trevor's skin. A single, tiny drop of red bulbed at the point of entry, but no blood flowed somehow. Satan's distinguished hands pressed the wing-like extensions back down and the needle-like protrusion withdrew. He pressed the device back together in a piston-like motion and as he reached the end of the motion, with a click, the familiar tip of a fine-line ball-point pen appeared where the needle had been.

Despite what had just clearly happened, what they knew it really was, the device in the devil's hand looked as though it could be nothing more than an expensively adorned pen. Its purpose appeared singular and clear. Trevor took it when it was offered, and began working his way through the contract before him, signing and dating and initialing where indicated by the black, pointed flags. The others just stood silently observing, listening to the rasping whispers of the pages made so loud in the largeness of the gymnasium, considering the situation alone with their thoughts as events moved forward outside their control.

They didn't try to stop him, but neither Jurrin nor Nirgal would have taken the devil's side. They didn't want to stay in Hell forever, but they didn't trust the deceiver. They knew they'd do everything in their power to help if they were allowed to participate in the duel; the proposed dodgeball game. Even Jurrin had decided that the small possibility that Trevor's offspring had survived their strange aborted birth forced him to attempt to get back to Earth to find and destroy them, knowing that for now it meant helping Trevor escape from this everlasting trap. The Gollum still didn't believe it ought to be allowed to continue to exist much longer, but it knew that assisting the real Trevor to free his friends might be why it had lasted this long already, and with Trevor's full mind and memories to draw on, it knew that this was the only viable option. Finally Trevor reached the final page, the pen-like device in his hand nearly to the end of its reservoir of 'red ink,' and looked hard at the last two signature lines before signing and dating the top one of the pair.

He pulled up the wing-like sections at the end of the pen just as the devil had, exposing the long needle that had hidden within it. Old Scratch already had his arm bare and ready, extended in Trevor's direction, and Trevor did not hesitate. He pushed the tip of the needle into the engorged vessel it had drawn forth, burying it into his arm at just the right angle to stay in the vein, then Trevor pushed the plunger of the pen-syringe down, forcing the final drops of his own blood into Satan's blood flow. Trevor had not intended any harm or malice, he had simply done what he knew to be the right thing to do just as easily as he had understood that he really had no choice in accepting or rejecting the devil's manipulations; this is how things had to be.

Still, the accuser yelped and growled in pain, fighting the urge to pull his arm away, grimacing and bearing the searing fire that worked its way up and down and along his internal circulatory infrastructure in a way that seemed somehow more intense than the fires of Hell ever were. He was shaking as Trevor took the next step, drawing the plunger back to draw out Satan's blood, and he nearly wept again after the needle was removed. Trevor flipped down the wing-like extensions that had turned the pen into a plunger, pushed it back down and together, clicking the pen tip back into place. The blood-ink in the shaft was a red so dark it appeared nearly black, and almost seemed to be swirling. Trevor placed the pen in the deceiver's trembling grip and turned the contract to face him.

There was a moment of hesitation.

Satan seemed almost too eager for this to believe that it was all really happening, and he paused for what felt to all of them like well too long to be considered reasonable.

No one else moved, waiting to see what the dark figure might be waiting for.

Then in a flourish of nervous speed, the hand swooped down and signed and dated the document with symbols of a pattern that none present recognized. The blood-ink was almost indistinguishably similar to the black printed on the page, but as soon as the pen was lifted, both signatures there seemed to shoot up swirling lines of fire, their two-dimensional profiles extended straight up like curved walls of light, flickering and fluttering along their tops for what couldn't have been more than a second before returning to normalcy as simple signatures on paper. Satan returned the contract to his pocket, it's reduction to a document small enough to consider such a thing made much more rapidly this time. Scratch handed the pen back to Trevor without a word, and it disappeared into one of his coat pockets. Trevor stood up and - not like it had disappeared, but like it had never been there - the desk was gone.

"So."

"So. Dodgeball?"

"Full teams. Who do you have available?"

Satan handed Trevor a small sphere of light from nowhere, and it disappeared into Trevor's hand, transferring to his mind the roster and playing history of every damned soul in Hell who had ever set foot on a dodgeball court, professional and amateur alike. "Alright. I'll need a few minutes to speak with these three and to put together a team. You can select from the remaining players, or from your demons, or you can play alone. I will win, there is no doubt in my mind, and you will do what you have promised."

"I will do what I have promised. I am bound by the same contract you are. Take your time. Let me know when you are ready." Satan walked across the court away from them, and sat in the stands about halfway up at the far end, an unreadable expression on his face. Something like glee, but terrible, suspicious, and something else. Only the Gollum noticed it, and he didn't try to understand it, only to remember it.

"Jurrin, are you with us? Can you play?"

"I wasn't exactly MVP, but I was on the high school's team when I attended, and at NRL University. It's been a while, but I'd like to do my part to get us out of this." Jurrin was lying through his teeth and Trevor and the Gollum both knew it, but they also knew there was no way to stop him from playing, and that he sincerely wanted to get out of Hell, so would do his best.

"Alright. The other players available basically represent the best of the best teams that ever played, and two of them helped finalize the basic gameplay while they were alive. I'm going to form a team that will be able to work together though, rather than just the best individual players, so Satan will almost certainly have Karnikophe and Sturitsky."

"They're here?"

"And you're passing on them?"

"Yes. They aren't team players. They'll work against Satan no matter which side they're on at the time. You'll see. Teamwork will be the key to success here."

"So who are we getting?"

"Don't worry about it. Most of them are women, and you've never seen them play. I just hope they'll still be good enough after all the time they've been down here. I'd hate to end up with a team too ravaged by torture to play a good game." Trevor paused briefly, took a slow breath, and concluded, "It doesn't really matter what I say to you right now, we won't have the chance to practice, we won't have a chance to get to know how to work together, we won't know how our opponents usually play, and no matter what else happens, we absolutely must win this match."

After that, everything seemed to move in fast forward, everything too intense for the details to stick. Suddenly the players Trevor had decided on were on the court, and introductions were made all around but very few names were retained one to the other. A couple here, another three players there, had played together in life. Before reunion hugs were finished on their side, Satan's team appeared on the other side of the court like a dark storm cloud gathering suddenly above the horizon.

A few of them had been professional dodgeball players, but Trevor and Jurrin and a few of their new teammates recognized that most of them were dark, evil wizards and magicians whose lives had more than made them deserving of their place in Hell. It was instantly clear that there were at least three true threefolds on the opposing team, their combined energies practically crackling with negative ethical charge. Not a team of experienced dodgeball players, but a collection of the most powerful forces of evil ever sent to Hell and a couple of hot-headed dodgeball players to hold things together.

The first game of the match started before they knew it, and was over almost sooner. Not through some trick or time manipulation, but because it was just too fast-paced, too intense, too disorganized and dangerous to seem anything but brief. If Trevor, Nirgal, and Jurrin had been killable or if any of the other players on either team had not already been dead, the usually unused statistic of mortality per team would have been factored into the game's scoring. None of the players on the devil's side were holding back even an ounce of their destructive, desecrating dark magic, and by the end of the first game, Trevor's team had also thrown caution to the wind.

This was not a normal match. This was a battlefield. No one could die. Fatal injuries were quickly but painfully repaired. Non-fatal injuries crippled players and sprayed blood through the air until someone who knew how could spare a second to heal them. Clothes were torn and burned and punched through with tiny holes from high-speed projectiles, stained with blood, and some fell to pieces. The court itself was pockmarked with holes and scorch marks and broken boards and fallen limbs and strips of clothing not recovered in the rush to keep playing. Ankles were twisted catching in holes and slipping on puddles of blood and tripping over lost fingers and feet and a few fleshless bones. Anyone not recovering or helping someone recover from hits and slips and accidents hurled whatever they could as fast as they could at their opponents.

It practically rained lightning on both sides the entire game; each side possessed experienced forkers, casting and splitting and dividing bolts of energy that coalesced into balls before dropping at near the speed of light across the court. Players were switching sides so fast it became quite quickly reasonable that neither side had had much time to become acquainted with their own teammates. Everyone just tried to throw as many various balls at the other side as they could, no matter which side they had started on - the feeling that there was a lot more at stake here than just winning or losing a simple game was palpable and driving. Quite a few times players were swapped one side to the other fast enough to be struck by effects of their own creation.

When the final buzzer of the first game sounded, fewer than half the players had been benched and the score calculation was complicated enough that a manual accounting would have taken days. There was no clear Condorcet winner, but Trevor's team had won by a series of small margins. Almost faster then the court could reset - the floor was cleaned and restored to its original playable state, the players' uniforms and 'bodies' were made whole and healthy again, the air was cleared of smoke and stink and sweat, and everyone was returned to their starting teams - the buzzer sounded again, and the second game began.

If anything, the second game went faster than the first one, was more deadly, more damaging, more malicious. Somehow though, Trevor was able to begin to get a handle on the pace of the game. Where he hadn't had the time to really pay attention to what individual players on Satan's side had been doing in the first game, even when he was on their side, Trevor was now able to watch the devil himself play the game like any normal man might have. Creating balls and throwing them, ducking and dodging and blocking incoming balls, trying to recover gracefully from inevitable strikes that hit him, still giving his all when converted to Trevor's side, the snake didn't seem to be doing anything but his best within the normal bounds of the game - he wasn't even using the sort of life-threatening, body-destroying, not-strictly-balls of magic that the most evil of the players on his own team were using. Trevor was doing the same thing, trying to play a fair game with chaos all around him, and almost began to trust the deceiver before the second game's ending buzzer went off. This time, with margins even closer than in the first game, pride's team had pulled out a narrow victory.

As the court reset and his team was re-united, Trevor shouted out audibly - and with a tactile ferocity as his words pressed the air against their skin - "WE MUST NOT LOSE THIS GAME!" They all understood, they all agreed, they all knew that there was more at stake here than even the wager that Satan had spelled out, and even if they didn't know what the full ramifications of victory would be, they all knew that their continued existence in any form might depend on their performance in the next twenty minutes. The last echo of Trevor's growlingly intense outburst coincided with the starting buzzer of the third game - there really was no time to recover or even to think between the games - and suddenly both sides were in motion again. The 'particles' of magical balls so densely filled the air of the gymnasium that it virtually became an emulsion.

This time the action was nothing short of blurred with speed. No one playing could really see what was going on at all, everyone was moving faster than they ever had before, and they only hoped their thrusts and blocks and area effects would do some good since they couldn't see to aim or even see their success or failure in the hazy uncertainty of rapid motion. Trevor, Nirgal, and the Gollum were more blurred than most as they used their time-contraction techniques to step outside the normal flow of time, and still the game seemed nearly too fast for them. About half way through the final game, though it seemed to be no time at all to Trevor, Old Scratch began to project his voice directly into Trevor's mind.

"It's almost over."

Trevor dove into a roll to keep his face from being chewed off his head by a ball of what appeared to be thousands of gnashing teeth that hurtled through the air from the dragon's side of the court, narrowly missing a man-sized hole in the floor to his right as he recovered his footing.

"Soon, you will be trapped in Hell. Forced into servitude. Responsible for untold suffering and infinite pain as you do what Hell requires."

Moving slightly faster than the lighting balls that fell all around him only because of the alternate time flow he occupied, Trevor narrowly avoided a conversion only to be struck hard by a fireball so hot it might have really been composed of a plasma, and pinwheeled on one foot from the force of the blow. The negative impression of a sphere was missing from his arm and shoulder, vaporized by the furious thermal energy of the striking projectile. Trevor's left arm was temporarily useless, and he tried to respond to the devil in thought as he restored his body to wholeness. "I am going to win this game, this match, this ridiculous duel of yours, and I am going to free my companions from your grip. I will not be yours to control." Satan's voice continued in Trevor's mind as though he had not heard the response; as though what Trevor asserted was meaningless.

"It is not personal. If another like us had reached my realm in such a manipulable position, they would have stood in your place. I am not doing this to hurt you, but out of love. You will understand soon enough."

Trevor could see that the blurred form of the accuser was playing as though there were nothing unusual going on, this monologue taking up no apparent concentration.

Trevor's response had distracted him nearly enough to be torn in half by a trio of sharpened, oblong balls that spun independently and around a common center in a plane parallel to their general direction of motion across the court and perpendicular to the floor, a swirling saw blade that would take a player out of the game while they recovered and score at least three hits against them at once. Potentially a lot more, if each 'saw ball' struck more than once in its course through the player's body. He tried to focus on winning the game, he hoped his double, his enemy-turned-compatriot and his friend would be able to play hard enough to win their freedom, and Trevor couldn't help but be distracted by the voice that continued its soliloquy in his head.

"At least the meaning of all those prophecies will either become clear or be ruled out as the knowledge that you indefinitely serve in Hell spreads to the living. No more speculation about your place in the world once your place is established in the underworld. And you really will be able to free your living companions. That was true enough."

Every player's vision was cut off as someone's area effect pulled all the light from the room and even the lightning storm arcing back and forth overhead was dulled to indeterminate dark grey streaks on a marginally darker background. Most of the players could still operate without using their eyes by using extended senses, but things were certainly made more difficult for the duration of the effect. Now instead of trying to hit and to dodge objects and beings blurred by speed, all the players were more fully separated from the strength of sight and had to rely on their other abilities and ingrained skills. Trevor sent a syllable of thought to Nirgal that they'd worked out to mean that he needed total defense so he could concentrate, and without waiting to feel for Nirgal's response, Trevor set to work to locate and counter the area effect. As he did, the seven-headed dragon's voice continued to echo through his mind, calm and confident.

"From what I know of your background - a background I now realize you yourself do not know - you will probably find a more elegant solution to your

366

entrapment in Hell than I ever could have conceived. I would love to see you escape the grip of this contract within a human generation or two; it would be a real triumph of will, of your mind over the requirements of Hell. Try not to give up hope."

Trevor was beginning to feel that Señor Diablo's mental speech had the taste of a goodbye, but having managed to dispell the blinding darkness effect just in time to be struck by three simultaneous lightning balls that had missed Nirgal's attempts to defend him, Trevor was distracted by his conversion. He knew he couldn't play with any less skill on the opposing team or it would effect his scoring, but Trevor needed to be on his own side to win. He hoped for lighting to strike him again, and played his best as the clock ran down. There was a massive scoreboard on the wall, but unlike normal high school level games, the math to comprehend the numbers displayed on it was not something Trevor could do in his head while focused on a game with the eternal damnation of souls he had led into Hell at stake. He didn't know how close the game might be, but he knew it was down to the final seconds as he found himself converting back to his own side of the court.

"Thank you for this, Trevor. I'm not going to leave you unprepared for the task ahead of you. The next thing you feel hit you will be nearly every memory and thought I've had since I was assigned to Earth millennia ago. Then, by my calculation, you'll feel the misery of victory and the realization that it didn't matter who won or lost the duel; only that you played my game."

Trevor saw a ball of light no bigger than the cue ball in billiards and similar in pale color arcing towards him from where the devil stood stock still, untouched by the maelstrom of activity swirling around him. Trevor stood just as still, just as untouched by the remaining effects of the game, and watched the ball of light approach him with inescapable momentum.

"Our paths may cross again, someday."

The ball of light struck Trevor square between the eyes and absorbed into his consciousness.

"May it be on better terms."

The end-game buzzer sounded, the match was over, all balls in motion disappeared.

"Thank you and goodbye."

Old Scratch vanished.

✹ ✹ ✹

Trevor had indeed been granted the power to free his companions from Hell, as promised. He had also been trapped in Hell, forced into an indefinite period of servitude, as promised. Trevor had been told that one would be the outcome if he won and the other would be the result of a loss, but per the terms of the contract he had signed, the same thing would happen to Trevor whether he won the duel or lost it. He had been manipulated, he had known he was being manipulated, but he had not guessed at the scope of the trap.

Trevor had agreed in a binding contract to take over Hell entirely from Old Scratch, and to fulfill all the responsibilities and requirements expressed and implied in the former dark prince's long history at the helm of the pit of damnation. There was much more to it, there were endless details in the six hundred and sixty-six page contract they had both signed in blood, but the main point was that at the conclusion of their duel, ownership and control of Hell would transfer completely to Trevor. And as the final buzzer had filled the air of the gymnasium, and as the former ruler's memories of its long history, and the events leading up to it in Heaven and on Earth before, poured out into Trevor's mind, Old Scratch had disappeared, freed from his loving obligation to Hell by the entrapment of another to take his place.

With Satan's memories and thoughts Trevor also acquired Satan's love of God and felt first-hand the conflicted and emotionally taxing crush created by that love and its history. Trevor completely understood Satan's earlier breakdown within the first moment after he had taken over the role of Satan for himself. He also understood why there had been nothing for the dark one to lose in opening himself up before Trevor - Trevor would soon know all there was to know about him, no secrets between them.

If Trevor had not been fast on his toes, if he had been granted the knowledge of and responsibility over Hell but not the power to control it, if he was not already getting ridiculously used to dealing with one new challenge after another, with absorbing and adapting to one absorbed mind on top of another, if any number of things had gone wrong or caught him off guard, there might have been chaos in Hell that day. Instead, almost instantly after the former devil had disappeared, so did every damned soul that had been playing on either side, shifted through a higher-order dimension to the various planes of Hell where each soul belonged. Nirgal and the Gollum asked almost at once, "What happened?"

"We won. Sort of." Trevor was trying to figure out how to clarify what had happened.

"What do you mean? Where's Satan? Do we get to leave now?"

"I uhhh... Yeah, I can get you out of Hell now. No problem."

The Gollum, who knew Trevor better than any of them, said "What aren't you telling us?"

"I got more than I bargained for. The duel, the dodgeball game, all of it was just a misdirection, a distraction from what was really going on. Old Scratch has gone home, he's back where he belongs at God's side."

"So who's in charge down here if he's gone?"

Jurrin was two steps ahead of Nirgal, "Haven't you figured that out yet? Trev is. What did you think he needed that thick a contract for?" Jurrin wasn't sure whether he should be glad that he might be allowed to go back to Earth and hunt down Trevor's offspring while Trevor remained in Hell or whether he should be worried about the damage Trevor could do in his new position.

Trevor pulled the contract out of his own coat pocket as though it had always been there and handed it over to Nirgal. "I know everything it says now, and why, but take a look at it, see if you could have worked out even that most basic idea without a thousand years' experience in contract law. It doesn't matter, I knew the risks of signing a contract proffered by the devil, and that there wasn't another option that might have freed you from this place. So you return to Earth and I'll rule Hell with all the love Old Scratch once did. It'll be as though nothing has changed down here. I can even take on his appearance," and Trevor did, transforming into an exact replica of the former Prince of Darkness, "and the demons and the damned may never know a change has occurred."

"We can't let you do that, Trev." Nirgal was flipping through the contract as though to find some way to get Trevor out of it, "there's got to be another way."

"There isn't. And I don't want there to be. Satan gave me all his memories and experiences since being assigned to Earth and ... I know why he was here. God didn't exactly force him into damnation, it was more of a ... request. The accuser had the ability to disobey, just as a child has the ability to disobey a parent who has grounded them or assigned them an unpleasant chore as punishment for something. He didn't disobey, though. He loved God so much that he always wanted to do whatever God asked. He loved God unconditionally, self-sacrificingly, and until God suggested that as long as the work was done by someone qualified to carry it out, Old Scratch didn't need to be the one to do it, he never considered trying to leave Hell."

"Wait." Nirgal's brow furrowed. "This was all God's idea? Trapping you in Hell to be the new devil was part of God's plan?"

"In a way, yes."

"God is fucked up."

"In her own way, yes. There's something more to that, something the snake didn't share with me, memories from before he came to Earth... Something I need time to figure out. But I think it explains why God behaves the way she does."

"She? God is a woman?" The incredulity in Nirgal's voice would have been well tempered had he been able to remember his encounter with a true goddess not long before. That a god, or someone calling themselves God, might be feminine would seem the most natural thing to him if he could recall the sensation of embodying a feminine fertility goddess. The modification of his memories had been rapid and complete, and even having been raised in a form of matriarchy, Nirgal's ingrained thoughts on the nature of God were masculine.

"Of course. She is the creator, the mother of all existence, right?"

"I guess so, but..."

"Don't worry about that part, Nirgal. It's no more important than that I'm the Prince of Lies now. What's important is that you return to your lives. Considering the price I've paid, it's the least you can do."

"Are we in a hurry? Do we have to abandon you here so soon? How's time work down here?"

"No, no, no hurry if you don't want to hurry. Time doesn't actually exist in Hell. Not in any conventional or linear way. Things take as long as those perceiving them believe they need to take... sort of. With relation to the outside world, it's as though all the time in Hell, all of eternity, was just a single instant of time. Except that all the time in the world outside Hell intersects with that single instant of time at once. The intersection of Hell's time and the world's time is like a prism where everything gets mixed up together."

"Does that mean you could send us back to Earth in what we consider to be the past or the future?" The Gollum was trying to conceive of all the possibilities that this model of time might represent with little success.

"Yes and no. Part of the problem has to do with the idea that while time is generally linear and forward-moving in the world you came from, it is largely based on perception and belief here in Hell." Trevor drew naturally on Old Scratch's long experience with these complications as he tried to explain. "At the point of intersection, the two overlap. So all the souls that would eventually reach Hell could have arrived at the same instant, at the beginning of Hell's time, but on the translation from linear time, their belief that they arrived in Hell in a linear fashion has dictated that they do, in fact, arrive in a linear fashion. Likewise, the few souls that have left Hell for the outside world, because of their own belief in linear time, have always found

371

themselves re-entering the linear time stream at the instant they left it - no matter their intentions. If there were some sort of natural law that governed it, some conservation of information that kept knowledge of the future from reaching the past or some conservation of energy that kept energy holes from forming in the linear timeline, that would be one thing, and perhaps less frustrating, but there isn't. Your own unconscious mind will return you to Earth at the instant the door to Hell was opened."

"What about location? Will we be in the wreckage of that church, or underground somewhere?"

"That's one aspect you do have some control over, the same as you can appear and disappear through space normally, you can control where you appear in space upon returning to Earth. But because you can, I'd like to suggest that you take the 'scenic route'." Trevor made finger quote-marks in the air as he said 'scenic route'. "You'd be surprised how many routes into Hell stand open and unguarded. With my consent, and only because of the unusual way you entered Hell will it be possible, but there's a particular route I'd like you to take to get out. When you're ready to leave I'll take you most of the way there."

"What are we supposed to tell everyone? How can we explain this?"

"You won't have to, Nirgal. I'll share everything with my Gollum, and he'll share it with Ms. Charming. She's on The Board, and an excellent communicator, not to mention that she stands in my defense." Trevor was addressing Nirgal's concern, but his eyes were on Jurrin as he said this. "It should be made clear that I didn't wrest power over evil from the devil. That this isn't some stepping stone on the way to taking over the world or destroying life as they know it. I was tricked into giving up my own freedom to be able to free you."

"What about everything before, with Hannah and your daughters and the churches?" Nirgal, after all that had happened, was back to his insecure self. He was not looking forward to having to face the most powerful people in his civilization without Trevor by his side.

"I'm sure they'll want to hear your version of events, Nirgal, but most of it can be covered effectively by the same means. The Gollum will have two perspectives on all that has happened, plus the background that Satan transferred to me, and he can give Sunshine as much or as little as she needs. This really doesn't have to be difficult. As far as my daughters are concerned, the forces that prevented their birth are not malevolent. I am confident that they will be safe for the time being."

"All time being equal, I'd like to leave as soon as possible. I don't relish the thought of spending more time in Hell - or with you - than I am required to." Jurrin sounded irritated and on the verge of fury. "Unless you're going to hold me here against my will, I'd like to leave sooner rather than later, and I have no interest in the scenic route."

"Certainly, Jurrin, you may leave at any time. I will gladly remind you that you will not have a head start on Nirgal and the Gollum, no matter how long they stay here with me - you will all reach Earth in the same instant you left."

"I'm not a fool, Trev." Jurrin's voice was practically growling now, "I understood you the first time." He rolled his eyes. "The powers above may be fools, but not me. Appointing an inexperienced hothead of a teenager to rule the underworld. You can be sure I'll have my ethical charge balanced far to the positive before I finally let go; you'll not be in charge of my afterlife, Trev."

Trevor held back his emotional reaction. "Whatever you want, Jurrin. You can leave at any time. It'll be like a leapfrog disappearance. Imagine a circle with everything that ever exists at the center, a radius of infinity and a circumference of zero. Imagine you're standing on the edge of that circle and first try to disappear outside the circle, then as soon as you're gone, try to disappear directly to the center. You'll end up where and when you're supposed to be."

"What a load of nonsense."

"It's that or the scenic route."

"Fuck you." And Jurrin was gone. Whether he had managed to visualize the circle and escape Hell or had just thrown himself to some other level of Hell, Jurrin was no longer in the gymnasium with them.

"Okay. So. Gollum, would you like to read my mind now, or later?" Trevor seemed almost cheerful once Jurrin was gone.

"I'd like to do a full synchronization, actually. Share minds both ways, get us both up-to-date." The Gollum had a small, sly smile and shot a wink to Nirgal that he totally failed to catch.

"Sounds good to me. Direct mental, or balls?"

"If we create persistent balls, Nirgal can join." The Gollum seemed to have Nirgal's attention, but only in part, as though he were thinking hard about something in the back of his mind. "Nirgal, would you like to join us in a three-way mental synchronization? It'll be good practice for embedding your thoughts and memories in an external substrate."

"Uhhh... sure," and without another word, a small but growing pinhole of light formed a few inches from the skin of his nose, between his eyes.

"Alright then," said the Gollum, and a golf-ball-sized sphere of shimmering memories formed all at once before him.

Trevor didn't say anything as he constructed a cluster of spheres ranging in size from that of a marble to the size of a healthy ostrich egg, each glowing more or less in various hues of off-white. Around the time Nirgal's snowballing sphere reached the size of a large grape, Trevor's cluster of shifting light collapsed into itself to form a single sphere, swirling with all the different hues of its components like one of those novelty glass balls filled with colored water and fine aluminum powder that Trevor had seen at certain gift shops at the mall. Neither Trevor nor Nirgal's spheres changed much after that.

The three of them were standing in a sort of triangular circle, and all at once the three glowing balls of memory rotated counter-clockwise until they were positioned in front of new faces, where they stopped. Reaching out with their minds, the three of them connected with the floating stored memories before them, absorbing

374

everything they had to offer. When all three of them were done, the three spheres rotated around again, positioning themselves before the final mind in their journey, and the absorption was repeated. Finally, the three spheres began moving again in a clockwise direction, but faster and faster, not stopping after a third of a turn but picking up rotational velocity until they separated out of the circle of light they were forming and crashed into the heads they had been spawned by. This last effect was mostly for show, but Trevor had always had a good sense of showmanship, and liked to add flare to even the most basic of proceedings.

"You had sex with who?" Trevor had somehow missed this detail in Satan's memories, but couldn't avoid it in Nirgal's.

"I uhhh... I don't really know." Nirgal's face flushed red. "Not who I thought it was, anyway." He concentrated on the copy of the devil's memories that Trevor had shared with him to try to work out the cast of his experience, and his face fell from embarrassment to sad horror. "If I'm remembering your memory of Satan's memories right, it must have been a succubus."

"The damned soul of a succubus, actually. It's not uncommon for the long-dead to agree to play along with the torture of the more-recently-dead, apparently. It gives them a temporary reprieve from their own tortured afterlives, and only those well beyond the rebellious stage of their damnation are even considered." Trevor paused, considering the history and details of this and similar procedures that were common in Hell. "Old Scratch was pretty sophisticated, actually. The fact that he was distracted by his imminent departure is probably what allowed that damned succubus to get out of hand with her former nature within her assigned role. The details you remember, though... That's very strange. I'll have to check on her later on, see what she remembers herself."

"Probably just having the time of her afterlife," replied the Gollum, "she hasn't had sexual contact since she got to Hell, you know."

"Of course not. Is there a better way to torture the soul of a creature whose entire life revolved around her sexual conquests than to deprive her of the ability to have sex?"

"Sure. Force her to have sex endlessly with ugly, unskilled, unendowed partners without allowing her to feel, taste, smell or hear anything, and without giving her the ability to move or react, even through experience or instinct. Pair her with the damned souls of former casanovas, men whose sense of being comes from being attractive and being able to sexually pleasure women; force them into these hideous, useless, uncoordinated forms and make them have endless sex with an unfeeling, unmoving, unresponsive partner."

"Well, if you can think of it, I'm sure I would have thought of it eventually. We're the same person, after all."

Nirgal disagreed, "Not exactly. It's living my life, remember? It's only got your mind."

"Well, we're the same in every way but our actual source of life, then. Do you suppose it makes a difference?"

"It makes a difference to me," said Nirgal, almost defensively, "every breath he breathes... Wait... Is that true here?"

"What do you mean?" asked the Gollum.

"I mean, if all the time in Hell is really just an instant, does the fact that all the time the Gollum lives is being subtracted from the end of my life matter? No matter how much time he spends here, it will never be more than an instant, right?" Nirgal was smiling, feeling clever again for the first time since he'd walked into that lie of a conference room.

"That certainly seems to make sense. Based on everything the former deceiver shared with us about the nature of time in Hell." Trevor found himself thinking of himself as the deceiver more and more, and the one that came before him, the one who had trapped him in this role, as 'former'. "So you've probably only lost the amount of time that passed between his creation and the end of the battle at the churches, plus however much time it takes for you two to convey the relevant information to Sunshine."

"Not more than a few hours," said the Gollum, "What a relief. I've felt I was stealing your life from you this entire time, but as long as I stay here, my continued existence doesn't subtract from yours at all." The Gollum took a contented, relieved breath.

"You're missing something important," insisted Nirgal, excitement overtaking his features, "You're both the same person! Don't you see?"

"You just told us we weren't the same person, and you were right."

"But you are the same person. Gollum, what's your name?"

"You know my name is Trev's name. You carved it into me." The Gollum didn't know where Nirgal was headed, and wished he would get to the point.

"And whose blood flows through your veins?"

"Trev's, I suppose. At least, it was Trev's when I was created. Some of it must have been replaced by natural processes by now."

"Sure, but the organs replacing it are Trev's organs, too. When I gave you Trev's name you became a functional duplicate of Trev, inside and out, mentally, physically, and emotionally. Right?"

Trevor could see by the white of Nirgal's knuckles around the object in his hands that what he suspected about Nirgal's point was almost certainly correct, but he remained silent while the Gollum fought to grasp it.

"Right. I breathe your breaths into Trev's lungs, I think Trev's thoughts, fine. Would you just tell me what I'm missing?"

Nirgal thrust the huge contract he still held with one hand out to the hairless copy of Trevor, pulling the pages back to reveal the final page of the document with his other hand. "So whose signature is that?"

"Trev's. We both saw him sign it."

"But if you had signed it, if you'd used the blood from your veins and the signature of your hand, would the signature be any different?"

"No, but--"

Nirgal continued, "And would the contract be any less legally binding if you had been the one who had signed it?"

"No, but it would bind--"

Nirgal didn't wait for the Gollum to complete his sentence, "And if there's no difference in the binding nature of the contract regardless of which of you had signed it or whose blood was used, is there any way to say which one of you is actually bound by the contract? You know the full details and meaning of every page, Gollum, does it make any differentiation that would make this contract only bind a particular copy or version of the entity which signed it thereupon?"

"No, but--"

But Nirgal didn't need to cut the Gollum off this time. The Gollum had no argument. Nirgal was right. It was brilliant and depressing and life-saving, all at once.

"Only if it's what you really want," said Trevor solemnly. "You're me, but you're your own being, too. I know you've been eager to be dispelled, to save Nirgal's life, but as long as you're in Hell you aren't taking away from his life. If you return to Earth, you'll get your chance to sacrifice your very existence for his, but while you stay here, you can live forever."

The Gollum seemed to be considering the matter, and Trevor continued. "Weirder still, because of the nature of time in and out of Hell, if you take the responsibility for my contract now and I return to Earth and live my life, then when I die and return to Hell--"

The Gollum tried to disagree with that, "You're not going to end up in Hell, and we both know it."

"None of that. Think about who's in charge, not to mention the fact that when I die I'll already be in Hell because you'll be in Hell." Trevor had had a head start on thinking about this while Nirgal had still be explaining the basic concept to the Gollum. "So I'll go live my life, and when I die and come to Hell I can take over from you. Then you can return to Earth if you like, and if you do, you'll return to the same instant you left, right? You won't miss a thing. And if we can work out how to do it, I might be able to return to Hell at the instant I left it, upon my death, and you won't have to rule in Hell at all."

"That's not the problem, and you know it. With all of Satan's mind in mine I can't help but love God's requirement that this job be done. You know how it feels, too, or you wouldn't be so eager to return to Hell to see it through."

"I know, and I can't help it. Same as Satan, though, I know that as long as the job is getting done by someone I can trust to do it right, I feel alright leaving it." Trevor wondered how Nirgal felt, if he was torn by the same desire to watch over the proper management of Hell and a desire to live his own life. Not only that, but about what Nirgal would think about his first sexual experience now that he knew that it was false in more than a couple of ways. Trevor supposed that Nirgal was not much alone in at least that aspect of it - many people find that their first time was surrounded by lies - his own experience with Kay and Elle had certainly not been borne out of honesty.

"Alright, so let's say I agree to take over Hell for you, Trev, what happens next?"

"I guess Nirgal and I return to Earth. If we're right and you're able to take responsibility for a contract I signed, I'll be able to leave Hell. If we're wrong and I have to do it all myself then I'm as trapped here as any of the damned."

"At least the damned don't actually have to stay in Hell until the very end," added Nirgal in a helpful tone before he realized that his observation was not exactly uplifting. He continued anyway, more moderately, "you can pardon them, or they can be destroyed, like the ones who touched Jurrin's armor."

"And I don't really have to stay through to the end, either, Nirgal. Not any more than Satan did. The Gollum will take part of the responsibility, and perhaps another will come along someday to take my place."

"You're right, I didn't mean to..."

"I know, Nirgal." Trevor put his arm around Nirgal's shoulders reassuringly, "This isn't exactly the sort of situation we're used to dealing with. Despite the extraordinary events that have been surrounding us lately, we're really only high school students."

"Sure, but two thirds of us are also the ruler of Hell, we all worked together to destroy an entire religion in a single day, and I don't know how closely you were paying attention during the match, but look at those numbers," Nirgal said, indicating with a gesture the wall of scores and calculations regarding the dodgeball games that had put the fate of the damned in the hands of a teenager, "If the world knew you'd played a match like that, and against Satan himself, they'd forget all about the tied match from the co-ed game."

Trevor tried to comprehend the figures and charts glowing in red from floor to ceiling on the wall of the gymnasium. To the trained eye, these figures would tell the entire story of all three games with more detail than any one - or two - players could recount from their own memory. Calling on powers he could no longer remember the origin of - his own ability, something he'd learned in class, something Sunshine had learned, something from the double-church and its long history, or even some power of Hell or of Satan himself - Trevor reached into the empty air between himself and the scoreboard and plucked forth a photograph of the entire tableau. Every glowing number and graph on the wall was clear and crisp in the image, as was the still-damaged floor, streaked with blood and littered with limbs from the final game, the three of them standing there facing the scoreboard, Trevor's arm around Nirgal's shoulders, everything in stunning detail. Trevor handed the photograph to Nirgal, saying "You hold on to this, in case I don't make it out of here. See what they say."

"Well," Nirgal gulped audibly, "they probably won't actually forget about the tied game."

"I know, Nirgal. But we should still have a record of this game. Our memories, the contract, and this photo. The actual contract can't leave Hell any more than I can." Trevor grinned, "Which means that a perfect copy of it should be able to leave Hell without incident."

Nirgal was still holding on to the original contract, and Trevor took it from him, returning it to his coat pocket. He nodded to the Gollum and they both pulled the left side of their coats open at once to reveal the top of the contract sticking out of both coats.

"Would you believe we're wearing the same coat, Nirgal?" asked the Gollum.

"Literally the same coat," continued Trevor, "Not a duplicate, but a trick of time manipulation?"

"I'd believe pretty much anything you told me, Trev." Nirgal didn't even try to figure out what they were talking about, how they could both be wearing the same coat at the same time, or how that related to the two copies of the contract in the coat's pocket. "On the first day I met you, just before lunch you said you were 'not feeling well' when you were struck down by a major magical attack that ought to have killed you and might have killed quite a few other students if they'd been less careful. Before we entered the first church, before the first battle really began, you told me I just needed to get warmed up, and minutes later I was using spells more powerful than anything I'd ever even seen. After that easy massacre you told me I could do something that had not been accomplished in thousands of years, and in seconds this new life had been created," Nirgal gestured toward the Gollum, who nodded. "You told us we were going to Hell, you said we would all be fine, and here we are, safe and ready to go home. Not to mention that we kicked Satan out of Hell with a soon-to-be-legendary dodgeball game and found a way to fulfill his contract without preventing you from living a normal life. If you told me you were more powerful than God I probably wouldn't doubt it. Saying that you two are wearing the same coat at the same time, able to take the same object out of two versions of the same pocket at once, is like telling me you know how to snap your fingers."

"If I discover I'm more powerful than God herself I'll be sure I have something more interesting to tell you at the same time. Wouldn't want to lose your interest." Trevor squeezed Nirgal's shoulder, pulling him closer before releasing him. "But for now, what say we take that scenic route? I know it won't be as interesting or surprising as it would have been if you hadn't absorbed all the snake's memories, but it should still be an interesting experience."

"I can't wait."

"I'll follow you most of the way up," said the Gollum, "I'd like to stay together as long as possible. I'm going to be down here on my own for a while, I think."

"Not really on your own. Every damned soul that ever lived is available for your companionship," reminded Trevor, "Which includes quite a few interesting and worthwhile individuals who would be more than happy to chat with you if it meant a break from otherwise everlasting pain."

"You know some of the most interesting souls trapped here were suicides. They torture themselves, and consistently turn down or ignore offers for temporary reprieves."

"So snap them out of it. Engage them in intelligent discourse. Convince them that all the time they thought they'd been in Hell was just a coma-induced dream, and that their suicide-induced coma has been broken. What else are you doing?"

"You know what I'll be busy with. You're looking forward to it, too. And I know I won't really be on my own, but Nirgal's our only real friend, and he'll be with you in the land of the living."

"But remember that after I live my life and return to Hell in death you'll be returning to Earth at the moment you left, the same moment we're returning to now." Trevor didn't understand how his duplicate could think so differently from him about such simple concepts. "There's this time for you, but then you won't be missing a thing. You'll be by our side on the other side."

"Maybe." The Gollum tried ineffectively to hide that his opinion on the subject did not allow for his return to Earth, but the others let it slide. "You'll know before I do, of course. Anyway, let's get going."

At a thought, Gollum shifted their plane of Hell to one in which the gymnasium was not there. This was the most common form of transportation used by the ruler of Hell and the most powerful demons, and was how the various shifting environments they had each experienced had changed. Rather than creating a room or a gymnasium or

382

even an illusion of the same around them, rather than disappearing them through three-dimensional space to some location where such a place existed already, they simply shifted through the unbounded higher-order dimension of Hell to a plane where such a place not only existed but existed where they were already located. Having infinite planes allowed for such arrangements to be possible and reasonable. The plane that they now found themselves on was effectively an unadulterated one.

It was over eight hundred fahrenheit degrees. The air was thickly layered with the smell like rotten eggs of the burning brimstone all around. The 'sky' above seemed to have a yellow-orange glow, but was only marginally brighter than the glowing-hot stone of the ground beneath their feet and the flowing rivers of molten rock that divided the land. What land was solid was twisted and jagged and was almost as painful to look at as it promised to be to cross. There seemed to be no end of it, though the Gollum knew that his earlier discussion about the size of Hell had been more accurate than it probably ought to have been considering his verifiable knowledge at the time. Now this fiery place, this barren place, this pit of pain and anguish, this horrible eternity was his home and his kingdom. As they all looked up, straight up into the glowing yellow-orange distance above them, only the Gollum wondered whether his never leaving Hell might keep Nirgal alive forever, and what a terrible thing that might be. What he did not know about the history of the one he was and was not, what the Gollum would slowly work out from the contextual clues and otherwise meaningless information tucked within the cracks and corners of the devil's memories and what Trevor would find out all at once and all too soon, related directly to an understanding of that very thing.

As they lifted off the scorching surface of Hell, floating higher and higher into Hell's rapidly thinning atmosphere, the Gollum forgot that line of thought for a time, instead enjoying the sensation of timelessness that floating up and up and up in a cloudless sky with an indistinguishably shrinking landscape below created for them. None of them spoke as they rose, up and up and up, even as the glowing yellow-orange shifted to orange, then to orange-red, then to red and through darker and darker shades or red all around them.   They didn't speak when the temperature cooled below five hundred degrees or even below the two hundred and twelve degrees that had kept their sweat as steam almost continuously since the doors to Hell had opened to Trevor's knock. As the edge of the sky drew nearer and nearer on all sides, even when it was inevitably clear that they were moving up within a vast funnel or cone shape, the three young figures only communicated non-verbally. When the walls were within a few hundred feet of them and nearly black, the air almost cold around them, and the surface of Hell was invisibly far below them, a distant, fading glow rather than a solid surface they had been standing on, they considered how to say goodbye.

By then they could all easily make out the writhing shapes of demons and damned souls crowding over the walls around them like some horrible infestation of mutant insects and deformed monsters and they knew they would soon be able to make out the edges of the pit in the darkness above them. Their intention to leave by this direct route - the route that had always been available to Trevor but not to the others for reasons he could not yet understand - had held it looking out at the instant in time they had reached Hell together. If she sun had been shining, they would have noticed the true proximity of the door between worlds much sooner, but the stars in the sky above were indistinguishable at great distances from the glistening skins of the creatures clinging to the surface of the passage, and the three boys were nearly at the threshold before any of them spoke.

"I guess this is it," said Trevor ineffectually. As soon as the words left his tongue he wanted them back, but he couldn't think of something better to say.

"I guess so," echoed the Gollum, equally tongue-tied.

Nirgal didn't even attempt to speak. He took Trevor into his arms in a huge, hearty, floating hug between friends. After just the right amount of time, Nirgal released Trevor, turned to the Gollum, and drew him into another hug. The

384

second hug was somehow more sincere, more full, more meaningful and thankful than the first. Finally they separated and Trevor and the Gollum took Nirgal's wise cue and embraced each other in a warm physical word of goodbye.

Then as Trevor and Nirgal continued their upward journey without looking back, the Gollum began his way back down to the surface of Hell, his eyes not shifting away from his two departing companions.

Trevor and Nirgal emerged from the pit into the cool, fresh night air and looked around and around to recalibrate, to regain their bearings. Just as they had known from the dark prince's memories that they would, they had returned to Earth on their own high school campus. By the time it occurred to either of them to look down into the pit to see if they could see the Gollum, their view had been negated. Like the skin of a soap bubble re-closing after some small thing emerges from it, their ability to see back along the expanding cone-shaped opening that the pit represented the termination of was sealed off by their passing beyond its threshold, and only darkness could be seen there now.

They heard noise coming from the nearby gymnasium, and Trevor and Nirgal approached it curiously wondering who would be at school so late at night. Rhythmic sounds like a musical back beat penetrated the walls, and a low sort of white noise accompanied it. There was light shining around the edges of the doors, broken presumably by the moving shadows of passing feet. They approached cautiously, their bodies still somewhat tensed and battle-ready after all their recent excitement. Neither one of them thought to peek mentally through to the other side of the doors before reaching out to open them.

What greeted them on the other side of the doors would have caused them each days or weeks of anxiety if they had known it was coming and had the opportunity to thoroughly consider appropriate preparations for facing it.

Some of the entities they saw inside the school's transformed gymnasium had been working to put together this culminating event for months, some had been in rigorous physical training to be fit for the challenges they now faced, and others had spent hundreds or thousands of dollars outfitting themselves with the gear and attire they felt they required to see the night through. Trevor and Nirgal were caught totally by surprise, and they nearly fled the scene at once.

"Trev!" A voice shouted out from among the assembled masses, "We didn't think you were going to make it!"

Other voices joined in the notice of them as heads turned and bodies stopped moving.

"It's almost midnight."

"What's he wearing?"

"I heard he died."

"Who's that with him?"

"Where are the twins?"

"Do you think he'll dance with me?"

"He looks like he's already seen the End of the World!"

"Does it smell like eggs to you?"

The murmuring voices continued, and as the harmless nature of the gathering they had interrupted sunk in, Trevor realized that he ought to change his clothes before going any further into the gym. He thought for a moment, and without so much as a flickering instant to disappear and reappear in changed clothes and with cleaned skin and hair, Trevor was wearing a classic tuxedo as seen in the early 1900's. Its lines were all straight and long and seemed to make him look taller and thinner than he was. The jacket was single-breasted, with satin lapels and had long tails. The tie was a simple straight self-tied black linen bow. He also carried, rather than wore, a tall black top hat.

Upon seeing Trevor's sudden change, Nirgal realized that he ought also to redress himself. Nirgal actually disappeared and reappeared a moment later, returning in a more traditionally modern style of black-tie formal wear. With everyone's eyes on Trevor, no one seemed to notice

386

Nirgal and his change at all, and Nirgal knew he was really back home at last. He settled quickly into his comfortable role as Trevor's nye-invisible, nearly forgettable sidelong companion.

As the students asked overlapping unanswered questions, each one trying to speak over top of the others, chaperoning teachers tried to work their way through the dense encircling crowd to reach Trevor and make sense of the chaos. "Everyone get back! Give him room!"

Trevor was pleased to see that Feagan was not among those in charge here, but realized before long that due to the nature of time continuity, Feagan had only followed the lanky stranger out of the crumbling church a minute or two before Trevor had walked into the End of the World Ball, and that had been somewhere on Earth where the sun was still shining. As Mr. Tauer and Mrs. McCallum's faces emerged from the rabble, Trevor thought of Ms. Charming. He wanted to let her know what had happened, but when he reached out with his mind to contact her, she wasn't there. Trevor created a pea-sized, pearl-colored sphere of a message for Sunshine, then plucked a bluebird out of thin air and told it to "Take this message to Sunshine Charming III, bluebird. She's probably inside the Wolyd Centre." The bird plucked the floating pearl-like thought from the air and flew out the still-open doors behind them.

"What was that about, Trev?" asked Mr. Tauer, "Something to do with your uhh... Special project?"

Not knowing how much anyone here knew about what he was supposed to have been doing all day, Trevor only nodded confirmation as he changed the subject. "I can't answer everyone's questions at once. Actually, I can't answer most of these questions, right now. What does everyone think happened with Kay and Elle? They aren't going to be named Queen, I hope."

"How did you?!" Mrs. McCallum seemed to have expected Trevor's having been voted King of the End of the World to remain a secret, and she shot a scornful look at Nirgal. Nirgal was just surprised that anyone had noticed he was there at all, and forgot to feel guilty for revealing the truth.

"That's not important. I just want everyone to have a good time tonight, alright, and if you name one or both of them Queen it will become very awkward for everyone. From the sounds of things, people were expecting us to show up together." Trevor spoke frankly, knowing that between the general noise and confusion and the small word-scramble effect he'd surrounded the four of them in, no one in the crowd would know what he was saying. "Is there a runner-up? Don't tell me who it is, just nod... alright. Go with the runner-up, that's your new Queen. But midnight is half an hour away, so don't worry about it too much." Trevor had been taking in the decorations, modifications, and additions to the gymnasium that had been created for the ball, and his eyes seemed to have locked on a stage that had been built at mid-court under the scoreboard wall and the unattended instruments that told him that the badly-DJ'd music he was hearing was not the only entertainment there tonight. "Where's the band? On a break?"

"Yeah, yes," Mr. Tauer was good at directing a classroom discussion, but not the best at handling all the details of a hurrah of this size. Trevor could see a couple more adults giving up on standing watch at the corners of the room and approaching the tight swell of bodies that Mr. Tauer and Mrs. McCallum had been unable to break up. "They're on a smoke-break." He pointed straight up, as though they might be hovering just under the ceiling, "We made them take it outside, told them to stay at least fifty feet up."

"Second hand smoke kills, you know," concluded Mrs. McCallum.

"Sure, fine, but I need one of you to go get them back in here now." He mentally broke the word-scrambling effect. "I'll be over there," and as soon as his arm had extended out to point at the stage long enough to get the collective heads of the entire graduating class and their dates to turn in that direction, Trevor was standing on the stage with a microphone in one hand and the other pointing back at the audience.

The force of moving bodies was like hundreds of iron filings caught in a magnetic field that suddenly reversed

388

polarity along a line between where he had just been standing and where he was now standing. The crowd as a whole would have looked more like a strange amoeba from the band's height above them if not for the roof of the gymnasium blocking their view - a seemingly contiguous blob let go of one wall and slipped wholly over to the perpendicular wall, wrapping its innumerable 'feet' around the variegated edge of the stage that had been retrofitted out from the wall. Trevor stood quietly, microphone in hand, and waited for everyone to calm down and stop moving around so much and quiet down enough that he didn't really need to use the microphone at all.

"Good evening, everyone!" A cheer and applause broke out, and Trevor gestured downward with both hands, his palms outspread and parallel to the ground, trying to get them to quiet down again. They quieted, not as much as before, but enough for Trevor to be heard over their whispers. "I hope you're all having a good time tonight. I wanted to thank all of you personally for inviting me to join your little get-together tonight, but thanking you all at once seems like it might save a few hours for partying, so here goes: Thanks, everyone! You guys are the best!"

Trevor's own skill at 'working a crowd' would not have even got him on stage if he'd never met Ms. Charming in the first place - back before that strange day changed his life, Trevor hadn't much known how to talk to a single person with real charisma. With everything he'd learned and absorbed since then, not to mention the seemingly endless fascination he'd retained in the minds of many of his classmates throughout the school year, Trevor's public speaking ability was more than sufficient to distract this crowd from what he couldn't say.

"Now, I know you have a lot of questions for me, but I think that with finals finally over, we've all had enough of questions for a while. What we really need right now is to forget all about questions and answers and passing and failing and getting into the college of our choice. What I think you'll all agree we need right now is to let it all hang out and party like there's no tomorrow. This IS the end of the world, right?"

The crowd was hooked, they hooted and cheered approval and "Right" and "Yeah" and Trevor knew it wasn't what you said that got people's attention, it was how you said it that mattered. Like encouraging or discouraging a dog, the message was all in your tone, parsing, and pace. Trevor saw what he presumed was the band floating in through the doors ahead of Mr. Tauer and proceeding in his direction over the heads of the raucous crowd. He raced through his mind to try to decide what song would best carry their energy and keep their minds off the potentially depressing stories he would inevitably have to share with someone before too much more time passed.

Almost as though it had picked itself from his memory without his help, a song came to mind, up-beat and meaningless. As the musicians took their places around him, donning their instruments and readying to play, Trevor communicated the song he wanted to them. Two of them had never heard it, had never heard of They Might Be Giants at all, but Trevor had listened to his copy of Miscellaneous T until the CD literally wore out, and he had no trouble passing each of them a flawless memory of how the song was played. He tried to be quick, and Trevor had just barely managed to get the opening notes beat by the drummer and played by the keyboardist before the crowd's energy had a chance to lower from a roar to a disconnected rabble.

Everyone's ears perked up.

After a few bars, when Trevor's voice joined the building music with the bass and guitar, the audience cheered. "Don't, don't, don't let's start," Trevor sang out, "This is the worst part."

"Could believe for all the world that you're my precious little girl..." and the crowd was moving to the beat, and a few who knew the song just cheered out louder as Trevor continued to sing and the band continued to play. "...I've got a weak heart, and I don't get around how you get around..."

The beat was fast and the crowd was moving, spreading out, taking the room they needed to bounce to the beat. "...When you are alone you are the cat you are the phone, you are an animal..." Trevor was bobbing his head to

390

the beat himself, a smile on his face as he sang out surprisingly in tune with the musicians. "...mean nothing more than meow to an animal..." Even the students and dates and chaperones who had never heard a note of the song before found themselves enraptured by Trevor's happy-go-lucky rendition and the incongruous appearance of this teenager in a hundred-year-old formal fashion singing a bouncy pop song that seemed to be about nothing more than that smile on his face. "...but don't try to stop the tail that wags the hound."

With a little mental urging, Trevor had most of the audience singing along with the next lines:

"D, world destruction"

"O-ver an overture"

"N, do I need"

"Apostrophe T, need this torture?"

"Don't, don't, don't let's start..." and the song continued with everyone dancing or hopping and bopping about, some with partners and most alone, the last couple of weeks' strangeness with Trevor and his girlfriends pushed out of their minds by the relentlessly happy beat.

"No one in the world ever gets what they want and that is beautiful," Trevor sang knowingly, "Everybody dies frustrated and sad and that is beautiful." His eyes belied a deep understanding of the words that most of these ears would fail to process, "They want what they're not and I wish they would stop..." the band played their hearts out, fueled by Trevor's charismatic but odd performance almost as much as they were by the audience's energy and response. This local band, with two graduates from this year among them, had never experienced anything like it before, had never heard an audience sing along with one of their songs the way they sang along with Trevor.

"D, world destruction"

"O-ver an overture"

"N, do I need"

"Apostrophe T, need this torture?"

"Don't, don't, don't let's start..." the crowd, like most crowds and mobs, had a shorter memory and lower intelligence the larger and more connected it grew. Where the individual graduates had questions aplenty for Trevor, as the song played on and they became more connected by the beat and the energy building in the room, their collective thoughts became less complicated and challenging. Even the chaperones, losing focus and allowing their bodies to move to the beat of the music, forgot they were supposed to be supervising the teenagers they had begun to dance along with.

"I don't want to live in this world any more," Trevor was barely paying attention to himself anymore, trying to figure out why he'd picked this particular song, "I don't want to live in this world..." It was a particularly odd selection after having risked so much to do what he thought would allow him to return to living in this world. Trevor had an intuition that it related somehow to a detail or contextual inference he wasn't seeing clearly in the former devil's memories. He finished the song without a drop in energy, but he felt inside that he was no longer emotionally involved in his performance. Before the final notes of the song could wind down to nothing, Trevor made sure that the band transitioned smoothly into another high-energy, low-thought song, probing their minds gently to see what they could pull off on their own.

He found a song that they had been practicing and toying with the idea of playing but had almost - not not entirely for certain - decided would be too clichéd to play, and as the final beats of Don't Let's Start pounded out for eight seconds after his final word, he convinced/induced them to play it. The drummer was suddenly pounding out rapid-fire machine-gun blasts of beats and Trevor shouted into the microphone "Here's to the end!" just before the band's normal singer could begin singing.

"That's great it starts with an earth-quake, birds and snakes and aeroplanes..." and Trevor tossed his mic into the air and dove out off the stage onto the crowd, "...eye of a hurricane, listen to yourself churn, world serves its own needs..." and the crowd was more than able to surf Trevor's ridiculously formally dressed form over their heads and around above the crowd as they rocked to the beat of R.E.M.'s It's The End Of The World As We Know It (And I

Feel Fine). Even where the density of dancers diminished and a normal crowd-surfer would fall to his pain, the extra help that years of magical training had embedded in the hands and minds of the graduating seniors kept him sometimes literally afloat until he reached the edge of the assembled rockers and curved gently down onto his feet.

Looking back over the crowd he could see that several others had been lifted up to surf the waves of arms and energy that pulsed through the throbbing body of the mob, powered by the frenetic pace of a song that hadn't had much coherent meaning when it was recorded in the late eighties and meant even less to the non-mundane, especially in the modern world almost twenty years later. Still, a few of the words that came through clearly seemed in touch with the theme of the ball, and Trevor felt that he'd effectively deflected a potentially problematic situation. Trevor's throat was a little hoarse from shouting and singing, but at least he was no longer the center of attention.

Trevor made his way to the refreshment table and poured himself a glass of the bubbling, smoking red punch available there. If he had been to a party or dance with bubbling red punch as recently as nine months before that night, he would have thought the effect related to harmless dry ice in the bottom of the punch bowl. While he trusted that the 'fruit punch' would be safe enough for everyone when supplied at an official school function, Trevor was keenly aware that it probably had intended effects more interesting or severe than simple refreshment and enjoyment. After all he'd been through in the last couple of weeks, Trevor didn't even hesitate before lifting the opaque liquid to his lips and quaffing the meager six ounces afforded by the stylized glasses in a single open-throated motion. He refilled his glass, grabbed and filled a second and turned around just in time to hand the second glass to an attractive young woman Trevor did not recognize just as she stepped within his reach.

"You were great up there, Trev." The young woman smiled warmly and stood closer than strangers usually stand. Trevor wondered whether he ought to remember her from a common class or extra-curricular activity of some kind, but his mind had absorbed more new knowledge since he'd last left campus than even most non-corporeal Mentalism specialists absorbed in their lifetimes and he hoped that that was why he couldn't recall her nearly symmetrical, smooth-skinned face.

"Thanks, but it was nothing. I was just trying to get everyone back in the swing of things."

"You did more than that," her hand briefly touched the inside of Trevor's elbow as she continued, "the ball didn't have much swing in its step before you showed up."

Now Trevor felt sure that he either knew this young woman or she was very, very forward, and he didn't want to go on too long without revealing his possible lapse of memory. "You'll have to excuse me for this, but I've had a pretty hard week and I can't remember --" he paused to exaggerate running his eyes over her face and figure as though trying comically to remember her, "-- what was your name?"

The young woman giggled, her hand lifting automatically to the edge of her tiny mouth in an endearing gesture. "Oh, I'm sorry, I didn't mean to confuse you. We've never met." She extended her arm the short distance to put her right hand next to his and Trevor automatically lifted it halfway up to his lips as he leaned the other half over and raised his eyes to meet hers, pausing in expectation of her introduction. "My name is Kaerelene. Kaerelene B'vough. Pleased to meet you, Trev."

"I'm pleased to meet you too, Kaerelene," and Trevor closed his eyes and gently touched with only the lightest contact of his lips the soft skin of her hand. "Are you a student here? I don't remember seeing you around campus." He returned to standing as he released her hand to her, and they both sipped at their drinks.

"Well, I actually graduated mid-year, last semester was my last semester." Her smile now took on a character of coyness or false modesty. "And when we attended at the same time I spent most of mine in the library or the labs doing special research. I was on a sort of self-paced curriculum."

"What was the focus of your study?" Trevor had begun his query with genuine interest, but before the sentence had finished spilling from his lips and tongue, her clues had led him to find everything there was to know about her from Ms. Charming's memories. He tried to turn his faux pas to his advantage with a single syllable exhaled as appropriately as the Principal's namesake, "Charm?"

Kaerelene giggled demurely and, smiling, gracefully allowed herself to be led onto the dance floor, their emptied glasses vanishing back to the table clean and dry. "In a manner of speaking, yes." Her skill at being led around a dance floor was significantly stronger than Trevor's skill at leading her, but like so much else, it came back to him from a place he'd never been and saved him the embarrassment that a high school dance is supposed to generate in everyone who attends. "But I gather you already know quite a bit more about my studies than I'd admit to in public. The way you're talked about, I'm surprised my charms are working on you at all."

"Did it occur to you that I might not mind the charms and graces of a beautiful young woman such as yourself?"

"What about Kay?" The tone of Kaerelene's voice made it clear that her concerns were not genuine and that she knew that he would not expect them to be. "I heard about how your saved her life."

"She's not the person I thought she was," he played along verbally as their feet stepped in time with the music and their eyes stayed locked with each other across the narrowing space between them, "and she's not quite the person she thought herself to be, either. Though," Trevor's voice paused a full measure as their bodies kept a different kind of conversation going between them, "I suppose you probably heard about that part as well, Kaerelene." Their faces were less than inches apart as the music transitioned to a strange sort of techno-tango and their bodies' ministrations followed the change quite naturally.

"It's like the band read my mind."

"That was me," Trevor had intercepted her mental command to the musicians for this particular music without her knowing - he had put in a polite request for the same music only moments earlier - and with the multi-mind camouflage techniques he'd so recently absorbed, Trevor effortlessly made her believe her commands had been taken individually by each member of the band as though their minds had submitted easily to force. The intensity of the back and forth of their steps stepped up as Kaerelene discovered that she could no more command the minds of the students around her than penetrate Trevor's mental defenses.

"Now why would a man of your stature, power and magnetism react so defensively to a pretty young thing like that?" Kaerelene's voice was becoming breathy. A normal man wouldn't know whether she was trying intentionally to be seductive or was growing weary from the fast pace and deep intensity of their dancing. Without even having to read her mind, Trevor knew that she was merely trying to appear weak before her real aggression began, to keep him off guard. It was literally a textbook technique. "Have you been betrayed by some deceitful young woman you thought you could trust? Is that why you're so guarded?"

"And what is it you're really after, then, that you search so intently for a foothold into my mind and for unwitting allies on every side?" Trevor managed to avoid breaking out in a sweat from the exertion and intensity of the dance because he'd spent the day quite literally in the fires of Hell. Kaerelene's perspiration was not entirely the result of trying to keep up with him physically, but she did not allow the risks she felt looming to manifest on her face or falter her feet. "What do you want with me, Kaerelene?"

"Why, only to be with you, the same as every girl at school." Separation and intimate nearness, a flurry of perfect steps and a pregnant pause, forward, backward, they danced in harmony without either one resorting to mental cues to keep in step. "You're suddenly available. Of course I want to at least try to win you over while I've got this chance." Trevor believed her, but did not drop his guard. He really had been burned too badly to let someone in so easily, even though he wished on some level that he could. "Especially since we're about to be named King and Queen

396

of the ball," and as was correct for the dance at that exact moment anyway, they both turned their heads to face the same direction - the direction of Mrs. McCallum mounting the stairs of the stage with the crown and tiara floating close behind her - and then away and back again in time with the music.

"It's you? Is that how you knew..."

"About Kay and Elle?" The music came to an end, and as the dancers around them turned toward the stage, Trevor and Kaerelene's bodies remained pressed against each other, their breath hard and fast in what little space there was between their moist lips. "A lady never..."

Her whisper was drowned out by feedback and then a too-loud throat clearing noise from Mrs. McCallum as she began, "Ladies and gentlemen," and the crowd was quiet again in eager anticipation of the crowning of the King and Queen of the End of the World Ball.

"It's been a long journey for all of us," Mrs. McCallum began her speech, "and we could never have made it here without each other. All of you have made me, and the rest of your teachers --"

There was a terrible noise, a feeling like all the air in the gym compressed and relaxed and compressed again all around them, and the entire roof of the building exploded up and out into the night sky above and into smaller and smaller chunks before it began raining down again into the gym and all over campus like a sort of stone hail. As graduates and better, everyone there was more than well enough equipped to avoid injury, the stone and steel and wooden shrapnel landing, crushing and piercing into the hardwood floor instead of their shoulders and heads.

Every face was looking up but two, and Trevor didn't need to look up to know the three figures floating overhead. Kaerelene would have looked up if she had not been held frozen in Trevor's soft gaze, if she had been aware that the world had continued outside of his arms, his breath, the warm embrace of his enchanting eyes and that look in them of hope, of attraction, of the possibility of happiness in this world, with her. The three figures descended, and as two of them were recognized by the assembled crowd a gasp rose

397

to meet them. Trevor moved in and kissed Kaerelene, soft and perfect and open and unguarded, and she was present enough to kiss him in return, present enough to be lost in his kiss. As if under their own control, the crown and tiara that had been about to clatter to the ground behind Mrs. McCallum floated across the room, turned appropriately, and settled softly on the heads of the only two people who had not been distracted by something much more like the end of the world than the ball had been expected to see. As they touched down, an unseen clock rang out midnight and everyone in attendance - distracted from their distraction back to what they had been waiting to see - broke into applause and cheers as the King and Queen of the End of the World Ball kissed a long, slow, passionate kiss the like of which Trevor had experienced quite recently in time but what seemed quite long ago in his experience, and which once again changed the life of the woman whose lips his touched.

"Don't let me interrupt your little celebration," the lanky leading gentleman floating overhead belted out, apparently upset that he had not become the evening's main attraction with his unexpected and explosive entrance. "I can wait a few moments before I kill you."

Not one to be cowed by threats, Trevor did not immediately break off the kiss. His classmates couldn't make up their minds about whether to watch the kiss, the intruders, or their chaperones' reactions for clues as to how to react themselves. Then the kiss finally began to wind down, ending with gentle pecks, his lips not wanting to give hers up entirely, until Kaerelene herself disappeared entirely. Trevor looked up, directly into the eyes of the tall man who must have come almost directly from the church's implosion to the school, and as he did so, he noticed Ms. Charming appear in the corner of his vision, a bluebird fluttering away from her and dissolving into the night sky above.

"What are you thinking?" insisted Trevor, taking an impertinent tone to try to maintain some semblance of an upper hand. "You couldn't get to my daughters. You sent me to Hell and I took the place over and still had time to make it to a high school dance. And if you're thinking that

Heaven can hold me, I'm pretty sure I've got an inside man up there, too. Why don't you just give up now and go back to playing with scarantulas or whatever it is you do for fun?"

"You've been to Hell and back and you still have no idea what's going on, do you?" The long, slim figure was practically racked with diabolical laughter, shaking in the air above. "They must be getting better at doing total mind wipes, but from what I've seen I have a pretty good idea of why they exiled you."

"Does talking in riddles make you feel more powerful?"

"How much more clear can I get, Trev? You're a criminal. You were exiled to Earth to protect the rest of the universe from the obvious threat you represent. They wiped your mind clean and planted you among the humans in the hope that you wouldn't get out of hand." The floating figure gave Trevor a sideways look akin to incredulity, "the devil didn't explain any of this?"

Trevor's head rocked unconsciously back and forth, saying no for him though he held his tongue. This was what had been missing from Old Scratch's memories, what he'd been referring to when they'd first met, and Trevor wanted to know the whole story, but didn't want to have to turn to his enemy to learn it. Still, he didn't have much choice.

"It's true. You and I, God and the Devil, a pair of the twins who knew better than to be around when you arrived and thousands of others, we're all alike in our imprisonment on this backwards little planet. For one crime or another we've been found to be too disruptive to be allowed to remain in the universe at large and from the way you've been behaving since you first tapped into your true nature you're one of the most disruptive I've seen. I should have killed you the first morning after you impregnated that innocent human child."

"If you still think you can kill me, why are you bothering to tell me all this?" Trevor was searching the memories of the multitudes of minds and histories that were now crowding his head, searching for some corroborating evidence of what this dangerous character purported to be the true nature of his life, but there was so much, so much,

399

so very much memory to sift through and most of it untouched for decades in the minds it originated from.

"I am killing you by telling you, Trev. I'm waiting here to see how long it takes them to tear you from this fragile form, wipe your mind again and put you back someplace that will hopefully keep you out of my way. You aren't supposed to know any of what I'm telling you, but maybe you need to know a little more before they notice."

"If they, whoever 'they' are, are so quick to kill me and wipe my mind just for knowing that they already have, why haven't they come for you? You obviously know more than you've told me, and so did Señor Diablo. How have you escaped the repercussions you wait so eagerly to see carried out on me?"

"To begin with, I haven't taken over, destroyed, or thrown into upheaval three exile microcosms, as you've done in the last year. They know they can't keep our true natures from distorting the world around us, so they allow us to lead whatever bizarre lives we like as long as we keep to ourselves." He waved an arm broadly before him to indicate the sea of faces staring up at him. "This culture you've stumbled into was started generations ago by long-dead exiles, and their fingerprints are still all over it, right down to their obsession with measuring the so-called 'ethical implications' of their every action.

"The culture you stormed into and massacred was an outgrowth of the loving connection between two identical twins, only one of which was a criminal exiled to this world. They've drawn countless humans into their bizarre alternate views of the world, but they kept mostly to themselves, so there was no need to stop them.

"And Hell. That's one of the oldest, started before they really began policing our effect on the humans, and it shows. Heaven and Hell have worked their way into the consciousness of nearly every culture in the world, and if they hadn't been so singularly separate from life itself, they might have been purged several administrations ago. But as you must surely know if you've taken over Hell as you've said, the denizens of Heaven and Hell aren't allowed any regular means of contact with the world.

400

"Speaking of which, how did you get out of there if you're in charge? It took the devil millennia to find someone stupid enough to take over his role there."

"I've still got a trick or two up my sleeve. Of course, I have to wonder what's taking your 'them' so long. You got here within minutes, and you're what, some petty criminal? Maybe a thorn in their side yourself? Are they waiting for me to take you out? Maybe even waiting for me to destroy a couple more of your so-called microcosms they've wanted disappeared anyway?"

"You don't know what you're talking about. They'll be here. Everyone here knows too much, it's a potential disaster for their precious prison planet, they've got to extract you, wipe this lot out, and maybe slap me on the wrist for not taking you out sooner."

"What, you're on their side now? A turncoat?"

"Not in so many words, but you won't be the first misbehaver I've assisted them with."

"So nice to know I've been misbehaving. You'd think the warden would have told me what the rules are if I'm expected to live by them." Trevor could feel the fabric of space and time opening up behind him and to his right in a sort of intuitive, sub-experiential way that must have been inherited through a memory-set he'd taken on recently. It was unlike any sensation that had ever crossed his subconscious, and he wondered if what the man had said was about to turn out to be true, if he was about to die, lose all these memories, lose so much that wasn't remembered by any other living soul. He maintained eye contact with the hovering threat in front of him but did not see any indication that what was going on behind him was visible to those eyes.

"If I knew your crime, I'd tell you what you'd done to deserve to have everything taken away from you, then as now. That would get them here that much faster, of course, but none of my sources were able to peek through the cover-up that hid your exile from the universe. It must have been something worse than the rest of us, something that deserved a more severe punishment..." His long face went slack. Trevor thought that whatever force was growing behind him must have been perceived, but the moment of silence

401

stretched and stretched and he didn't want to give anything away by reacting or turning to see. He stood stock still.

"...no," continued the dazed-looking face of the once-menacing dark wizard, "you couldn't be..." Trevor sensed the substance of space and time around him virtually sigh with relief and knew that the violence behind him must have ceased.

A young woman's voice confidently came to them from the exact spot Trevor expected it to, and hearing that voice brought a sudden calm to his whole being, every voice and memory in his head suddenly in harmony and every fiber of his being suddenly at ease. "He very much could be. Now and quite literally forever."

In the dark stranger's palpably silent failure to respond, the thousands of small sounds of fabric sliding across fabric, across skin, of hair and hanging jewelry rearranging, of every head but Trevor's changing focus from the sky above to the figure standing just behind Trevor's peripheral vision on his right-hand side was audible to the point of assault instead of faint enough to forget to sense; a cacophony where inaudible whispers belonged. People began to hold their breath to keep from interrupting the tension and anticipation so clearly about to coalesce into an unknowable conclusion before their very eyes.

"The question isn't whether you can kill him, because you can't." Her voice was confident, assured, almost disruptively youthful. "It's whether they'll continue with the masquerade that they could ever hold or punish him after they learn how he brought us here." Her left arm reached out and up and came gently, lovingly, to rest on Trevor's right shoulder blade, her fingertips only softly curving with the barest beginning of his shoulder as she put her hand on him in a gesture they had shared so many times before. It was a gesture his whole heart remembered at once without letting his mind in on the story, and Trevor's eyelids shuffled shut in complete contentment, the muscles of his neck relaxing, releasing his head from its skyward gaze, his diaphragm allowing his lungs to let go the air they'd been holding captive since the last word he'd spoken. Everything that he'd thought had gone before became as dust brushed

402

away to reveal the treasured, secret surface so long lost below; Trevor felt wholly at home.

Beginning to realize the depth of his irrelevance as the pieces of the puzzle came together quite literally before him but unable to reconcile the obvious truth within the structure of self-importance his mind had wrenched and carved itself into through the years of his imprisonment, the dark and powerful exile found a thorn of inconsistency to stick in his own side, distracting himself from the idea that he'd destroyed his own house of cards by coming out of the shadows to face Trevor head-on. "What do you mean by 'us'?" His response, in a tone that was meant to be scathing but came out almost trembling, was directed solely at the woman; he was ignoring Trevor in equal measure to his being now ignored, but not because he was at peace. The prisoner addressed her because some part of him knew with certainty that there was nothing he could ever do to stop Trevor in his tracks or alter the direction of his inescapable flow through history. He addressed her because addressing Trevor suddenly didn't seem wise at all. "Trev didn't exile himself, he was brought by force. I personally spoke to the officer of the court that delivered him here. You don't know what you're talking about."

"There is more going on here than you know, perhaps more than I know, but I was not mistaken. When I said 'us' I referred to myself and the other one he brought here despite every power the court and the rest of the universe could put between us. The other one is my sister," and without missing a beat or a breath or opening his eyes or touching her mind, Trevor continued her sentence, her thought, saying "my daughter," and just as fluidly the sentence was completed, "myself," by a third figure that no one had noticed slipping through reality to stand behind and to the left of Trevor until she was lifting her right arm to place her right hand on his left shoulder blade in a reflection that created a symmetry of support behind the wearied warrior. The woman on the right continued as though all the words had been hers, "We were brought here by the same force that the denizens of the universe found so repellant as to exile Trevor to this place and me to another, but the

403

strange circumstances of our surrogate mother's seizure by a cult of colocation created something unexpected.

"The intention of the force brought to bear was to return me to Trevor despite all odds and obstacles; his wife, carried across space and time and the boundaries of beingness by the power of his love in the form of an impossible daughter. Then, when those greedy doubled madmen brought their own forces into play, another new life was created from the whole cloth of the literal incarnation of our love for each other before I had come to fully inhabit it." The stranger, Sunshine standing on the sideline, and a few others that were aware enough of the rest of the story to follow along, felt their eyes widen and their jaws drop with the strange truth revealing itself in their minds. "There is no way you will ever understand the intensity and the beauty and the unique love... There is nothing that will fit in your limited perception of reality which can ever shadow the experience of a mother sharing the inside of a womb with her own daughter, growing and experiencing every moment of development first-hand in harmony with a child created out of your own unstoppable, unconditional love. You probably don't even know what it means to love. No mother or father or brother or sister, no woman or man or beast has ever held your heart for so much as a moment, has it? All you know how to love is your own empty pursuit of power, isn't it?"

"I watched... I watched you being born..." Nirgal's half-breathed muttering was heard by every eager ear around, "...it couldn't have been half an hour ago..."

The crowd's attention was slowly becoming fragmented and scattered. Some people kept their eyes on the three figures overhead, two of whom most had seen before and either trusted and now felt betrayed by or had suspected and now felt triumphant in their former paranoia.

Some people kept their eyes on Trevor and the two women with him; a strangely familiar sight, this young man with two nearly identical and alarmingly beautiful young women, but altogether different from the trio they'd grown familiar with.

A few people were looking at, moving toward, and even beginning to question Nirgal about what was going on; he was simultaneously the one in focus here they least expected to be at the center of world-changing events and the one they considered most approachable and addressable. It was as though the immediacy of events still transpiring had slipped their minds as they reached out to their classmate for answers.

Sqrat was trying to think of a place to disappear to that would be far enough away and secret enough that maybe they wouldn't come after him right away, and Ms. Charming had recognized the look on his face of a trapped animal just waiting for an opportunity to scurry away and had incanted a powerful location-tracing enchantment on him under her breath.

Feagan had felt his master begin to slip, to lose faith in himself and lose concentration from the situation at hand, and had found himself having to forcibly hold a man he used to have respect for in an upright and stationary position so that none of them appeared to be weak or to be giving up. They weren't weak, the three of them together, Feagan knew it, and he was adamant that he would force action if that was what he had to do. This had gone on too long and cost too much to give up without a fight, at least in Feagan's mind, and he was preparing himself mentally to begin a real war here if the tall figure he held aloft before him didn't get things back together and start things on his own.

Trevor's head was still turned low, his eyes still closed, his heart more content than he could remember.

And above everyone, through the rough opening that had not long ago been a ceiling, a roof, a starlike point of light began moving against the night sky, began growing. And few of the hundred-fold present noticed it, spinning, glowing, growing and growing as it approached and filled the boxed-in sky above them, at least not until its lights were shining bright enough to fill the room as daylight never had, so near and so brilliant, so much brighter than the room's destroyed lights had once been and shockingly brighter than moonlight. Those that did not give over their attention to the light had it taken from them by the sudden noise: Trevor

405

raised his head solemnly, slowly upward, his eyes still closed. Feagan flipped around in the air to face whatever foe approached from his rear when the lights filled the room, and was so blown away by the noise that he literally dropped his master's body. Deflected automatically by the students below, the limp form of the formerly formidable foe fell limp and lifeless to lay forgotten on the floor. Sqrat had disappeared in the instant after the lights filled the room, when Ms. Charming's eyes flitted momentarily away, and he never heard the noise. Nirgal, who had been stumbling and stuttering through the best answers he could give about what he knew for sure would be okay to give, had stopped and stared well before the lights had completed their downward journey, and those who queried him followed suit one after the other until the noise halted all. The noise had begun incongruently, like the low, deep, gut-quaking rumble one would expect a spaceship's engine to make, but only after the ship had stopped moving. If that rumble had been the only component of the noise it might not have commanded all attention so readily; layered within it were sounds akin to electronic animals dying, and at volumes that seemed only fractional adjustments on a dial away from blown speakers.

Somewhere in between the layers of rumbling, dying, loud and captivating noise there was something else. Buried nearly beyond hearing and perhaps expressed only in broadcast thought or a desire for meaning within the chaos that had interrupted an otherwise pleasant evening for most of those who remained present and awake, was a voice, calm and steady and low.

"We apologize for this interruption, and formally regret any inconvenience this matter may cause. Rest assured that the anomaly is being addressed with all due haste and that a return to normalcy is imminent. Formal complaints may be registered as applicable with officers of the court at your next scheduled potential release hearings. Detrimental effects on natives, as such, cannot be efficaciously measured or repaired and no formal effort will be made to do so, though the interred are welcome to do whatever they feel is appropriate for such beings as their terms and restrictions so permit. As always, your

406

cooperation in matters such as these is appreciated and will not go unnoticed by the court. Thank you for your patience."

The noise was gone, the ship was silently reversing course, and the crowd was slowly coming out of the trance-like state it had been put in. That Trevor and the two women who had appeared at his side were gone was not particularly shocking to anyone; that was what most everyone had expected would happen when they heard that "the anomaly is being addressed." Enough people had seen Sqrat disappear before the noise that a consensus was quickly reached that he was simply a coward, not taken by the craft. The collapsed bodies of Feagan and the other had drawn a tight and wondering crowd. The students who had been trying to pry information from Nirgal shouted out for him, and no one could find him.

Then here and there, a little at a time before it seemed to be everyone at once, people began to notice that they couldn't communicate mentally. They couldn't levitate. They couldn't disappear. Sunshine couldn't track down Sqrat, she couldn't summon an animal to deliver a message to the Wolyd Centre, she couldn't even activate her permanently enchanted panic button to alert The Board to emergency. Where everyone had been confident and steadfast in the face of their enemies, either from experience or from youth, now a panic broke out as everyone found themselves as powerless as the general public they had so long ago dropped out of. It was mayhem.

"When are you going to unlock his memories? You have no right to hold his mind captive offworld." Toni was very nearly shouting at the uniformed young man who was trying to lead the four of them from the foyer of the ship to the captain's quarters as he had been ordered. He was not restricted from speaking, he was simply too scared to say something somehow wrong, and his stunned silence came across as stiff-necked discipline. At least, that's how he hoped he appeared. Toni kept berating him, "his rights are

407

guaranteed to be restored as soon as he sets foot off the exile planet under the supervision of the courts. There's supposed to be an experienced guildmaster or at least a cartographerobot present in the foyer during any exile extraction." As Toni scuttled backwards down the long and curving corridor of the ship, practically barking in the young officer's face, her daughter led Trevor along on one side while Nirgal -who appeared to be taking yet another unexpected change of venue in stride- helped him along on the other side. Trevor's eyes were now open, but he walked as though in a trance. His body followed the guidance of his best friend and his daughter, but his eyes never left Toni's beautiful face as she darted and bounced ahead of all of them. "It's the law. We demand our rights! You can't treat us this way."

"Calm down, mother."

"You know the law as well as I do. We can't let them get away with something like this, or they'll see it as an open door to further abuses!"

"Look at his rank, mother, he's only just made corporate. He probably doesn't know half as much about the situation as..." she peeked around her father to address Nirgal, "what was your name?"

"N-n-n-Nirgal. M-m-my name is Nirgal." Nirgal's voice betrayed a lack of confidence that his feet and face had been able to hide, and the stutter his proximity to Trevor's confidence had all-but-erased. "P-p-p-p-p... P-p-pleased to m-meet you."

"Oh, we haven't met yet, I'm--"

Toni cut her off with another burst that was almost, but not quite, shouting in the young officer's face. "A rank amateur? Some errand boy? They rip us out of a situation rife with problems we're more than responsible to clean up on our own without even a 'Hello, how do you do,' they don't provide a guildmaster to restore my husband's memories, and to top it all off the sapling of a nothing they do send is some lone, inexperienced, deaf-mute who wouldn't know the letter of the law from a punch in the jaw! Why, I oughta--" but Toni was cut off by her own grandstanding as she stumbled backwards into the Captain's door.

The uniformed gentleman waited for her to step aside, placed his hand in a slot beside the door that contained both the biometric equipment to identify him with certainty as well as the necessary equipment to hold him and dismember him if either was requested by the computer or an authorized citizen on the other side of the door. His hand was released and the door slid aside. With his still-intact hand, he gestured to indicate that they should enter the Captain's quarters, and they obeyed without a word - though Toni shot him a look that pierced straight through him as she walked by - and the door slid closed behind them, leaving the officer relieved to be alone in the corridor and hoping he wouldn't have to face that woman again. He turned and, whistling, sauntered back down the corridor and out of sight.

About the Author

Teel denies claims by certain members of the underworld and a particular staffer at FOX News that the Trevor character from his Untrue Tales From Beyond Fiction series is modeled after his own adolescence. Teel goes on to assert that as far as any reputable being knows, he has not yet saved mankind from any religious organizations trying to take over the world, has not taken over the underworld himself, and has not left the Earth in an unidentified corporate space craft. The fact that he also refers to the entire series as included in his ongoing attempt to document his life in memoirs is an idea that should not be considered a contradiction of this.

Teel is a lifelong resident of Arizona, and like most lifelong residents of Arizona, he longs to journey to faraway places. Places with exotic things like weather, and trees. Places from which he can return happy and secure in the knowledge that while you always have to shovel snow, you never have to shovel heat. He has recently published a collection of poetry exploring one such journey called Worth 1k - Volume 1.

You can find out more about him, and find his other novels and his poetry, at Modern Evil Press:

http://modernevil.com

Or email him: teel@modernevil.com

Acknowledgements

This novel would not have been possible without the help of a few special people: Thanks Starbucks baristas. Without your valuable help in making and serving coffee, not to mention not kicking me out after taking up the same table for hours on end, day after day, I would have had to write these books at home. Thanks again go to Angela, who helped me edit, and to Pat, who also gave me some valuable feedback.

Books by Teel McClanahan III

Lost and Not Found

Dragons' Truth

The Vintage Collection

Worth 1k --- Volume 1
A collection of poetry instead of pictures

Untrue Tales From Beyond Fiction
Recollections of an Alternate Past
-a series-

Book One:
An Introduction To Dodgeball, or
Conception and Induction, or
How To Begin An Apocalypse

Book Two:
The Twofold Invasion, or
Penetration and Destruction, or
How To Make Love With Twins

Book Three:
Escape From Exile, or
Confusion and Contraction, or
How To Get Out Of Hell